Shadows of the
Pomegranate Tree

Shadows of the Pomegranate Tree

TARIQ ALI

VERSO

London · New York

First published by Chatto & Windus 1991
This edition published by Verso 1993
© Tariq Ali

3 5 7 9 10 8 6 4

Verso
UK: 6 Meard Street, London W1F 0EG
USA: 180 Varick Street, New York, NY 10014-4606

Verso is the imprint of New Left Books

British Library Cataloguing in Publication Data
A catalogue record for this book is available from the British Library

Library of Congress Cataloging-in-Publication Data
A catalog record for this book is available from the Library of Congress

ISBN 0-86091-676-6

Printed and bound in the USA by
R. R. Donnelley & Sons

For Aisha, Chengiz and Natasha

THE BANU HUDAYL in 1499 AD

The clan of Hassan al-Hudayl left Dimashk in 237 AH - 932 AD - and reached the Western outposts of Islam in the same year. They settled near Gharnata and in the following year began to build the village which bore their name. The mansion was constructed three years later by stonemasons who had built the Medina al-Zahara near Qurtuba.

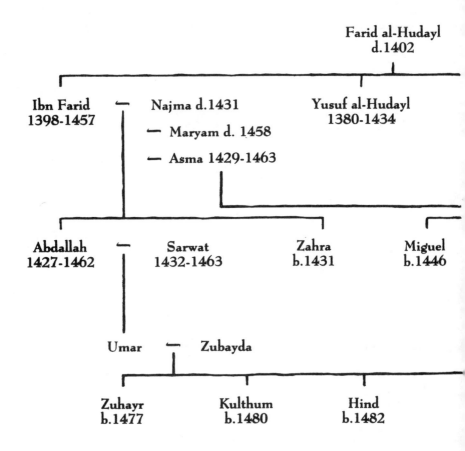

Farid al-Hudayl
d.1402

Ibn Farid
1398-1457

Najma d.1431

Maryam d. 1458

Asma 1429-1463

Yusuf al-Hudayl
1380-1434

Abdallah
1427-1462

Sarwat
1432-1463

Zahra
b.1431

Miguel
b.1446

Umar

Zubayda

Zuhayr
b.1477

Kulthum
b.1480

Hind
b.1482

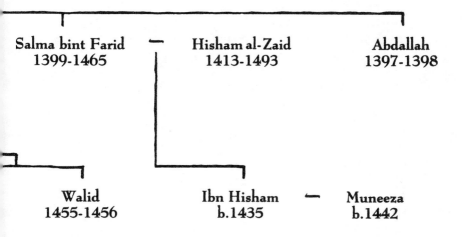

| Salma bint Farid | — | Hisham al-Zaid | Abdallah |
| 1399-1465 | | 1413-1493 | 1397-1398 |

| Walid | Ibn Hisham | — | Muneeza |
| 1455-1456 | b.1435 | | b.1442 |

Yazid
b.1490

Author's Note

In Moorish Spain, as in the Arab World today, children received a given name, and were further identified by the name of their father or mother. In this narrative Zuhayr bin Umar is Zuhayr, son of Umar; Asma bint Dorothea is Asma, daughter of Dorothea. A man's public name might simply identify him as the son of his father – Ibn Farid, Ibn Khaldun, son of Farid, of Khaldun. The Moors in this story use their own names for cities which now bear Spanish names, including several that were founded by the Moors themselves. These names, and some common Moorish words, are explained in the Glossary on p. 242

Prologue

The five Christian knights summoned to the apartment of Ximenes de Cisneros did not welcome the midnight call. Their reaction had little to do with the fact that it was the coldest winter in living memory. They were veterans of the Reconquest. Troops under their command had triumphantly marched into Gharnata seven years before and occupied the city in the name of Ferdinand and Isabella.

None of the five men belonged to the region. The oldest amongst them was the natural son of a monk in Toledo. The others were Castilians and desperate to return to their villages. They were all good Catholics, but did not want their loyalty taken for granted, not even by the Queen's confessor. They knew how he had had himself transferred from Toledo where he was the Archbishop to the conquered city. It was hardly a secret that Cisneros was an instrument of Queen Isabella. He wielded a power that was not exclusively spiritual. The knights were only too well aware how a defiance of his authority would be viewed by the Court.

The five men, wrapped in cloaks but still shivering from the cold, were shown into Cisneros' bed-chamber. The austerity of the living conditions surprised them. Looks were exchanged. For a prince of the Church to inhabit quarters more suited to a fanatical monk was unprecedented. They were not yet used to a prelate who lived as he preached. Ximenes looked up at them and smiled. The voice which gave them their instructions had no clang of command. The knights were taken aback. The man from Toledo whispered loudly to his companions: 'Isabella has entrusted the keys of the pigeon-house to a cat.'

Cisneros chose to ignore this display of insolence. Instead, he raised his voice slightly.

'I wish to make it clear that we are not interested in the pursuit of any personal vendettas. I speak to you with the authority of both Church and Crown.'

This was not strictly true, but soldiers are not accustomed to questioning those in authority. Once he was satisfied that his instruction had been fully understood, the Archbishop dismissed them. He had wanted to make it clear that the cowl was in command of the sword. A week later, on the first day of December in the year 1499, Christian soldiers under the command of five knight-commanders entered the one hundred and ninety-five libraries of the city and a dozen mansions where some of the better-known private collections were housed. Everything written in Arabic was confiscated.

The day before, scholars in the service of the Church had convinced Cisneros to exempt three hundred manuscripts from his edict. He had agreed, provided they were placed in the new library he was preparing to endow in Alcala. The bulk of these were Arab manuals of medicine and astronomy. They represented the major advances in these and related sciences since the days of antiquity. Here was much of the material which had travelled from the peninsula of al-Andalus as well as Sicily to the rest of Europe and paved the way for the Renaissance.

Several thousand copies of the Koran, together with learned commentaries and theological and philosophical reflections on its merits and demerits, all crafted in the most exquisite calligraphy, were carted away indiscriminately by the men in uniform. Rare manuscripts vital to the entire architecture of intellectual life in al-Andalus, were crammed in makeshift bundles on the backs of soldiers.

Throughout the day the soldiers constructed a rampart of hundreds of thousands of manuscripts. The collective wisdom of the entire peninsula lay in the old silk market below the Bab al-Ramla.

This was the ancient space where once Moorish knights used to ride and joust to catch the eye of their ladies; where the populace would assemble in large numbers, children riding on the shoulders of fathers, uncles and elder brothers as they cheered their favourites; where catcalls greeted the appearance of those who paraded in the armour of knights simply because they were creatures of the Sultan. When it was clear that a brave man had allowed one of the courtiers to win out of deference to the King

2

or, just as likely, because he had been promised a purse full of gold dinars, the citizens of Gharnata jeered loudly. It was a citizenry well known for its independence of mind, rapier wit, and reluctance to recognize superiors. This was the city and this the place chosen by Cisneros for his demonstration of fireworks that night.

The sumptuously bound and decorated volumes were a testament to the arts of the Peninsulan Arabs, surpassing the standards of the monasteries of Christendom. The compositions they contained had been the envy of scholars throughout Europe. What a splendid pile was laid before the population of the town.

The soldiers who, since the early hours of the morning, had been building the wall of books had avoided the eyes of the Gharnatinos. Some onlookers were sorrowful, others tempestuous, eyes flashing, faces full of anger and defiance. Others still, their bodies swaying gently from side to side, wore vacant expressions. One of them, an old man, kept repeating the only sentence he could utter in the face of the calamity.

'We are being drowned in a sea of helplessness.'

Some of the soldiers, perhaps because they never had been taught to read or write, understood the enormity of the crime they were helping to perpetrate. Their own role troubled them. Sons of peasants, they recalled the stories they used to hear from their grandparents, whose tales of Moorish cruelty contrasted with accounts of their culture and learning.

There were not many of these soldiers, but enough to make a difference. As they walked down the narrow streets, they would deliberately discard a few manuscripts in front of the tightly sealed doors. Having no other scale of judgement, they imagined that the heaviest volumes must also be the weightiest. The assumption was false, but the intention was honourable, and the gesture was appreciated. The minute the soldiers were out of sight, a door would open and a robed figure would leap out, scoop up the books and disappear again behind the relative safety of locks and bars. In this fashion, thanks to the instinctive decency of a handful of soldiers, several hundred important manuscripts survived. They were subsequently transported across the water to the safety of personal libraries in Fes, and so were saved.

In the square it was beginning to get dark. A large crowd of reluctant citizens, mainly male, had been assembled by the soldiery. Muslim grandees and turbaned preachers mingled with the shopkeepers, traders, peasants, artisans and stall-holders, as well as pimps, prostitutes and the mentally unstable. All humanity was represented here.

Behind the window of a lodging house the most favoured sentinel of the Church in Rome was watching the growing palisade of books with a feeling of satisfaction. Ximenes de Cisneros had always believed that the heathen could only be eliminated as a force if their culture was completely erased. This meant the systematic destruction of all their books. Oral traditions would survive for a while, till the Inquisition plucked away the offending tongues. If not himself, then someone else would have had to organize this necessary bonfire – somebody who understood that the future had to be secured through firmness and discipline and not through love and education, as those imbecile Dominicans endlessly proclaimed. What had they ever achieved?

Ximenes was exultant. He had been chosen as the instrument of the Almighty. Others might have carried out this task, but none so methodically as he. A sneer curled his lip. What else could be expected from a clergy whose abbots, only a few hundred years ago, were named Mohammed, Umar, Uthman and so on? Ximenes was proud of his purity. The childhood jibes he had endured were false. He had no Jewish ancestors. No mongrel blood stained his veins.

A soldier had been posted just in front of the prelate's window. Ximenes stared at him and nodded, the signal was passed to the torch-bearers, and the fire was lit. For half a second there was total silence. Then a loud wail rent the December night, followed by cries of: 'There is only one Allah and he is Allah and Mohammed is his Prophet.'

At a distance from Cisneros a group was chanting, but he could not hear the words. Not that he would have understood them anyway, since the language of the verses was Arabic. The fire was rising higher and higher. The sky itself seemed to have become a flaming abyss, a spectrum of sparks that floated in the air as the delicately coloured calligraphy burnt itself out. It was as if the stars were raining down their sorrow.

Slowly, in a daze, the crowds began to walk away till a beggar stripped himself bare and began to climb on to the fire. 'What is the point of life without our books of learning?' he cried through scorching lungs. 'They must pay. They will pay for what they have done to us today.'

He fainted. The flames enveloped him. Tears were being shed in silence and hate, but tears could not quench the fires lit that day. The people walked away.

The square is mute. Here and there, old fires still smoulder. Ximenes is walking through the ashes, a crooked smile on his face as he plans the next steps. He is thinking aloud.

'Whatever revenge they may plan in the depths of their grief, it will be useless. We have won. Tonight was our real victory.'

More than anybody else in the Peninsula, more even than the dread figure of Isabella, Ximenes understands the power of ideas. He kicks to ashes a stack of burnt parchments. Over the embers of one tragedy lurks the shadow of another.

Chapter 1

'IF THINGS GO on like this,' Ama was saying in a voice garbled by a gap-toothed mouth, 'nothing will be left of us except a fragrant memory.'

His concentration disrupted, Yazid frowned and looked up from the chess-cloth. He was at the other end of the courtyard, engaged in a desperate attempt to master the stratagems of chess. His sisters, Hind and Kulthum, were both accomplished strategists. They were away in Gharnata with the rest of the family. Yazid wanted to surprise them with an unorthodox opening move when they returned.

He had tried to interest Ama in the game, but the old woman had cackled at the thought and refused. Yazid could not understand her rejection. Was not chess infinitely superior to the beads she was always fingering? Then why did this elementary fact always escape her?

Reluctantly, he began to put away the chess pieces. How extraordinary they are, he thought, as he carefully replaced them in their little home. They had been especially commissioned by his father. Juan the carpenter had been instructed to carve them in time for his tenth birthday last month, in the year 905 A.H., which was 1500, according to the Christian calendar.

Juan's family had been in the service of the Banu Hudayl for centuries. In AD 932 the head of the Hudayl clan, Hamza bin Hudayl, had fled Dimashk and brought his family and followers to the western outposts of Islam. He had settled on the slopes of the foothills some twenty miles from Gharnata. Here he had built the village that became known as al-Hudayl. It rose on high ground and could be seen from afar. Mountain streams surrounded it, and turned in springtime into torrents of molten snow. On the outskirts of the village the children of Hamza cultivated the land and planted orchards. After Hamza had been dead for almost fifty years, his descendants built themselves a palace. Around it lay farmed land, vineyards, and almond, orange, pomegranate and mulberry orchards that gave the appearance of children clustering about their mother.

Almost every piece of furniture, except of course for the spoils looted by Ibn Farid during the wars, had been carefully crafted by Juan's ancestors. The carpenter, like everyone else in the village, was aware of Yazid's status in the family. The boy was a universal favourite. And so he determined to produce a set of chess statuettes which would outlast them all. In the event Juan had surpassed his own wildest ambitions.

The Moors had been assigned the colour white. Their Queen was a noble beauty with a mantilla, her spouse a red-bearded monarch with blue eyes, his body covered in a flowing Arab robe bedecked with rare gems. The castles were replicas of the tower house which dominated the entrance to the palatial mansion of the Banu Hudayl. The knights were representations of Yazid's great-grandfather, the warrior Ibn Farid, whose legendary adventures in love and war dominated the culture of this particular family. The white bishops were modelled on the turbaned Imam of the village mosque. The pawns bore an uncanny resemblance to Yazid.

The Christians were not merely black; they had been carved as monsters. The black Queen's eyes shone with evil, in brutal contrast with the miniature madonna hanging round her neck. Her lips were painted the colour of blood. A ring on her finger displayed a painted skull. The King had been carved with a portable crown that could be easily lifted, and as if this symbolism was not sufficient, the iconoclastic carpenter had provided the monarch with a tiny pair of horns. This unique vision of Ferdinand and Isabella was surrounded by equally grotesque figures. The knights raised blood-stained hands. The two bishops were sculpted in the shape of Satan; both were clutching daggers, while whip-like tails protruded from behind. Juan had never set eyes on Ximenes de Cisneros, otherwise there can be little doubt that the Archbishop's burning eyes and hooked nose would have provided an ideal caricature. The pawns had all been rendered as monks, complete with cowls, hungry looks and pot-bellies; creatures of the Inquisition in search of prey.

Everyone who saw the finished product agreed that Juan's work was a masterpiece. Yazid's father, Umar, was troubled. He knew that if ever a spy of the Inquisition caught sight of the chess-set, the carpenter would be tortured to death. But Juan was adamant: the child must be given the present. The carpenter's father had been charged with apostasy by the Inquisition some six years ago while visiting relatives in Tulaytula. He had later died in prison from the deep wounds sustained by his pride during torture by the monks. As a finale, fingers had been snapped off each hand. The old carpenter had lost the urge to live. Young Juan was bent on revenge. The design of the chess set was only a beginning.

Yazid's name had been inscribed on the base of each figure and he had grown as closely attached to his chess pieces as if they were living creatures. His favourite, however, was Isabella, the black Queen. He was both frightened and fascinated by her. In time, she became his confessor, someone to whom he would entrust all his worries, but only when he was sure that they were alone. Once he had finished packing the chess-set he looked again at the old woman and sighed.

Why did Ama talk so much to herself these days? Was she really going mad? Hind said she was, but he wasn't sure. Yazid's sister often said things in a rage, but if Ama really were mad, his father would have found her a place in the maristan at Gharnata next to Great-Aunt Zahra. Hind was cross only because Ama was always going on about it being time for their parents to find her a husband.

Yazid walked across the courtyard and sat down on Ama's lap. The old woman's face, already a net of wrinkles, creased still further as she smiled at her charge. She abandoned her beads without ceremony and stroked the boy's face, kissing him gently on his head.

'May Allah bless you. Are you feeling hungry?'

'No. Ama, who were you talking to a few minutes ago?'

'Who listens to an old woman these days, Ibn Umar? I might as well be dead.'

Ama had never called Yazid by his own name. Never. For was it not a fact that Yazid was the name of the Caliph who had defeated and killed the grandsons of the Prophet near Kerbala? This Yazid had instructed his soldiers to stable their horses in the mosque where the Prophet himself had offered prayers in Medina. This Yazid had treated the Companions of the Prophet with contempt. To speak his name was to pollute the memory of the Prophet's family. She could not tell the boy all this, but it was reason enough for her always to refer to him as Ibn Umar, the son of his father. Once Yazid had questioned her about this in front of all the family and Ama had thrown an angry glance at their mother, Zubayda, as if to say: it's all her fault, why don't you ask her? but everyone had begun to laugh and Ama had walked out in a temper.

'I was listening to you. I heard you talk. I can tell you what you said. Should I repeat your words?'

'Oh my son,' sighed Ama. 'I was talking to the shadows of the pomegranate trees. At least they will be here when we are all gone.'

'All gone where, Ama?'

'Why to heaven, my child.'

'Will we all go to heaven?'

'May Allah bless you. You will go to the seventh heaven, my pure little slice of the moon. I'm not so sure about the others. And as for that sister of yours, Hind bint Umar, unless they marry her off soon she won't even get to the first heaven. No, not her. I dread that something evil will overtake that child. I fear that she will be exposed to wild passions and shame will fall on the head of your father, may God protect him.'

Yazid had begun to giggle at the thought of Hind not even getting through the first heaven, and his laughter was so infectious that Ama began to cackle as well, revealing the total complement of her eight remaining teeth.

Of all his brothers and sisters, Yazid loved Hind the most. The others still treated him like a baby, seemed constantly amazed that he could think and speak for himself, picked him up and kissed him as though he were a pet. He knew he was their favourite, but he hated it when they never answered his questions. That was the reason he regarded them all with contempt.

All that is except Hind, who was six years older than him, but treated him as her equal. They argued and they fought a great deal, but they adored each other. This love for his sister was so deep-rooted that none of Ama's mystical premonitions bothered him in the slightest or affected his feelings for Hind.

It was Hind who had told him the real reason for Great-Uncle

Miguel's visit, which had so upset his parents last week. He too had been upset on hearing that Miguel wanted them all to come to Qurtuba, where he was the Bishop, so that he could personally convert them to Catholicism. It was Miguel who, three days ago, had dragged all of them, including Hind, to Gharnata. Yazid turned to the old woman again.

'Why doesn't Great-Uncle Miguel speak to us in Arabic?'

Ama was startled by the question. Old habits never die and so, quite automatically, she spat at the sound of Miguel's name and began to feel her beads in a slightly desperate way, muttering all the time: 'There is only one Allah and he is Allah and Mohammed is His prophet . . .'

'Answer me, Ama. Answer me.'

Ama looked at the boy's shining face. His almond-coloured eyes were flashing with anger. He reminded her of his great-grandfather. It was this memory which softened her as she answered his question.

'Your Great-Uncle Miguel speaks, reads and writes Arabic, but . . . but . . .' Ama's voice choked in anger. 'He has turned his back on us. On everything. Did you notice that this time he was stinking, just like them?'

Yazid began to laugh again. He knew that Great-Uncle Miguel was not a popular member of the family, but nobody had ever spoken of him so disrespectfully. Ama was quite right. Even his father had joined in the laughter when Ummi Zubayda had described the unpleasant odours emanating from the Bishop as being reminiscent of a camel that had consumed too many dates.

'Did he always stink?'

'Certainly not!' Ama was upset by the question. 'In the old days, before he sold his soul and started worshipping images of bleeding men stuck on wooden crosses, he was the cleanest person alive. Five baths a day in the summer. Five changes of clothes. I remember those times well. Now he smells like a horse's stable. Do you know why?'

Yazid confessed his ignorance.

'So that nobody can accuse him of being a Muslim under his cassock. Stinking Catholics! The Christians in the Holy Lands were clean, but these Catholic priests are frightened of the water. They think to have a bath is a betrayal of the saint they call the son of God.

'Now get up and come with me. It's time to eat. The sun is setting and we can't wait any longer for them to return from Gharnata. I've just remembered something. Did you have your honey today?'

Yazid nodded impatiently. Since he was born, and his brother and sisters before him, Ama had forced a spoonful of wild, purifying honey down their throats every morning.

'How can we eat before you've said the evening prayers?'

She frowned at him to register disapproval. The thought that she could ever forget her sacred ritual. Blasphemy! Yazid grinned and she could not stop herself from smiling at him as she lifted herself up slowly and began to walk to the bathroom to do her ablutions.

Yazid remained seated under the pomegranate tree. He loved this time of day, when the birds were noisily preparing to retire for the night. The cuckoos were busy announcing their last messages. In an alcove on the outside of the tower house, overlooking the outer courtyard and the world beyond, the doves were cooing.

Suddenly the light changed and there was total silence. The deep blue sky had turned a purplish orange, casting a magical spell on the mountain-tops still covered with snow. In the courtyard of the big house, Yazid strained his eyes, trying to observe the first star, but none was yet visible. Should he rush to the tower and look through the magnifying glass? What if the first star appeared while he was still mounting the stair? Instead, Yazid shut his eyes. It was as if the overpowering scent of jasmine had flooded his senses like hashish and made him drowsy, but in reality he was counting up to five hundred. It was his way of killing time till the North Star appeared.

The muezzin's call to prayer interrupted the boy. Ama limped out with her prayer-mat and pointed it in the direction of the sunrise and began to say her prayers. Just as she had prostrated herself in the direction of the Kaaba in Mecca, Yazid saw al-Hutay'a, the cook, signalling to him frantically from the paved path at the edge of the courtyard in the direction of the kitchen. The boy ran towards him.

'What is it, Dwarf?'

The cook put his finger to his lips and demanded silence. The boy obeyed him. For a moment both the dwarf-cook and the child remained frozen. Then the cook spoke. 'Listen. Just listen. There. Can you hear?'

Yazid's eyes lit up. There in the distance was the unmistakable noise of horses' hoofs, followed by the creaking of the cart. The boy ran out of the house as the noises became louder. The sky was now covered with stars and Yazid saw the retainers and servants lighting their torches to welcome the family. A voice echoed from afar.

'Umar bin Abdallah has returned. Umar bin Abdallah has returned . . .'

More torches were lit and Yazid felt even more excited. Then he saw the three men on horseback and began to shout.

'Abu! Abu! Zuhayr! Hind! Hind! Hurry up. I'm hungry.'

There they all were. Yazid had to admit an error. One of the three men on horseback was his sister Hind. Zuhayr was in the cart with his mother and Kulthum, a blanket wrapped round him.

Umar bin Abdallah lifted the boy off his feet and hugged him. 'Has my prince been good?'

Yazid nodded as his mother rained kisses on his face. Before the others could join her in this game, Hind grabbed him by the arm and the two ran off into the house.

'Why were you riding Zuhayr's horse?'

Hind's face became tense and she paused for a moment, wondering whether to tell him the truth. She decided against, not wishing to alarm Yazid. She, better than anyone else in the family, knew the fantasy-world in which her younger brother often cocooned himself.

'Hind! What's wrong with Zuhayr?'

'He developed a fever.'

'I hope it's not the plague.'

Hind shrieked with laughter.

'You've been listening too much to Ama's stories again, haven't you? Fool! When she talks about the plague she means Christianity. And that is not the cause of Zuhayr's fever. It's not serious. Our mother says he'll be fine in a few days. He's allergic to the change of seasons. It's an autumnal fever. Come and bathe with us. It's our turn first today.'

Yazid put on an indignant look.

'I've already had a bath. Anyway Ama says I'm getting too old to bathe with the women. She says . . .'

'I think Ama is getting too old. The nonsense she talks.'

'She talks a lot of sense as well, and she knows a great deal more than you, Hind.' Yazid paused to see if this rebuke had left any impact on his sister, but she appeared unmoved. Then he saw the smile in her eyes as she offered him her left hand and walked briskly through the house. Yazid ignored her extended hand, but walked by her side as she crossed the courtyard. He entered the bath chambers with her.

'I won't have a bath, but I will come and talk to all of you.'

The room was filled with serving women, who were undressing Yazid's mother and Kulthum. Yazid wondered why his mother seemed slightly worried. Perhaps the journey had tired her. Perhaps it was Zuhayr's fever. He stopped thinking as Hind undressed. Her personal maid-servant rushed to pick the discarded clothes from the floor. The three women were soaped and scrubbed with the softest sponges in the world, then containers of clean water were poured over them. After this they entered the large bath, which was the size of a small pond. The stream which flowed through the house had been piped to provide a regular supply of fresh water for the baths.

'Have you told Yazid?' asked their mother.

Hind shook her head.

'Told me what?'

Kulthum giggled.

'Great-Uncle Miguel wants Hind to marry Juan!'

Yazid laughed. 'But he's so fat and ugly!'

Hind screamed with pleasure. 'You see, Mother! Even Yazid agrees. Juan has a pumpkin instead of a brain. Mother, how could he be so totally stupid! Great-Uncle Miguel may be slimy, but he's no fool. How could he have produced this cross between a pig and a sheep?'

'There are no laws in these matters, child.'

'I'm not so sure,' ventured Kulthum. 'It might be a punishment from God for becoming a Christian!'

Hind snorted and pushed her older sister's head below the water. Kulthum emerged in good spirits. She had become engaged only a few months ago, and it had been agreed to have the wedding ceremony and departure from the parental home in the first month of the next year. She could wait. Her intended, Ibn Harith, was someone she had known since they were children. He was the son of her mother's cousin. He had loved her since he was sixteen years old. She wished they were in Gharnata instead of Ishbiliya, but it could not be helped. Once they were married she would try and drag him nearer her home.

'Does Juan stink as much as Great-Uncle Miguel?'

Yazid's question went unanswered. His mother clapped her hands and the maid-servants who had been waiting outside entered with towels and scented oils. As Yazid watched thoughtfully, the three women were dried and then rubbed with oil. Outside Umar's voice could be heard muttering impatiently, and the women hurriedly left the chamber and entered its neighbour where their clothes awaited them. Yazid followed them, but was immediately dispatched by his mother to the kitchen with instructions for the Dwarf to prepare the food, which should be served in exactly half an hour. As he set off, Hind whispered in his ear: 'Juan smells even more than that old stick Miguel!'

'So you see, Ama is not always wrong!' cried the boy triumphantly as he skipped out of the room.

In the kitchen, the Dwarf had prepared a feast. There were so many conflicting scents that even Yazid, who was a great friend of the cook, could not decipher what the stunted genius had prepared for the evening meal to celebrate the family's safe return from Gharnata. The kitchen seemed crowded with servants and retainers, some of whom had returned with Umar from the big city. They were talking so excitedly that none of them saw Yazid enter except the Dwarf, who was roughly the same height. He rushed over to the boy.

'Can you guess what I've cooked?'

'No, but why are they all so excited?'

'You mean you don't know?'

'What? Tell me immediately, Dwarf. I insist.'

Yazid had unintentionally raised his voice and had been noticed, with the result that the kitchen became silent and only the sizzling of the meat-balls in the large pan could be heard. The Dwarf looked at the boy with a sad smile on his face.

'Your brother, Zuhayr bin Umar . . .'

'He's got a slight fever. Is it something else? Why did Hind not tell me? What is it, Dwarf? You must tell me.'

'Young master. I don't know all the circumstances, but your brother does not have a slight fever. He was stabbed in the city after a rude exchange with a Christian. He's safe, it is only a flesh wound, but it will take some weeks for him to recover.'

Forgetting his mission, Yazid ran out of the kitchen, through the courtyard and was about to enter his brother's room when he was lifted off the ground by his father.

'Zuhayr is fast asleep. You can talk to him as much as you like in the morning.'

'Who stabbed him, Abu? Who? Who was it?'

Yazid was dismayed. He was very close to Zuhayr and he felt guilty at having ignored his older brother and spent all this time with Hind and the women. His father attempted to soothe him.

'It was a trivial incident. Almost an accident. Some fool insulted me as we were about to enter your uncle's house . . .'

'How?'

'Nothing of moment. Some abuse about forcing us soon to eat pig-meat. I ignored the creature, but Zuhayr, impulsive as always, slapped the man's face, upon which he revealed the dagger he had been concealing under his cloak and stabbed your brother just under the shoulder . . .'

'And? Did you punish the rascal?'

'No my son. We carried your brother inside the house and tended to him.'

'Where were our servants?'

'With us, but under strict instructions from me not to retaliate.'

'But why, Father? Why? Perhaps Ama is right after all. Nothing will be left of us except fragrant memories.'

'Wa Allah! Did she really say that?'

Yazid nodded tearfully. Umar felt the wetness on his son's face and held him close. 'Yazid bin Umar. There is no longer any such thing for us as an easy decision. We are living in the most difficult period of our history. We have not had such serious problems since Tarik and Musa first occupied these lands. And you know how long ago that was, do you not?'

Yazid nodded. 'In our first century and their eighth.'

'Exactly so, my child. Exactly so. It is getting late. Let us wash our hands and eat. Your mother is waiting.'

Ama, who had heard the entire conversation in silence from

the edge of the courtyard outside the kitchen, blessed father and son under her breath as they walked indoors. Then, swaying to and fro, she let loose a strange rattle from the back of her throat and spat out a malediction.

'Ya Allah! Save us from these crazed dogs and eaters of pigs. Protect us from these enemies of truth, who are so blinded by sectarian beliefs that they nail their God to a piece of wood and call it father, mother and son, drowning their followers in a sea of falsehood. They have subjected and annihilated us through the force of their oppression. Ten thousand praises to you, O Allah, for I am sure you will deliver us from the rule of these dogs who in many towns come daily to pull us from our homes . . .'

How long she would have carried on in this vein is uncertain, but a young serving woman interrupted her.

'Your food is getting cold, Ama.'

The old woman rose to her feet slowly and with her slightly bent back followed the maid into the kitchen. Ama's status among the servants was unambiguous. As the master's wet-nurse who had been with the family since she was born, her authority in the servants' quarters was unchallenged, but this did not solve all the problems of protocol. Apart from the venerable Dwarf, who boasted that he was the most skilled cuisinier in al-Andalus and who knew exactly how far he could go in discussing the family in the presence of Ama, the others steered away from sensitive subjects in her presence. It was not that Ama was a family spy. Sometimes she would let her tongue loosen and the servants would be amazed by her boldness, but despite these incidents her familiarity with the master and the sons made the rest of the household uneasy.

In fact, if the truth be told, Ama was extremely critical of Yazid's mother and the way she brought up her children. If she let her thoughts travel uncensored on this subject Ama finally ended up praying that the master would take a new wife. She regarded the lady of the manor as over-indulgent to her daughters, over-generous to the peasants who worked on the estate, over-lenient to the servants and their vices and indifferent to the practices of their faith.

On occasion Ama went so far as to voice a moderate version of these thoughts to Umar bin Abdallah, stressing that it was precisely weaknesses of this order which had brought Islam to the sorry pass in which it now found itself in al-Andalus. Umar simply laughed and later repeated every word to his wife. Zubayda was equally entertained by the thought that the frailties of al-Andalusian Islam were symbolized in her person.

The sounds of laughter emanating from the dining chamber tonight had nothing to do with Ama or her eccentricities. The jokes were a sure sign that the Dwarf's menu for the evening had found favour with his employers. On an ordinary day the family ate modestly. There were usually no more than four separate dishes and a plate of sweetmeats, followed by fresh fruit. Tonight they had been presented with a heavily spiced and scented barbecue lamb; rabbits stewed in fermented grape-juice with red peppers and whole cloves of garlic; meat-balls stuffed with brown truffles which literally melted in the mouth; a harder variety of meat-balls fried in coriander oil and served with tri-angular pieces of chilli-paste fried in the same oil; a large con-tainer full of bones floating in a saffron-coloured sauce; a large dish of fried rice; miniature vol-au-vents and three different salads; asparagus, a mixture of thinly sliced onions, tomatoes, cucumbers, sprinkled with herbs and the juice of fresh lemons, chick-peas soaked in yoghurt and sprinkled with pepper.

It had been Yazid trying to extract the marrow from a bone and blowing it by mistake on to his father's beard that had caused the laughter. Hind clapped her hands and two serving women entered the room. Her mother it was who asked them to clear the table and distribute the large amount of left-over food amongst themselves.

'And listen. Tell the Dwarf we will not try his sweetmeats or cheese-cakes tonight. Just serve the sugar-cane. Has it been dipped in rose-water? Hurry up. It's late.'

It was already too late for young Yazid, who had fallen asleep leaning on the floor-cushion. Ama, who had suspected this, walked into the room, put her finger on her lips to stress the need for silence and signalled to the rest that Yazid was fast asleep. Alas, she was too old to pick him up any longer. The thought saddened her. Umar realized instinctively what was pass-ing through his old wet-nurse's head. He recalled his own child-hood, when she barely let his feet touch the ground and his mother became worried that he might never learn to walk. Umar rose, and gently lifting his son, he carried him to his bed-chamber, followed by Ama wearing a triumphant smile. It was she who undressed the boy and put him to bed, making sure that the bed-covers were firmly in place.

Umar was in a thoughtful frame of mind when he joined his wife and daughters to partake of a few slices of sugar-cane. Strange how that memory of Ama picking him up and putting him to bed all those years ago had made him reflect yet again on the terminal character of the year that had just begun. Terminal, that is, for the Banu Hudayl and their way of life. Terminal if the truth be told, for Islam in al-Andalus.

Zubayda, sensing his change of mood, attempted to penetrate his mind.

'My lord, answer me one question.'

Distracted by the voice he looked at her and smiled vacantly.

'In times such as these, what is the most important consideration? To survive here as best we can, or to rethink the last five hundred years of our existence and plan our future accordingly?'

'I am not yet sure of the reply.'

'I am,' declared Hind.

'Of that I am sure,' replied her father, 'but the hour is late and we can continue our discussion another day.'

'Time is against us, Father.'

'Of that too I am sure, my child.'

'Peace be upon you, Father.'

'Bless you my daughters. Sleep well.'

'Will you be long?' asked Zubayda.

'Just a few minutes. I need to breathe some fresh air.'

For some minutes after they had left, Umar remained seated, engrossed in his meditations, staring at the empty table. Then he rose and, wrapping a blanket round his shoulders, walked out into the courtyard. The fresh air made him shiver slightly even though there was no chill and he clutched the blanket tightly as he began to walk up and down.

The torches were being extinguished inside, and he was left to measure his paces in starlight. The only noise was that of the stream which entered the courtyard at one corner, fed the fountain in its centre and then flowed out at the other end of the house. In happier days he would have collected the scent-laden flowers from the jasmine bushes, placed them tenderly in a muslin handkerchief, sprinkled them with water to keep them fresh and placed them at the side of Zubayda's pillow. In the morning they would still be fresh and aromatic. Tonight such thoughts were very remote from his mind.

Umar bin Abdallah was thinking, and the recurring images were so powerful that they made his whole body ·tremble momentarily. He imagined the wall of fire. Memories of that cold night flooded back. Uncontrollable tears watered his face and were trapped by his beard. The fall of Gharnata eight years ago had completed the Reconquest. It had always been on the cards and neither Umar nor his friends had been particularly surprised. But the surrender terms had promised the Believers, who comprised a majority of the citizenry, cultural and religious freedom once they recognized the suzerainty of the Castilian rulers. It was stated on paper and in the presence of witnesses that Gharnata's Muslims would not be persecuted or prevented from practising their religion, speaking and teaching Arabic or celebrating their festivals. Yes, Umar thought, that is what Isabella's prelates had pledged in order to avoid a civil war. And we believed them. How blind we were. Our brains must have been poisoned by alcohol. How could we have believed their fine words and promises?

As a leading noble of the Kingdom, Umar had been present when the treaty was signed. He would never forget the last farewell of the last Sultan, Abu Abdullah, the one the Castilians called Boabdil, to the al-Pujarras where a palace awaited him. The Sultan had turned and looked for the last time towards the city, smiled at the al-Hamra and sighed. That was all. Nothing was said. What was there to say? They had reached the terminus of their history in al-Andalus. They had spoken to each other with their eyes. Umar and his fellow nobles were prepared to acccept this defeat. After all, as Zubayda never ceased to remind him, was not Islamic history replete with the rise and fall of kingdoms? Had not Baghdad itself fallen to an army of Tatar illiterates? The curse of the desert. Nomadic destinies. The cruelty of fate. The words of the prophet. Islam is either universal or it is nothing.

He suddenly saw the gaunt features of his uncle's face. His uncle! Meekal al-Malek. His uncle! The Bishop of Qurtuba. Miguel el Malek. That gaunt face on which the pain was ever present and could not be concealed either by the beard or the false smiles. Ama's stories of Meekal as a boy always contained the phrase, 'he had the devil in him', or 'he behaved like a tap turned on and off by Satan.' It was always said with love and affection to stress what a naughty child Meekal had been. The youngest and favourite son, not unlike Yazid. So what had gone wrong? What had Meekal experienced that forced him to run away to Qurtuba and become Miguel?

The old uncle's mocking voice was still resounding in Umar's head. 'You know the trouble with your religion, Umar? It was too easy for us. The Christians had to insert themselves into the pores of the Roman Empire. It forced them to work below the ground. The catacombs of Rome were their training-ground. When they finally won, they had already built a great deal of social solidarity with their people. Us? The Prophet, peace be upon him, sent Khalid bin Walid with a sword and he conquered. Oh yes, he conquered a great deal. We destroyed two empires. Everything fell into our lap. We kept the Arab lands and Persia and parts of Byzantium. Elsewhere it was difficult, wasn't it? Look at us. We have been in al-Andalus for seven hundred years and still we could not build something that would last. It's not just the Christians, is it Umar? The fault is in ourselves. It is in our blood.'

Yes, yes, Uncle Meekal, I mean Miguel. The fault is also in ourselves, but how can I even think about that now? All I see is that wall of fire and behind it the gloating face of that vulture, celebrating his triumph. The curse of Ximenes! That cursed monk dispatched to our Gharnata on the express instructions of Isabella. The she-devil's confessor sent here to exorcise her demons. She must have known him well. He undoubtedly knew what she wanted. Can't you hear her voice? Father, she whispers in her tone of false piety, Father, I am troubled by the unbelievers in Gharnata. I sometimes get the urge to crucify them into submission so that they can take the path of righteousness. Why did she send her Ximenes to Gharnata? If they were so confident of the superiority of their beliefs why not trust in the ultimate judgement of the believers?

Have you forgotten why they sent Ximenes de Cisneros to Gharnata? Because they did not think that Archbishop Talavera was going about things the right way. Talavera wanted to win us over by argument. He learnt Arabic to read our books of learning. He told his clergy to do the same. He translated their Bible and catechisms into Arabic. Some of our brethren were won over in this fashion, but not many. That's why they sent Ximenes. I described it to you only last year my Bishop Uncle, but you have forgotten already. What would you have done if they had been really clever and appointed you Archbishop of Gharnata? How far would you have gone, Meekal? How far, Miguel?

I was present at the gathering when Ximenes tried to win over our *qadis* and learned men in theological dispute. You should have been there. One part of you would have been proud of our scholars. Ximenes is clever. He is intelligent, but he did not succeed that day.

When Zegri bin Musa replied point by point and was applauded even by some of Ximenes' clergymen, the prelate lost his temper. He claimed that Zegri had insulted the Virgin Mary when all that our friend had done was to ask how she could have remained a virgin after the birth of Isa. Surely you can see that the question followed a certain logic, or does your theology prevent you from acknowledging all known facts?

Our Zegri was taken to the torture-chamber and treated so brutally that he agreed to convert. At that stage we left, but not before I had seen that glint in Ximenes' eyes, as if he realized at that instant that his was the only way to convert the population.

The next day the entire population was ordered out on to the streets. Ximenes de Cisneros, may Allah punish him, declared war on our culture and our way of life. That day alone they emptied all our libraries and built a massive wall of books in the Bab al-Ramla. They set our culture on fire. They burnt two million manuscripts. The record of eight centuries was annihilated in a single day. They did not burn everything. They were not, after all, barbarians, but the carriers of a different culture which they wanted to plant in al-Andalus. Their own doctors pleaded with them to spare three hundred manuscripts, mainly concerned with medicine. To this Ximenes agreed, because even he knew that our knowledge of medicine was much more advanced than everything they knew in Christendom.

It is this wall of fire that I see all the time now, Uncle. It fills my heart with fear for our future. The fire which burnt our books will one day destroy everything we have created in al-Andalus, including this little village built by our forefathers, where you and I both played as little boys. What has all this got to do with the easy victories of our Prophet and the rapid spread of our religion? That was eight hundred years ago, Bishop. The wall of books was only set on fire last year.

Satisfied that he had won the argument, Umar bin Abdallah returned to the house and entered his wife's bed-chamber. Zubayda had not yet gone to sleep.

'The wall of fire, Umar?'

He sat down on the bed and nodded. She felt his shoulders and recoiled. 'The tenseness in your body hurts me. Here, lie down and I will knead it out of you.'

Umar did as she asked and her hands, expert in the art, found the points in his body. They were as hard as little pebbles and her fingers worked round them till they began to melt and she felt the tense zones beginning to relax once again.

'When will you reply to Miguel on the question of Hind?'

'What does the girl say?'

'She would rather be wed to a horse.'

Umar's mood registered a sharp change. He roared with laughter. 'She always did have good taste. Well there you have your answer.'

'But what will you tell His Bishopness?'

'I will tell Uncle Miguel that the only way Juan can be sure of finding a bed-partner is for him to become a priest and utilize the confessional!'

Zubayda giggled in relief. Umar had recovered his spirits. Soon he would be back to normal. She was wrong. The wall of books was still on fire.

'I am not sure that they will let us live in al-Andalus without converting to Christianity. Hind marrying Juan is a joke, but the future of the Banu Hudayl, of those who have lived with us, worked for us for centuries. That is what worries me deeply.'

'Nobody knows better than you that I am not a religious person. That superstitious old wet-nurse of yours knows this only too well. She tells our Yazid that his mother is a blasphemer, even though I keep up a pretence. I fast during Ramadan. I . . .'

'But we all know that you fast and pray to preserve your figure. Surely this is not a secret.'

'Make fun of me, but what matters the most is the happiness of our children. And yet . . .'

Umar had become serious again. 'Yes?'

'And yet something in me rebels against the act of conversion. I begin to feel agitated, even violent, when I think about it. I would rather die than cross myself and pretend that I am eating human flesh and drinking human blood. The cannibalism in their ritual repels me. It goes very deep. Remember the shock of the Saracens when the Crusaders began to roast prisoners alive and eat their flesh. It makes me ill to even think of it, but it flows from their faith.'

'What a contradictory woman you are, Zubayda bint Quddus. In one breath you say that what matters most to you is the well-being of our children, and in the same breath you exclude the only act which might guarantee them a future in their own ancestral home.'

'What has that got to do with happiness? All your children, including little Yazid, are ready to take up arms against Isabella's knights. Even if you allow your own sceptical mind to be crushed by Miguel, how will you convince your own children? For them your conversion would be as big a blow as the wall of fire.'

'It is a political and not a spiritual matter. I will communicate with the Maker just as I have always done. It is simply a question of appearances.'

'And when Christian nobles come on feast-days will you eat pork with them?'

'Perhaps, but never with my right hand.'

Zubayda laughed, but she was also shocked. She felt that he was close to a decision. The wall of fire had affected his brain. Very soon he would follow in Miguel's footsteps. Once again he surprised her.

'Did I ever tell you what several hundred of us found ourselves chanting that night while they were destroying our inheritance?'

'No. Have you forgotten that you were silent for a whole week after you returned from Gharnata? Not a word did you speak to anyone, not even Yazid. I pleaded, but you could not bring yourself to speak of it.'

'No matter. We wept like children that night, Zubayda. If our tears had been properly channelled they would have extinguished the flames. But suddenly I found myself singing something I had learnt as a youth. Then I heard a roar and I realized I was not the only one who knew the words of the poet. That feeling of solidarity filled me with a strength which has never left me. I'm telling you this so that you understand once and forever that I will never convert voluntarily.'

Zubayda hugged her husband and kissed him gently on the eyes.

'What were the words of the poet?'

Umar stifled a sigh and whispered by her side:

> 'The paper ye may burn,
> But what the paper holds ye cannot burn;
> 'tis safe within my breast.
> Where I remove, it goes with me;
> Alights when I alight,
> And in my tomb will lie.'

Zubayda remembered. Her private tutor, a born sceptic, had told her the story hundreds of times. The lines came from Ibn Hazm, born five hundred years before, just when the light of Islamic culture was beginning to illuminate some of the darkest crevices in the continent of Europe.

Ibn Hazm, the most eminent and courageous poet in the entire history of al-Andalus. A historian and biographer who had written four hundred volumes. A man who worshipped true knowledge, but was no respecter of persons. His caustic attacks on the preachers of orthodox Islam led to them excommunicating him after Friday prayers in the great mosque. The poet had spoken those words when the Muslim divines had publicly committed some of his works to the flames in Ishbiliya.

'I learnt about him too, but he has been proved wrong, hasn't he? The Inquisition goes one step further. Not content with burning ideas, they burn those who supply them. There is a logic. With every new century there are new advances.'

She heaved a sigh of relief, confident in the knowledge that her husband was not going to be rushed into a decision which he would regret for the rest of his life. She stroked his head as if to reassure him, but he was already asleep.

Despite her best efforts, Zubayda's mind would not slow down and let her sleep. Her thoughts had now wandered to the fate of her eldest son, Zuhayr. Fortunately the wound had not been serious, not this time, but given his headstrong character and impetuosity, anything could happen. Gharnata was too dangerous. The best solution, thought Zubayda, would be for him to marry her favourite niece, Khadija, who lived with her family in Ishbiliya. It would be a good match. The village needed a celebration, and a big family wedding was the only way now to provide a diversion without provoking the authorities. And with these innocent plans for tomorrow's pleasures the lady of the house lulled herself into sleep.

Chapter 2

How BEWITCHING, HOW magnificent, is a September morning in al-Hudayl. The sun has not yet risen, but its rays have lit the sky and the horizon is painted in different shades of purplish orange. Every creature wallows in this light and the accompanying silence. Soon the birds will start chattering and the muezzin in the village will summon the faithful to prayer.

The two thousand or so people who live in the village are used to these noises. Even those who are not Muslims appreciate the clockwork skills of the muezzin. As for the rest, not all respond to the call. In the master's house, it is Ama alone who stretches her mat in the courtyard and gets down to the business of the day.

Over half the villagers work on the land, either for themselves or directly for the Banu Hudayl. The rest are weavers, who work at home or on the estate, the men cultivating the worm and the women producing the famous Hudayl silk, for which there is a demand even in the market at Samarkand. Add to these a few shopkeepers, a blacksmith, a cobbler, a tailor, a carpenter, and the village is complete. The retainers on the family estate, with the exception of the Dwarf, Ama and the tribe of gardeners, all return to their families in the village every night.

Zuhayr bin Umar woke early feeling completely refreshed, his wound forgotten, but the cause of it still burning in his head. He looked out of the window and marvelled at the colours of the sky. Half a mile from the village there was a hillock with a large cavity marking the rocks at the summit. Everybody referred to it as the old man's cave. On that hill, set in the cave, was a tiny, whitewashed room. In that room there lived a man, a mystic, who recited verses in rhymed prose and whose company Zuhayr had begun to value greatly ever since the fall of Gharnata.

No one knew where he had come from or how old he was or when he had arrived. That is what Zuhayr believed. Umar recollected the cave, but insisted that it had been empty when he was a boy and, had, in fact, been used as a trysting place by the peasants. The old man enjoyed enhancing the mystery of his presence in the cave. Whenever Zuhayr asked him any personal questions, he would parry the thrust by bursting into poetry. Despite it all, Zuhayr felt that the old fraud was genuine.

This morning he felt an urgent desire to converse with the dweller in the cave. He left his room and entered the hammam. As he lay in the bath he wished Yazid would wake up and come and talk to him. The brothers enjoyed their bath conversations a great deal, Yazid because he knew that in the bath Zuhayr was a captive for twenty minutes and could not escape, Zuhayr because it was the only opportunity to observe the young hawk at close quarters.

'Who's in the bath?'

The voice belonged to Ama. The tone was peremptory.

'It's me, Ama.'

'May Allah bless you. Are you up already? Has the wound . . . ?'

Zuhayr's laughter stopped her in her tracks. He got out of the bath, robed himself and stepped out into the courtyard.

'Wound! Let us not joke, Ama. A Christian fool attacked me with a pen-knife and for you I am already on the edge of martyrdom.'

'The Dwarf is not yet in the kitchen. Should I make you some breakfast?'

'Yes, but when I return. I'm off to the old man's cave.'

'But who will saddle your horse?'

'You've known me since I was born. Do you think I can't ride a horse bareback?'

'Give that Iblis a message from me. Tell him I know full well that it was he who stole three hens from us. Tell him if he does so again, I will bring a few young men from the house and have him whipped publicly in the village.'

Zuhayr laughed indulgently and patted her on the head. The old man a common thief? How ridiculous Ama was in her stupid prejudices.

'You know what I'd love for breakfast today?'

'What?'

'The heavenly mixture.'

'Only if you promise to threaten that Iblis in my name.'

'I will.'

Fifteen minutes later Zuhayr was galloping towards the old man's cave on his favourite mount, Khalid. He waved to villagers on their way to the fields, their midday meal packed in a large handkerchief, attached to a staff. Some nodded politely and kept on walking. Others stopped and saluted him cheerfully. News of his confrontation in Gharnata had reached the whole village, and even the sceptics had been forced to utter the odd word of praise. There is no doubt that Zuhayr al-Fahl, Zuhayr the Stallion, as he was known, cut a very fine figure as he raced out of the village. Soon he was a tiny silhouette, now disappearing, now restored to view, as the topography dictated.

The old man saw horse and rider walking up the hill and smiled. The son of Umar bin Abdallah had come for advice once again. The frequency of his visits must displease his parents. What could he want this time?

'Peace be upon you, old man.'

'And upon you, Ibn Umar. What brings you here?'

'I was in Gharnata last night.'

'I heard.'

'And ... ?'

The old man shrugged his shoulders.

'Was I right or wrong?'

To Zuhayr's great delight the old man replied in verse:

> *'Falsehood hath so corrupted all the world*
> *That wrangling sects each other's gospel chide;*
> *But were not hate Man's natural element,*
> *Churches and mosques had risen side by side.'*

Zuhayr had not heard this one before and he applauded. 'One of yours?'

'Oh foolish boy. Oh ignorant creature. Can you not recognize the voice of a great master? Abu'l Ala al-Ma'ari.'

'But they say he was an infidel.'

'They say, they say. Who dares to say that? I defy them to say it in my presence!'

'Our religious scholars. Men of learning ...'

At this point the old man stood up, left his room, followed by a mystified Zuhayr, and adopted a martial pose as he recited from the hill-top in the loudest voice he could muster:

'*What is Religion? A maid kept so close that no eye may view her;*
The price of her wedding-gifts and dowry baffles the wooer.
Of all the goodly doctrine that from the pulpit I have heard
My heart has never accepted so much as a single word!'

Zuhayr grinned.
'Al-Ma'ari again?'
The old man nodded and smiled.
'I have learnt more from one of his poems than from all the books of religion. And I mean *all* the books.'
'Blasphemy!'
'Just the simple truth.'
Zuhayr was not really surprised by this display of scepticism. He always pretended to be slightly shocked. He did not wish the old man to think that he had won over a new disciple so easily. There was a group of young men in Gharnata, all of them known to Zuhayr and one of them a childhood friend, who rode over twenty miles to this cave at least once a month for lengthy discussions on philosophy, history, the present crisis and the future. Yes, always the future!

The mellow wisdom they imbibed enabled them to dominate the discussion amongst their peers back in Gharnata, and occasionally to surprise their elders with a remark so perceptive that it was repeated in every mosque on the following Friday. It was from his friend Ibn Basit, the recognized leader of the philosopher's cavalry, that Zuhayr had first heard about the intellectual capacities of the mystic who wrote poetry under the name of al-Zindiq, the Sceptic.

Before that he had unquestioningly accepted the gossip according to which the old man was an eccentric outcast, fed by the shepherds out of kindness. Ama often went further and insisted that he was no longer in full possession of his mind and, for that very reason, should be left to himself and his satanic devices. If she had been right, thought Zuhayr, I would be confronting a primal idiot instead of this quick-witted sage. But why and how had this hostility developed? He smiled.

The old man had been skinning almonds, which lay soaked in a bowl of water, when Zuhayr arrived. Now he began to grind them into a smooth paste, adding a few drops of milk when the mixture became too hard. He looked up and caught the smile.

'Pleased with yourself, are you? What you did in the city was thoughtless. A deliberate provocation. Fortunately your father is less foolish. If your retainers had killed that Christian, all of you would have been ambushed and killed on the way back.'

'In Heaven's name, how do you know?'

The old man did not reply, but transferred the paste from a stone bowl into a cooking pan containing milk. To this concoction he added some wild honey, cardamoms and a stick of cinnamon. He blew on the embers. Within minutes the mixture was bubbling. He reduced the fire by pouring ash on the embers and let it simmer. Zuhayr watched in silence as his senses were overpowered by the aroma. Then the pan was lifted and the old man stirred it vigorously with a well-seasoned wooden spoon and sprinkled some thinly sliced almonds on the liquid. Only then was it poured into two earthenware goblets, one of which was promptly presented to Zuhayr.

The young man sipped it and made ecstatic noises.

'Pure nectar. This is what they must drink in heaven all the time!'

'I think once they are up there,' muttered al-Zindiq, pleased with his success, 'they are permitted something much stronger.'

'But I have never tasted anything like this . . .'

He stopped in mid-sentence and put the goblet down on the ground in front of him. He had tasted this drink somewhere once before, but where? Where? Zuhayr stared at the old man, who withstood the scrutiny.

'What is the matter now? Too few almonds? Too much honey? These mistakes can ruin the drink, I know, but I have perfected the mixture. Drink it up my young friend. This is not the nectar which the Rumi gods consumed. It is brain juice of the purest kind. It feeds the cells. Ibn Sina it was, I think, who first insisted that almonds stimulated our thought-processes.'

It was a feint. Zuhayr saw that at once. The old man had

blundered. Zuhayr now remembered where he had last tasted a similar drink. In the house of Great-Uncle Miguel, near the Great Mosque, in Qurtuba. The old man must have some connection. He must. Zuhayr felt he was close to solving some mystery. What it was he did not know. The old man looked at the expression on the face in front of him and knew instinctively that one of his secrets was close to being uncovered. Before he could embark on a major diversion, his guest decided to go on the offensive.

'I have a message for you from Ama.'

'Ama? Ama? What Ama? Which Ama? I do not know any Ama.'

'My father's wet-nurse. She's always been with our family. The whole village knows her. And you, who claim to know everything that goes on in the village, do not know her? It is unbelievable!'

'Now that you explain it becomes clear. Of course I know who she is and how she always talks of matters which do not concern her. What about her?'

'She instructed me to inform you that she knew who had stolen three of our egg-laying hens . . .'

The old man began to roar with laughter at the preposterousness of such a notion. He, a thief?

'She said that if you did it again she would have you punished in front of the whole village.'

'Can you see any hens in this cave? Any eggs?'

'I don't really care. If you need anything from our house all you have to do is let me know. It will be here within the hour. I was just passing on a message.'

'Finish your drink. Should I heat some more?'

Zuhayr lifted the goblet and drained it in one gulp. He inspected the old man closely. He could be any age above sixty or perhaps sixty-five. His head was shaved once a week. The snow-white stubble growing on it meant that he was late for his weekly visit to the village barber. He had a very sharp, but small nose, like the beak of a bird, a wrinkled face of olive-brown hues, whose colour varied with the seasons. His eyes dominated everything else. They were not large or striking in the traditional sense, but the very opposite. It was their narrowness which gave them a hypnotic aspect, especially in the middle of heated discussions, when they began to shine like bright lamps in the dark or, as his enemies often said, like those of a cat on heat.

His white beard was trimmed, too neatly trimmed for an ascetic – an indication perhaps of his past. Usually, he was dressed in loose white trousers and a matching shirt. When it was cold he added a dark-brown blanket to the ensemble. Today, as the sun poured into his one-room abode, he was sitting there without a shirt.

It was the wrinkles on his withered chest which gave the real indication of his age. He was, undoubtedly, an old man. But how old? And why that irritating, sphinx-like silence, which contrasted so strangely with his open-minded nature and the fluency of his speech, whenever Zuhayr queried his origins? Not really expecting an answer, the son of Umar bin Abdallah none the less decided to pose the question once again.

'Who are you, old man?'

'You mean you really don't know?'

Zuhayr was taken aback.

'What do you mean?'

'Has that Ama of yours never told you? Clearly not. I can see the answer in your face. How incredible! So, they decided to keep quiet after all. Why don't you ask your parents one day? They know everything there is to know about me. Your search for the truth might be over.'

Zuhayr felt vindicated. So his instincts had been right after all. There was some link with the family.

'Does Great-Uncle Miguel know who you are?'

The old man's features clouded. He was displeased. His gaze fixed itself on the remains of the almond drink, and he sunk deep in thought. Suddenly he looked up.

'How old are you, Zuhayr al-Fahl?'

Zuhayr blushed. From al-Zindiq's lips, the nickname he had acquired sounded more like an accusation.

'I will be twenty-three next month.'

'Good. And why do the villagers call you al-Fahl?'

'I suppose because I love horse-riding. Even my father says that when he sees me riding Khalid he gets a feeling that the horse and I are one.'

'Complete nonsense. Mystical rubbish! Do you ever get that feeling?'

'Well, no. Not really, but it is true that I can get a horse, any horse you know, not just Khalid, to go faster than any of the men in the village.'

'Ibn Umar, understand one thing. That is not the reason they call you al-Fahl.'

Zuhayr was embarrassed. Was the old devil launching yet another line of attack to protect his own flank?

'Young master, you know what I'm talking about. It isn't just riding horses, is it? You jump on their women whenever you get the chance. I am told that you have a taste for deflowering the village virgins. The truth now!'

Zuhayr stood up in a rage.

'That is a lie. A gross calumny. I have never entered a wench against her will. Anyone who says otherwise I challenge to armed combat. This is not a joking matter.'

'Nobody has suggested that you force them. How could they be forced when it is your right? What use are wide open legs, if the mind remains closed? Why has my question annoyed you so much? Your father is a decent man, not given to excesses of any sort, but episodes such as these have been taking place in your family for centuries. Hot-blooded fool, sit down. Did you not hear me, sit down.'

Zuhayr did as he was told.

'Do you know Ibn Hasd, the cobbler?'

Zuhayr was perplexed by the question – what had that venerable figure to do with such a discussion? – but he nodded.

'Next time you meet him, study his features closely. You might see a resemblance.'

'To whom?'

'A general family resemblance, that's all.'

'Which family?'

'Yours, of course. Look for the mark of the Banu Hudayl.'

'Crazy old man. Ibn Hasd is a Jew. Like his forefathers . . .'

'What has that got to do with it? His mother used to be the most beautiful woman in the village. Your great-grandfather, Ibn Farid, espied her bathing in the river one day. He waited for her to finish and then forced her. The result was Ibn Hasd, who really is Ibn Mohammed!'

Zuhayr laughed. 'At least the old warrior had good taste. Somehow I can't imagine him as a . . .'

'Al-Fahl?' suggested the old man helpfully.

Zuhayr stood up to take his leave. The sun was high in the sky and he began thinking of Ama's heavenly mixture. The old man had outwitted him once again.

'I will take my leave now and I will do as you say. I will ask my father about your history.'

'Why are you in such a hurry?'

'Ama promised to make some heavenly mixture and . . .'

'Amira and her heavenly mixtures! Does nothing ever change in that cursed house? You have a weakness, Zuhayr al-Fahl. A weakness that will be your undoing. You are too easily convinced. Your friends lead you where they want, you become their tail. You do not question enough. You must think for yourself. Always! It is vital in these times when a simple choice is no longer abstract, but a matter of life or death.'

'You of all people have no right to say that. Have I not been questioning you for over two years? Have I not been persistent, old man?'

'Oh yes. I cannot deny that, but why then are you leaving just as I am about to tell you what you wish to know?'

'But I thought you said that I should ask . . .'

'Exactly. It was a ruse to distract you and, as always, it worked. Foolish boy! Your father will never tell you anything. Your mother? To tell the truth I do not know. She is a spirited lady and much respected, but on this matter I think she will follow your father. Remain with me, Ibn Umar. Soon I will tell you all.'

Zuhayr began to tremble in anticipation. The old man heated some water and prepared a container of coffee, after which he moved the cooking utensils to one side and dragged a large, well-used, hand-woven rug to the centre of the cave. He sat down cross-legged and beckoned Zuhayr to join him. When they were both seated, the old man poured out two bowls. He sipped noisily and began to speak.

'We thought the old days might end everywhere else, but never in our Gharnata. We were convinced that the kingdom of Islam would survive in al-Andalus, but we underestimated our own capacity for self-destruction. Those days will never return, and do you know why? Because the self-styled defenders of the faith quarrelled amongst themselves, killed each other, and proved incapable of uniting against the Christians. In the end it was too late.

'When Sultan Abu Abdullah was looking for the last time on his lost kingdom, he started to weep, whereupon his mother, the Lady Ayesha, remarked: "You may well weep like a woman, for what you could not defend like a man." I always felt this was unfair. By that time the Christians had overwhelming military superiority. We used to think that the Sultan of Turkey might send us help, and look-outs were posted in Malaka, but nothing came. All that was just fifteen years ago. The times I am going to tell you about are almost a hundred years old.

'Your great-grandfather, Ibn Farid, was an exceptional soldier. It is said that he was more feared by the Christian knights than even Ibn Kassim, and that, believe me, is saying a lot. Once at the siege of Medina Sid he rode out alone on his steed and galloped to the tent of the Castilian King. "Oh King of the Christians," he shouted. "I challenge each and every one of your knights to personal combat. The Emir has instructed me to tell you that if I am felled by one of your men we will open the gates to you, but if, by the time the sun sets, I am still on my horse, then you must retreat."

'Their King, knowing your great-grandfather's reputation, was reluctant to agree, but the Christian knights rebelled. They felt that to refuse such an offer was an insult to their manhood. So the offer was accepted. And what had to happen, happened. When the sun had set, the lord of the Banu Hudayl was dripping with blood, but he was still on his horse. Nearly sixty Christian knights lay dead. The siege was lifted . . . for a week. Then they came back, took the garrison by surprise, and ultimately won, but Ibn Farid had returned to al-Hudayl by that time.

'Your grandfather Abdallah was only two years old when his much-loved mother, the Lady Najma, died giving birth to your Great-Aunt Zahra. Her younger sister, the Lady Maryam took her place and became a mother to the two children. And what a mother. It is said that the children grew up believing that she was their real mother.'

Zuhayr was beginning to get impatient. 'Are you sure this is the story of *your* life? It sounds more like mine. I was brought up on fairy stories about my great-grandfather.'

Al-Zindiq's eyes narrowed as he glared at Zuhayr. 'If you

interrupt me once more, I will never discuss the matter with you again. Is that clear?'

Zuhayr indicated his agreement to these harsh conditions and the old man resumed the tale.

'But there were problems. Ibn Farid showed great respect and affection to his new wife, but passion there was none. Maryam could substitute for her sister in every other way, but not in your great-grandfather's bed. He simply lost the use of that implement with which every man has been endowed. Many physicians and healers came to see him. Restorative potions of the most exotic sort arrived and were poured down his throat to revive his lost ardour. Nothing happened. Beautiful virgins were paraded before his bed, but nothing moved.

'What they did not realize was that diseases of the mind cannot be cured like those of the body. You see, my young friend, when the spirits are low the cock does not crow! Are you sure you don't know any of this?'

Zuhayr shook his head.

'I am truly surprised to learn that. Both Ama and the Dwarf know every detail. One of them should have told you.' And the old man expressed his disapproval of the pair he had named by sniffing violently and spitting the phlegm out of the cave with both skill and accuracy.

'Please do not stop now. I must know it all,' said Zuhayr, in a voice which was both pleading and impatient. The old man smiled as he poured out some more coffee.

'One day when Ibn Farid was visiting his uncle in Qurtuba, the two of them rode out of the city to the village of a Christian nobleman whose family and yours had been friends since the fall of Ishbiliya. The nobleman, Don Alvaro, was not at home. Nor was his lady. But while they were waiting a young serving maid brought in some fruit and drinks. She must have been fifteen or sixteen years old at the most.

'Her name was Beatrice and she was a beautifully shaped creature. Her skin was the colour of ripe apricots, her eyes were the shape of almonds, and her whole face smiled. I saw her soon afterwards and even as a boy it was difficult not to be affected by her beauty. Ibn Farid could not take his eyes off her. His uncle realized straight away what had happened. He attempted to leave, but your great-grandfather refused to stir from the house. His uncle later told the family that even then he had a presentiment that Ibn Farid was heading for the precipice, but all his warnings and fears and evil portents were of no avail. Ibn Farid was known for his obstinacy.

'When Don Alvaro returned with his sons, they were delighted to see the visitors. A feast was prepared. Beds were made ready. There was no question of the two men being permitted to return to Qurtuba that night. A messenger was dispatched to inform the family that Ibn Farid would not be returning till the next day. You can guess how delighted he was. Finally, late at night, the great warrior meekly asked his host about the maid.

' "You too, my friend, you too?" said Don Alvaro. "Beatrice is the daughter of Dorothea, our cook. What is it that you desire? If you want to bed the wench it could, no doubt, be arranged."

'Imagine Don Alvaro's surprise when his generous response led to Ibn Farid rising from his cushions, red in the face with anger, and challenging his host to a duel. Don Alvaro realized that the matter was serious. He stood up and hugged Ibn Farid. "What is it you desire my friend?" Everyone became silent. Ibn Farid's voice was choked with emotion. "I want her for my wife, that is all." His uncle fainted at this stage, though he had probably just succumbed to the alcohol. What could Don Alvaro say? He said the girl's father was dead and he would have to ask Dorothea, but he was candid enough to make it clear that, since the woman was in his employment, a refusal was most unlikely.

'Your great-grandfather could not wait. "Summon her now!" Don Alvaro did as he was told. A perplexed and puzzled Dorothea arrived and bowed to the assembled company. "Oh Dorothea," Don Alvaro began, "my guests have enjoyed your food a great deal and this great knight, Ibn Farid, compliments you on your cooking. He also compliments you on the beauty of young Beatrice. We who have seen her grow up these last few years take her features for granted, but to any outside she appears devastating. Have you any plans for her marriage?" Poor woman, what could she say? She too was very striking, with her magnificent frame and flowing red hair which reached her knees. She was stunned by the enquiry. She shook her head in disbelief. "Well then," Don Alvaro continued, "I have good news for you. My friend, Ibn Farid, wants her for his wife.

Understand? His wife for all time, not a concubine for one night! He will pay you a handsome dowry. What do you say?"

'You can imagine, Ibn Umar, the state of that poor woman. She started weeping, which moved Ibn Farid, and he spoke and explained to her once again that his intentions were fully honourable. She looked then at Don Alvaro and said: "As you please, my Lord. She has no father. You decide." And Don Alvaro decided at that very moment that on the next morning Beatrice would become your great-grandmother number three. More wine was consumed. Such joy, we were later told, had not been seen on the face of your ancestor since the day your grandfather was born. He was in the seventh heaven. He began to sing, and he did so with such obvious joy and passion that the infection spread and they all joined him. He never forgot that poem and it was sung in your home regularly from that time on.'

Zuhayr stiffened.

'Was it the Khamriyya? The Hymn to Wine?'

The old man smiled and nodded. Zuhayr, deeply moved by the story of Ibn Farid's passion, suddenly burst into song.

'Let the swelling tide of passion my senses drown!
Pity love's fuel, this long-smouldering heart,
Nor answer with a frown,
When I would fain behold thee as thou art.
For love is life, and death in love the heaven
Wherein all sins are readily forgiven . . .'

'Wa Allah!' the old man exclaimed. 'You sing well.'

'I learnt the words from my father.'

'And he from his, but it was the first time that was the most important. Should I continue or have you had enough for today? The sun is already shining on the peaks. Your heavenly mixture awaits you at home. If you are tired . . .'

'Please continue. Please!'

And the old man continued.

'The next morning, after breakfast, Beatrice converted to Islam. When offered a choice of Muslim names she appeared puzzled, and so it came about that even her new name was decided by her husband-to-be. Asma. Asma bint Dorothea.

'Poor child. She had been informed about her impending nuptials when she woke up, early that morning, to clean the kitchen and light the fire. She was in tears. Some hours later, the wedding ceremony took place. It was your great-grandfather's uncle who, as the only other Muslim present, had to perform the ritual. Ours is a simple religion. Birth, death, marriage, divorce do not involve any elaborate rituals, unlike the system devised by the monks.

'Ibn Farid was in a hurry because he wanted to present the family with an irreversible fact. Any delay, he felt, could have been fatal. The brothers of Najma and Maryam belonged to that section of the family which specialized in settling disputes with other clans. They were expert assassins. Naturally they would regard it as an outrage that their sister was being bypassed in favour of a Christian slave-girl. Concubines are, as you know, permissible. But this was different. A new mistress of the household was being chosen without their knowledge or consent. She would, no doubt, bear him children. Given time to think they might have tried to kill Beatrice. Ibn Farid was known throughout al-Andalus as "the lion" for his courage, but he could play the fox with equal skill. If he was actually married, he knew that he would have the advantage of his brothers-in-law. Of course his uncle was angry, but he did not quarrel with his nephew in the house of Don Alvaro. That came later.

'So Ibn Farid and Asma bint Dorothea returned to Qurtuba. They rested for a day and a night before beginning the two-day journey to the kingdom of Gharnata and the safety of al-Hudayl. Unknown to Ibn Farid news had already reached the house, through a special messenger, dispatched by his uncle.

'The atmosphere in the house was one of mourning. Your grandfather Abdallah, was then eighteen years old, already a man. Your great-aunt, Zahra, was four years younger, the same age as myself. They were walking up and down in the courtyard through which the stream flows, and they were both in a state of great agitation. I was watching them get more and more upset without knowing the cause. When I asked your grandfather he shouted at me: "Son of a dog, get out of here. It is none of your concern." He had never spoken like that to me before. As the Lady Maryam came out of her room, both of them rushed up to her and embraced her, weeping all the while. My insolence was happily forgotten. I loved your grandfather very much, and what he said to me that day hurt me badly. Later, of course, I understood the reason for his anger, but till that day I had always played with him and Zahra as an equal. Something had changed. Once calm had returned we both tried to return to our habits of the old days, but it was never the same again. I could never forget that he was the young master and he was constantly reminded that I was the son of a serving woman, who had now been assigned the duty of attending to the needs of the Lady Asma.'

At last, thought Zuhayr, he is beginning to talk about himself; but before he could ask a question, the old man had moved on.

'Lady Maryam was the most gentle of women, even though her tongue could be very cruel if any of the maids, except of course for your Ama, attempted even the tiniest degree of familiarity. I remember her so well. Sometimes she used to go and bathe in a large freshwater pool made by the river. She was preceded by six serving women and followed by another four maid-servants. They held sheets on either side of her to ensure total privacy. The party usually proceeded in silence unless Zahra happened to be with her. Then aunt and niece chattered away and the maids were permitted to laugh at Zahra's remarks. The servants respected Maryam, but did not like her. Her dead sister's children worshipped her blindly. For your grandfather and great-aunt she could do no wrong. They knew their father was not happy with her. They felt, the way children usually do, that whatever the problem was it went very deep, but they never stopped loving her.'

The old man stopped abruptly and peered into his listener's troubled eyes.

'Something is worrying you, young master? Do you wish to leave now and return another day? The story cannot run away.'

Zuhayr's eyes had picked up a small figure on the horizon and the dust indicated it was a rider galloping on a mission. He suspected it was a messenger from al-Hudayl.

'I fear we are about to be interrupted. If the man on horseback is a messenger from our house, I will return at sunrise tomorrow. Could you satisfy my curiosity on one question, before I leave today?'

'Ask.'

'Who are you, old man? Your mother served in our house, but who was your father? Could you be a member of our family?'

'I am not sure. My mother was a piece of the dowry, a serving girl who came with the Lady Najma from Qurtuba when she married Ibn Farid. She must have been sixteen or seventeen years old at the time. My father? Who knows? My mother said that he was a gardener on your estates, who was killed in one of the battles near Malaka the year I was born. It is true that she was married to him, but Heaven alone knows if he was my father. In later years, after the sudden and mysterious death of Asma bint Dorothea and the strange circumstances of my own mother's demise, I would hear stories about my real father. It was said the seed which produced me was planted by Ibn Farid. It would certainly explain his behaviour in later years, but if that had been the case my mother would have told me herself. I stopped caring much about it.'

Zuhayr was intrigued by this turn of events. He now remembered vaguely the stories Ama used to tell about the tragedy of the Lady Asma, but he could not even recall their outlines. He was desperate to stay and hear it all, but the dust seemed closer.

'You are still concealing one important fact.'

'What may that be?'

'Your name, old man, your name.'

The old man's head, which had been held erect for all this time, suddenly slumped as he contemplated the patterns on the rug. Then he looked up at Zuhayr and smiled.

'I have long forgotten the name my mother gave me. Perhaps your Ama or the Dwarf will remember. For too many decades my friends and enemies have known me as Wajid al-Zindiq. That was the name I used when I wrote my first book. It is a name of which I am still very proud.'

'You claimed you knew why they called me al-Fahl. I will have to think hard to come up with something equally sharp to explain to you why you acquired such a name.'

'The answer is simple. It describes me well. I am, after all, a sceptic, an ecstatic freethinker!'

Both of them laughed. As the horseman arrived outside the cave, they stood up and Zuhayr, impulsive as usual, hugged the old man and kissed his cheeks. Al-Zindiq was moved by the

41

gesture. Before he could say anything the messenger coughed gently.

'Come in, man. Enter. Is it a message from my father?' said Zuhayr.

The boy nodded. He was barely thirteen years old.

'Excuse me, my lord, but the master says you must return at once. They were expecting you back for breakfast.'

'Good. You climb on that mule you call a horse and ride back. Tell them I am on my way. Wait. I've changed my mind. Go back now. I will overtake you in a few minutes. I will greet my father myself. There are no messages.'

The boy nodded, and was about to leave when al-Zindiq stopped him. 'Come here, son. Are you thirsty?'

The boy looked at Zuhayr, who nodded slightly. The boy eagerly took the cup of water he was being offered and drank it in one gulp.

'Here, take a few dates for your ride back. You will have time to eat them after the young master has overtaken you.'

The boy gratefully accepted the fruit, bowed to the men and was soon to be seen coaxing his horse to retrace their route to the mountain.

'Peace be upon you, Wajid al-Zindiq.'

'And you, my son. Could I request a favour?'

'Whatever you like.'

'When your father permitted me to live here a quarter of a century ago he insisted on one condition and that alone. My lips were to remain sealed on all affairs concerning his family. If he were ever to discover that this condition had been breached, his permission would be withdrawn. And so would the supplies of food which your mother has so kindly organized for me. My future depends on your silence. There is nowhere else left for me to go.'

Zuhayr was outraged.

'But this is unacceptable. It is unjust. It is not like my father. I will . . .'

'You will do nothing. Your father may have been wrong, but he had his reasons. I want your pledge that you will remain silent.'

'You have my word. I swear on the al-koran . . .'

'Your word alone is sufficient.'

'Of course, al-Zindiq, but in return I want your promise that you will complete the story.'

'I had every intention of doing so.'

'Peace be upon you then, old man.'

Al-Zindiq walked to where Khalid was tethered and smiled appreciatively as Zuhayr jumped on to his bare back. Al-Zindiq patted the horse.

'Riding a horse without a sack . . .'

'I know,' shouted Zuhayr, '. . . is like riding on a devil's back. If that were true, all I can say is that the devil must have a comfortable back.'

'Peace be upon you, al-Fahl. May your house flourish,' shouted the old man with a grin on his face as Zuhayr galloped down the hill.

For a while al-Zindiq stood there silently appreciating the skill of the departing horseman.

'I used to ride like that once. You remember don't you, Zahra?'

There was no reply.

Chapter 3

Y AZID HAD WOKEN up from his afternoon sleep, trembling slightly, with sweat pouring down his face. His mother, lying next to him, was anxious at seeing her last-born in this state. She wiped his face with a linen cloth soaked in rose-water and felt his forehead. It was as cool as the afternoon breezes in the courtyard. There was no cause for alarm.

'Are you feeling unwell my son?'

'No. I just had a strange dream. It was so real, Ummi. Why are afternoon dreams more real? Is it because our sleep is lighter?'

'Perhaps. Want to tell me about it?'

'I dreamt of the Mosque in Qurtuba. It was so beautiful, Mother. And then Great-Uncle Miguel entered and began to pour bottles of blood everywhere. I tried to stop him, but he hit me . . .'

'What we see in dreams outdoes reality,' Zubayda interrupted him. She did not like the continuous attacks on Miguel which the children were fed by Ama, and so she tried to divert her son's mind. 'But all that one could dream of the Great Mosque in Qurtuba falls short of the truth. One day we shall take you to see its magnificent arches. As for Miguel . . .' She sighed.

Zuhayr, on his way to the bath, had overheard the conversation and entered his mother's room silently, just in time to hear Yazid's condemnation of the Bishop of Qurtuba.

'I don't like him. I never have. He always squeezes my cheeks too hard. Ama says one can't expect anything better. She said that his mother, the Lady Asma, didn't like him either. You know, Mother, once I heard Ama and the Dwarf talking to each other about the Lady Asma. Ama said that it was Miguel who killed her. Is that true?'

Zubayda's face turned ashen. She gave an unconvincing little laugh. 'What foolishness is this? Of course Miguel did not kill his mother! Your father would be shocked to hear you talk in this fashion. Your Ama talks a lot of nonsense. You must not believe everything she says.'

'Are you sure of that, Mother?' asked Zuhayr in a mocking tone.

His voice startled both of them. Yazid leapt up and jumped straight into his arms. The brothers embraced and kissed each other. Their mother smiled.

'The cub is safely back with its protector. You were greatly missed this morning. Yazid has been wandering about annoying everyone including himself. What did that old man have to say that was so interesting?'

Zuhayr's answer to the predictable question had been carefully worked out on his ride back to the house.

'The tragedy of al-Andalus. The failure of our way of life to survive. He thinks we are at the terminus of our history. He is a very learned man, Mother. A true scholar. What do you know about him? He simply refuses to talk about himself.'

'Ask Ama,' said Yazid. 'She knows all about him.'

'I am going to tell Ama that in future she must keep her imagination under control and be careful when Yazid is present.'

Zuhayr smiled, and was about to enter the discussion on Ama and the merits of her many pronouncements, but he suddenly caught his mother's eye and the warning was clear. She had sat up in bed and a peremptory command soon followed.

'Go and bathe, Zuhayr. Your hair is full of dust.'

'And he smells of horse-sweat!' added Yazid, pulling a face.

The brothers left and Zubayda clapped her hands. Two maids-in-waiting entered the room. One carried a mirror and two combs. Without a word they began to gently massage the head of their mistress, two pairs of hands working in perfect symmetry. The twenty fingers, delicate and firm at the same time, covered the entire area from the forehead to the nape. In the background Zubayda could only hear the sound of water. When she felt her inner balance restored she signalled that they should cease their labours.

The two women settled down on the floor and, as Zubayda shifted her body and positioned herself on the edge of the bed, they began to work on her feet. The younger of the two, Umayma, was new to this task and her nervousness revealed itself in her inability to use the force necessary to knead her mistress's left heel.

'What are they saying in the village?' inquired Zubayda. Umayma had only recently been promoted to wait on her and she wanted to put the girl at her ease. The young maid-servant blushed on being addressed by her mistress and mumbled a few incoherent thoughts about the great respect everyone in the village had for the Banu Hudayl. Her older and more experienced colleague, Khadija, came to the rescue.

'All the talk is about Zuhayr bin Umar slapping the face of the infidel, my lady.'

'Zuhayr bin Umar is a rash fool! What does the talk say?'

Umayma had succeeded in suppressing a giggle, but Zubayda's informality reassured her and she responded clearly.

'The younger people agree with Ibn Umar, my lady, but many of the elders were displeased. They wondered whether the Christian had not been put up to the provocation and Ibn Hasd, the cobbler was worried. He thought they might send soldiers to attack al-Hudayl and take all of us prisoner. He said that . . .'

'Ibn Hasd is full of doom in good times, my lady.'

Khadija was worried lest Umayma gave too much away, and wanted to steer the conversation to safer waters, but Zubayda was insistent.

'Quiet. Tell me girl, what did Ibn Hasd say?'

'I cannot remember everything my lady, but he said that our sweet daydreams were over and soon we would wake up shivering.'

Zubayda smiled.

'He is a good man even when he thinks unhappy thoughts. A stone from the hand of a friend is like an apple. Have you taken my clothes to the hammam?'

Umayma nodded. Zubayda dismissed the pair with a tilt of her head. She knew full well that the cobbler was only expressing what the whole village felt. There was a great feeling of uncertainty. For the first time in six hundred years, the villagers of al-Hudayl were being confronted with the possibility of a life without a future for their children. There were a thousand and one stories circulating throughout Gharnata of what had happened after the Reconquest of Qurtuba and Ishbiliya. Each refugee had arrived with tales of terror and random bestiality. What had left a very deep imprint was the detailed descriptions of how land and estates and property in several towns had been seized by the Catholic Church and the Crown. It was this that the villagers feared more than anything else. They did not want to be driven off the lands which they and their ancestors before them had cultivated for centuries. If the only way to save their homes was to convert, then many would undergo that ordeal in order to survive. First among them would be the family steward, Ubaydallah, whose only gods were security and wealth.

Zubayda determined to discuss these problems with her husband and reach a decision. The villagers were looking towards the Banu Hudayl for an answer. She knew they must be frightened by Zuhayr's impulsiveness. Umar must go to the mosque on Friday. People wanted to be reassured.

As Zubayda walked through the courtyard she saw her sons playing chess. She observed the game for a minute and was amused to notice that the giant scowl disfiguring Zuhayr's features was a sure sign that Yazid was on the verge of victory. His young voice was excited as he announced his triumph: 'I always win when I have the black Queen on my side!'

'What are you saying, wretch? Control your tongue. Chess must be played in total silence. That is the first rule of the game. You chatter away like a crow on heat.'

'Your Sultan is trapped by my Queen,' said Yazid. 'I only spoke when I knew the game was over. No reason to get ill-tempered. Why should a drowning man be worried by rain?'

Zuhayr, angry at being defeated by a nine-year-old, laid his King on the table, gave a very weak laugh and stalked off.

'I'll see you at dinner, wretch!'

Yazid smiled at the Queen. He was collecting the pieces and stowing them in their special box when an old retainer, his face pale with fear as if he had seen a ghost, ran into the courtyard. Ama came out of the kitchen. He whispered something in her ear. Yazid had never seen the old woman look so worried. Could it be that a Christian army was invading al-Hudayl? Before he could rush to the tower and find out for himself, his father appeared on the scene, followed by Ama.

Yazid, not wanting to be left out, walked over casually to his father and held his hand. Umar smiled at him, but frowned at the servant.

'Are you sure? There can be no mistake?'

'None, my Lord. I saw the party with my own eyes pass through the village. There were two Christian soldiers accompanying the Lady and people were worried. It was Ibn Hasd who recognized her and told me to ride as fast as I could and let you know.'

'Wa Allah! After all these years. Go, man. Eat something before you return. Ama will take you to the kitchen. Yazid, go and tell your mother I wish to speak to her. After that inform your brother and sisters that we have a guest with us tonight. I want them to join me here so that we can greet our visitor as a family. Run, boy.'

Zahra bint Najma had exchanged a word with the cobbler, but otherwise she had not replied to the greetings addressed to her by the village elders. She had nodded slightly to acknowledge their presence, but nothing more. Once her cart had passed through the narrow streets of the village and reached the clump of trees from which the house was so clearly visible, she told the carter to follow the rough path that ran parallel to the stream.

'Go with the water till you see the house of the Banu Hudayl,' she said, her frail voice beginning to shake with emotion. She had never thought that she would live to see her home again. The tears, controlled for decades, burst with the quiet fury of a swollen river overflowing its banks. They are nothing now but memories, she told herself.

She had thought that in the course of half a century she had purged her system so thoroughly that hardly anything was left inside. How deceptive existence can be. Her first glance at the house told her that nothing had been erased. As she saw the familiar landscapes she remembered everything so vividly that it began to hurt again. There was the orchard of pomegranate trees. She smiled as the cart-horse slowed down, exhausted by the long journey, and drank some water from the stream. Even though it was autumn she could shut her eyes and smell the orchards.

'*Are you sure you weren't observed?*' *His voice nervous and excited.*

'*Only by the moon! I can hear your heart beating.*'

No more words were said that night till they had parted just before dawn.

'You will be my wife!'

'I want none other.'

She opened her eyes and drank in the last rays of the sun. Nothing had changed here. There were the giant walls and the tower. The gates were open as usual. Winter was already in the air. The scent of the soil overpowered her senses. The gentle noise and silken water of the stream that flowed through that courtyard and into the tanks that serviced the hammam – it was just as she recalled it all those years ago. And Abdallah's boy, Umar, was now master of this domain.

She felt the Christian soldiers with her grow suddenly tense, and soon she saw the cause. Three horsemen, dressed in blinding white robes and turbans, were riding towards her. The cart stopped.

Umar bin Abdallah and his two sons, Zuhayr and Yazid, reined in their horses and saluted the old lady.

'Peace be upon you, my father's sister. Welcome home.'

'When I left you were four years old. Your mother was always telling me to be more strict with you. Come here.'

Umar dismounted and walked to the cart. She kissed him on his head.

'Let us go home,' she whispered.

As they reached the entrance to the house, they saw the older servants waiting outside. Zahra disembarked as Ama limped forward and hugged her.

'Bismallah, bismallah. Welcome to your old home, my lady,' said Ama as the tears flowed down her face.

'I'm glad you're still alive, Amira. I really am. The past is forgotten and I do not wish it to return,' Zahra replied as the two ancients looked at each other.

Then she was escorted indoors, where Zubayda, Hind and Kulthum bowed and made their welcomes. Zahra inspected each of them in turn and then turned round to see if Yazid was following her. He was and she grabbed his turban and threw it in the air. This gesture relieved the tension as everyone laughed. Zahra knelt on the cushion and hugged Yazid. The boy, feeling instinctively that the act was genuine, reciprocated the affection.

'Great-Aunt Zahra, Ama told me you've been locked up in

the maristan in Gharnata for forty years, but you don't seem mad at all.'

Umar frowned at his son as a wave of nervousness gripped the family, but Hind roared with laughter.

'I agree with Yazid. Why did you not come sooner?'

Zahra smiled.

'At first I did not think that I would be welcome. Then I just did not think.'

Ama, followed by two young maids, walked in with towels and clean clothes.

'May Allah bless you, my lady. Your bath is ready. These girls will help you.'

'Thank you, Amira. After that I must eat something.'

'Dinner is ready, Aunt,' Zubayda interjected. 'We were waiting to eat with you.'

Ama took Zahra by the arm and they walked out into the courtyard, followed by the two maid-servants. Hind waited till they were out of earshot.

'Father! Great-Aunt Zahra is not mad, is she? Was she ever mad?'

Umar shrugged his shoulders and exchanged a rapid glance with Zubayda. 'I do not know, child. We were all told that she had lost her mind in Qurtuba. They sent her back here, but she refused to marry and started wandering about the hills on her own reciting blasphemous verses. I must confess I was never convinced about her illness. It seemed too convenient. My father adored her and was very unhappy at the decision, but Ibn Farid was a very hard man. We must make her last years happy ones.'

Hind was not prepared to change the subject.

'But Father, why did you never go to the maristan and visit her. Why?'

'I felt it might be too painful for her. I did think about it sometimes, but something always stopped me. My father used to go and see her, but each time he returned home in such a state of depression that he could not smile for weeks. I suppose I did not wish to reawaken those memories. But she is here now, my daughter and I'm sure that she will answer all your questions. Aunt Zahra was never renowned for her discretion.'

'I don't want you to imagine that we ignored her existence,' said Zubayda. 'Till last week fresh clothes and fruit were being sent to her every week on our behalf by your father's cousin Hisham.'

'I'm glad to hear that,' said Yazid in a very adult tone, which, much to his annoyance, made them all laugh and he had to turn away to conceal his own smile.

If there had been any doubts left about Zahra's sanity, they were all dispelled during dinner. She talked and laughed with such ease that it seemed as if she had always been part of their household. At one stage, when the discussion had inevitably moved to the tragedy of al-Andalus, the old lady revealed a politically perceptive streak that surprised Zubayda.

'Why did we go into decline? We fell prey to the fool's sense of honour! Do you know what that is Hind? Yazid? Zuhayr? No? Fools regard forgiveness as wrong.'

It was Hind who finally asked the question in everyone's mind.

'Great-Aunt, how did you get permission to leave the maristan? What happened?'

The old lady seemed genuinely surprised. 'You mean you don't know?'

Everyone shook their heads.

'We always were isolated from the rest of the world in this place. The whole of Gharnata is talking about what happened in the maristan. I thought you knew.' She began to chuckle. 'I'd better tell you, I suppose. Is there anything to sweeten the palate, niece?'

Before Zubayda could reply, Ama, who had been waiting patiently for them to finish the main part of the meal, spoke. 'Would my lady like some heavenly mixture?'

'Heavenly mixture! You remembered, Amira?'

'Yes, I did remember,' said Ama, 'but I was going to make some anyway for Zuhayr's breakfast, except that he did not return from his long ride till after midday. All the ingredients have been ready since the morning. The cornflour is kneaded and waiting to be shaped into cakes and baked. I will not be long.'

Seeing that they were all looking at her expectantly, Zahra realized that it was time to tell them, and so she began to recount the momentous incidents which had brought about a sudden change in her life.

'Ten days ago some friars arrived and began to enquire about the religion of the inmates. The majority were followers of the Prophet. The rest were Jews and there were a few Christians. The monks told the authorities that the Archbishop from Tulaytula . . .'

'Ximenes!' hissed Zuhayr. His great-aunt smiled.

'The same. He had instructed his monks to start the forced conversions. What better place to choose than the maristan? They did not need to threaten us, but they did. From henceforth only those who believed in the virginity of Mary and the divine status of Jesus would be permitted to stay. As you know alcohol is not permitted, and when the inmates saw these priests with their flasks of wine, they happily drank the blood of Christ. So the conversions proceeded smoothly.

'When it came to me, I told them: "Nothing is easier for me than abstinence from things unlawful, but I have news for you. I do not drink the devil's piss and yet I am already a convert of my own free will. In fact, much revered fathers, that is the reason my family sent me here. They thought I must have lost possession of my faculties when I announced that I had become a devoted follower of your Church." The poor priests were puzzled. I suppose they could have thought that I was really mad and chosen to ignore my story. For that reason, I pointed to the crucifix around my neck. And do you know something, children? It worked.

'The next morning I was taken to meet the Captain-General at the al-Hamra. Imagine, an inmate of a maristan meeting the representative of the Castilian King! He was most courteous. I told him what had happened to me. When he realized that I was the daughter of Ibn Farid he nearly fainted. He told me that he had heard stories of your great-grandfather's valour from his father and he immediately proceeded to tell me some of them. I knew them all, but I did not let him realize that and listened attentively to every word, smiling and gesturing at the right moments. The fact that it was my father's temper that had landed me in the maristan was somehow ignored by both of us. He asked me what I thought of the situation in Gharnata. I told him that forty years ago I had asked the Almighty to do me a very big favour and I was still praying for my desire to be granted before I died. "What is that favour, madame?" the Captain-

General enquired. "To give me strength not to meddle with that which does not concern me." '

Yazid started giggling at the way she was mimicking both the Captain-General and herself, and everyone laughed, even Kulthum, who had been overawed by the arrival of this mythical figure. Zahra, delighted with the effect of her stories, continued the tale. 'You may think this was an act of cowardice on my part, and you would be right. You see, my children, I wanted to get out. If I had told the truth . . . if I had let him know what I felt when that evil Ximenes burnt our books, I might still have been in the maristan or sent to some convent. You know they took all of us from the maristan to witness the bonfire of our culture. I thought then of this house and all the manuscripts in our library – Ibn Hazm, Ibn Khaldun, Ibn Rushd, Ibn Sina. At least here they would survive. I could have told the Captain-General all that, but they would never then have believed that I was sane. And my air of indifference had the effect I desired.

'The Captain-General rose, bowed and kissed my hand. "Rest assured, my dear lady, that you shall be escorted to your family estates as soon as you wish with an armed guard." Then he took his leave and I was brought back to the maristan. You can imagine my state. I had not left that building for four whole decades. I was preparing calmly for death and then all this happened. Incidentally, you must send those books away. Ship them to the University in al-Qahira or to Fes. Here they will never survive. Now I have nothing more to say. I only hope that I do not come as a burden.'

'This is your home,' replied Umar, slightly pompously. 'Perhaps you should never have left it.'

Hind hugged and kissed Zahra. The old woman was greatly moved by the spontaneity of the gesture.

'I never knew that you had become a Christian, Great-Aunt.'

'Nor did I,' replied Zahra, making Yazid scream with laughter.

'Did you make it all up to get out of there? Did you?'

Zahra nodded and all of them laughed, but something was worrying Yazid.

'Then where did you get the crucifix?'

'Made it myself. Time never intruded in that place. I carved many figures in wood to keep myself from really going mad.'

Yazid left his place and went and sat near Zahra, clutching her hand tightly as if to make sure that she was real.

'I can tell already that my nephew, like his father, is a good man. Your children are relaxed in your presence. It was never like that with us. Hmmmm. I can smell something good. That Amira has not lost her touch.' Ama entered with the maize cakes wrapped in cloth to keep them warm. She was followed by the Dwarf, who was carrying a metal container full of bubbling hot milk. Umayma came last with a pot full of raw, brown sugar. The Dwarf bowed to Zahra, who returned his greetings.

'Is your mother dead or alive, Dwarf?'

'She died some fifteen years ago, my lady. She was also praying for you.'

'She should have prayed for herself. Might have been still alive.'

Ama was beginning to prepare the heavenly mixture. Her hands were hidden in a large bowl where she was tearing the soft cakes apart. They crumbled easily. She added some fresh butter and carried on softening the mixture with her hands. Then she signalled to Umayma, who came forward and began to pour on the sugar while Ama's wrinkled hands continued to mix the ingredients. Finally the fingers withdrew. Zahra clapped her hands and proffered her bowl. Ama cupped her right hand and served her a large handful. The procedure was repeated for the others. Then the hot milk was poured on and the sweet course was taken. For a moment they were too busy savouring the delights of this simple concoction to thank its author.

'Heaven. It is simply heaven, Amira. What a wonderful heavenly mixture. Now I can die in peace.'

'I have never tasted such a heavenly mixture before, Ama,' said Yazid.

'This heavenly mixture could never have been created for me alone, Ama, could it?' asked Zuhayr.

'The taste of this heavenly mixture reminds me of my youth,' muttered Umar.

Ama was satisfied. The guest and the three men of the house had praised her in public. She had no cause to grumble tonight, Hind thought to herself as she laughed inwardly at the absurdity of this ritual, which dated back to Ibn Farid's first marriage.

Hind's bed-chamber had once belonged to Zahra. Now it had

been prepared again for the old lady. Hind had moved to a spare chamber in the women's section of the house, near her mother. Zahra was taken to her room by all the women in the family and Ama. She stood by the doorway in the courtyard and looked at the sky. A tear escaped, and then another.

'I used to dream about this courtyard every month. Remember the shadows of the pomegranate tree during the full moon, Amira? Remember what we used to say? If the moon is with us, what need do we have for the stars?'

Ama took her arm and gently propelled her through the door as Zubayda, Hind and Kulthum wished her a good night's sleep.

In another section of the courtyard, Umayma was on her way home after preparing the Lady Zubayda's bed-chamber, when an arm grabbed her and pulled her into a room.

'No, master,' she whispered.

Zuhayr felt her breasts, but as his hands began to roam elsewhere the girl stopped him.

'I cannot tonight, al-Fahl. I am unclean. If you don't believe me, dip your hand in and see for yourself.'

His hands fell to his side. He did not reply and Umayma flitted through the door and disappeared.

Hind and Kulthum had returned to their mother's bed-chamber. They were sitting on the bed watching Zubayda dismantle her hair and then undress.

Umar walked in through the door that connected their chambers.

'What a strange evening it has been. She was only two years younger than my father. I see a lot of him in her. They were so very close. I know how much he missed her. What a tragedy. What a waste of a life. Zahra could have been something truly great. Did you know she wrote poetry? And it was good. Even our grandfather, at a time when he was still very angry with her, had to admit that to himself . . .'

There was a knock on the door and Zuhayr entered the room.

'I heard voices and I knew it must be a family conference.'

'A family conference would be impossible without Yazid,' retorted Hind. 'He is the only one who takes them seriously. Abu was talking about our great-aunt before you galloped into the conversation.'

'That is what I came to hear. It is not every day that a ghost returns to life. What a woman she must have been. Banished from this house for over fifty years. How well she behaved tonight. No resentments. No anger. Just relief.'

'She has no cause to be angry with us,' said their father. 'We did her no harm.'

'Who did harm her, father? Who? Why? What was Great-Aunt Zahra's crime?'

Hind's impatient voice was edged with an anger she did not attempt to conceal. Without knowing anything about Zahra, except for the odd enigmatic remark from Ama or gossip she had picked up from their cousins in Ishbiliya, she had been touched by the dignity of the old woman. None of the stories tallied with the reality they had experienced today as the real Zahra had sought refuge from the turmoil of Gharnata in her ancestral home.

Umar looked at Zubayda, who nodded gently, and he accepted that there was a strong case for telling the children all he could remember of the mystery surrounding Zahra. There were many things he did not know. Of all those left alive, only Ama knew all the details, and perhaps one other person – barring Great-Uncle Miguel, who seemed to know everything.

'It was all such a long time ago,' began Umar bin Abdallah, 'that I'm not sure I remember all the details. What I am about to tell you was told to me by my mother, who liked Zahra and became very attached to her.

'I don't know exactly when Zahra's tragedy began. My mother used to say that it was the day your great-grandfather Ibn Farid, may he rest in peace, returned to al-Hudayl with his new wife, the Lady Asma. She was only a few years older than Zahra and made no attempt to alter the style or the pattern of life here. She left the management of the household to Grandmother Maryam. It is said that during her first months she was so much in awe of everything that she found it difficult to issue a command to a servant.

'Zahra and father were very close to their Aunt Maryam. It was she who had brought them up after their mother died. And so, in their hearts, she took their mother's place. Brother and sister saw Asma's entry into our house as an intrusion. Nothing improper ever took place, but a gulf had opened between them and their father. There is no doubt the servants played an unhealthy part in this whole affair. They were, after all, aware of Asma's origins. She had been a Christian kitchen girl, whose mother was still a cook, even though Ibn Farid invited her to leave Don Alvaro's service and join his household. All this provided endless seams of gossip for the whole village, and especially the kitchen in this house. You would have thought that there would be some fellow-feeling amongst the cooks, at the sudden elevation of one of their kind, but not a bit of it. The Dwarf's father, in particular, spread a great deal of venom, till one day Ibn Farid sent for him and threatened to execute him personally in the outer courtyard. The threat worked. Slowly, things calmed down. The fever began to abate.

'The trouble was that the servants had not even bothered to lower their voices when the children were present and the disease was infectious. Zahra became extremely disaffected. Ibn Farid had been the centre of her life. He had married Asma and Zahra felt betrayed. Simply in order to snub her father, she turned down every suitor. She withdrew more and more into herself. She could go for days without talking to anyone.

'Of course Ibn Farid had foreseen the effect of his marriage in the village. He was not unaware of the problems. For that reason he had hired a whole retinue of maids in Qurtuba to serve Asma, knowing that their primary loyalty would be to their new mistress. At their head he placed an older woman who had served in our family for many years but had run foul of Grandmother Najma's tongue and had been exiled from the house. She had become a washerwoman in the village.

'This woman had a son whose father was either a seller of figs in Qurtuba or one of our retainers who died in a siege near Malaka or . . . heaven alone knows. He was an extremely intelligent boy, and well educated thanks to the generosity of the Banu Hudayl. He studied with the same tutors as did my father and Aunt Zahra. Unlike them, he read a great deal and knew the work of the masters of philosophy, history, mathematics, theology and even medicine. He knew the books in our library better than anyone in the family. His name was Mohammed ibn Zaydun. He was also good-looking.

'Your great-aunt fell in love with him. It was Ibn Zaydun who brought her out of her depression. It was he who encouraged her to write poetry, to think of the world outside this house and even beyond the frontiers of al-Andalus. He explained the circumstances of Ibn Farid's marriage and convinced Zahra that it was not the fault of the Lady Asma. Thus he brought them together.

'I think it was the knowledge that this servant's boy had succeeded where he himself had failed so abysmally that caused Ibn Farid to develop an intense dislike for Ibn Zaydun. On one occasion he was heard to say: "If that boy is not careful with his tongue it might cost him his neck." He began to punish the boy. He insisted that Mohammed be sent to work in the fields and learn a trade like anyone else. He suggested that Juan's father could teach him carpentry or Ibn Hasd the skills of shoemaking. The boy was wise beyond his years. He felt the anger of his master, but he also understood the cause and began to shun the inner courtyard. Both Zahra and Asma pleaded with Ibn Farid not to be so rough on the young man. I think it was Grandmother Asma who finally succeeded in persuading my grandfather to let Ibn Zaydun teach Zahra and my father the principles of mathematics in a methodical way.

'My father was rarely present. He was often away hunting or staying with our family in Gharnata. And so it was that Mohammed ibn Zaydun and Zahra bint Najma were in each other's company every single day. What had to happen happened . . .'

Hind's eyes were gleaming with excitement.

'But why did they not just run away? I would have done so.'

'All in good time, Hind. All in good time. There was a problem in the shape of another young woman. Like Zahra she was very beautiful, but unlike Zahra she was the daughter of an old retainer and worked as a young serving girl. Not so different from our Umayma. She was extremely intelligent, but without any formal learning, and she too wanted Ibn Zaydun for her husband. Naturally, Ibn Farid thought this was an excellent idea and instructed the parents of both to arrange the nuptials.

'Zahra went mad. Perhaps I should not use that word. Let us say that she was in a very discomposed state when Ibn Zaydun told her what was being planned. She forced him to meet her that night in the pomegranate grove just outside the house . . .'

Hind shrieked with laughter, which was so infectious that

everyone began to smile except Zuhayr. Her father demanded an explanation.

'Some things never change, do they brother? Fancy them meeting in the pomegranate grove!'

Zuhayr's complexion changed colour. His father understood the reference, smiled and diverted attention from his first-born by continuing Zahra's story.

'That night they acted as if they were husband and wife. The next morning Zahra went to Grandmother Asma and told her what had happened. Asma was shocked and told Zahra that on no account could she let her marry the son of her maid-servant . . .'

'But . . .' Hind was beginning to interrupt till she saw the frown on her father's face and stopped.

'Yes Hind, I know, but there is never any logic in such matters. Asma did not want Zahra to repeat her own experience. It is a contradiction of course, but not uncommon. Your mother will remember that when Great-Uncle Rahim-Allah married a court-esan, she turned out to be the most puritanical of the great-aunts. Fiercely loyal to her husband and unbending in her attitude to adultery and other such vices. It is, I suppose, one of the consequences of what the master Ibn Khaldun might have referred to as the dilemma of shifting social locations. Once you have climbed all the way up the ladder from the lowest rung, you can never stop looking down upon those less fortunate than yourself.

'To return to the story. One night when Zahra and Ibn Zaydun were trysting in their favourite spot, unknown to them they had been followed by Zahra's rival. She watched everything. Everything. The next morning she reported the whole affair directly to Ibn Farid. He did not doubt her word for a moment. He must have felt that his instinctive dislike of the washer-woman's son had been vindicated. He was heard to roar at the top of his voice: "Fifty gold dinars to the person who will bring that boy to me."

'I think if Ibn Zaydun had been caught that day, my grand-father would have had him castrated on the spot. Fortunately for our lover, he had been dispatched early in the morning on an errand to Gharnata. On hearing of what lay in store for him if he returned, his mother, warned by Grandmother Asma, sent a friend from the village to warn the boy. Ibn Zaydun simply disappeared. He was never seen in the village again while Ibn Farid was alive . . .'

'Father,' Kulthum enquired in her soft, obedient voice, 'who was Great-Aunt's rival?'

'Why, child, I thought all of you might have guessed after the events of this evening. It was Ama!'

'Ama!' all three of them shouted.

'Shhhh!' said Zubayda. 'She'll come running if she hears you shouting in that fashion.'

They looked at each other in silence. It was Hind who spoke first.

'And Great-Aunt Zahra?'

'Your great-grandfather sent for her in the presence of both my grandmothers. They pleaded with him to forgive her. Zahra herself was defiant. Perhaps we can ask her now, but my mother told me that Zahra is supposed to have said: "Why should you be the only one to marry someone of your choice? I love Asma both as the wife of your choice and as my friend. Why could you not accept Ibn Zaydun?" It was then that he struck her and she cursed him and cursed him till Ibn Farid, feeling ashamed of himself, but not to the extent of begging her forgiveness, turned his back on her and walked out of the room. The very next day she left this house. Never came back till last night. What she did in Qurtuba, I do not know. You will have to ask someone else.'

While the children of Umar bin Abdallah were reflecting on their great-aunt's tragic story, the subject of all their thoughts was preparing to dismiss Ama and retire for the night. Zahra had carefully avoided all mention of Ibn Zaydun. She did not want any apologies. They would have been half-a-century too late in any case. It was all over and she genuinely did not bear any grudges. The two old women had spent the evening discussing the state of the Banu Hudayl. Zahra had wanted to know everything, and in Ama she had found the only person who could tell everything.

Ama had told her the circumstances, not sparing any detail, in which her brother Abdallah had died, after he had been thrown by a horse he had trained and bred himself, and how his wife had only survived him for a year.

'Even on his death-bed he thought about you and made young Umar swear on the al-koran that a regular supply of food and clothes would be sent to you. He never got over your absence.'

Zahra sighed and a sad smile tugged at her face.

'Our childhood memories were so closely intertwined you know . . .'

Then she stopped, as if the memory of her brother had led her to others. The look on her face reminded Ama of the old days. She must be seeing him in her mind's eye, Ama thought to herself. I wish she would talk about him. What is there to hide now?

It was as if Zahra had read her old rival's thoughts. 'Whatever became of Mohammed ibn Zaydun?' Zahra tried to sound very casual, but her heart was beating faster. 'Is he dead?'

'No, my lady. He is alive. He changed his name, you know. He calls himself Wajid al-Zindiq and lives on a hill a few miles from here. Zuhayr ibn Umar sees him regularly, but does not know his past. He too is sent food from the house. Umar bin Abdallah insisted we did that, once we had discovered the identity of the man who had moved into that cave on the hill. This very morning Zuhayr was with him for several hours.'

Zahra was so excited by this piece of news that her heartbeats sounded like gunshots in Ama's ears.

'I must sleep now. Peace be upon you, Amira.'

'And upon you, my lady. May God bless you.'

'He has not done that for a very long time, Amira.'

Ama left the room with the lamp. As she stepped outside she heard Zahra say something. She was about to return to the chamber, but it was obvious that Ibn Farid's daughter was thinking aloud. Ama remained rooted to the tile in the courtyard on which she stood.

'The first time. Remember Mohammed?' Zahra was talking to herself. 'It was like the opening of a flower. Our eyes were shining, full of hope and our hearts were leaping. Why did you never come back to me?'

Chapter 4

'THERE IS NO other way. If necessary we must permit Providence to avail itself of the darkness of the dungeon and pour the light of the true faith on the benighted minds of these infidels. Friar Talavera my illustrious predecessor, tried other methods and failed. Personally, I believe that the decision to publish the Latin-Arabic dictionary was misguided but enough said on that question. That phase is mercifully over, and with it, I trust, the illusion that these infidels will come to us through learning and rational discourse.

'You look displeased, Excellency. I am fully aware that a softer policy might suit the needs of our temporal diplomacy, but you will excuse my bluntness. Nothing more or less than the future of thousands of souls is at stake. And it is these which I am commanded by our Holy Church to save and protect. I am convinced that the heathen, if they cannot be drawn towards us voluntarily, should be driven in our direction so that we can push them on to the path of true salvation. The ruins of Mahometanism are tottering to their foundations. This is no time to stay our hand.'

Ximenes de Cisneros spoke with passion. He was hampered by the fact that the man sitting on a chair facing him was Don Inigo Lopez de Mendoza, Count of Tendilla, Mayor and Captain-General of Granada, which the Moors called Gharnata, Don Inigo had deliberately chosen to be dressed in Moorish robes for this particular meeting. It was a style that greatly distressed the Archbishop.

'For a spiritual leader, Your Grace reveals a remarkable capacity for interceding in matters temporal. Have you thought about this matter seriously? Their majesties did agree the terms of surrender, which I drafted, did they not, Father? I was present when a solemn undertaking was given to their Sultan by the Queen. We agreed to leave them in peace. Friar Talavera is still greatly respected in the Albaicin because he kept to the terms that had been agreed.

'I will be blunt with you, Archbishop. Till your arrival we had no serious problems in this kingdom. You failed to win them over by force of argument and now you wish to resort to the methods of the Inquisition.'

'Practical methods, Excellency. Tried and tested.'

'Yes, tried and tested on Catholics whose property you wanted to possess and on Jews who have never ruled over a kingdom and who bought their freedom by paying out gold ducats and converting to our religion. The same methods will not work here. Most of the people we call Moors are our own people. Just like you and me. They have ruled over a very large portion of our peninsula. They did so without burning too many bibles or tearing down all our churches or setting synagogues alight in order to build their mesquitas. They are not a rootless phenomenon. They cannot be wiped out with a lash of the whip. They will resist. More blood will be spilled. Theirs and ours.'

Cisneros stared at the Count with a look of pure contempt. If it had been any other grandee of the kingdom, the Archbishop would have declared to his face that he spoke thus because his own blood was impure, tainted with an injection from Africa. But this wretched man was no ordinary noble. His family was one of the most distinguished in the country. It boasted several poets, administrators and warriors in the service of the true faith. The Mendozas had employed genealogists who traced their descent back to the Visigothic kings. Cisneros had yet to be convinced by this last detail, but the pedigree was impressive enough, even without the Visigoth connections. Cisneros knew the family well. He himself had been a protégé of the king-making Cardinal Mendoza. After all, the whole country was aware of the fact that the Captain-General's paternal uncle had, as Cardinal and Archbishop of Seville, aided Isabella to outwit her niece and usurp the Castilian throne in 1478. The Mendoza family was therefore held in very high regard by the present King and Queen.

Cisneros knew he had to be careful, but it was the Count who had violated the norms which governed relations between Church and State. He decided to remain calm. There would be other opportunities to punish the man's arrogance. Cisneros spoke in the softest voice he could muster for the occasion. 'Is Your Excellency charging the Inquisition with corruption on a grand scale?'

'Did I mention the word corruption?'

'No, but the implication . . .'

'Implication? What implication? I merely pointed out, my dear Friar Cisneros, that the Inquisition was amassing a gigantic fortune for the Church. The confiscated estates alone could fund three wars against the Turks. Could they not?'

'What would Your Excellency do with the property?'

'Tell me, Father, is it always the case that the children of your so-called heretics are also guilty?'

'We take for granted the loyalty of the members of a family to each other.'

'So a Christian whose father is a Mahometan or a Jew is never to be trusted.'

'Never is perhaps too strong.'

'How is it then that Torquemada, whose Jewish ancestry was well known, presided over the Inquisition?'

'To prove his loyalty to the Church he had to be more vigilant than the scion of a noble family whose lineage can be traced to the Visigoth kings.'

'I begin to understand your logic. Well, be that as it may, I will not have the Moors subjected to any further humiliations. You have done enough. Burning their books was a disgrace. A stain on our honour. Their manuals on science and medicine are without equal in the civilized world.'

'They were saved.'

'It was an act of savagery, man. Are you too blind to understand?'

'And yet Your Excellency did not countermand my orders.'

It was Don Inigo's turn to stare at the priest with anger. The rebuke was just. It had been cowardice on his part, pure cowardice. A courtier, freshly arrived from Ishbiliya, had informed him that the Queen had sent a secret instruction to the Archbishop which included the order to destroy the libraries. He now knew that this had been a fabrication. Cisneros had deliberately misled the courtier and encouraged him to misinform the Captain-General. Don Inigo knew he had been tricked, but it was no excuse. He should have countermanded the order, forced Cisneros out into the open with the supposed message from Isabella. The priest was smiling at him. 'The man's a devil,' the Count told himself. 'He smiles with his lips, never his eyes.'

'One flock and one shepherd, Excellency. That is what this country needs if it is to survive the storms that confront our Church in the New World.'

'You are blissfully unaware of your own good fortune, Archbishop. Had it not been for the Hebrews and the Moors, the natural enemies who have helped you to keep the Church in one piece, Christian heretics would have created havoc in this peninsula. I did not mean to startle you. It is not a very profound thought. I thought you would have worked that out for yourself.'

'You are wrong, Excellency. It is the destruction of the Hebrews and the Moors which is necessary to preserve our Church.'

'We are both right in our different ways. I have many people waiting to see me. We must continue this conversation another day.'

And in this brusque fashion the Count of Tendilla informed Ximenes de Cisneros that his audience was over. The priest rose and bowed. Don Inigo stood up, and Cisneros saw him resplendent in his Moorish robes. The priest flinched.

'I see my clothes displease you just as much as my thoughts.'

'The two do not appear to be unrelated, Excellency.'

The Captain-General roared with laughter. 'I do not grudge you the cowl. Why should my robes annoy you? They are so much more comfortable than what is worn at court. I feel buried alive in those tights and doublets whose only function appears to be the constriction of the most precious organs which God saw fit to bestow. This robe which I wear is designed to comfort our bodies, and is not so unlike your cowl as you might imagine. These clothes are designed to be worn in their Alhambra. Anything else would clash with the colours of these intricate geometric patterns. Surely even you can appreciate that, Friar. I think there is a great deal to be said for communicating directly with the Creator without the help of graven images, but I am approaching blasphemy and I do not wish to upset or detain you any further . . .'

The prelate's lips curled into a sinister smile. He muttered something under his breath, bowed and left the room. Don

Inigo looked out of the window. Underneath the palace was the Albaicin, the old quarter where the Muslims, Jews and Christians of this town had lived and traded for centuries. The Captain-General was buried in his own reflections of the past and present when he heard a discreet cough and turned round to see his Jewish major-domo, Ben Yousef, carrying a tray with two silver cups and a matching jar containing coffee.

'Excuse my intrusion, Excellency, but your guest has been waiting for over an hour.'

'Heavens above! Show him in, Ben Yousef. Immediately.'

The servant retreated. When he returned it was to usher Umar into the audience-chamber.

'His Graciousness, Umar bin Abdallah, Your Excellency.'

Umar saluted Don Inigo in the traditional fashion.

'Peace be upon you, Don Inigo.'

The Count of Tendilla moved towards his guest with arms outstretched and hugged him.

'Welcome, welcome, Don Homer. How are you, my old friend? No formalities between us. Please be seated.'

This time Don Inigo sat on the cushions laid near the window and asked Umar to join him there. The major-domo poured coffee and served the two men. His master nodded to him and he moved backwards out of the chamber. Umar smiled.

'I am glad you retained his services.'

'You did not come all this way to compliment me on my choice of servants, Don Homer.'

Umar and Don Inigo had known each other since they were children. Their grandfathers had fought against each other in legendary battles which had long since become part of the folk-lore on both sides, then the two heroes had become close friends and begun to visit each other regularly. Both grandfathers knew the true costs of war and were greatly entertained by the myths surrounding their names.

In the years before 1492, Inigo had called his friend Homer simply because he had difficulties in pronouncing the Arabic 'U'. The use of the prefix 'Don' was more recent. It could be dated very precisely to the Conquest of Gharnata. There was no point in taking offence. In his heart, Umar knew that Don Inigo was no longer his friend. In his mind he suspected that Don Inigo felt the same about himself. The two men had not met for several months. The whole sad business was a charade, but appearances had to be maintained. It could not be admitted that all chivalry had been extinguished by the Reconquest.

Good relations had been kept up through the regular exchange of fruits and sweetmeats on their respective feast-days. Last Christmas had been the only exception. Nothing had arrived at the Captain-General's residence at the al-Hamra from the family of Hudayl. Don Inigo was hurt but not surprised. The wall of fire had preceded Christ's birthday by a few weeks. Umar bin Abdallah was not the only Muslim notable to have boycotted the celebrations.

It was with the express purpose of repairing the breach that now existed between them, that Don Inigo had sent for his old friend. And here he was, just as in the old days, sipping his coffee as he stared through the carved tracery of the window. Except that in years gone by, Umar would have been seated with the Sultan Abu Abdallah as a member of his council, giving advice to the ruler regarding Gharnata's relations with its Christian neighbours.

'Don Homer, I know why you are angry. You should have stayed at home that night. What was it that your grandfather once told mine? Ah, yes, I remember. When the eye does not see the heart cannot grieve. I want you to know that the decision was not mine. It was Cisneros, the Queen's Archbishop, who decided to burn your books of learning.'

'You are the Captain-General of Gharnata, Don Inigo.'

'Yes, but how could I challenge the will of Queen Isabella?'

'By reminding her of the terms which she and her husband signed in this very room, in your presence and mine, over eight years ago. Instead you remained silent and averted your eyes as one of the greatest infamies of the civilized world was perpetrated in this city. The Tatars who burned down the Baghdad library over two centuries ago were illiterate barbarians, frightened of the written word. For them it was an instinctive act. What Cisneros has done is much worse. It is cold-blooded and carefully planned . . .'

'I . . .'

'Yes, you! Your Church put the axe to a tree that afforded free shade for all. You think it will benefit your side. Perhaps, but for how long? A hundred years? Two hundred? It is possible, but in the long run this stunted civilization is doomed. It will be overtaken by the rest of Europe. Surely you understand that it is the future of this peninsula which has been destroyed. The men who set fire to books, torture their opponents and burn heretics at the stake will not be able to build a house with stable foundations. The Church's curse will damn this peninsula.'

Umar felt himself going out of control and stopped suddenly. A weak smile appeared on his face.

'Forgive me. I did not come here to preach a sermon. It is always presumptuous of the vanquished to lecture their victors. I came, if you want the truth, to discover what your plans are for dealing with us.'

Don Inigo stood up and began to pace up and down in the large audience-chamber. There were two options before him. He could deploy a troop of honeyed words and calm his friend, assure him that whatever else happened or did not happen, the Banu Hudayl would always be free to live as they had always lived. He would have liked to say all that and more, but he knew that it was not true, even though he wanted it to be true. It would only make Homer more angry, since he would see it as yet another example of Christian deception. The Count decided to abandon diplomacy.

'I will be blunt with you, my friend. You know what I would like. You see how I am dressed. My entourage consists of Jews and Moors. For me, a Granada without them is like a desert without an oasis. But I am on my own. The Church and the court have decided that your religion must be wiped out from these lands for ever. They have the soldiers and the weapons to ensure that this is done. I know that there will be resistance, but it will be foolish and self-defeating for your cause and ultimately we will defeat you. Cisneros understands this better than anyone else on our side. You were about to say something?'

'If we had used our iron fists to deal with Christianity the way you treat us now, this situation might never have arisen.'

'Spoken like the owl of Minerva. Instead you attempted to bring civilization to the whole peninsula regardless of faith or creed. It was noble of you and now you must pay the price. The war had to end sooner or later with the final victory of one side and the definitive defeat of the other. My advice to your family is to convert at once. If you do so I pledge that I will personally be present and will even drag Cisneros to your estates with me to bless you all. That would be the best protection I could afford your family and your village. Do not take offence, my friend. I may sound cynical, but in the end what is important is for you and yours to remain alive and in possession of the estates which have been in your family for so long. I know that the Bishop of Qurtuba has tried to persuade you as well, but . . .'

Umar rose and saluted Don Inigo.

'I appreciate your bluntness. You are a true friend. But I cannot accept what you say. My family is not prepared to swear allegiance to the Roman Church or any other. I thought about it many times, Don Inigo. I even considered murder. Do not be startled. I tried to kill our past, to exorcise memory once and for all, but they are stubborn creatures, they refuse to die. I have a feeling, Don Inigo, that if our roles had been reversed your answer would not have been so different.'

'I am not so sure. Just look at me. I think I would have made a reasonably good Mahometan. How is your little Yazid? I was hoping you would bring him with you.'

'It was not an appropriate time. Now, if you will excuse me, I must take my leave. Peace be upon you, Don Inigo.'

'Adios, Don Homer. For my part I would like our friendship to continue.'

Although Umar smiled, he said nothing as he left the chamber. His horse and his bodyguard were waiting outside the Jannat-al-Arif, the summer gardens where he had first encountered Zubayda, but Umar was in no mood for nostalgia. Mendoza's crisp message still echoed in his ears. Not even the magical sound of water as he approached the gardens could distract him today. Till a few weeks ago he had thought of Gharnata as an occupied land which might be liberated once again at the right time. The Castilians had many enemies at home and abroad. The minute they were embroiled in another war, that would be the time to strike. Everything else must be subordinated to that goal. This is what Umar had told his Muslim fellow grandees at several gatherings since the surrender of the town.

The wall of fire had changed all that, and now the Captain-General had confirmed his worst thoughts. The worshippers of icons were not content with a simple military presence in Gharnata. It was naïve to have imagined that they would adhere to the agreements in the first place. They wanted to occupy minds, to pierce hearts, to remould souls. They would not rest till they had been successful.

Gharnata, once the safest haven for the followers of the Prophet in al-Andalus, had now become a dangerous furnace.

'If we stay here,' Umar spoke to himself, 'we are finished.'

He was not simply thinking about the Banu Hudayl, but the fate of Islam in al-Andalus. His bodyguard, seeing him from a distance and surprised at the brevity of the interview, ran to the gate of the garden with his master's sword and pistol. Still engrossed in his thoughts, Umar rode down to the stables, where he dismounted and then walked a few hundred yards to the familiar and comforting mansion of his cousin Hisham in the old quarter.

While his father had been at the al-Hamra, Zuhayr had spent the morning in the public bath with his friends. After cleansing themselves with steam, they were taken in hand by the bath attendants, thoroughly scrubbed with hard sponges, and washed with soap before entering the bath, where they were alone. Here they relaxed and began to exchange confidences. Zuhayr's small shoulder scar was being admired by his friends.

There were over sixty such baths in Gharnata alone. The afternoons were reserved for women and the men had no choice but to bathe in the mornings. The bath where Zuhayr found himself today was restricted by tradition for the use of young noblemen and their friends. There had been occasions, especially during the summer when parties of mixed bathers had arrived and bathed, without attendants, in the light of the moon, but such occasions had been rare and seemed to have ended with the conquest.

In the old days, prior to the fall of Gharnata, the bath had been a centre for social and political gossip. Usually the talk dwelled on sexual adventures and feats. Sometimes erotic poetry was recited and discussed, especially in the afternoon sessions. Now hardly anything seemed to matter except politics – the latest series of atrocities, which family had converted, who had offered money to bribe the Church, and, of course, the fateful night which was burned in their collective memory and which caused even those who had previously expressed a total indifference to politics to sit up and take stock.

The political temperature in Zuhayr's bath was subdued. Three more *faqihs* had died under torture two days before. Fear was beginning to have its effect. The mood was one of despair and fatalism. Zuhayr, who had been listening patiently to his friends, all of them scions of the Muslim aristocracy in Gharnata, suddenly raised his voice.

'The choices are simple. Convert, be killed, or die with our swords in our hands.'

Musa bin Ali had lost two brothers in the chaos which had preceded the entry of Ferdinand and Isabella into the city. His father had died defending the fortress of al-Hama, which lay to the west of Gharnata. His mother clung to Musa with a desperation which he found irksome, but he knew that he could not override his responsibility to her and his two sisters. Whenever Musa spoke, which was not often, he was heard in respectful silence.

'The choices underlined by our brother Zuhayr bin Umar are correct, but in his impatience he has forgotten that there is another alternative. It is the one which Sultan Abu Abdullah chose. Like him we could cross the water and find a home on the coast of the Maghreb. I may as well tell you that it is what my mother wants us to do.'

Zuhayr's eyes flashed with anger.

'Why should we go anywhere? This is our home. My family built al-Hudayl. It was barren land before we came. We built the village. We irrigated the lands. We planted the orchards. Oranges and pomegranates and limes and palm trees and the rice. I am not a Berber. I have nothing to do with the Maghreb. I will live in my home, and death to the unbeliever who tries to take it away from me by force.'

The temperature in the baths rose dramatically. Then a young man with a carefully chiselled face, pale olive skin and eyes the colour of green marble coughed suggestively. He could not have been more than eighteen or nineteen years of age. Everyone looked at him. He was new to the town, having arrived from Balansiya only a few weeks ago and before that from the great university of al-Azhar in al-Qahira. He had come to do some historical research on the life and work of his great-grandfather

Ibn Khaldun, and study some of the manuscripts in the libraries in Gharnata. Unfortunately for his project, he had arrived on the very day that Cisneros had chosen to burn the books. The man with the green eyes had been heartbroken. He had wept all night in his tiny room in the Funduq al-Yadida. By the time morning came he had already decided upon the course which the remainder of his life would take. He spoke in a soft tone, but it was the music in his Qahirene speech, as much as his message, that entranced his fellow bathers.

'When I saw the flames in the Bab al-Ramla consuming the work of centuries, I thought that it was all over. It was as if Satan had plunged his poisoned fist through the heart of the mountain and reversed the flow of the stream. Everything we had planted lay withered and dead. Time itself had petrified and here, in al-Andalus, we were already on the other side of hell. Perhaps I should pack my bags and return to the East . . .'

'None of us would hold that against you,' said Zuhayr. 'You came here to study, but there is nothing to study except a void. You would be well advised to return to the university of al-Azhar.'

'My friend is giving you sage advice,' added Musa. 'We are all now impotent. The only thing we can glory in is the vigour of our fathers.'

'There I disagree,' replied Zuhayr. 'Only he who says "Behold, I am the man" not "My father or grandfather was" can be considered truly noble and courageous.'

The man with green eyes smiled.

'I agree with Zuhayr bin Umar. Why should you who have been knights and kings desert your castles to the enemy and become mere pawns? Tear away the curtains of doubt and challenge the Christians. Cisneros imagines that you have no more fight left inside you. He will thrust you further and further towards the edge, and then with one last push he will watch you fall into the abyss.

'I was told by friends in Balansiya that throughout the country the Inquisitors are preparing themselves to deliver the fatal blow. They will soon forbid us our language. Arabic will be banned on pain of death. They will not let us wear our clothes. There is talk that they will destroy every public bath in the country. They will prohibit our music, our wedding feasts, our religion.

All this and more will fall on our heads in a few years' time. Abu Abdullah let them take this town without a struggle. This was a mistake. It has made them too confident.'

'What do you suggest, stranger?' enquired Zuhayr.

'We must not let them imagine that what they have done to us is acceptable. We must prepare an insurrection.'

For a minute nothing stirred. They were all frozen by his words. Only the sound of water flowing through the hammam punctuated their thoughts and their fears. Then Musa directly challenged the young scholar from Egypt.

'If I were convinced that an uprising against Cisneros and his devils would succeed and enable us to turn back even one page of history, I would be the first to sacrifice my life, but I remain unconvinced by your honeyed words. What you are proposing is a grand gesture that will be remembered in the times which lie ahead. Why? What for? What good will come of it in the end? Gestures and grand words have been the curse of our religion, from the very beginning.'

Nobody responded to his objections and Musa, feeling that he now had the advantage over the Qahirene, pressed his arguments further.

'The Christians hunt different beasts in different ways and during different seasons, but they have begun to hunt us the whole year round. I agree we must not let our lives become distorted with fear, but nor should we sacrifice ourselves unnecessarily. We have to learn from the Jews how to live in conditions of great hardship. The followers of Islam still live in Balansiya, do they not? Even in Aragon? Listen friends, I am not in favour of any foolishness.'

Zuhayr spoke angrily to his friend.

'Would you convert to Christianity, Musa, just in order to live?'

'Have not Jews done so throughout the land in order to retain their positions? Why should we not imitate them? Let them tighten the screws as much as they like. We will learn new methods of resistance. Here in our heads.'

'Without our language or our books of learning?' asked the great-grandson of Ibn Khaldun.

Musa looked at him and sighed. 'Is it true that you are in the line of the master Ibn Khaldun?'

Ibn Daud smiled and nodded his head.

'Surely,' continued Musa, 'you must know better than us the warning your noble forebear directed against men such as yourself. Scholars are of all men those least fitted for politics and its ways.'

Ibn Daud grinned mischievously. 'Perhaps Ibn Khaldun was referring to his own experiences which were less than happy. But surely, however great a philosopher he may have been, we must not treat him as a prophet whose word is sacred. The question which confronts you is simple. How should we defend our past and our future against these barbarians? If you have a more efficient solution, pray speak your mind and convince me.'

'I do not have all the answers, my friend, but I know that what you are recommending is wrong.'

With these words Musa got out of the bath and clapped his hands. Attendants rushed in with towels and began to dry his body. The others followed suit. Then they repaired to the adjoining chamber, where their servants were waiting with new robes. Before departing, Musa embraced Zuhayr and whispered in his ear: 'Poison finds its way into even the sweetest cups of wine.'

Zuhayr did not take his friend too seriously. He knew the pressures of everyday life on Musa, and he understood, but that was not sufficient reason for cowardice at a time when everything was at stake. Zuhayr did not wish to quarrel with his friend, but nor could he keep silent and conceal his own thoughts. He turned to the stranger.

'By what name are we to call you?'

'Ibn Daud al-Misri.'

'I would like to talk with you further. Why do we not return to your lodgings? I will help you pack your bags and then find you a horse to ride back with me to al-Hudayl. Trust in Allah. You might even find some of Ibn Khaldun's manuscripts in our library! You do ride?'

'That is very kind of you. I accept your hospitality with pleasure and, yes, I do ride.'

To the rest of the party Zuhayr issued a more general invitation. 'Let us meet in my village in three days' time. Then we will make our plans and discuss the methods of their execution. Is that agreed?'

'Why not stay the night and we can talk now?' asked Haroun bin Mohammed.

'Because my father is in town and has pressed me to spend the night at my uncle's house. I pleaded a desire to return home. It would be unwise to deceive him so openly. Three days?'

An agreement was reached. Zuhayr took Ibn Daud by the arm and escorted him to the street outside. They walked briskly to the lodging house, collected Ibn Daud's belongings and then repaired to the stables. Zuhayr borrowed one of his uncle's horses for his new friend and before Ibn Daud had time to recover from the suddenness of the proceedings, they were on their way to al-Hudayl.

Zuhayr's uncle, Ibn Hisham, lived in a handsome town house, five minutes away from the Bab al-Ramla. The entrance to the house was no different from those of the other private dwellings on the street, but if one were to pause and look closely to either side it would become clear that the two adjoining entrances were in fact non-existent. False doors inlaid with turquoise tiles were designed to deceive. No stranger could imagine that what lay beyond the latticed doorways was a medium-sized palace. An underground passage beneath the street connected the different wings of the mansion and also served as an escape route to the Bab al-Ramla. Merchants did not take risks.

It was to this small palace that Umar bin Abdallah had repaired after his unsatisfactory exchange earlier that day with the Captain-General of Gharnata.

Ibn Hisham and Umar were cousins. Ibn Hisham's father, Hisham al-Zaid, was the son of Ibn Farid's sister. He had settled in Gharnata after the death of his uncle Ibn Farid, who had been his guardian since the early death of his parents, killed by bandits during a journey to Ishbiliya. While rising to become the chief economic adviser to the Sultan in the al-Hamra, he had utilized his position and talents to build his own fortune. In the absence of any rivalry over the property in al-Hudayl, the relationships between the two cousins had been warm and friendly. After the premature demise of Umar's father, it had been his uncle Hisham al-Zaid who had stepped in and helped his nephew get over the emotional loss. More importantly he had also taught Umar the art of running an estate, explaining the difference between trade in the towns and land cultivation in the following words:

'For us in Gharnata it is the goods we sell and exchange which matter most. Here in al-Hudayl what is crucial is your ability to communicate with the peasants and understand their needs. In the olden days the peasants were united to Ibn Farid and his grandfather through war. They fought under the same banner. That was important. Times have changed. Unlike the goods we buy or sell, your peasants can think and act. If you remember this simple fact you should not have any serious trouble.'

Hisham al-Zaid had died one year after the fall of the city. He had never known any disease, and the talk in the market ascribed his death to a broken heart. This may have been so, but it was also the case that he had celebrated his eightieth birthday some weeks before his departure.

Ever since his return from the al-Hamra, Umar had been in a dejected state of mind. He had bathed and rested, but his silence during the evening meal had weighed on everyone present. Ibn Hisham's offer to send for some dancing girls and a flask of wine had been abruptly refused. Umar could not understand how his cousin's family was in such good humour. It was true that people grew accustomed to adversity, but his instincts detected that there was something else at work. When he had told them about his meeting with Don Inigo they had refrained from expressing an opinion. Ibn Hisham and his wife Muneeza had exchanged strange looks when he had poured scorn on the Captain-General's suggestion that every Muslim should convert immediately to Christianity. It was, Umar felt, as if they were being pulled away from him by hidden currents. Now, as the two men sat on the floor facing each other, they found themselves alone for the first time since his arrival. Umar was on the verge of an explosion.

He had barely opened his mouth when a loud knock sounded on the door. Umar saw Ibn Hisham's face grow tight. He paused for the servant to come and announce the new arrival. Perhaps Don Inigo had had a change of heart and had sent a messenger asking him to return post-haste to the al-Hamra. Instead of the servant, however, a familiar robed figure entered the room. Suddenly everything became clear to Umar.

'My Lord Bishop. I had no idea you were in Gharnata.'

The old man signalled for a chair, and took his seat. Umar began to pace up and down. Then his uncle spoke in a voice which was in marked contrast to his infirm appearance.

'Sit down, nephew. I was fully aware that you were in Gharnata today. That is why I am here. Fortunately the son of my late cousin Hisham al-Zaid, may he rest in peace, has more sense than you. What ails you, Umar? Is the headship of the Banu Hudayl so great a burden that you have lost the use of your mind? Did I not tell you when they burnt the books that it would not stop at that? Did I not try and warn you of the consequences of clinging blindly to a faith whose time in this peninsula is over.'

Umar was boiling with rage.

'Over is it, Uncle? Why don't you lift your beautiful purple gown for a minute? Let us inspect your penis. I think we might discover that a tiny bit of skin has been removed. Why did you not cling on blindly to that piece of skin, Uncle? Nor were you shy of using the implement itself. Your son Juan is how old? Twenty? Born five years after you became a priest! What happened to his mother, our unknown aunt? Did they force her to leave the convent, or did the Mother Superior double as a midwife in her spare time? When did you see the light, Uncle?'

'Stop this, Umar!' his cousin shouted. 'What is the use of all this talk? The Bishop is only trying to help us.'

'I am not angry with you, Umar bin Abdallah. I like your spirit – it reminds me very much of my own father. But there is a law for those who engage in politics. They must pay some attention to the real world and what goes on there. Every circumstance that accompanies and succeeds an event must be studied in detail. That is what I learnt from my tutor, when I was Yazid's age. We used to have our lessons in that courtyard through which the water flows and which your family loves so much. It was always in the afternoon, when it was drenched in sunshine.

'I was taught never to base my views on speculation, but to make my thoughts conform to the realities that existed in the world outside. It was impossible for Gharnata to continue its existence. An Islamic oasis in a Christian desert. That is what you said to me three months before the surrender. Do you recall my reply?'

'Only too well,' muttered Umar, mimicking the old man. ' "If what you say is true, Umar bin Abdallah, then it cannot go on like this. The oasis must be captured by the warriors of the desert." Yes, Uncle. I remember. Tell me something . . .'

'No! You tell me something. Do you want our family estates to be confiscated? Do you want Zuhayr and yourself killed, Zubayda and the girls annexed to form part of your murderer's household, Yazid enslaved by some priest and misused as an altar boy? Answer me!'

Umar was trembling. He sipped some water and just stared at Miguel.

'Well?' the Bishop of Qurtuba continued. 'Why do you not speak? There is still time. That is why I used all my powers of persuasion to organize your meeting in the al-Hamra this morning. That is why I have persuaded Cisneros to come and perform the baptisms in the village. That is the only road to survival, my boy. Do you think I converted and became a Bishop because I saw a vision? The only vision I saw was of the destruction of our family. My decision was determined by politics, not religion.'

'And yet,' said Umar, 'the Bishop's gown sits easily on you. It's as if you had worn it since birth.'

'Mock as much as you like, my nephew, but make the right decision. Remember what the Prophet once said: Trust in God, but tether your camel first. I will give you another piece of information, though if it were to become known the Inquisition would demand my head. I still make my ablutions and bow before Mecca every Friday.'

Both Miguel's nephews were startled, which made him chuckle.

'In primitive times one must learn the art of being primitive. That is why I joined the Church of Rome, even though I still remain convinced that our way of seeing the world is much closer to the truth. I ask you to do the same. Your cousin and his family have already agreed. I will baptize them myself tomorrow. Why do you not stay and observe the ceremony? It is over before you can say . . .'

'There is no Allah but Allah and Mohammed is his Prophet?'

'Exactly. You can carry on saying that to yourself every day.'

'Better to die free than live like a slave.'

'It is stupidity of this very sort which led to the defeat of your faith in this peninsula.'

Umar looked at his cousin, but Ibn Hisham averted his face.

'Why?' Umar shouted at him. 'Why did you not tell me? It is like being stabbed in the heart.'

Ibn Hisham looked up. Tears were pouring down his face. How strange, thought Umar, as he saw the distress on his cousin's face, when we were young his will was stronger than mine. I suppose it is his new responsibilities, but I have mine and they are greater. For him it is his business, his trade, his family. For me it is the lives of two thousand human beings. And yet the sight of his cousin saddened Umar, and his own eyes filled with tears.

For a moment, as they looked at each other, their eyes heavy with sorrow, Miguel was reminded of their youth. The two boys had been inseparable. This friendship had continued long after they were married. But as they grew older and became absorbed in the cares of their own families, they saw less of each other. The distance between the family home in the village and Ibn Hisham's dwelling in Gharnata seemed to grow. Yet still, when they met, the two cousins exchanged confidences, discussed their families, their wealth, their future and, naturally, the changes taking place in their world. Ibn Hisham had felt great pain at concealing his decision to convert from Umar. It was the most important moment of his life. He felt that what he was about to do would ensure protection and stability for his children and their children.

Ibn Hisham was a wealthy merchant. He prided himself on his ability to judge human character. He could smell the mood of the city. His decision to become a Christian was on the same level as the decision he had taken thirty years ago to put all his gold into importing brocades from Samarkand. Within a year he had trebled his wealth.

He had no wish to deceive Umar, but he was frightened that his cousin, whose intellectual stubbornness and moral rigour had always inspired a mixture of respect and fear in their extended family, would convince him that he was wrong. Ibn Hisham did not wish to be so persuaded. He confessed all this, hoping that Umar would understand and forgive, but Umar continued to stare at him in anger and Ibn Hisham suddenly felt the temperature of those eyes pierce his head. In the space of a few minutes the gulf between the two men had grown so wide that they were incapable of speaking to each other.

It was Miguel who finally broke the silence. 'I will come to al-Hudayl tomorrow.'

'Why?'

'Are you denying me the right to enter the house where I was born? I simply wish to see my sister. I will not intrude in your life.'

Umar realized that he was in danger of consigning the family code to oblivion. This could not be done and he retreated straight away. He knew that Miguel was determined to speak to Zubayda and convince her of the necessity of conversions. The old rogue thought she might be easier to convince of his nefarious plans. Old devil. He is as transparent as glass.

'Forgive me, Uncle. My mind was on other matters. You are welcome as always to your home. We shall ride back together at sunrise. Pardon me, I had forgotten you have a baptism to perform. You will have to make your own way, I'm afraid. Now I have a favour to ask of you.'

'Speak,' said the Bishop of Qurtuba.

'I would like to be alone with my uncle's son.'

Miguel smiled and rose. Ibn Hisham clapped his hands. A servant entered with a lamp and escorted the cleric to his chamber. Both of them felt more relaxed in his absence. Umar looked at his friend, but his eyes were distant. Anger had given way to sorrow and resignation. Foreseeing their separation, which could well be permanent, Ibn Hisham stretched out his hand. Umar clasped it for a second and then let it drop. The grief felt by both of them went so deep that they did not feel the need to say a great deal to each other.

'Just in case you had any doubts,' Ibn Hisham began, 'I want you to know that my reasons have nothing to do with religion.'

'That is what saddens me deeply. If you had converted genuinely I would have argued and felt sad, but there would have been no anger. No bitterness. But do not worry, I will not even attempt to change your mind. Has the rest of the family accepted your decision?'

Ibn Hisham nodded.

'I wish time would stop forever.'

Umar laughed out aloud at this remark, and Ibn Hisham flinched. It was a strange laugh like a distant echo.

'We have just come through one disaster,' said Umar, 'and are on the edge of another.'

'Could anything be worse than what we have just experienced, Umar? They set our culture on fire. Nothing more they can do has the power to hurt me. Being tied to a stake and stoned to death would be a relief by comparison.'

'Is that why you decided to convert?'

'No, a thousand times no. It was for my family. For their future.'

'When I think of the future,' Umar confessed, 'I no longer see the deep blue sky. There is no more clarity. All I see is a thick mist, a primal darkness enveloping us all, and in the distant layer of my dreams I recognize the beckoning shores of Africa. I must rest now and say farewell. For tomorrow I will leave before all of you are out of bed.'

'How can you be so cruel? We will all be up for the morning prayers.'

'Even on the day of your baptism?'

'Especially on that day.'

'Till the morning then. Peace be upon you.'

'Peace be upon you.'

Ibn Hisham paused for a moment.

'Umar?'

'Yes.'

He moved quickly and embraced Umar, who remained passive, his arms by his side. Then as his cousin began to weep again, Umar hugged him and held him tight. They kissed each other's cheeks and Ibn Hisham led Umar to his room. It was a chamber reserved exclusively for the use of Umar bin Abdallah.

Umar could not sleep. His head was alive with anxious voices. The fatal poison was spreading every day. Despite his public display of firmness, he was racked with uncertainties. Was it fair to expose his children to decades of torture, exile and even death? What right had he to impose his choice on them? Had he raised children only to hand them over to the executioners?

His head began to roar like the noise of an underground river. The savage torments of memory. He was mourning for the forgotten years. The springtime of his life. Ibn Hisham had been with him when he first saw Zubayda, a cape round her shoulders, wandering like a lost soul in the gardens near the al-Hamra. As long as he lived he would never forget that scene. A ray of sunlight had filtered through the foliage to turn her red hair to gold. What struck him at once was her freshness – not a trace of the voluptuous indolence that marred so many of the women in his family. Entranced by her beauty, he had been rooted to the spot. He wanted to go and touch her hair, to hear her speak, to see how the shape of her eyes might alter when she smiled, but he controlled himself. It was forbidden to pluck ripening apricots. On his own he might have let her go and never seen her again. It was Ibn Hisham who had given him the courage to approach her and, in the months that followed, it was Ibn Hisham who kept watch over their clandestine trysts.

Both sides of the pillow were warm when Umar finally fell asleep. His last conscious thought had been a determination to rise well before dawn and ride back to al-Hudayl. He was not prepared for the emotional upheaval of a second parting. He did not want to see the helpless eyes of his friend pleading silently for mercy.

And there was another reason. He wanted to relive the journeys of his lost youth: to ride home in the cleansing air, far removed from the reality of Miguel's sordid baptisms; to feel the first rays of the morning sun, deflected by the mountain peaks; and to feast his eyes on the inexhaustible reserves of blue skies. Just before sleep finally overpowered him, Umar had a strong sensation that he would not see Ibn Hisham again.

Chapter 5

'TRUTH CANNOT CONTRADICT truth. True or false, Zuhayr al-Fahl?'

'True. How could it be otherwise? It is written in the al-koran, is it not?'

'Is that the only reason it is true?'

'Well . . . I mean, if it is written in the al-koran . . . Listen old man, I did not come here today to debate blasphemy!'

'I will ask you another question. Is it legitimate to unite what is given by reason and that which is provided by tradition?'

'I suppose so.'

'You suppose so! Do they teach you nothing these days? Bearded fools! I pose a dilemma which has confused our theologians for centuries and all you can say is "I suppose so." Not good enough. In my day young men were taught to be more rigorous. Have you never read the writings of Ibn Rushd, one of our greatest thinkers? A truly great man who the Christians of Europe know as Averroës? You must have read his books. There are four of them in your father's library.'

Zuhayr felt embarrassed and humiliated.

'I was taught them, but in such a way that they made no sense to me. My teacher said that Ibn Rushd may have been a learned man, but he was a heretic!'

'How the ignorant spread ignorance. The accusation was false. Ibn Rushd was a great philosopher, imbued with genius. He was wrong, in my opinion, but not for the reasons given by the fool who was hired to teach you theology. In order to resolve what he thought was the contradiction between reason and tradition, he accepted the teachings of the mystics. There were apparent meanings and hidden meanings. Now it is true that appearance and reality are not always the same, but Ibn Rushd insisted that allegorical interpretations were a necessary corollary to the truth.

That was a great pity, but I do not think that in stating it he was inspired by any base motives.'

'How do you know?' asked Zuhayr with irritation. 'He may have felt that it was the only way to extend knowledge and survive.'

'He was completely sincere,' al-Zindiq asserted with a certainty derived from old age. 'He once said that what had hurt him the most in his life was when he took his son for Friday prayers and a crowd of turbulent illiterates threw them out. It was not just the humiliation, which undoubtedly upset him, but the knowledge that the passions of the uneducated were about to drown the most modern religion in the world. As for myself, I think Ibn Rushd was not heretical enough. He accepted the idea of a Universe completely in thrall to God.'

Zuhayr shivered.

'Are you cold boy?'

'No, it is your words that frighten me. I did not come here to discuss philosophy or trade theological insults with you. If you wish to test your ideas we can organize a grand debate in the outer courtyard of our house between you and the Imam from the mosque, but with all of us as the judges. I am sure my sister Hind will defend you, but be careful. Her support is not dissimilar to that provided by a rope to a hanging man!'

Al-Zindiq laughed. 'I am sorry. When you arrived so suddenly without warning I was working on a manuscript. My whole life's work, which is an attempt to draw together all the strands of the theological wars which have plagued our religion. My head was so full of those thoughts that I began to inflict them on you. Now tell me all about your visit to Gharnata.'

Zuhayr sighed with relief. He recounted the events of the last few days without sparing a single detail. As he spoke about how they had decided not to accept any further humiliations without resistance, al-Zindiq's ear caught the note of a familiar passion. How often he had heard young men in their prime eager to lay down their lives to protect their honour. He did not want another life wasted. He looked at Zuhayr and an image of the young man in a white shroud flashed through his head. Al-Zindiq trembled. Zuhayr misjudged the slight movement. He thought that, for once, he had infected the sage with some of his excitement.

'What is to be done, al-Zindiq? What is your advice?'

Zuhayr was expecting his friends from Gharnata later that day. It would inspire them with so much confidence if they knew that the old man had decided to back their project. He had been talking for well over an hour, outlining Musa's objections to their plan and Ibn Daud's response to such feeble-mindedness. It was time he let al-Zindiq talk.

Zuhayr had never needed the old man as much as he did now, for underneath the bravado, the great-grandson of Ibn Farid was racked with serious doubts. What if they all perished in the attempt? If the result of their deaths was the rebirth of Muslim Gharnata, then the sacrifice would have been worth every life, but was that likely? Suppose their rashness led to the elimination of every believer in the old kingdom, their lives cut short by the knights of Ximenes de Cisneros? Zuhayr was still not sure that it was the right time to depart from this world.

Al-Zindiq began his counter-offensive by asking what appeared to be an innocent question.

'So Ibn Daud al-Misri says he is the great-grandson of Ibn Khaldun?'

Zuhayr nodded eagerly.

'Why that suspicious tone? How can you doubt his word without having ever seen him?'

'He sounds headstrong and rash. His great-grandfather would not have suggested such a course of action. He would have argued that without a strong sense of social solidarity in the camp of the believers, there could be no victory. It was the absence of this solidarity amongst the followers of the Prophet that led to the decline in al-Andalus. How can you recreate what no longer exists? Their armies will crush you. It will be like an elephant stepping on an ant.'

'We know that, but it is our only hope. Ibn Daud said that a people which is defeated and subjugated by others soon disappears.'

'Spoken like his great-grandfather! But does he not understand that we have already been defeated and are now being subjugated? Bring him to me. Bring them all to me tonight and let us discuss the matter again and with the seriousness that it deserves. It is not your lives alone that could be lost. A great deal more is at stake. Does your father know?'

85

Zuhayr shook his head.

'I would like to tell him, but Great-Uncle Miguel has arrived to see Great-Aunt Zahra . . .'

Zuhayr stopped himself, but it was too late. The forbidden name had been uttered. He looked at al-Zindiq who smiled. 'I was wondering when you intended to mention her. The village is talking of nothing else. It does not matter now, boy. It was a long time ago. I was going to tell you the last time, but your servant's arrival sealed my lips. So now you know why al-Zindiq is banished, but also provided with food.'

'If you loved her, why did you not go to Qurtuba and find her? She would have married you.'

'The heat and cold that remains in our body is never constant, Ibn Umar. At first I was frightened of her father – he had threatened to slay me if I was seen near Qurtuba. But there was something else.'

'What?'

'Perhaps Zahra did love me all those years ago. Perhaps. She had strange ways of demonstrating her affection.'

Zuhayr was perplexed.

'What do you mean?'

After three months in Qurtuba she was seen climbing atop every Christian nobleman who smiled at her. This went on for many years. Too many years. When I heard the stories of her adventures I fell ill for a long time, but I recovered. It cured me. The malady disappeared. I felt free again, even though my heart forgot what the sun used to look like.'

'And you forgot Great-Aunt Zahra?'

'I did not say that, did I? How could I ever forget? But the gates were tightly closed. Then I heard other stories about similar incidents with other men. After that I stuffed my ears with cotton wool. Many, many years later Amira told me that the lady was in the Gharnata maristan.'

'I think what she did not tell you was that Great-Aunt Zahra was as sane as you or me. She was sent there on the express orders of her father, the year before he died. He believed that her behaviour was designed explicitly to punish him for forbidding her to marry you. That is what my mother told me.'

'Great men like Ibn Farid always saw themselves at the centre of everything. Could he not see that the Lady Zahra was punishing herself?'

'She was quite moved to see her brother, you know. Even though Ama told us that she used to loathe Miguel. When we asked why, Ama's face became as hard as a rock. Did Miguel play any part in your banishment, al-Zindiq? I'm sure he must have spied on you.'

Al-Zindiq cupped his face in his hands and stared downwards at the earth. Then he raised his head and Zuhayr saw the pain clearly reflected in his eyes. His wrinkled face had suddenly become taut. How strange, thought Zuhayr, he reacts exactly like Ama.

'I am sorry, old man. I did not mean to revive hurtful memories. Forgive me.'

Al-Zindiq spoke in a strange voice.

'For you, Miguel is an apostate who betrayed the colour green for their hymns and wooden icons. You see him swaggering around as the Bishop of Qurtuba, blaspheming against your religion, and you are ashamed that he is related to you. Am I not correct?'

Zuhayr nodded earnestly.

'Yet what if I were to tell you that as a boy, Meekal al-Malek was full of life and fun? Far from spying on me and running to tell tales to his father, he wanted Zahra and me to be happy. He would play chess with such passion that if he had done nothing else he would still be remembered as the inventor of at least three opening moves which could not be matched by the masters of the game in this peninsula, let alone the likes of me or even the Dwarf's father, who was a player of some distinction. He would often engage in philosophical battles with his tutors, which revealed such a precocious streak that it frightened all of us, especially his mother. There was so much promise in him that Ibn Farid used to say to the Lady Asma: "Do not let the maids stare at him in admiration. They will afflict him with the Evil Eye." Later, after what happened, many of us recalled what his father had said so many years ago. It was my mother, Lady Asma's maid and confidante, who used to look after Miguel. He was often in our quarters and I was very fond of him.'

'How then did his ship sink to the bottom?' asked Zuhayr.

'What is the mystery? How did he get ill? What happened, al-Zindiq?'

'Are you sure you want to know? There are some things which are best left alone.'

'I must know, and you are the only one who will tell me.'

The old man sighed. He knew that this was not true. Amira probably knew much more than he had ever been told, but whether either of them knew everything was open to question.

Two women, and they alone, had known the whole truth. Lady Asma and her trusted serving woman. My much-loved mother, thought this lonely old man on the top of the hill. Both were dead, and Wajid al-Zindiq was certain that his mother had been poisoned. The family of Hudayl did not trust in fate. They had felt that only the cemetery could ensure total silence. Who had taken the decision? Al-Zindiq did not believe for a moment that it could have been Umar's father, Abdallah bin Farid. It was not in his character or temperament. Perhaps it had been Hisham of Gharnata, a great believer in tying up loose ends. It made no difference except that the exact details of what happened had died with her.

Some years later, al-Zindiq and Amira had sat down one evening and pieced together everything they knew regarding the tragedy. There was still no way of knowing whether their version was accurate or not, and it was for that reason that al-Zindiq was reluctant to talk.

'Al-Zindiq, you promised you would tell me everything.'

'Very well, but remember one thing, al-Fahl. What I am about to recount may not be the whole truth. I have no way of knowing.'

'Please! Let me be the judge.'

'When your great-grandfather died, both your grandmothers were distraught. The Lady Maryam had not shared his bed for many years, but still she loved him. Ibn Farid died in his sleep. When the Lady Asma went to his bed she pressed his shoulders and the back of his head as was her norm, but there was no response. When she realized that life had flown out of him she screamed: "Maryam! Maryam! A calamity has befallen us." My mother said it was the most heart-rending cry she had ever heard. Both wives consoled each other as best they could.

'A year later the Lady Maryam was buried. It was a slow and

terrible death. Her tongue was covered with a black growth and she was in terrible pain. She pleaded for poison, but your grandfather would not hear of it. The best physicians from Gharnata and Ishbiliya were sent for, but they were helpless before the scourge which had planted itself in her mouth and was spreading throughout her body. Ibn Sina once said that this disease has no known cause and no known cure. He was of the opinion that in some cases the cause lay in the accumulation of bad humours trapped in the patient's mind. I have not studied such cases and am, therefore, not in a position to comment. In any event, whatever the cause, Lady Maryam died almost exactly a year after Ibn Farid. My mother used to say that her heart had been in mourning for twenty years before the death of her husband.

'Lady Asma was now left alone. Zahra was in the maristan. Meekal was a growing boy and not much inclined to stay within the confines of the house. Your grandfather was a kind man, but not renowned for his agility of mind. His wife, your grandmother, was similar in character. Lady Asma spent a lot of time with your father, who was then about eight years old. He became a substitute for the love she used to lavish on her late husband. Outside the family it was my mother who became her closest friend. Her own mother, the old cook Dorothea, despite repeated requests, refused to come and live in the house. Whenever she did come the quality of the food served in the house improved immeasurably. She would make short, but memorable visits. Unforgettable because she used to bake small almond cakes, which melted in our mouths. She was truly a very fine cook and the Dwarf's father learnt a great deal from her. He also fell in love with her, and there were stories that – but let me not digress. The fact is that if Dorothea had come and lived with Asma after Ibn Farid's death, the tragedy might never have happened.'

Zuhayr had been so absorbed in the story that he had, till now, controlled his curiosity. As a young boy, listening to the unending tales of family history, he had often irritated his father by persistent questions in pursuit of some tangential detail. Dorothea's refusal to relinquish her master and to follow her daughter to al-Hudayl had been puzzling him for some time, and so he interrupted the story-teller.

'I find that odd, al-Zindiq. Why? I mean in Don Alvaro's

house she was just a cook. Here she would have lived in comfort till she died.'

'I do not know, Ibn Umar. She was a very decent woman. I think she simply felt embarrassed at being the mother-in-law of such a notable as Ibn Farid. Perhaps, from a distance, it was easier to accept her sudden elevation. Much to Ibn Farid's annoyance she would refuse to stay in the house. My mother would vacate our room in the servants' quarters and that is where she slept.'

'What was the tragedy, al-Zindiq? What happened? I have a feeling that time may defeat us once again, and I would not like that to happen.'

'You mean why did Lady Asma die and who killed my mother?'

'Exactly. Lady Asma was not old was she?'

'No, and there lay the problem. She was still young, full of life and proud of her body. She had only borne two sons.'

'Great-Uncles Miguel and Walid.'

'Exactly. Walid's death was a terrible shock to us all. Just imagine if your Yazid were suddenly to contract a fever and die. You see, even the thought pains you. Lady Asma was ready to bear many more children when your great-grandfather decided to retire from this life. Mother told me that there were many suitors for the widow of Ibn Farid, but they were all refused. Your grandfather Abdallah would not hear of his father's wife being treated like any other woman. So Lady Asma lived in seclusion surrounded by her family.

'Your great-uncle Hisham had married just before Ibn Farid died and resumed his trading activities in Gharnata – activities, I may say, which were regarded with displeasure by all except his mother. For a son of the Banu Hudayl to become a tradesman in the market-place was nothing short of sacrilege. An insult to the honour of the family. It had its poets and philosophers and statesmen and warriors, and even a crazed painter whose erotic art, it is said, was greatly appreciated by the Caliph in Qurtuba, but they had all been based firmly on the land. Now the nephew of Ibn Farid was negotiating with merchants and haggling with owners of ships and actually enjoying every minute of his life. If Hisham had only pretended to be unhappy he might have been forgiven. Ibn Farid was livid, but having expelled one child he did not wish to break with another, and in any case the Lady Asma would not have tolerated any nonsense.'

'But this sounds like madness. Were not the Banu Hudayl descended from Bedouin warriors, who certainly traded and haggled with caravans every day of their lives, before coming to the Maghreb? Do you not agree?'

'Wholeheartedly. Think of it, my al-Fahl. Descendants of nomadic warriors who marched from Arabia to the Maghreb had lost the urge to travel and become so attached to the land that a member of the family deciding otherwise was treated as a heretic.'

Zuhayr, who was very close to the children of Ibn Hisham, was intrigued by the displeasure their grandfather had incurred.

'I am not sure I agree with you. I mean, even in the desert our forefathers had contempt for the town-dwellers. I remember Ama telling me as a child how only parasites lived in towns.'

Al-Zindiq laughed. 'Yes, she would. Amira was always an effective carrier of other people's prejudices. But you see, my al-Fahl, towns have a political importance which villages such as yours lack. What do you produce? Silks. What do they produce? Power. Ibn Khaldun once wrote . . .'

Zuhayr suddenly realized that the old fox was about to trap him into a lengthy discussion on the philosophy of history and the interminable debate on urban existence versus rural life, and so he stopped him.

'Al-Zindiq, how did Lady Asma die? I do not wish to ask this question again.'

The old man smiled with his eyes and his face was wreathed in wrinkles. In the space of a second those very same eyes were filled with a foreboding of disaster. He wanted to change the subject, but Zuhayr was staring at him. His soft bearded face wore a grim expression and suddenly revealed a firmness which surprised al-Zindiq. He breathed heavily.

'Six years after Ibn Farid died, the Lady Asma became pregnant.'

'How? who?' asked Zuhayr in a hoarse, agonized whisper.

'Three people knew the truth. My mother and the other two. My mother and Lady Asma are dead. That leaves one person.'

'I know that, you old fool.' Zuhayr was angry.

'Yes, yes, young Zuhayr al-Fahl. You feel upset. You knew none of these people, but still your pride is hurt.'

Strange, thought al-Zindiq, how much it has affected this boy. What has it to do with him? The infernal power of yesterday's ghosts still fuelling our passions? It is too late to stop now. He stroked Zuhayr's face and patted his back as he gave him a glass of water.

'You can imagine the atmosphere in the house when this became known. The old ladies of the family, many of whom had been presumed dead from gluttony long ago, suddenly reappeared, descending on the house from Qurtuba, Balansiya, Ishbiliya and Gharnata. Bad news always travels fast. The Lady Asma did not come out of her room. My mother acted as the mediator between her and these old witches. An old midwife from Gharnata, considered an expert in the art of removing unwanted children from the womb, began her work, with my mother at her side. Her operation was successful. The embarrassment was removed. A week later, Lady Asma died. Some poison had entered the stream of her blood. But that was not all. When your grandfather and grandmother went to see her, Lady Asma whispered in your grandmother's ear that she wanted to die. She had lost the will to live. The shame was unbearable. Hisham and his wife were in the house with their son, who was another great favourite of the Lady Asma and used to spend weeks at the house. That is how Ibn Hisham became so close to your father. As for Meekal, he fell very ill himself. He did not go and see his mother on her death-bed. Nor did she send for him.'

'But who was, it al-Zindiq? How can pure water in a jug turn overnight into sour milk?'

'My mother did not see it happen, but the Lady Asma told her everything there was to know. Three weeks later my mother herself was dead. She had never been ill in her life. I had come to the village and asked for permission to attend Lady Asma's funeral. This was considered improper, but I did manage to speak to my mother. She insisted on speaking in riddles. She would not name the person, but from a combination of what she said to me that night and what Amira had observed with her own eyes, what had happened became clear to us – or so we imagined.'

Zuhayr's breathing had become heavier, and the blood rose to his face in anticipation as al-Zindiq paused to drink some water.

'Tell me, old man. Tell me!'

'You know that house well, Zuhayr bin Umar. Lady Asma was in the rooms where your mother now lives. Tell me something. Is any strange man or even a male servant ever allowed into those quarters?'

Zuhayr shook his head.

'Which males can come and go as they please, apart from your father?'

'I suppose Yazid and myself.'

'Exactly.'

For a minute Zuhayr could not comprehend what he had been told. It hit him like an unexpected blow on the skull. He looked at the old story-teller in horror.

'You do not mean . . . you cannot mean . . .' But the name refused to trip off his tongue. It was al-Zindiq who finally had to speak the name.

'Meekal. Miguel. What difference does it make?'

'Are you sure?'

'How can I be? But it is the only supposition. Everyone noticed weeks before the pregnancy was discovered that Meekal was behaving in a very strange fashion. He had stopped going to the baths in the village to peep at the naked women. He stopped laughing. His beardless face became heavy and morose. His eyes were heavy with lack of sleep. Physicians arrived from Gharnata, but what could they do? The illness was beyond their cures. So they prescribed sea air, fresh fruits and herbal infusions. Your great-uncle was sent off to Malaka for a month. Just being away from that house must have had a beneficial effect.

'When he returned he did look much better. But, to the surprise of all those who had no idea of the inner torment which was consuming him, he never went near his mother's chamber. I think she spoke with him once. At her funeral he was inconsolable. He wept for forty days. After that he fell ill for a long time. His health never returned. The Meekal I knew had also died. The tragedy claimed three lives. The Bishop of Qurtuba is a ghost.'

'But how could it happen, al-Zindiq?'

'That is no mystery. Ever since he was a baby, Meekal was the favourite. He used to bathe with his mother and the other ladies. Amira told me that even though he was sixteen, he would walk in while the Lady Asma was having a bath and often took off his clothes and jumped in with her.

'She was not yet past her prime. I do not know who initiated what happened, but I can understand her dilemma. She was still a woman, and she still yearned for that one particular joy which had disappeared from her life since the death of Ibn Farid. When it happened it was so warm, so ecstatic, so comfortable, so familiar, that she forgot who she was and who he was and where they were. Then immediately afterwards the memory became a pain, which in her case, could only be removed by death. Who are we to judge her, Zuhayr? How can we ever understand what she felt?'

'I don't know – I don't want to know – but it was madness.'

'Yes, that it was and the people around her became stern and inflexible. I have a suspicion that the old midwife was encouraged to facilitate the death of both mother and child.'

'Lady Asma must have regretted converting to our religion.'

'Why do you say that?'

'Well, if she had remained a worshipper of icons she could have pretended to the world that the appearance of a child in her body was a divine mystery.'

'You are beginning to sound bitter. It is time you went home.'

'Come with me, al-Zindiq. You will be welcomed.'

The old man was startled by the suddenness of the invitation. 'I thank you. I would like to see Zahra, but some other day.'

'How can you bear this solitude day after day?'

'I look at it differently. From here I see the sun rise as no other person does, and from here I enjoy the sun set as few others will. Look at it now. Is not that the colour of paradise? And there are my manuscripts, growing by the year. Solitude has its own pleasures my friend.'

'But what about its pains?'

'In every twenty-four hours there is always one which is full of anguish and self-pity and confusion and the desire to see other faces, but an hour passes quickly enough. Now fly away my young friend. You have important business to conduct tonight, and do not forget to bring to me the young man who claims he is the descendant of Ibn Khaldun.'

'Why so sceptical?'

'Because Ibn Khaldun's entire family perished in a shipwreck while travelling from Tunis to al-Qahira! Now go, and peace be upon you.'

Chapter 6

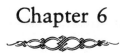

'DWARF, WHEN I grow up I want to be a cook, just like you.'
The chief cook, who was sitting over a giant pan grinding a concoction of meat, pulses and wheat with a large wooden pestle, looked at the young boy sitting directly opposite him on a tiny stool and smiled.

'Yazid bin Umar,' he said, as he carried on pounding the meat, 'it is very hard work. You have to learn how to cook hundreds of dishes before anyone will employ you.'

'I will learn, Dwarf. I promise.'

'How often have you had *harrissa*?'

'Hundreds and thousand of times.'

'Exactly so, young master, but do you know how it is cooked or what ingredients are used to flavour the meat? No, you do not! There are over sixty recipes for this dish alone. I cook it in the style recommended by the great teacher al-Baghdadi, but using herbs and spices of my own choice.'

'That's not true. Ama told me that it was your father who taught you everything you know. She says he was the Sultan of cooks.'

'And who taught him? That Ama of yours is getting too old. Just because she has known me since I was your age, she thinks I have no creative skills of my own. My father was certainly more inventive in the realm of sweets. His date and vermicelli mixture cooked in milk over a low heat to celebrate all the big weddings and festivals was famous throughout al-Andalus. The Sultan of Gharnata was here for your grandfather's wedding. After tasting the dessert he wanted to take my father away to the al-Hamra, but Ibn Farid, may his soul rest in peace, said "Never."

'But in the kingdom of real food he was not as good a cook as my grandfather, and he knew that fact very well. You see, young master, a genius can never rely on the recipes of others.

How many pinches of salt? How much pepper? Which herbs? It is not just a question of learning, though that is important, but of instinct.That is the only secret of our craft. It happens like this. You are beginning to cook a favourite dish and you realize that there are no onions in the kitchen. You grind some garlic, ginger, pomegranate seeds and pimentos into a paste and use them instead. Add a tiny cup of fermented grape juice and you have a brand-new dish. The Lady Zubayda, whose generosity is known to all, tastes it when the evening meal is served. She is not deceived. Not even for a single moment. Straight away she realizes that it is something completely new. After the meal I am summoned to appear before her. She congratulates me and then questions me in some detail. Naturally I let her into my secret, but even as I am speaking to her I have forgotten the exact measures of the ingredients I have used. Perhaps I will never cook that dish again, but those who have tasted it once will never forget the unique blend of flavours. A truly good dish, like a great poem, can never be repeated exactly. If you want to be a cook, try and remember what I have just told you.'

Yazid was greatly impressed.

'Dwarf? Do you think you're a genius?'

'Of course, young master. Why else would I be telling you all this? Look at the *harrissa* I am cooking. Come here and observe it carefully.'

Yazid moved his stool close to the cook and peered into the pan.

'This has been cooking the whole night. In the old days they would only use lamb, but I have often used the meat of calves or chicken or beef, simply in order to vary the flavour. Otherwise your family would begin to get bored with my cooking, and that would upset me greatly.'

'What have you put in this *harrissa*?'

'The meat of a whole calf, three cups of rice, four cups containing the hearts of wheat, a cup of brown lentils, a cup of chickpeas. Then I filled the pan with water and let it cook overnight. But before I left the kitchen I put some dried coriander seeds and black cardamoms in a little muslin bag and lowered it into the pan. By the morning the meat had melted completely and now I am grinding it into a paste. But before I serve it for your Friday lunch, what else will I do?'

'Fry some onions and chillies in clarified butter and pour them on the *harrissa*.'

'Very good, young master! But the onions must be burnt and floating in the clarified butter. Perhaps next week I will add something to this dish. Perhaps a few eggs fried in butter and sprinkled with herbs and black pepper would mix well with *harrissa*, but it might be too heavy on the stomach just before Friday prayers. What if the pressure was so great that when they bowed their heads before Mecca the other end of their bodies began to emit a foul-smelling wind? That would not be appreciated by those directly in the line of fire.'

Yazid's laughter was so infectious that it made the Dwarf grin. Then the boy's face became very serious. A tiny frown appeared on the large forehead. The eyes became intense. A thought had crossed his head.

'Dwarf?'

'Yes?'

'Don't you sometimes wish that you were not a dwarf, but a big tall man, like Zuhayr? Then you could have been a knight instead of being in this kitchen all day?'

'Bless your heart, Yazid bin Umar. Let me tell you a story. Once upon a time, in the days when our Prophet, peace be upon him, was still alive, a monkey was caught pissing in a mosque.'

Yazid started giggling.

'Please do not laugh. It was a very serious offence. The care-taker rushed up to the monkey and shouted: "You blaspheming rascal! Aren't you frightened that God will punish and transform you into some other creature?" The monkey was unashamed. "It would only be a punishment," replied the insolent creature, "if he were to turn me into a gazelle!" So you see, my dear young master, I would much rather be a dwarf creating wonder-ful dishes in your kitchen than a knight constantly in fear of being hunted by other knights.'

'Yazid! Yazid! Where is that little rascal, Amira? Go and find him. Tell him I want to see him.'

Miguel's voice echoed in the courtyard and reached the kitchen. Yazid looked at the Dwarf and put his finger on his lips. There was total quiet except for the bubbling of the two large pots containing stock from the bones of meat and game. Then he went and hid behind the platform which had been specially erected in the kitchen to enable the Dwarf to reach the pots and pans. It was no use. Ama walked in and marched straight to the hiding place.

'Wa Allah! Come on out and greet your great-uncle. Your mother will be very angry if you forget your manners.'

Yazid re-emerged. The Dwarf's face expressed sympathy.

'Dwarf?' asked the boy. 'Why does Great-Uncle Miguel stink so much? Ama says . . .'

'I know what Ama thinks, but we must have a more philosophical answer. You see, young master, any person who inserts himself between the onion and the peel is left with a strong smell.'

Ama glared at the cook and took Yazid by the hand. He broke loose and ran out of the kitchen towards the house. His plan was to avoid the courtyard altogether and try and hide in the bath-chamber by using the secret entrance from the side of the house. But Miguel was waiting for him, and the boy realized he had lost this battle.

'Peace be upon you, Great-Uncle.'

'Bless you, my child. I thought we might have a game of chess before lunch.'

Yazid cheered up immediately. In the past, whenever he had suggested a game, the adult world had resisted any incursions into their time and space. Miguel had barely spoken to him on his rare visits, let alone anything else. The boy rushed indoors and returned with his chess-set. He laid the chess-cloth on the table and carefully undid the box. Then, turning his back on the Bishop, he took a Queen in each hand and proffered his closed fists to his great-uncle. Miguel chose the fist which concealed the black Queen. Yazid cursed under his breath. It was at this stage that Miguel noticed the peculiar character of the chess-set. He began to inspect the pieces closely. His voice was hoarse with fear when he spoke.

'Where did you get this from?'

'A birthday gift from my father.'

'Who carved it for you?'

Juan the carpenter's name was about to be revealed when Yazid remembered that the man sitting before him was a servant of the Church. A stray remark of Ama's had lodged in his brain as a warning, and now the child's introspective wisdom came into play.

'I think it was a friend in Ishbiliya!'

'Do not lie to me, boy. I have heard so many confessions in my life that I can tell by the inflections in a person's tone whether or not he is telling the truth, and you are not. I want an answer.'

'I thought you wanted to play chess.'

Miguel looked at the troubled face of this boy with the shining eyes who sat opposite him and he could not help recalling his own childhood. He had played chess in this very courtyard and on this same piece of cloth. On the three occasions he had played against a master from Qurtuba, Miguel remembered the whole family standing round the table watching with excitement as the master was defeated every time. Then the applause and laughter as his brother would hoist him into the air to celebrate. Most pleased of all was his mother, Asma. He shuddered at the memory and looked up to see Hind, Kulthum and the young visitor from Egypt, Ibn Daud, smiling at him. Hind had seen everything from a distance and had realized that Yazid was in some sort of trouble. It was not too difficult to deduce that this was connected with the chess pieces. Even in his reverie Miguel was clutching the black Queen in his hand,

'Have you started the game, Yazid?' she asked innocently.

'He won't play. He keeps calling me a liar.'

'Shame on you, Great-Uncle Miguel,' said Hind as she hugged her brother. 'How can you be so cruel?'

Miguel turned towards her, his aquiline nose twitching slightly as a weak smile distorted his cheeks.

'Who carved these pieces? Where are they from?'

'Why, Ishbiliya, of course!'

Yazid looked at his sister in wonderment and then went and retrieved the black Queen from Miguel's clutches. Hind laughed.

'Play him, Great-Uncle Miguel. You might not win.'

Miguel looked at the boy. Yazid was no longer frightened. A mischievous glimmer had returned to his face. Despite himself the Bishop was once again reminded of his youth. These surroundings, this courtyard and a cheeky nine-year-old looking at him with a hint of insolence. Miguel was reminded of his own challenges to every Christian nobleman who called on his father.

Often they succumbed, and how the whole household would celebrate his triumphs.

Strange how that world, so long dead for him, continued to exist in the old house. Miguel felt like playing Yazid after all. He was about to sit down, when Ama signalled that lunch had been served.

'Did you wash your hands, Miguel?' Zahra's shrill voice took the family of Umar bin Abdallah by surprise, but her brother smiled as he looked at her. He knew that voice well.

'I am not ten years old, Zahra.'

'I don't care whether you're ten or ninety. Go and wash your hands.'

Yazid saw Hind trying to stop herself from laughing and began to giggle in an uncontrolled fashion. This reduced his sister to tears as she still held back her mirth. It was when Zubayda became infected that Miguel realized he had to act fast to stop the entire lunch from degenerating into a circus. He laughed feebly.

'Amira! You heard Zahra. Come.'

Ama brought a container filled with water, and a young man-servant carried in a basin, followed by a kitchen-boy holding a towel. Miguel washed his hands amidst a bemused silence. When he had finished his sister applauded.

'It was the same when you were a boy. If I shut my eyes I can just hear your screams, with Umm Zaydun and your mother, bless her heart, soaping your head and your body, washing you thoroughly and then flinging you into the bath.'

Zuhayr tensed at this reference to the Lady Asma. He looked at Zahra and Miguel, but there was no trace of emotion. Miguel looked at his sister and nodded.

'I am delighted to see you back in this house, sister.'

The midday meal was consumed with great passion. The Dwarf, eavesdropping as usual from the adjacent chamber, was satisfied with the level of praise. Compliments flew across the room like tame birds. The peak of perfection for the Dwarf was reached when both Miguel and Zahra spontaneously confirmed that his *harrissa* was infinitely superior to that prepared by his late and much-lamented father. Only then did the master-cuisinier retire to his kitchen at ease with his craft and the world.

'I am told that you live in great style in the Bishop's palace in

Qurtuba, attended by priests and your fat son. Why, Miguel?'
Zahra asked her brother. 'Why did it have to end like this for
you?'

Miguel did not reply. Zuhayr studied them closely as they
ate. Surely Zahra must know the real reason for Miguel's decision to cut himself completely from the old ways. Then Umar
announced that it was time for the men to depart. Ibn Daud,
Yazid and Zuhayr sprang to their feet and excused themselves.
They left the room to prepare themselves for the ride to the
mosque and Friday prayers.

Zahra and Miguel washed their hands and moved to the
courtyard, where a wooden platform covered with carpets had
been placed for them to enjoy the winter sunshine. Ama brought
a tray whose compartments contained almonds, walnuts, dates
and raisins and placed it before them.

'Allah be praised. It does my heart good to see both of you
at home.'

'Amira,' instructed Miguel as he picked a date, removed its
seed and replaced it with an almond, 'please ask my niece to
join us for a few minutes.'

Ama limped back in to the house as Zahra repeated her
question.

'Why, Miguel? Why?'

Miguel's heart began to pound. His face, which had become
so accustomed to concealing all emotions, suddenly filled with
anguish.

'You really don't know, do you?'

Zahra shook her head. They saw Zubayda approaching, and
what Miguel might or might not have told her remained buried
in his heart.

'Sit down my child,' said Miguel. 'I have something important
to say to you, and it is best said while the men are away.'

Zubayda sat down next to him.

'I am intrigued, Uncle Miguel. My ears await your message.'

'It is your brain which I wish to address. Yazid's chess-set is
the most dangerous weapon you have in this house. If it were
to be reported to the Archbishop in Gharnata he would inform
the Inquisition, especially if it was carved in Ishbiliya.'

'Who told you it was carved in Ishbiliya?'

'Yazid and Hind.'

Zubayda was moved by the instinct of her children to protect Juan the carpenter. Living in the village had made her complacent, and her first reaction had been to tell Miguel the truth, but she paused for reflection and decided to follow the line laid down by Yazid.

'They must know.'

'You are a fool, Zubayda. I am not here to spy on my family. I want you to burn those chess pieces. They might cost the boy his life. In this beautiful village the music of the water lulls us into a world of dreams. It is easy, too easy, to become complacent. I used to think we would be safe here for all time to come. I was wrong. The world in which you were born is dead, my child. Sooner or later the winds which carry the seeds of our destruction will penetrate the mountains and reach this house. The children must be warned. They are impatient. Headstrong. In the eyes of that little boy I see my own defiance of long ago. Hind is a very intelligent girl. I understand why you don't wish her to marry my Juan. Do not protest, Zubayda. I may be old, but I am not yet senile. In your place I would do the same. My motives were not the advancement of my son, but the safety of your children. And, I suppose, sentiment. Juan would marry in the family.'

Despite herself, for she found the Bishop repulsive, Zubayda was not unmoved. She knew that he spoke the truth.

'Why do you not speak to all of them tonight, Uncle Miguel? It might have a deeper impact than anything I could say. Then we can discuss what to do with Yazid's chess-set. The boy will be heart-broken.'

'I will happily speak to you all tonight. That is, after all, the main reason for my visit.'

'I thought you came to see me, Your Holiness. You crooked old stick!' interjected Zahra, with a cackle.

Zubayda, observing the pair, was reminded of something her mother had once taught her as a child, and it made her laugh. The couple turned on her with fierce looks.

'Share the joke this minute,' demanded Zahra.

'I cannot, Aunt. Do not compel me. It is too childish for words.'

'Let us be the judges. We insist,' said Miguel.

Zubayda looked at them and began to laugh again at the

ridiculousness of it all, but she realized she had no choice but to speak.

'It was the way Yazid's great-aunt used the word holiness, I suppose. It reminded me of a childhood rhyme:

'A fierce argument raged between the Needle and the Sieve;
Said the Needle: "You seem a mass of holes – how ever do
you live?"
Replied the sieve with a crafty smile: "That coloured thread
I see is not an ornament but passes through your head!" '

Zubayda saw their stern looks dissolve into laughter.

'Was he the needle?' asked Zahra.

Zubayda nodded.

'And she the sieve?' enquired Miguel.

Zubayda nodded again. For a moment they kept their balance and looked at each other in silence. Then a wave of laughter arose inside each of them but surfaced simultaneously.

As it subsided Ama, sitting underneath the pomegranate tree, felt tears trickling down her face. It was the first time Miguel had laughed in this house since the death of his mother.

The relaxed atmosphere in the courtyard of the old family house of the Banu Hudayl could not have been more different to the tension which gripped the village mosque that Friday. The prayers had passed off without incident, though Umar had been irritated on arrival to notice that despite his instructions to the contrary, half a dozen places in the front row had been kept for his family out of deference. In the early days people had stood and prayed where they could find a place. The true faith recognized no hierarchy. All were considered equal before God in the place of worship.

It had been Ibn Farid who insisted that the front row be kept empty for his family. He had been impressed by the Christian nobility's practice of reserving special pews in church. He knew that such a practice was repugnant to Islam, but he had insisted nonetheless on some recognition of the Muslim aristocracy by the mosque.

Umar stood discreetly at the back with the Dwarf and other servants from the house, but Zuhayr and Yazid had been pushed to the front by helping hands, and they had dragged Ibn Daud with them.

The prayers were now over. A young, blue-eyed Imam, new to the village, began to prepare himself for the Friday sermon. His old predecessor had been a very learned theologian and greatly respected as a human being. The son of a poor peasant, he had studied at the madresseh in Gharnata, acquired a great deal of knowledge, but never forgotten his origins. His successor was in his late thirties. His rich brown beard emphasized the whiteness of his turban as well as his skin. He was slightly nervous as he waited for the congregation to settle down and for the non-Muslim latecomers to be accommodated. The Jewish and Christian members of the tiny village community were permitted to attend the meeting after the Friday prayers were over. Yazid was delighted to see Juan the carpenter and Ibn Hasd enter the precincts of the mosque. They were accompanied by an old man robed in dark red. Yazid wondered who this person could be and nudged his brother. Zuhayr recognized Wajid al-Zindiq and trembled slightly, but did not say anything.

Suddenly Yazid frowned. Ubaydallah, the much-feared steward of the al-Hudayl estates, had moved up and seated himself just behind Zuhayr. Ama had told Yazid so many odious tales about this man's corruption and debauchery that they had instilled a blind hatred in the boy. The steward smiled at Zuhayr as they exchanged greetings. Yazid glowered in anger. He was desperate to talk to Juan and tell him that Great-Uncle Miguel had been asking questions about the chess-set, but Zuhayr frowned and put his heavy arm on the boy's shoulder to stop him wriggling.

'Behave with dignity and never forget that we are under the public gaze,' he whispered angrily into Yazid's ear. 'The honour of the Banu Hudayl is at stake. Tomorrow we may have to lead these people in a war. They must never lose their respect for us.'

'Rubbish,' muttered Yazid under his breath, but before his brother could retaliate the preacher had coughed to clear his throat and then begun to speak.

'In the name of Allah the beneficent, the merciful. Peace be upon you my brothers . . .'

He began to drone about the glories of al-Andalus and its Muslim rulers. He wanted there to be no doubt that the Islam which had existed in the Maghreb had been the only true Islam. The Umayyad Caliph of Qurtuba and his successors had defended the true faith as prescribed by the Prophet and his Companions. The Abbasids in Baghdad had been moral degenerates.

Yazid had heard talk like this in mosques ever since he had started attending Friday prayers. All the preachers reminded him of Ama, except that he could stop Ama with a question and divert her from all this lofty talk. That was impossible in the mosque.

Nor was Yazid the only member of the congregation to be distracted by the preacher's performance. At the back of the mosque the veterans of the Friday congregation were beginning to whisper to each other. It was difficult not to feel sorry for the young man trying to impose his will on a gathering which was not kind to newcomers or beginners, and for that reason Umar bin Abdallah put his finger to his lips and glared at the offenders. There was silence. The encouragement was sufficient to free the man with the brown beard. He became fired with a new enthusiasm and departed from the text he had so painstakingly prepared, abandoning the quotations from the al-koran which he had spent half the night learning and rehearsing. Instead he gave voice to his real thoughts.

'In the distance we can hear the solemn bells of their churches begin to ring with a tone so ominous that the noise eats my insides. They have already prepared our shrouds and it is for that reason that my heart is heavy, my spirit is oppressed and my mind is permanently troubled. It is only eight years since they conquered Gharnata, but so many Muslims already feel dead and dumb. Has the end of our world arrived? All the talk of our past glories is true, but what use are they to us now? How is it that we who held this peninsula in the palm of our hand have let it slip away?

'Often I hear our elders speak of the even worse calamities which befell the Prophet, peace be upon him, and how he overcame all of them. This is, of course, true, but at that time his enemies had not understood correctly the impact of the true word. We are paying the price for having become a universal religion. The Christian kings are not frightened of us alone, but when they hear that the Sultan of Turkey is considering sending his fleet to help us, then they begin to tremble. That is where the danger lies and that is why, my brethren, I fear the worst. Ximenes confides to his intimates that the only way to defeat us is to destroy everything . . .'

Every word he spoke was heard in silence. Even Yazid, an extreme critic of confessional performances, was struck by the integrity of the preacher. It was obvious that he was speaking from the heart. His brother was less impressed. Zuhayr was irritated by the pessimistic note which had been struck. Was the man going to offer any solution to the problem or simply demoralize the congregation?

'I think of our past. Our standards fluttering in the air. Our knights waiting for the command that will send them into the battle. I remember the stories we have all heard of our bravest of knights, Ibn Farid, may his soul rest in peace, challenging their warriors and slaying them all in the course of a day. I think of all this and pray to the Almighty for succour and support. If I were convinced that the Sultan in Istanbul would really dispatch his ships and soldiers I would willingly sacrifice every inch of this body to save our future. But, my brothers, I fear that all these hopes are empty. It is too late. We have only one solution. Trust in God!'

Zuhayr was frowning. To finish without an exhortation was an extremely unorthodox procedure at the best of times. Given the present situation it was an unheard-of abdication of a theologian's duty. Perhaps he was pausing to think. No. He had finished. He had taken his place in the front row and sat down three places away from Yazid.

Usually the congregation broke up after the *khutba*, but on this particular Friday it was as if a paralysis had set in. Nobody moved. How long they would have remained still and silent is a matter for conjecture, but Umar bin Abdallah, realizing that some action was needed, stood up and, like a lone sentinel stationed on a mountain top, observed the landscape around him. No one followed his example. Instead they all moved in unison, as if rehearsed, to create a path for him. Slowly he walked along this corridor. When he reached the front he turned round and faced them all. Yazid looked up at his father, his eyes gleaming with expectation and pride. Zuhayr's features were masked, but underneath his heart was beating rapidly.

For a moment Umar bin Abdallah was buried deep in reflection. He knew that at moments like this, when the sense of impending disaster hangs over a people, each word and every sentence acquires an exaggerated importance. For that reason everything has to be carefully chosen and the cadences united with the words. Rhetoric has its own laws and its own magic. This man who had grown up in the patterned tranquillity of the family estates, who had been bathed in water scented with the oil of orange blossoms, had been always surrounded by the delicate scent of mountain herbs and had, from his childhood, learnt the art of presiding over the lives of other men and women, understood what was expected of him.

The cellars of his memory were overflowing, but there was nothing there which could be raided to provide even the slightest degree of comfort to these people seated before him.

Umar began to speak. He recounted all that had been happening in Gharnata under the Christian occupation. He described the wall of fire in vivid detail, and as he spoke his eyes filled with tears, their grief shared by the congregation; he told of the fear which reigned in every Muslim household; he evoked the uncertainties which hung over the city like a dark mist. He reminded them that clouds were not shifted by the howls of dogs, that the Muslims of al-Andalus were like a river which was being re-channelled under the stern gaze of the Inquisition.

Umar spoke for an hour and they listened to every word. He could not by any means be described as an orator. His soft voice and modest style contrasted favourably with the noise made by many of the preachers, who sounded like hollow drums and whose recitation of the holy texts was accompanied by exaggerated mannerisms. These not only lost them the attention of their audiences after the first few minutes, but had the undesired effect of providing merriment for the benefit of Yazid and his friends.

Umar knew that he could not go on much longer with his litany of disasters. He had to suggest a course of action. As the leading notable of the village it was his duty, and yet he hesitated. For if the truth be told, Umar bin Abdallah was still not sure in which direction to take his people. He stopped speaking and let his eyes wander as they searched out the elders of the village. There was no help coming from that direction and so Umar decided that honesty was the only approach. He would trust them with his uncertainties.

'My brothers, I have a confession to make. I have no way of communicating directly with our Creator. Like you I am lost, and so I have to tell you that there is no easy solution to all our problems. One of our greatest thinkers, the master Ibn Khaldun, warned us many years ago that a people which is defeated and subjugated by another soon disappears. Even after the fall of Qurtuba and Ishbiliya we did not learn anything. There is no excuse for falling into the same hole thrice. Those of us who, in the past, sought refuge in the Sultan's shadow were fools because it quickly faded.

'There are three ways out of the maze. The first is to do what many of our brethren have done elsewhere. To say to oneself that a sane enemy is better than an ignorant friend and convert to their religion, while in our hearts believing what we wish to believe. What do you think of such a solution?'

For a few seconds they were stunned. It was a dangerously heretical idea, and the village was so isolated from Gharnata, let alone the rest of the peninsula, that they could not follow his line of reasoning. They recovered rapidly and a spontaneous chant rose from the ground on which they sat and reached for the sky.

'There is only one Allah and he is Allah and Mohammed is His Prophet.'

Umar's eyes moistened. He nodded his head and, with a sad smile, addressed them once again.

'I thought that would be your response, but I feel it is my duty to warn you that the Christian kings who now rule over us may not permit us the freedom to worship Allah for much longer. In any case the choice must be yours.

'The second possibility is to resist any incursion on our lands and fight to the death. Your death. My death. The death of all of us and the dishonouring of our mothers, wives, sisters and daughters. It is an honourable choice, and if that is what you decide I will fight alongside you, though I must be honest. I will send the women and children in my family to a safe refuge before the battle and I would advise you to do the same. What is your feeling on this matter? How many of you wish to die sword in hand?'

Once again they were silent, but this time without anger. The old men looked at each other. Then, from somewhere in the middle of the assembly, five young men stood up. In the front row Zuhayr al-Fahl jumped to his feet. The sight of the young master offering his life for the cause created a miniature sensation. A few dozen young men rose to their feet, but not Ibn Daud. His thoughts had wandered to Hind, whose infectious laughter was still ringing in his head. Yazid was torn between his father and his brother. He agonized for a few minutes and then stood up and clutched Zuhayr's hand. This gesture, in particular, moved everyone present, but only a minority was on its feet. Umar was greatly relieved. Suicide was not a course that he favoured. He signalled to his sons that they should sit down and their followers followed suit. Umar cleared his throat.

'The last option is to leave our lands and our homes in this village which our forefathers built when there was nothing but large rocks which covered the earth. It was they who cleared the ground. It was they who found the water and planted the seed. It was they who saw the earth yield a rich harvest. My heart tells me this is the worst of all choices, but my head warns that it may be the only way to preserve ourselves. It may not happen, but we should be mentally prepared to leave al-Hudayl.'

A half-scream in a choked voice interrupted Umar.

'And go where? Where? Where?'

Umar sighed.

'It is safer to climb the stairs step by step. I do not yet know the answer to your question. All I wish to do is to make it clear to you that the cost of believing in what we believe will involve sacrifices. The question we will have to ask ourselves is whether to live here as unbelievers or to find a place where we can worship Allah in peace. I have nothing more to say, but if any of you wish to speak and present us with a more acceptable choice then now is the time. Speak while your lips are free.'

With these words Umar sat down next to Yazid. He hugged his young son and kissed him on the head. Yazid clasped his father's hand and held on to it, much as a drowning person grasps anything that is afloat.

Umar's words had made a deep impression. For a while nobody spoke. Then Ibn Zaydun, who called himself Wajid al-Zindiq, rose in his place and enquired if he could speak his mind. Umar turned round and nodded vigorously. The older men present frowned and stroked their beards. They knew Ibn Zaydun as a sceptic who had poisoned a large number of young minds. But, they reasoned to themselves, this was a crisis and even heretics had a right to speak their minds. The voice, which was so familiar to Zuhayr al-Fahl, now began to crackle with indignation.

'For twenty years I have tried to tell you that it was necessary to take precautions. That blind faith alone would not get us anywhere. You thought that the Sultans would last till the Day of Judgement. When I warned you that he who eats the Sultan's soup ends up with his own lips on fire, you mocked me, denounced me as a heretic, an apostate, an unbeliever who had lost his mind.

'And now it is too late. All the wells are poisoned. There is no more pure water in the whole of this peninsula. That is what Umar bin Abdallah has been trying to tell you for the last hour. Instead of looking to the future we Muslims have always turned to the past. We still sing songs of the time when our tents first rose in these valleys, when we united in a staunch defence of our creed, when our pure white banners returned from the battle-field a different colour, drenched in the blood of the enemy. And how many cups of wine were drained in this village alone to celebrate our victories.

'After seventy years, I am tired of living. When death comes stumbling my way, like a night-blind camel, I will not move aside. Better to die in complete possession of my senses than be trampled on when my mind has already ceased to exist. And what holds true for an individual applies equally to a community . . .'

'Old man!' cried Zuhayr in agony. 'What makes you think that we are ready to die?'

'Zuhayr bin Umar,' al-Zindiq replied with a steady voice. 'I was speaking in symbols. The only way for you and your children and their children to survive in the lands now occupied by the Castilians is to accept that the religion of your fathers and their fathers is on the eve of its demise. Our shrouds have already been prepared.'

This remark annoyed the faithful. There were some angry faces as a familiar chant was hurled at the sceptic.

'There is only one Allah and he is Allah and Mohammed is his Prophet.'

'Yes,' replied the old man. 'That is what we have been saying for centuries but Queen Isabella and her Confessor do not agree with you. If you go on repeating this the Christians will tear open your hearts with straight and hard-shafted spears.'

'Al-Zindiq,' shouted Ibn Hasd from the back of the mosque. 'Perhaps what you say is true, but in this village we have lived at peace for five hundred years. Jews have been tormented elsewhere, but never here. Christians have bathed in the same baths as Jews and Muslims. Might the Castilians not leave us alone if we do nothing to harm them?'

'It is unlikely, my friend,' replied the sage. 'What is good for the liver is bad for the spleen. Their Archbishop will argue that if even one example is permitted to survive it will encourage others. After all if we are allowed to carry on as before on these estates, sooner or later, when other kings and queens, less given to violence, are on the throne, our existence might well encourage them to relax the restrictions against the followers of Hazrat Musa and Mohammed, may peace be upon him. They wish to leave nothing of us. That is all I wish to say. I thank you Umar bin Abdallah for letting my voice be heard.'

As al-Zindiq began to walk away, Umar put Yazid on his lap and beckoned the old man to sit by his side. As he settled down on the prayer rug, Umar whispered in his ear: 'Come and eat with us tonight, Ibn Zaydun. My aunt wishes it so.'

For once al-Zindiq was taken by surprise as he held back his emotions and nodded silently. Then Umar rose once again.

'If there is nobody else who wishes to speak, let us disperse, but remember that the choice is yours. You are free to do as you wish and I will help in any way I can. Peace be upon you.'

'And peace be upon you,' came the collective reply.

Then up rose the young preacher and recited a surá from the al-koran, which they all, including the Christians and Jews present, repeated after him. All that is except al-Zindiq.

> 'Say: "O Unbelievers,
> I worship not that which ye worship,
> And ye worship not that which I worship,
> Neither will I worship that which ye worship,

Nor will ye worship that which I worship.
Ye have your religion and I have my religion." '

As the meeting dispersed, al-Zindiq muttered to himself: 'The creator must have been suffering from indigestion on the day he dictated those lines. The rhythm is broken.'

Ibn Daud had overheard him and could not restrain a smile. 'The punishment for apostasy is death.'

'Yes,' replied al-Zindiq, staring straight into the young man's green eyes, 'but no *qadi* alive would ever pass such a sentence today. Are you the one who calls himself the grandson of Ibn Khaldun?'

'I am,' replied Ibn Daud as they walked out of the mosque.

'Strange,' reflected al-Zindiq, 'when all his family perished on the sea.'

'He lived with another, my grandmother, in later years.'

'Interesting. Perhaps we can discuss his work tonight? After supper?'

'Zuhayr has told me that you have studied his books and much else besides. I have no desire to quarrel with you or compete with your knowledge. I myself am still at the stage of learning.'

Ibn Daud saluted his interlocutor and hurried to the spot where the horses had been tethered. He did not wish to keep his host waiting, but when he arrived he could only see Yazid and Zuhayr. The young boy was smiling. Zuhayr had a distant look on his face and frowned at Ibn Daud. He was angry with his new-found friend. In the hammam in Gharnata, Ibn Daud had fired their imaginations with his talk of an armed uprising against the occupiers. Here he had swayed with the wind. Zuhayr stared coldly at the Qahirene and wondered whether he believed in anything.

'Where is your respected father?' enquired the visitor, feeling slightly uneasy.

'Attending to his business,' snapped Zuhayr. 'Are you ready?'

Umar had been surrounded by the elders of the village. They were anxious to discuss the future in much greater detail and in the privacy of a familiar house. It was for this reason that they had all repaired to the house of Ibn Hasd, the cobbler, where they were greeted with almond cakes and coffee, flavoured with cardamom seeds and sweetened with honey.

Zuhayr had been deeply disturbed by the events in the mosque. His anger was directed against himself. For the first time ever he had understood how grim the situation really was, and that there appeared to be no possibility of escape. Now he knew that any insurrection in Gharnata was doomed. He had learnt more from the looks of defeat and despair on the faces inside the mosque than from all the talk of Great-Uncle Miguel or Uncle Hisham, and yet ... And yet everything had been planned. It was too late.

Zuhayr appeared to forget that a guest was riding by his side. He nudged his horse gently in the stomach and the creature responded by a sudden burst of speed, which took Yazid by surprise. At first he thought his brother was trying to race him back to the house.

'Al-Fahl! Al-Fahl! Wait for me,' he grinned, and was about to race after his brother, but Ibn Daud stopped him.

'I cannot ride like your brother and I need a guide.'

Yazid sighed and reined in his horse. He had realized that Zuhayr wanted to be alone. Perhaps he had arranged to meet some of the young men who wanted to fight. Yazid understood that he had to take his brother's place. Otherwise Ibn Daud might imagine that they were being deliberately discourteous.

'I suppose I had better accompany you home. My sister Hind would never forgive me if you were lost!'

'Your sister Hind?'

'Yes! She's in love with you.'

Chapter 7

IN NOMINE DOMINI Nostri Jesu Christi.
Most excellent, most Christian and most brave King and Queen of all Spain.
It is now eight whole years since the crescent was removed from the Alhambra and the last fortress belonging to the sect of Mahomet reconquered for our Holy Father. Your Highnesses asked me to respect the terms of the Capitulation signed by the Sultan and yourselves when he surrendered to a superior moral force. Her Majesty will recall her injunction to her most loyal servant: 'As our most trusted Bishop you will be seen not solely as the servant of the Church, but as the eyes and ears of your King in Granada. You will behave in such a fashion that it can never be said that you brought dishonour to our name.' I understood Her Majesty to mean that the followers of the false Prophet were to be treated kindly and permitted to worship in their usual fashion. I have never told Your Majesties an untruth. I believe that the kindness shown by my predecessor was misunderstood by the Moors. They showed no inclination to convert to our holy faith. It was for that reason that I decided they must be taught that the time was past for idolatries and heresies. Her Majesty will recall our discussions in Toledo, when I explained the nature of the al-koran. I stressed that the books of this sect and its rituals and superstitions were a bottomless sea. In every house, in every room, they display the commandments of their prophet in rhymed couplets. It was Her Grace who first expressed the view that such evil books and the poisonous doctrines contained within them should be consigned to the fires of hell. I do not believe that any other person in Granada could have organized the public burning of all the al-korans and everything else related to that book.
I am not suggesting that as an individual I am indispensable for the task assigned to me by Your Majesties and our Holy

Church. How can any single person be essential to a Church such as ours? Nonetheless I took a vow when I became Archbishop of Toledo. I pledged that I would convert every follower of Mahomet to believe in our Lord Jesus Christ. I plead for your help to fulfil my vow and to be given all the powers necessary to execute my mission.

The Captain-General, that most noble Count of Tendilla whose family produced our most astute Cardinal Mendoza, my honoured predecessor, argues incessantly that since Your Majesties have won the war it is only a matter of time before the Moors adopt our language, customs and religion. When I pointed out to him that three Moorish women had been seen by one of my priests in the act of urinating over crucifixes which had been removed from church, he replied: 'What else do you expect, Archbishop? After all, you decided to burn their books. This is their revenge. Blasphemous outrage, but better they do that than castrate you in the market-place.'

It is attitudes such as these which are heard within our own ranks. The Count has few enough Christians in his court, but those that attend on him mock openly at our Church, denounce it as corrupt, joke about the number of Bishops and friars who live in sin, procreate and then appoint their sons to positions inside the Church. Even Don Pedro Gonzales de Mendoza, the Cardinal who on his death-bed advised Your Majesty to appoint me in his place, the man who defended your cause before you came to the throne, the noble ancestor of our brave Captain-General; even this holy person had seven children by two ladies of the highest rank. Don Pedro, as Her Majesty knows, was commonly referred to as our 'third monarch' and could do no wrong in the eyes of those who served him. The other day a Moor accosted me in the gardens near the palace and asked in a most courteous fashion: 'Are your children healthy and well, Your Grace? How many of them are there?' He meant well, perhaps, but I felt like plucking out his blaspheming tongue and sending him to roast in hell.

I am aware, of course, that this is an ancient disease, much encouraged in the past by that most learned of Bishops, Gregory of Tours, whose family, six hundred years after the birth of Our Lord, controlled the Church in central France for many years.

Our Cardinals and Bishops, and those who serve under them,

have, for these last six centuries, been swimming in a sea of sin. Even after we had reclaimed most of our lands, Granada became an oasis in which the Mahometans could indulge day and night in the excesses of the flesh. Mahomet's followers have become accustomed to besporting themselves like farm animals. It is this example of never-ending iniquity which has infected our Church and done our cause the most grievous injury. That is another strong reason for not letting these evil fashions survive in our lands. I beg Your Majesties' permission to proclaim the edicts of our faith in this kingdom and to appoint an apostolic Inquisitor to begin his work amongst these people, so that any person can come forward and report to us if he has heard or seen any other person, alive or dead, present or absent, say or act in a manner which is heretical, rash, obscene, scandalous or blasphemous.

Failing this, I must inform Your Majesties that it will be necessary to destroy all the public baths in the city. It is bad enough that the Mahometans flaunt these dens of sensuousness in our faces every single day. You will recall how our soldiers, on discovering that Alhama possessed more baths than any other city in this peninsula, decided that the best way to save the town was to destroy it, and this they did with the words of our Saviour on their lips. The obscenities painted on the side of the baths added fervour to their already strong determination. It was in these circumstances that our crusaders eradicated every remnant of sin.

Matters in Granada are much more serious, and not simply on the spiritual level. These accursed baths are also their regular meeting places to talk amongst themselves and engage in plots of sedition and treason. There is a great deal of unrest in the city. Every day my faithful conversos bring me reports of conversations in the Albaicin and the Moorish villages which are dotted, like the plague, in the Alpujarras.

My own inclination would be to end the discontent by arresting the ringleaders and burning them at the stake. What a tragedy befell our Church with the death of Tomás de Torquemada. The noble Count, however, is of a totally different disposition. For him Torquemada was nothing more than a Jewish converso trying desperately to prove his loyalty to the new faith. The Count is opposed to any firm measures against the heathen in our midst. He imagines that by speaking their language and dressing as they do he will win them over to our ways. Her Majesty will perhaps understand that I can neither comprehend nor appreciate the logic underlying such behaviour. Many of our knights, who fought like lions when we took Alhama, are permanently engaged in carefree and jocund revelry in Granada. They believe that their war is over. They do not understand that the most decisive stage of our war has only just begun. It is for that reason that I request Her Majesty to authorize the measures listed below and kindly to inform the Captain-General of Granada, Don Inigo Lopez de Mendoza, that he is not to obstruct any action taken by the Church.

- We must instruct the Moriscos to cease speaking Arabic, either amongst themselves in private or for the purpose of buying and selling in the market. The destruction of their books of learning and knowledge should make such an edict easily enforceable.
- They must be barred from keeping slaves bred in captivity.
- They should not be permitted to wear their Moorish robes. Instead they must be made to conform in dress and the way they carry themselves to the Castilian manner.
- The faces of their women must under no circumstances be covered.
- They must be instructed not to keep the front doors of their homes closed.
- Their baths must be destroyed.
- Their public festivals and weddings, their licentious songs and their music must be disallowed.
- Any family which produces more than three children must be warned that all extra progeny will be placed in the care of the Church in Castile and Aragon so that they can be brought up as good Christians.
- Sodomy is so widespread in these lands that in order to root it out we must be severe in the extreme. It should, in normal circumstances, be punished with death. Where the act is committed on animals a period of five years as a galley-slave would be adequate punishment.

These measures may appear to contradict the terms of the Capitulation agreed by us, but this is the only lasting solution to the disease which has eaten into our souls for so long. If Your

Most Gracious Majesties are in agreement with my proposals I would suggest that the Holy Inquisition opens an office in Granada without further delay and its familiars be dispatched to this sinful city immediately to collect evidence. Two, or at the most, three autos de fe *will make these people understand that they can no longer trifle with the power which God has willed to rule over them.*

I await an early reply and remain Your Majesties' most faithful servant, Francisco Ximenes de Cisneros.

Ximenes folded the paper and affixed his seal to the parchment. Then he called for his most loyal friar, Ricardo de Cordova, a Muslim converso who had converted at the same time as his master, Miguel, and had been gifted by him to the Holy Church. He handed him the letter.

'Only for the eyes of the Queen or King. Nobody else. Clear?'

Ricardo smiled, nodded and left the room.

Ximenes was thinking. What was he thinking? His mind was dwelling on its own frailties. He knew that he was not smooth of speech or letter. He had never been adept at coupling fire with water. The grammar he had studied as a boy in Alcala had been of the most primitive variety. Later at the university in Salamanca he had devoted himself to a study of the civil and canonical law. Neither there nor in Rome had he .acquired a taste for literature or painting.

Michelangelo's frescos left him completely unmoved. Despite himself he had been greatly impressed by the abstract geometric patterns on tiles he had seen in Salamanca and later in Toledo. When he thought about such matters, which was not very often, he confessed to himself that it would have been far more natural to worship the Lord as a concept. He did not like the cluster of images inherited from paganism and clothed in the colours of Christianity.

If only he had possessed the epistolary skills of his illustrious predecessor, Cardinal Mendoza. His letter to Isabella and Ferdinand would have been written in the most flowery and fashionable language. The monarchs would have been so moved by the literary quality of the composition that they would have accepted the dagger concealed underneath the verbiage as a necessary adjunct, but he, Ximenes, could not and would not deceive his Queen.

He had become Isabella's confessor when Talavera was sent as Archbishop to Granada, and to her great pleasure and surprise had not betrayed any feeling of agitation or anxiety on being conducted to her presence. Nor had she noticed in his facial expression, or the manner in which he approached her, the slightest trace of servility. His sense of dignity and the piety which exuded from every pore of his body were unmistakably genuine.

Isabella knew that she had a fervent priest, his inflexible temperament akin to her own. Talavera had treated her with respect but had not been able to conceal his despair at what he took to be a combination of cupidity and prejudice. He had always tried to lecture her on the virtues of tolerance and the necessity of coexistence with their Muslim subjects. Ximenes was made of sterner stuff. A priest with an iron soul and, moreover, a mind like her own. Isabella invited him to take charge of her conscience. She poured out her heart to him. Ferdinand's infidelities. Her own temptations. Fears for a daughter whose mind appeared to desert her without warning. All this the priest heard with a sympathetic face. On one occasion alone had he been so stunned by her revelation that his emotions overpowered his intellect and a mask of horror covered his face. Isabella had confessed an unsatisfied carnal urge which had gripped her some three years before the Reconquest of Granada. The object had been a Muslim nobleman in Cordova.

Ximenes recalled that moment with a shudder, giving silent thanks to his Lord Jesus Christ for sparing Spain that particular calamity. If a Moor had entered the Queen's chamber, who could predict the turn that History might have taken? He shook his head violently as if the very thought was heretical. History could have moved in no other direction. If Isabella had blunted her own capacities, then a sharper instrument would have been found.

Ximenes was the first truly celibate Archbishop of Spain. One night in Salamanca, during his university days, he had heard the noises which often marked a male dormitory in those excitable times and realized that his fellow students were busy mimicking the behaviour of overheated animals. The pleasure that some of the mating couples were giving each other was there for all to hear. Ximenes had felt a twinge of excitement below his groin. The shock had been enough to send him to sleep, but when he woke the next morning, he was horrified to discover his nightshirt drenched in what could only be his own seed. What made it worse was a sinful coincidence. The liquid imprint bore an uncanny resemblance to the map of Castile and Aragon.

For two whole days, Ximenes had been beside himself with dread and anxiety. At church, later that week, he described the scene to his confessor, who, much to the disgust of the future Archbishop had roared with laughter and responded in a voice so loud that it had made Ximenes tremble in embarrassment.

'If I . . .' the friar had begun with a laugh, but then, observing the pale, trembling young man before him, he had hesitated to search for a more sombre conclusion to the sentence. 'If the Church were to treat sodomy as an unforgivable sin, every priest in Spain would go to hell.'

That encounter in the confessional, much more than the events in the dormitory, had led Ximenes to take a vow of celibacy. Even when he was working at Siguenza on the estates of Cardinal Mendoza, at a time when a priest was expected to pick any peasant woman or boy he desired, Ximenes resisted temptation. Unlike a eunuch, he could not even take pride in his master's penis. Instead he turned to monasticism, embracing the Franciscan order to underline his heartfelt commitment to an austere and pious life.

Cardinal Mendoza, when informed of the exceptional self-restraint of his favourite priest, grunted his disapproval: 'Parts so extraordinary' – it was generally assumed that this was a reference to the intellectual qualities of Ximenes – 'must not be buried in the shade of a convent.'

Ximenes walked up and down the room. From his arched window he could see the cathedral which the masons were building on the ruins of an old mosque overlooked by the palace. He was thinking elevated thoughts, but unforeseen and unwanted images will sometimes break into the mind's core, disrupting even the most lofty meditations. Ximenes had been informed of a deeply offensive act of sacrilege committed in Toledo a month before, when a follower of Islam, imagining that he was unobserved, had been caught in the act of dipping his bared penis into the holy font. On being apprehended by a couple of vigilant friars, he had made no effort to deny what he had done or plead for mercy or indicate that he deeply regretted his rash behaviour. Instead he claimed he was a recent converso and had been instructed by an old Christian friend to perform this special type of ablution before he offered prayers in the cathedral.

The offender had refused to name his friend. He was tortured. His lips remained sealed. The Inquisition found the story unconvincing and handed him over to the civil authorities for the final punishment. He had been burnt at the stake some days ago. The image of the offensive act continued to haunt Ximenes. He made a mental note to send for the papers of the Inquisition referring to this particular case.

Ximenes was not bereft of a conscience. The man who was proposing himself as the cruel executioner of Islamic Gharnata had once himself been a victim. He had spent time in an ecclesiastical prison on the orders of the late Cardinal Carillo. The Cardinal, who was soon to be succeeded by Archbishop Mendoza, had asked Ximenes to abdicate a minor position in the Spanish Church, to which he had been appointed by Rome, in favour of one of the circle of sycophants which surrounded Carillo. Ximenes refused. His punishment had been six months' solitary confinement. The experience had left the priest sensitive to questions such as the difference between guilt and innocence, and it was this that made him reflect on the death of the man in Toledo who had cleaned his private parts in the holy water. Perhaps he had been innocent, but no Catholic would have sent him to the cathedral with those instructions. It must have been one of those French heretics who had escaped punishment. The prelate's eyes began to gleam as he felt he had uncovered the real truth. He would study the papers closely.

There was a knock on the door.

'Enter.'

A soldier entered and whispered in his ear.

'Send him in.'

Ibn Hisham entered the room. He went straight to the Archbishop who extended his hand. Ibn Hisham bent on one knee and kissed the ring. Ximenes lifted him up and indicated a seat.

'My uncle Miguel left firm instructions that I must call on Your Grace and pay my respects.'

Ximenes looked at the newest converso from the ranks of Granada's nobility and attempted a smile.

'How were you christened by the Bishop of Cordova?'

'Pedro de Gharnata.'

'Surely you mean Pedro de Granada.'

Pedro nodded, his eyes betraying the sadness and humiliation which he had inflicted upon himself. He saw the half-triumphant, half-contemptuous look on the face of the man whose hand he had kissed and he wanted to be dead. Instead he smiled weakly, cursing himself for his servility.

Ximenes looked at him and nodded.

'Your visit was unnecessary. I have already intimated to your uncle that you would be permitted to carry on your trade. I am a man who keeps his word. Tell me something, Pedro. Did your daughter convert to our faith as well?'

Pedro de Granada began to sweat. The devil knew everything.

'She will on her return from Ishbi . . . I mean Sevilla, Your Grace. We are awaiting her return.'

'Bless you, my son. Now if you will excuse me it is time for evensong, and after that I have other business to which I must attend. Just one more thing. As you probably know, seven of our priests on their way to Holy Communion last week were ambushed. A deluge of human excrement contained in wooden buckets was emptied over their heads. Do you by any chance know the names of the young men who perpetrated this act?'

Pedro shook his head.

'No, I thought not. If you did you would have already reported the matter. Try and find out if you can. Such outrages cannot remain unpunished.'

The newly baptized Pedro de Granada agreed with these sentiments most forcefully.

'When God wants to destroy an ant, Your Grace, he permits her to grow wings.'

After Pedro had bowed and taken his leave, a wave of nausea overpowered Ximenes.

'Hateful, spineless, confused, witless wretches,' he thought to himself. 'Every day they come and see me. Some out of fear. Others to protect their future. Ready to betray their own mothers if . . . if . . . if . . . always an if . . . if the Church will guarantee their property; if the church will not interfere with their trade;

if the Church will keep the Inquisition out of Granada. Only then will they happily convert to our faith and bring to it their relentless pursuit of greed. God curse them all. Our Church does not need such pitiful wrecks. Pedro de Granada will remain a Mahometan till the day he dies. May God curse him and others like him.'

Chapter 8

AT A DISTANCE, on the slopes of the mountain, the white houses of the village were no longer visible, but the flickering of the oil lamps which hung outside them was magical from where Yazid was seated. He knew the lights would not go out till the men and women around him returned home.

The outer courtyard of the house was overflowing with visitors. They were sitting in a large circle on thick carpets which had been placed on the grass. Occasionally, a tiny flame would light the face of al-Zindiq or Miguel, who were seated in the centre of the circle. The coal fires burning in the stoves kept them all warm. There had been over two hundred people present that night when the 'debate' had first started.

This family, which for centuries had not thought about anything more demanding than the pleasures of the hunt, the quality of the marinade used by the cooks on the roast lamb being grilled that day, or the new silks which had arrived in Gharnata from China, was tonight confronting history.

Miguel had dominated the evening. At first he had sounded bitter and cynical. The success of the Catholic Church, its practical superiority, he had argued, lay in the fact that it did not even attempt to sweeten the bitter taste of its medicine. It did not bother to deceive; it was not searching for popularity; it did not disguise its shape in order to please its followers. It was disgustingly frank. It shook Man by the shoulders, and shouted in his ear:

'You were born in excrement and you will live in it, but we might forgive you for being so foul, so vile, so repulsive if you sink to your knees and pray every day for forgiveness. Your pitiful, pathetic existence must be borne with exemplary humility. Life is and will remain a torment. All you can do is to save your soul, and if you do that and keep your discontent well hidden, you might be redeemed. That and that alone will make your life on earth a mite less filthy than it was on the day you were born. Only the damned seek happiness in this world.'

Miguel had paused at this point and studied his audience. They appeared to be in a hypnotic trance and had stared back at him in amazement. In a soft, calm voice, he had taken them on a tour of their past, reminding them not just of the glories of Islam, but also of the defeats, the chaos, the palace despotisms, the internecine wars and the inevitable self-destruction.

'If our Caliphs and Sultans had wanted things to stay the same, they should have changed the way they governed these lands. Do you think it gave me pleasure to shift religions? Even tonight, I have made some of my own family angry, as you have observed, but I have reached a stage in my life where I can no longer conceal the truth.

'I love this house and this village. It is because I want them to remain and all of you to prosper that I ask you, once again, to think very seriously. It is already late, but if you do as I say we can still save you. In the end you will convert, but by then the Inquisition will be here and they will question all of you to determine which conversion is true and which is false. Since one of their aims is to confiscate your lands for the Church and the Crown, they will give themselves the benefit of the doubt. I cannot compel you, but those who are coming after me will not be so kind.'

Even though what he had to say was unpopular, it was felt by most of those present that he was nearer the truth than the hotheads who wanted to start a war, for underneath the detached calm which surrounded the seigneurial house, there was a great deal of tension.

Some of those with young children had drifted away after the opening speeches, but Yazid was still wide awake and enjoying every moment. He was sitting near his mother, sharing her large woollen cloak. Next to him was his sister Hind, who had, true to the Berber characteristics she had inherited from her mother's side, displayed an exuberance which had amazed everyone, except Yazid. She had interrupted her great-uncle several times, laughed sarcastically at his attempted witticisms and muttered the odd obscenity under her breath, but the night air had carried her voice and the village women had applauded. Miguel had responded without anger, secretly admiring Hind's courage, and publicly proclaiming that he loved her dearly. Her response to this avuncular declaration had been characteristic, but this time she had gone too far and isolated herself.

'When a serpent says he loves me I wear him as a necklace.'

Ama had cackled loudly, which had surprised Yazid since he knew Ama disapproved strongly of Hind's behaviour. But Ama had been alone. Even though Miguel was not universally popular, this sort of rudeness did not please the villagers, who felt it was a breach of hospitality to the son of Ibn Farid. The comparison to a snake had upset her great-uncle. His ears had been stung by the venom and he had been unable to prevent the telltale water from filling his eyes.

It was the sight of his uncle in tears that had in turn upset Umar, who had frowned at his wife from the other side of the stove. Zubayda deciphered the signal accurately. She whispered Hind to order, threatening her with marriage to Miguel's son, simple Juan, unless she disciplined her tongue immediately. The blackmail worked brilliantly. Hind had sidled up to Miguel and apologized in his ear. He had smiled and stroked her head. Peace had returned. Coffee had been served.

Hind was not at all upset, since her own views had been made clear to the assembled company and, in particular, to the stranger who sat in its midst. Ibn Daud, the green-eyed jewel from al-Qahira and the object of her affections, was deep in thought. Ibn Daud had been struck by Hind even before Yazid had blurted out his sister's secret. Her hot-tempered tongue and sharp, mischievous features had enchanted him, but tonight he was distracted by the debate. He had smiled at Hind's cheeky assault on her great-uncle, but it was al-Zindiq's sobering reflections which had become the centre of his preoccupations that evening.

Al-Zindiq had, in polar contrast to Miguel, savaged Christian beliefs and superstitions. He had mocked the old Church for its inability to resist pagan pressures. Why else make Isa a divinity and his mother an object of worship? The Prophet Mohammed, in contrast, had ultimately rejected the same pressures, resisted temptation and disavowed the worship of three female goddesses. That was as far as al-Zindiq was prepared to travel tonight with his co-religionists. He did not defend Islam with the intellectual vigour for which he was renowned, and which had been expected from him on this night. He was too honest a man to contradict those of Miguel's assertions that he regarded as indisputable. Instead he tried to enthuse his audience by reminding them that a star which waned in one firmament could rise in another. He described the Muslim victories in Istanbul in such graphic detail that a shiver of collective pride shook his audience. As for the decline of al-Andalus, he did not give much credence to some of the more popular explanations.

'Remember,' he asked them, 'the story of the Sultan of Tlemcen and the holy man? The Sultan was attired in his most extravagant clothes when he received Abu Abdallah al-Tunisi. "Is it lawful for me to pray in these fine clothes I am wearing?" he asked his learned visitor. Abu Abdallah laughed and explained his reaction in the following words. "I am laughing, O proud Sultan, at the feebleness of your intellect, your ignorance of yourself and your sorry spiritual state. For me you are like a dog sniffing around in the blood of a carcass and eating filth, but lifting its leg when it urinates lest the liquid soil its body. You ask me about your clothes when the sufferings of men are upon your head." The Sultan began to weep. He renounced his position and became a follower of the Holy Man.'

Al-Zindiq finished his story amidst cries of 'Wa Allah' and the expression of sentiments supporting the thesis that if all the Muslim kings of al-Andalus had behaved in like fashion, the followers of the Prophet would not be in such a sad state at the moment. This was the reaction al-Zindiq expected, and he now confronted them very directly.

'It sounds good, but would it have saved us? I don't think so. No amount of religion can succeed in changing the ways of kings unless it is based on something more, on something which our great teacher Ibn Khaldun called solidarity. Our defeats are a result of our failure to preserve the unity of al-Andalus. We let the Caliphate collapse and in its place we let poisonous weeds grow, till they had covered every inch of our garden. The big lords pounced on al-Andalus and divided it amongst themselves. Each became a big fish in a tiny pond, whereas exactly the opposite process was reshaping the kingdoms of Christianity. We founded many dynasties, but failed to find a way of ruling our people according to the dictates of reason. We failed to establish political laws, which could have protected all our citizens against the whims of arbitrary rulers. We who led the rest of the world in the realms of science and architecture, medicine and music, literature and astronomy, we who were a privileged people, could not find the road to stability and a government based on reason. That was our weakness and the Christians of Europe have learnt from our mistakes. It is that and not the way our kings dressed which has been the curse of Islam in these lands. I know that some of you think help will come from the Sultan in Istanbul. I do not believe so, my friends. I think the Turks will take the East and leave us in peace to be devoured by the Christians.'

Umar had been greatly impressed by both Miguel and al-Zindiq, but he was tired. There were more urgent matters involving his family which were worrying him and had prevented his total concentration on the proceedings of the evening. He wanted to bring the event to an end, but some traditions had acquired a semi-religious status and become part of the rules of the debate. In a tone which suggested otherwise, Umar asked if any other person present wished to speak. To his great annoyance, an old weaver rose to his feet.

'Peace be upon all of you and may God preserve you and your family, Umar bin Abdallah,' began the weaver. 'I have heard both His Excellency the Bishop of Qurtuba and Ibn Zaydun who calls himself al-Zindiq with great attention. I do not possess their knowledge, but I wish to make just one point. I think our defeat was settled within the first hundred years of Tarik ibn Ziyad landing on the rock which now bears his name. When two of our generals reached the mountains the Franks know as the Pyrenees, they stood on the summit and looked down on the land of the Gauls. Then they looked at each other. They did not utter a word, but both Generals were thinking the same thing. If they wanted to safeguard al-Andalus, they had to secure the country of the Franks. We tried. Yes, we tried. Many of the cities fell to us, but the most decisive conflict in our history was the confrontation between our armies and those of Charles Martel just outside the town they call Poitiers. We lost our chance to win the Frankish kingdom that day, but we also lost al-Andalus, though few of us still recognize this fact. The only way to have saved this land for our Prophet would have been to construct a mosque in Notre-Dame. That is all I wanted to say.'

Then Umar thanked him profusely for raising their sight to a more lofty understanding of their present impasse and bade everyone present a happy night.

As the congregation began to disperse, Ama took Yazid by the hand and led him into the house, but not before she had noticed that an unusually large number of men were shaking Miguel by the hand with unusual warmth. These included his natural brother Ibn Hasd and, as the two men stood together, Hind was once again struck by how alike they looked when seen in profile. Zubayda stood by her husband exchanging greetings with the men and women of the village as they said their farewells.

Unlike his father and grandfather, Umar's relationships with the peasants and weavers whose families dominated Hudayl were cordial, even friendly. He attended their weddings and funerals, displaying a knowledge of their names and the number of children in each family which surprised and pleased them. 'This lord is a lord,' a weaver would say to his wife. 'Of that there can be no doubt. He benefits from our labours just as his fathers did, but he is a decent lord.'

There was no time tonight for such niceties. Umar was in an impatient mood. He had not spoken a great deal during the discussion and he was now eager for them all to return to their homes. Zubayda had informed him during the evening meal, which had been taken early that day in order to accommodate the debate, that their first-born was engaged in an undertaking which was as rash as it was foolish and she feared for his life. Serving women from the village had informed her that Zuhayr was recruiting young men for 'the battle'. Zuhayr had not been present, and when enquiries had been made as to his whereabouts, the groom reported that he had saddled the young master's favourite steed, but had been given no indication as to his destination. All he knew was that Zuhayr al-Fahl had taken two blankets with him. When the groom had left the room, Hind had been unable to control a smile. That was all Umar needed to make a deduction.

'Discourteous dog! His great-uncle will debate his great friend Ibn Zaydun on matters of life and death for his family, his faith, our future, and where is our knight? Busy on some hillside impregnating a wretched maid-servant.'

From inside the house Zuhayr observed the departures, feeling regret that he had absented himself from this important occasion. He was feeling sated and tinged with disgust at his own lack of discipline and his affinities to the animal kingdom, but ... but, he thought as he relived the experience, Umayma was so different from those painted whores in Gharnata, whose flesh was manhandled every hour of the day and night. Umayma made him feel irresponsible. She excited his sensuality. She neither expected nor demanded anything more. If he had not gone to her this evening he might never have seen her again. Within three months she would be married to Suleiman, the bald, cross-eyed weaver who spun the finest silk in the village, but who was hardly a match for him, Zuhayr al-Fahl, in the crafts which really mattered.

'Well?' said Umar, startling his son. 'Where were you? Missing the meal was unimportant, but absenting yourself from the debate at such a time? Your absence was noted. Ibn Hasd and Suleiman the weaver were both enquiring after your health!'

'Peace be upon you, Father,' muttered Zuhayr, trying desperately not to show his unease. 'I was out with friends. An innocent evening, I assure you.'

Umar looked at his son and could not restrain a smile. The boy was such an unaccomplished liar. He had his mother's light-brown eyes and, as he stood there facing him, Umar felt a strong charge of emotion. There was a time when they had been close. It was Umar who had taught Zuhayr to ride and hunt, Umar who had taken him to swim in the river. The boy had often accompanied his father to the court at the al-Hamra. Now he felt he had left the boy alone for far too long, especially since the birth of Yazid. How different they were and how he loved them both.

He slumped on to a large cushion. 'Sit down, Zuhayr. Your mother tells me that you have made some plans. What are they?'

Zuhayr's face became very serious. He suddenly looked much older than his years.

'I'm leaving, Father. Early tomorrow morning. I wanted to bid farewell to all of you tonight, but Yazid is fast asleep and I could not leave without hugging him. I'm leaving for Gharnata. We can't allow the monks to bury us alive. We must act now before it is too late. Plans for an insurrection are under way. It is a duel with Christianity, Father. Better to die fighting than live the life of a slave.'

Umar's heart began to pound. He saw a vision. A clash with the Captain-General's soldiers. Confusion. Swords are raised, shots are heard, and his Zuhayr lies on the grass with a hole in his head.

'It is a crazy plan, my child. Most of these young men who rant in the baths of Gharnata will run at the first sight of the Castilians. Let me finish. I have no doubt that you will find a few hundred boys to fight on your side. History is full of young fools getting drunk on religion and rushing to do battle with the infidel. Far easier to drink poison underneath a tree by the river and die peacefully. But better still to live, my son.'

Zuhayr's mind was not free of doubt, but he knew better than to admit that to his father. He truly did not wish to be talked out of the endeavour which he and his friends had been planning ever since the bonfire on the Bab al-Ramla. His face remained deadly serious.

'Contrary to what you imagine, Father, I have no great hopes for the success of our uprising, but it is necessary.'

'Why?'

'So that things stay the same in our kingdom of Gharnata. It is bad, but better it should stay like this than be handed over to Torquemada's animals, who they call priests and familiars. If our last Sultan, may God curse him, had not capitulated without a fight, things might have been different. Isabella treats us like whipped dogs. Our challenge will show them and others of our faith throughout this peninsula that we will die on our feet, not our knees; that there is still some life underneath the ruins of our civilization.'

'Foolish, foolish boy!'

'Ask Ibn Daud what he saw in Sarakusta and Balansiya on his way to Gharnata. Every Muslim who fled from the Christians has said the same.'

Despite himself, Umar felt an unusually strong sense of pride in his son. He had underestimated Zuhayr.

'What are you talking about boy? You're very unlike yourself. Talking in riddles.'

'I'm talking about the looks on the faces of their priests as they depart to supervise the torture of innocents and the making of orphans in the dungeons of the Inquisition! Unless we fight now everything will die, Father. Everything!'

'Perhaps everything will die in any case, whether you fight or not.'

'Perhaps.'

Umar knew that Zuhayr, deep inside himself, was tormented by uncertainties. He sympathized with his son's dilemma. Having spoken up at the mosque, and having boasted of victories that lay ahead in the company of his friends, the boy felt trapped. Umar determined to prevent his son's departure.

'You are still a young man, Zuhayr. At your age death appears to be an illusion. I will not let you throw your life away. Anything could happen to me, now that I have decided that conversion is impossible. Who would look after your mother and sisters? Yazid? They have taken power and authority away from us, but the estates are still intact. We can enjoy our wealth in peace and dignity. Why should al-Hudayl disturb the Castilians? Their eyes are on a new world, on its mountains of silver and gold. They have defeated us and resistance is futile. I forbid you to leave!'

Zuhayr had never fought in a real battle. His experience was limited to the intensive training he had received in the arts of war as a boy. He was an expert swordsman and his daredevil exploits on horseback were well known to all those who attended the tournaments in Gharnata on the Prophet's birthday. But he could not forget that he had yet to cross swords with a real enemy.

As he looked into his father's grim face, Zuhayr realized that this was his last opportunity to change his mind. He could simply inform his fellow conspirators that his father had forbidden him to leave the house. Umar was widely respected and they would all understand. Or would they? Zuhayr could not tolerate the thought that one of his friends might accuse him of cowardice. But that was not his only concern. Zuhayr did not believe that al-Hudayl would be safe as long as Ximenes held sway in Gharnata. That made him feel that Umar was dangerously out of tune with the times.

'Abu,' began Zuhayr plaintively, 'nothing matters to me as much as the safety of our home and the estates. That is why I must go. My mind is set. If you instruct me to stay here against my will and my judgement, then of course I will not disobey, but I will be unhappy, and when I am unhappy, Abu, I think of death as a consolation.

'Can you not see that the monks will destroy everything? Sooner or later they must reach al-Hudayl. They want to reduce al-Andalus to a desert. They want to burn our memory. How then can they permit even a single oasis to survive? Do not compel me to stay. You must understand that what I want to do is the one course that might save our home and our faith.'

Umar was unconvinced, and the argument continued, with Zuhayr growing ever more adamant as the hours went by. Finally Umar perceived that his son could not be kept at home against his will. His face softened. Zuhayr knew at once that he had won his first battle. He understood his father's temperament. Once Umar agreed to something, he sat back and did not meddle.

The two men stood up. Umar hugged his son and kissed his cheeks. Then he walked to a large chest and from it removed a beautifully engraved silver scabbard which contained the sword of Ibn Farid. He drew the weapon and, holding it with both his hands, lifted it above Zuhayr's head and handed it to him.

'If fight you must, then best to do it with a weapon tried and tested in many battles.'

Zuhayr's eyes became moist.

'Come,' said Umar bin Abdallah. 'Let us go and break the news to your mother.'

As Zuhayr, proudly carrying the sword of his great-grand-father, followed his father through the inner courtyard, they ran into Miguel and Zahra. Four different voices resounded in unison.

'Peace be upon you.'

Miguel and Zahra saw their father's sword and understood everything.

'God protect you, child,' said Zahra, kissing his cheeks.

Zuhayr did not reply, but stared at the odd couple. The encounter had disturbed him. Then his father tapped him gently on the shoulder and they walked away. It had all lasted a few seconds. Zuhayr thought it was a bad omen.

'Will Miguel . . . ?' he began to ask his father, but Umar shook his head.

'Unthinkable,' he whispered. 'Your great-uncle Miguel would never put the Church before his own family.'

For a while Zahra and Miguel stood still, like sentinels on guard duty. Remnants of a generation which had ceased to exist. The sky above them was full of stars, but neither it nor the solitary lamp on the wall, just above the entrance to the bath-chamber, gave much light. In the night shadows, with their bent spines draped in thick woollen shawls, they resembled a pair of stunted, weatherbeaten pine trees. It was the Bishop who broke the silence.

'I fear the worst.'

Zahra was about to say something when Hind and Ibn Daud, followed by three maid-servants, entered the courtyard. None of them saw the old lady or Miguel. The young man bowed and was about to walk away to his room, till he heard a voice.

'Ibn Daud!'

It was Hind who replied.

'Wa allah! You frightened me, Great-Uncle. Peace be upon you, Great-Aunt.'

'Come,' said Miguel to Ibn Daud, 'you can walk me to my room, which is next to where you sleep. I never thought the day would come when I would stay in the chambers reserved for guests in this house.'

'Nonsense,' said Zahra. 'Where else could they put you? In the stables? Hind, I need you to press me tonight. The cold is eating into my bones and I have been feeling a pain in my chest and shoulders.'

'Yes, Great-Aunt,' said Hind, dismissing the servants with a nod and looking longingly at the back of the young man with green eyes. Ibn Daud was escorting the Bishop through the corridor which linked the courtyard to a set of rooms which had been added to the house by Ibn Farid. There visiting Christian knights had been feasted and provided with nocturnal entertainments.

How strange, Zahra is thinking, that this child who I barely know and who has just reached her eighteenth year, reminds me so much of my own youth. Her father sees her still as a flower in bud. How wrong he is, how wrong all fathers are and will remain. She is in full bloom, like the orange-blossoms in spring. Those blossoms whose scent excites the senses. As if to make sure, Zahra lifted herself with the aid of a pillow-cushion and looked down on her great-niece, who was diligently but gently pressing the toes on her left foot. Even in the weak glow of the lamplight, Hind's skin, normally the colour of wild honey, was flushed and animated. Her eyes were shining and her mind was elsewhere. They were familiar symptoms.

'Does he love you as much?'

The suddenness of the question startled the girl.

'Who could you be talking about, Great-Aunt?'

'Come, child, it is not like you to be so coy. Everything is written on your face. Here I was thinking that you were excited by what happened this evening. Miguel told me what you shouted at him. He's not really upset – admires you for it – but you've forgotten it all, haven't you? Where have you been?'

Hind, unlike her calm and contented older sister Kulthum, was temperamentally incapable of dissimulation. At the age of nine she had shocked a religious scholar from Ishbiliya, who also happened to be her mother's first cousin, by challenging his interpretation of the al-koran. The theologian had been denouncing every possible pastime in which Muslim nobles indulged as 'forbidden', and had developed the argument to demonstrate how all this sensual irresponsibility had led to the decline of al-Andalus. Hind had interrupted him in mid-flow with a memorable intervention, still recalled with pleasure by the Dwarf and his friends in the village.

'Uncle,' the young girl had asked with a sweet smile, which was completely out of character. 'Did not our Prophet, peace be upon him, once say in a *hadith* which has never been questioned, that the angels loved only three sports?'

The theologian, deceived by her smile and delighted that one so young could be so well versed in the scriptures, had stroked his beard and responded warmly.

'And what were these, my young princess?'

'Why horse-racing, shooting at a mark and copulation, of course!'

The uncle from Ishbiliya had choked on the meat which he had, till then, been consuming quite happily. Zuhayr had excused himself and collapsed with laughter in the kitchen. Zubayda had been unable to control a smile and Umar had been left to divert the conversation, which he had accomplished with some finesse.

Kulthum alone had remained silent and offered her uncle a glass of water. For some reason this gesture had left a deep impact on the scholar. It was his son whom Kulthum was due to marry next month.

Zubayda had told the tale to Zahra. It had made the old woman laugh, and it was that memory which now caused her to smile at her great-niece.

'My ears are getting impatient, child.'

Hind, who had so far not dared confide her secret to anyone except her favourite maid-servant, was desperate to unburden herself to a member of the family. She decided to tell Zahra the whole story. Her eyes began smiling again.

'From the very first day it was, Great-Aunt. From the very first day I saw him I knew that I wanted no other man.'

Zahra smiled and nodded thoughtfully. 'The first love may not be the best, but it is usually the deepest.'

'The deepest and the best! It has to be the best!'

Hind's eyes were burning like lamps. She described Ibn Daud's arrival at al-Hudayl. The impression he had made on the whole family. Her father had taken an immediate liking to the young scholar and had immediately offered him a job as a private tutor to the family. They had all attended his first lecture. Ibn Daud had explained the philosophy of Ibn Khaldun as it was interpreted in al-Qahira. Zubayda had questioned him in some detail on how Ibn Khaldun's theories could explain the tragedy of al-Andalus. 'Loose stones,' he had replied, 'could never construct a stable city wall.'

'Hind,' pleaded Zahra. 'I am too old to appreciate every detail. I accept without dispute that the boy is both intelligent and attractive, but if you go on like this I might not be alive to hear you finish your story! What happened tonight? After the meeting?'

'Father was worried about Zuhayr, and before I realized the whole family had disappeared inside the house. I walked up to Ibn Daud, told him that I needed fresh air and asked him to take a walk by my side.'

'You asked him?'

'Yes, I asked him.'

Zahra threw back her head and laughed. Then she cupped Hind's face with her withered hands and stroked her face.

'Love can be a snake disguised as a necklace or a nightingale which refuses to stop her song. Please continue.'

And Hind described how a maid-servant had led the way with a lamp, while two others had followed them at a discreet distance till they had reached the pomegranate grove.

'*The* pomegranate grove?' asked Zahra faintly, trying to control her heartbeats. 'The clump of trees just before the house is visible when you're returning from the village? When you lie flat on the ground does it still feel as if one is underneath a tent of pomegranates with a round window at the top? And when you open your eyes and look through it, do the stars still dance in the sky?'

'I do not know, Great-Aunt. I did not have the opportunity to lie down.'

The two women looked at each other and laughed.

'We talked,' continued Hind, 'about our house, the village, the snow on the mountains, the coming spring, and after we had exhausted every possible formality, we fell silent and looked at each other. It seemed like a year before he spoke again. He took my hand and whispered that he loved me. At this point the maids began to cough loudly. I warned them that if they did that again I would send for the Inquisition to roast them alive. Then they could cough all the way to hell. I looked him straight in the eyes and confessed my love for him. I took his face between my hands and kissed him on the lips. He said he would ask Father for my hand in marriage tomorrow. I advised caution. Better that he let me prepare the path. On the way back I felt my body ache and realized that it was for want of him. I offered to go to his room tonight, but he nearly fainted at the thought. "I am your Father's guest. Please do not even suggest that I abuse his hospitality and betray his trust. It would be a disgrace." Thanks be to God that you are here, Great-Aunt Zahra. I could not have kept it to myself much longer.'

Zahra sat up in her bed and hugged Hind. Her own life flashed by and made her shiver. She did not want this girl, on the threshold of her life, to make the same mistakes, to be scarred by the same emotional wounds. She would talk to Umar and Zubayda on behalf of the young couple. The boy was clearly poor, but times had changed. To her great-niece she offered only words of encouragement.

'If you are sure of him, then you must not let go. I do not want any talk a hundred years from now of a green-eyed youth who wandered round these mountains, desolate and heart-broken, confiding to the river his yearning for a woman named Hind.

'Look at me, my child. A pain still oppresses my heart. I was burnt by love. It devoured my insides till there was nothing left at all and I began to open my legs to any *caballero* who wished to enter, not caring whether I enjoyed or disliked the experience. It was my way of destroying all that was sensitive in myself. It was when they found me naked on the tracks outside Qurtuba that they decided to send me to the maristan in Gharnata. Never make my mistakes. Far better that you run away with this boy and discover in six months that all he wanted was to feast on these two peaches than to accept a refusal from your parents. The first will cause you misery for perhaps a few months, even a year. The second will lead to despair, and despair gnaws at one's soul. It is the worst thing in the world. I will talk to your mother and father. Times have changed and, in any case, your Ibn Daud is not the son of a servant in this house. Now go to your own room and dream of your future.'

'I will, Great-Aunt, but there is a question which, with your permission, I must ask you.'

'Ask!'

'There is a story in the village about Great-Uncle Miguel . . .'

'Oh yes! That old business about the weaver's daughter. It is not a secret. What of it?'

'Nothing. It was never a secret in the first place. What I meant to ask is if what they say about Miguel and his mother, the Lady Asma, is true?'

Zahra shut her eyes very tight, hoping that darkness would obscure the memory of that pain, which Hind wanted her to relive. Slowly her face relaxed and her eyelids were raised.

'I do not know the answer. I had already been expelled from this house and was living in Qurtuba at the time. We used to call Asma "Little Mother", which made us all laugh, even Ibn Farid. I was very upset when I heard that Asma was dead. Meekal? Miguel?' Zahra shrugged her shoulders.

'But Great-Aunt . . .' began Hind.

The old woman silenced her with a gesture. 'Listen to me

138

carefully, Hind bint Zubayda. I never wanted to know. The details were of no interest. Asma, whom I loved like a sister, could not be brought back to life. Nor could Ibn Zaydun's mother. Perhaps everything they say did take place, but the actual circumstances were known to only three people. Two of them are dead and I do not think that anyone has ever asked Meekal. Perhaps when he converted, he told the whole truth in the confessional, in which case a third person was taken into confidence. What difference does it make to anything now? When you grow up you will, no doubt, hear of similar tragedies which have befallen other families. Or other branches of our family. Do you remember that cousin of your mother from Ishbiliya?'

Hind's face revealed her consternation.

'You must remember! The very religious cousin from Ishbiliya who was shocked by your knowledge of the *hadith*?'

'Him?' said Hind with a grin. 'Ibn Hanif. Kulthum's future father-in-law! What about him?'

'If ever they raise the business of poor Asma to try and humiliate our Kulthum, you can ask them the name of Ibn Hanif's true father. It was certainly not Hanif.'

Every mischievous fibre in Hind's body was now alert. This unexpected revelation had even relegated Ibn Daud for a few minutes.

'Tell me please, Aunt! Please!'

'I will, but you must never tell Kulthum, unless you feel she needs the information. Do you promise?'

Hind nodded eagerly.

'Ibn Hanif's father was also his mother's father. Nobody in that family felt it necessary to take their own life. I do not think that Ibn Hanif is even aware of the fact. How could he be? His mother and father took the secret with them when they died. But the old servants in the house knew. Servants know everything. That is how the story travelled to this house.'

Hind was shaken by this information. In Asma's case death had, at least, wiped the slate clean, but in Ishbiliya . . .

'I am tired, child, and you need to sleep,' said Zahra, signalling her dismissal from the room.

Hind, realizing that it was useless to pursue this matter, rose from the bed, bent down and kissed Zahra's withered cheeks.

'Peace be upon you, Great-Aunt. I hope you sleep well.'

After the girl had left, Zahra was assailed by the memories of her own youth. Hardly a day passed now without the magnification of some episode from the past in her thoughts. In the eerie calm of the maristan in Gharnata she had concentrated on the three or four good years in her life – these she would relive and even put down on paper. But three days before her return to the village of the Banu Hudayl, she had destroyed everything on a tiny replica of the bonfire lit by Ximenes in the market. She had done so in the belief that her life was not of any great interest to anyone except herself and she was about to die. It did not occur to her that in erasing what she regarded as the mummified memories of her own history she was also condemning a unique chronicle of a whole way of life to the obscurity of the flames.

She had been truly happy to return to her old home and find it inhabited by Umar and his family. For decades she had controlled her own emotions, deliberately depriving herself of contacts with the whole family, so that now she found herself overcome by a surfeit of affection. It was when she was on her own that she was haunted by the painful aspects of her life.

Take, for instance, the meeting with Ibn Zaydun at dinner tonight. Despite herself she had felt her heart flutter like a caged bird, just as when she first set eyes on him all those years ago. When the family had tactfully left them alone to sip their mint-flavoured tea, she had felt unable to communicate with him. Even when he had told her in that selfsame voice, which she had never stopped hearing and which had not changed, that he had written her a long letter every week since they had been parted, she had felt strangely unmoved. Was this the man for whom she had destroyed her whole life?

He had felt the emotion disappearing in her and had gone on his knees to declare that he had never stopped loving her, that he had never looked at another woman again, that every single day he had experienced an hour of pain. Zahra had been unaffected. She realized that her bitterness, her anger at his cowardice all those years ago when he had bowed to his status as the son of a house-slave and abandoned her to her class, had never left her. This resentment, displaced during her confinement by more pleasing images from the days of their turbulent and clandestine courtship, had nonetheless continued to grow and grow, so that now she felt nothing for him. This realization pleased her. Enslaved for so many years by the poison of love, she was free again. 'I wonder,' she thought to herself, 'what might have happened if we had met again twenty years ago. Would I have got rid of him so easily?'

Ibn Zaydun knew that their phantom relationship was over and, as he wished her well and took his leave, he saw the coldness in her eyes, which made him feel empty and worse. 'In this cursed house,' he thought, 'I am once again nothing but the son of my mother who worked for them and was killed for her pains.' It was the first time that this sensation had overpowered him in her presence.

Zahra undid the clasps which held her snow-white hair. It unfolded like a python and reached halfway down her back. She had made a real effort to dress well tonight and the effect had stunned them all. She chuckled at the memory and undid the diamond brooch which held her shawl together. The diamond had been a gift from Asma. She had been told by some fool that worn close to the skin it cured every madness.

Lovely, ill-fated Asma. Zahra remembered the day her father's party had returned from Qurtuba. She and Abdallah had not known what to expect as they had stood near the entrance to the house from the outer courtyard, holding tight to the hands of their mother's sister, the replacement wife they believed had been grievously injured by Ibn Farid's acquisition of a Christian concubine. Their first impression of Asma had been one of stunned astonishment. She looked so young and innocent. She was of medium height, but well built and generously proportioned. A virtuous face presided over a voluptuous body. Her skin was as smooth as milk but the colour of peaches, and her mouth looked as if it had been carefully painted with the juice of pomegranates. Underneath a mass of raven-black hair was a pair of shy, almost frightened brown eyes. They could all see how Ibn Farid had been bewitched by her.

'How could you possibly love my father?' Zahra had asked her some years later, just before Meekal was born and after they had become close friends. The old woman smiled as she remembered the peals of tinkling laughter which had greeted this question. Asma's face, creased with dimples, had finally returned to its normal flawless posture. 'Do you want to know how it was?' she had asked. 'Yes! Yes!' Zahra had shouted, imagining some fantastically erotic description. 'It was the way he farted. It reminded me of the kitchen where my mother worked. I felt I was at home again and loved him for that reason.' Zahra's shock had given way to incredulous laughter. Without realizing it, Asma had humanized the huge and brooding figure of Ibn Farid.

Zahra pulled the quilt, stuffed with sheep's wool and covered with her favourite silk, over herself. Sleep would not come. It was as if the final act of expelling Ibn Zaydun from her memory had cleared some space for everyone else. Her father appeared before her now. Not in the guise of the haughty lord with a despotic temperament, ordering her to bend to his will and abandon her lover or suffer his punishment, but as a friendly giant, full of fun, teaching her to ride a horse so that she could race against Abdallah. How patient he had been and how she had worshipped him. In the same week he had taught her to shoot at a mark. Her shoulders had ached for a whole week after that, which had made him laugh. Then Miguel had come and Ibn Farid, delighted with the child of his love, had left Abdallah and Zahra to their own devices. Who knows, she thought, if he had not ignored us so completely, I might not have fallen under the spell of Ibn Zaydun and Abdallah might not have become so obsessed with racing horses.

Suddenly her mind pictures a young woman. Zahra does not remember her at all, but she is very familiar. She has Abdallah's forehead and her own eyes. It must be their mother. Zahra screams to Death: 'I have been waiting for you a long time. You're going to come soon. Why not now? I can't bear the agony of waiting much longer.'

'Aunt Zahra! Aunt Zahra!'

She opened her eyes and saw Zubayda's worried face.

'Can I get you something?'

Zahra smiled weakly and shook her head. Then recalling something, she lifted her diamond brooch and handed it to Zubayda.

'I am dying. This is for your daughter Hind. Make sure that boy from al-Qahira loves her. Then let them be wed. Tell Umar it was his dying aunt's last wish.'

'Should I fetch Uncle Miguel?' asked Zubayda, wiping the tears off her face.

'Let him sleep in peace. He would only try and give me the last rites, and I insist on dying a Muslim. Tell Amira to bathe me properly as she used to do in the old days.'

Zubayda was pressing Zahra's legs and feet.

'You're not dying, Aunt Zahra. Your feet are as warm as burning embers. Whoever heard of anyone dying with warm feet?'

'What a child you are, Zubayda,' replied her aunt in a weak voice. 'Have you never heard of the poor innocents who are being burnt at the stake?'

The shock on Zubayda's face made Zahra laugh. The mirth was infectious and Zubayda joined her. Without warning the laughter disappeared and the life ebbed away from her. Zubayda clutched the old lady to her bosom and hugged her.

'Not yet, Aunt Zahra. Do not leave us so soon.'

There was no reply.

Chapter 9

Z AHRA WAS BURIED the very next day. Her body had been carefully and lovingly bathed by Ama long before the sun rose. As the early morning breezes danced to welcome the first rays of the sun, the job was finished.

'Why did you want *me* to do this, Zahra? My last punishment? Or was it a final gesture of friendship? If it hadn't been for you, my lady, I would have married that man on the mountain who now gives himself airs and calls himself al-Zindiq. Borne him three children. Perhaps four! Made him happy. I'm talking like an old fool. Forgive me. I suppose God meant us to live apart. There! You're all ready now for the last journey. I'm so glad you came back here. In Gharnata they would have put you in a wooden box and stuck a cross over your grave. What would Ibn Farid have said when you met him in the first heaven? Eh?'

Dressed in a pure white shroud, Zahra's body lay on the bed, waiting for burial. News of her demise had travelled to the village and, such had been her reputation amongst the weavers and peasants, who saw in her a noblewoman prepared to marry one of them for love, that they had rushed to the house, before they began their day's work, to pay their last respects and help lay the old woman's body to rest.

Slowly four pairs of hands lifted the bed and placed it gently on four sets of sturdy shoulders. Umar and Zuhayr lifted the head, while Ibn Daud and the Dwarf's strapping twenty-year-old son brought up the rear. Al-Zindiq and Miguel were in the centre, too old to offer their shoulders, but too close to the dead woman to leave her exclusively to a younger generation. Yazid followed closely behind his father. He had liked the old woman, but since he barely knew her, he could not grieve like Hind.

The women had mourned earlier. Early that morning Ama's wails as she sang the praises of Zahra had woken every section of the household. Streams of sorrow had poured out of Hind's eyes as she sought the comfort of Zubayda's lap. They had all spoken about her human qualities. How she had been as a child, a young woman, and then there had been silence. Nobody wished to discuss what had befallen her in Qurtuba, or to mention that the bulk of her life had been lived in the maristan in Gharnata.

The funeral procession was moving very slowly on purpose. The family cemetery was situated just outside the perimeter of the high stone walls which guarded the house. Zahra would be buried with her family. A space had been reserved for her next to her mother, Lady Najma, who had died sixty-nine years ago, a few days after Zahra's birth. She lay buried underneath a palm-tree. On the other side of her was Ibn Farid, the father she had loved and hated so much. The *hadiths* had insisted that followers of the Prophet should be buried simply and, in strict accordance with this tradition, none of the graves were marked. The Banu Hudayl claimed descent from one of the Companions of the Prophet and, regardless of whether this was true or pure invention, even the most irreligious members of the clan had insisted on the tradition of a simple mound of mud over their graves. Nothing more. The tiny, hand-made hillocks were covered with carefully tended grass and a dazzling array of wild flowers.

Zahra was lifted from the bed and laid in the freshly dug grave. Then Miguel, thinking he was Meekal, scooped up a handful of mud and threw it on his sister's corpse and cupped his hands together to offer prayers to Allah. Everyone followed suit. Then each of the mourners embraced Umar bin Abdallah in turn and departed. It was only when Miguel saw Juan the carpenter crossing himself that he was reminded of his own ecclesiastical identity. He dutifully fell on his knees and prayed.

The Bishop of Qurtuba must have been in that posture for several minutes, for when he opened his eyes he found himself alone by the freshly built mound. It was at this moment that his powers of self-control seemed to desert him. He broke down and wept. A pain, long suppressed, had welled up inside him. Two little waterfalls poured down his cheeks and sought refuge in his beard. Miguel knew perfectly well that whoever is born must die. Zahra had reached her sixty-ninth year. All complaints to the Almighty were out of order.

It was the suddenness of his sister's departure that had shaken him, just like the time, all those years ago, when she had left the house without saying goodbye to him. He had wanted so much to tell her all that had happened to him after that fateful day of shame; to describe the explosion of passions which had propelled him into an unknown space to defy the time-honoured taboo, and the horrendous aftermath; to discuss for the first time the death of Asma, a death which had deprived him of someone to blame for his own inner torment and unhappiness; the layers of guilt which still lay congealed somewhere in his mind; the disintegration of the old household and the birth of its successor. For the last three days he had been thinking of nothing else. Miguel now realized that he himself would die without one last conversation with the only member of the family who had belonged to the same vanished world. It was an unbearable thought.

'All of it happened after you had left us in disgrace, Zahra,' Miguel moaned in a soft voice. 'If you had stayed everything might have been different. You took truth and generosity with you. We were left with fear and sorrow and malice. Your absence disfigured us all. I think our father really died of grief. He missed you more than he would ever admit. Almost half a century has now passed and I have not been able to talk about any of this with even a single human being. This failing heart of mine was preparing to unburden itself to you. On the day I was ready to talk, you, my sister, went and died. Peace be upon you.'

As he rose and looked one more time at the piece of earth that covered his dead sister, a familiar voice disturbed his solitude and startled him.

'I did talk to her, Your Excellency!'

'Ibn Zaydun!'

'I was weeping on the other side of the grave. You did not see me.'

The two men embraced. Al-Zindiq told Miguel of how he had finally been rejected by Zahra; how the pride of the Hudayl clan had at long last reclaimed its prodigal daughter; how the real kernel had been thoroughly camouflaged; how, in the weeks before her death, she had actually suffered at the memory of their love; how she had come to feel that the worst of her injuries had been self-inflicted, and how she had begun to regret the break with Ibn Farid and her family, for which she accepted sole responsibility.

'I always knew,' Miguel commented, 'that our father was the most important thing in her life.'

The happiness Miguel felt on hearing this news was as great as the sadness it had caused al-Zindiq. Bishop and sceptic, for a moment they remained motionless, facing each other. They had once belonged to the same sunken civilization, but the universe which each inhabited had been separated by an invisible sea. The woman who had tried to bridge the gap between their two worlds, and had been punished for her pains, lay buried a few yards from where they stood.

The fact that, during her last days on this earth, she had, in her heart, returned to the family, consoled her brother. For al-Zindiq, sad, embittered al-Zindiq, it was but another example of the deep-rooted divisions in al-Andalus, which had torn the children of the Prophet asunder. They had failed to build a lasting monument to their early achievements.

'All that is left,' al-Zindiq whispered to himself, 'is for us to be inquisitioned. Yes! And to the very marrow of our sorry bones!'

Miguel heard, but kept silent.

As the two men returned to the house, one to join his family, the other to have breakfast in the kitchen, Zuhayr was on his way to Gharnata. He was riding at a fair pace, but his thoughts were on those whom he had left behind. The parting with his young brother had upset him the most. Yazid, as if guided by a mysterious instinct, had felt that he would not see his older brother ever again. He had hugged Zuhayr tight and wept, pleading with him not to go to Gharnata and certain death. The sight, witnessed by the entire household, had brought tears to the eyes of all, including the Dwarf, which had surprised Yazid and helped to distract him from the principal cause of his distress.

'I will remember this red soil forever,' thought Zuhayr, stroking Khalid's mane as he rode away from the village. When he reached the top of a hill, he reined in the horse and turned round to look at al-Hudayl. The whitewashed houses were glistening in the light, and beyond them were the thick stone walls of the house where he had been born.

'I will remember you forever: in the winter sun like today, in the spring when the fragrance of the blossoms makes our sap rise to the surface, and in the heat of the summer when the gentle sound of a single drop of water soothes the mind and cools the senses. Then, a few drops of rain to settle the dust, followed by the scent of jasmine.

'I will remember the taste of the water from the mountain springs which flow through our house, the deep yellow of the wild flowers which crown the gorse, the heady mountain air filtered through the pines and the majesty of the palms as they dance to the breezes from heaven, the spicy breath of thyme, the fragrance of the wood fires in winter. And how on a clear summer's day the blue sky is suddenly overpowered by darkness and little Yazid, clutching a piece of glass which belonged to our great-grandfather, waits patiently on the terrace outside the old tower for the stars to become visible once again. There he stands observing the universe till our mother or Ama drags him downstairs to bed.

'All this,' Zuhayr told himself, 'will always be the passionate heart of my life.'

He pulled on the reins and, turning his back on al-Hudayl, gently pressed his heels on the horse's belly, causing the animal to gallop towards the road which led to the gates of Gharnata.

Zuhayr had been brought up on a thousand and one tales of chivalry and knighthood. The example of Ibn Farid, whose sword he was carrying, weighed heavily on his young shoulders. He knew those days were over, but the romance of a last battle, of riding out into the unknown, taking the enemy by surprise and, who knows, perhaps even winning a victory, was deeply embedded in his psyche. It was this which had inspired his impulsive behaviour.

But, as he often told himself and his friends, his actions were not exclusively inspired by fantasies associated with the past or dreams of glory for the future. Zuhayr may not have been the most astute of Umar and Zubayda's children, but he was, undoubtedly, the most sentimental.

When he had been half Yazid's age news had come to the village of the destruction and capture of al-Hama by the

Christians. Al-Hama, the city of baths, where he used to be taken to see his cousins once every six months. For them the baths and the hot-water springs were part of everyday life. For Zuhayr a visit to the famous springs, where the Sultan of Gharnata himself used to bathe, was a very special treat. They had all died. All the men, women and children had been massacred, and their bodies thrown to the dogs outside the city gates.

The Castilians had waded in blood and, if their own chroniclers were to be believed, they relished the experience. The entire kingdom of Gharnata, including many Christian monks, had been mortified by the scale of the massacre. A loud wail had been heard rising from the village as the citizens had rushed to the mosque to offer prayers for the dead and swear vengeance. All Zuhayr could think of that day was the cousins with whom he had played so often. The thought of two boys his own age and their three older sisters being killed without mercy had filled him with pain and hatred. His father's sombre face as he announced the news: 'They have destroyed our beautiful al-Hama. Ferdinand and Isabella now hold the key to Gharnata. It won't be long before they take our city.'

Zuhayr had entered the deepest recesses of his memory and had begun to hear the old voices. Ibn Hasd was describing the reaction in Gharnata as news of the carnage in al-Hama reached the palace. Zuhayr pictured the old Sultan Abul Hassan. He had only seen him once, when he was two or three, but he could never forget that weather-beaten, scarred face and the trim white beard. It was this old man whose courageous but crazed attack and capture of the frontier town of Zahara had provoked the Christian response against al-Hama. He had rushed with his soldiers to save the town, but it was too late. The Christian knights had forced him to retreat. The Sultan had sent town-criers all over Gharnata, preceded by drummers and players of tambourines, whose loud but sombre music had alerted the citizens that a statement from the palace was on its way. People had crowded the streets, but the town-crier had uttered only one sentence:

'*Ay de mi al-Hama*. Woe is me, Al-Hama.'

The memory of those atrocities raised Zuhayr's temperature, and he began to sing a popular ballad which had been composed to mark the carnage.

'The Moorish Sultan was riding
through the city of Gharnata, ₁
from the Bab al-Ilbira
to the Bab al-Ramla.
Dispatches were brought him:
Al-Hama had been taken
Ay de mi al-Hama!

He threw the letters in the fire,
and killed the messenger;
he ran his hands through his hair
pulled at his beard in a rage.
He got off his mule
and rode on a horse;
along up Zacatin
climbed to the al-Hamra;
he ordered his trumpets top blast,
and his silver bugles,
so the Moors would hear
as they ploughed the fields.
Ay de mi al-Hama!

Four by four, five by five,
a large company assembled.
An old sage spoke up
from the depths of his thick grey beard:
"Why do you call us, Sultan?
What do your trumpets announce?"
"So you can hear, my friends,
of the great loss of al-Hama.
Ay de mi al-Hama"

"It serves you right, good Sultan,
good king, you well deserved it;
you killed the princes
who were the flower of Gharnata;
you took the turncoats
from Qurtuba the renowned.
And so, king, you deserve
very great punishment,

your own and your kingdom's ruin
and soon the end of our Gharnata.
Ay de mi al-Hama!" '

The ballad reminded him of his dead cousins. Their laughter
rang in his ears, but the joyful recollections did not stay long.
He saw them now as dismembered bodies and felt a chill. In
turn he became frenzied, disdainful and bitter as he spurred his
steed on faster and faster. Suddenly he found himself removing
Ibn Farid's sword from the scabbard. He held it above his head
and imagined that he was at the head of the Moorish cavalry,
riding out to relieve al-Hama.

'There is only one God and Mohammed is his Prophet!'
shouted Zuhayr at the top of his voice. To his astonishment
there was a resounding echo, but in dozens of voices. He reined
in his horse. Both beast and master stood still. The sword was
gently sheathed. Zuhayr could hear the noise of hoofs and then
he saw the dust. Who could they be? For a moment he thought
they were Christian knights who had responded to his cry in
order to entrap him. He knew that no other horse in the kingdom
could outpace his steed, but it would be cowardly, against the
rules of chivalry, to run away. He waited till the horsemen
neared the road and then rode out to meet them. To his great
relief all fourteen wore turbans, and on each of these there
was planted the familiar crescent. There was something unusual
about their attire, but before Zuhayr could determine where the
strangeness lay, he found himself being addressed by the stranger
who appeared to be the commander of this small group by virtue
of his age.

'Peace be upon you brother! Who are you and where are you
headed?'

'I am Zuhayr bin Umar. I come from the village of al-Hudayl
and I am on my way to Gharnata. Wa Allah! You are all
followers of the Prophet. I was frightened when I first saw the
dust raised by your horses. But pray who are you and in which
direction do you travel?'

'So!' replied the stranger. 'You are the great-grandson of Ibn
Farid. Al-Zindiq has told us a great deal about you, Zuhayr al-
Fahl!'

At this the stranger roared with laughter and his followers

joined him. Zuhayr smiled politely and studied each in turn. Now he saw what had first struck him as eccentric. On the left ear of every single one of them there hung a silver ear-ring in the shape of a crescent. Zuhayr's heart froze, though he tried hard to control his fear. The men were bandits, and if they realized he was carrying gold coins in his purse they would deprive him of the burden, but they might also steal his life. He would much rather die in battle against the Christians. He repeated his question.

'You say you know my teacher, al-Zindiq. This makes me happy, but I still do not know who you are or what your business is.'

'We ride through this land far and wide,' came the jovial reply. 'We have flung away our pride and have no cares or troubles. We can slow down the speeding torrent, tame a troublesome steed. We can drink a flask of wine without pausing for breath, consume a lamb while it still roasts on the spit, pull the beard of a preacher and sing to our hearts' content. We live unconstrained by the need to protect and preserve our reputation, for we have none. We all bear one name in common. The name of al-Ma'ari, the blind poet who lived between Aleppo and Dimashk some four hundred years ago. Come and share our bread and wine and you shall learn some more. Come now, Zuhayr al-Fahl. We shall not detain you long.'

Zuhayr was startled by the nature of this response, but it calmed his fears. They were far too eccentric to be cold-blooded killers. He nodded his agreement to the offer and as they wheeled their horses he rode alongside them. After a few miles they reached the boulders. These were carefully removed and they turned off the track through the concealed entrance. After a ten-minute ride he found himself in an armed encampment. It was a village of tents, strategically placed near a tiny stream. A dozen women and half that number of young children were seated outside one of the tents. The women were grinding corn. The children were playing an intricate game with stones.

The captain of this band, who now introduced himself formally as Abu Zaid al-Ma'ari, invited Zuhayr into his tent. The interior was austere, apart from a rug on which lay a few ragged cushions. As they sat a young woman entered with a flask of wine, two tiny loaves of brown bread and a selection of

cucumbers, tomatoes, radishes and onions. She put these in front
of the two men and hurried out, only to return with a bowl full
of olive oil. It was at this point that Abu Zaid introduced her
to Zuhayr.

'My daughter, Fatima.'

'Peace be upon you,' muttered Zuhayr, charmed by the young
woman's carefree demeanour. 'Will you not break bread with
us?'

'I will join you later with the others after we have eaten,'
replied Fatima, flashing her eyes at Abu Zaid. 'I think my father
wishes to speak to you alone.'

'Now my young friend,' began Abu Zaid al-Ma'ari as his
daughter left them alone, 'it is not fate that has brought us
together, but al-Zindiq. As you can see we are men who live by
what we can steal from the rich. In line with the teachings of
the great al-Ma'ari, we do not distinguish between Muslim,
Christian or Jew. Wealth is not the preserve of one religion.
Please do not be afraid. I noticed the alarm in your eyes when
you first caught sight of the silver crescent which pierces our left
ear. You wondered, did you not, whether your gold was safe?'

'To be frank,' confided Zuhayr, dipping the bread in the olive
oil, 'I was more worried for my life.'

'Yes, of course,' continued Abu Zaid, 'and you were right to
be so worried, but as I had begun to tell you it was that old
man in the mountain cave who told me that you had embarked
on a wild venture to Gharnata. He pleaded with me to try and
stop you; to persuade you either to return to your ancestral
home or to join our little band. We are thinking of leaving this
region and moving to the al-Pujarras, where there are many
others like us. There we will wait for the right moment. Then
we shall seize the time and join the battle.'

'In these times,' confessed Zuhayr as he sipped the fermented
juice of dates, 'it is much harder to make new friends than to
keep old enemies. I will think carefully before I decide whether
or not to accept your kind proposal.'

The bandit leader chuckled, and was about to respond when
his daughter, carrying an earthenware jug full of coffee, and
followed by three of her five brothers, interrupted his thoughts.
The aroma of the brew, which had been freshly boiled with
cardamoms, filled the tent and reminded Zuhayr of the home

which he had left only an hour ago. The new entrants settled down cross-legged on the rug as Fatima poured out the coffee.

'I do not think,' Abu Zaid informed the assembled company, 'that our young friend will join our ranks. He is a *caballero*, a knight who believes in the rules of chivalry. Am I not correct?'

Zuhayr was embarrassed at being discovered so quickly.

'How can you talk like that, Abu Zaid al-Ma'ari? Have I not just told you that I will think before I make up my mind?'

'My father is a good judge of people,' Fatima broke in. 'His instinct can tell him in a flash whether you are the sort of person who plays chess with an extra piece. It is obvious even to me that you are not such a man.'

'Should I be?' Zuhayr asked her plaintively.

'What is good for the liver is often bad for the spleen,' she replied.

Her brother, who could not have been more than eighteen years of age, felt that Fatima had been far too diplomatic.

'My father has always taught us that people are like metal. Gold, silver or copper.'

'Yes, that is true,' roared Abu Zaid, 'but a knight might think, and with good reason from his own point of view, that he is the gold, while a bandit is the copper. Since we are discussing the relative values of metals, let me put another point to our young guest from al-Hudayl. Would he agree with us that nothing cuts iron, but iron?'

'Why of course!' said Zuhayr, pleased that the discussion had taken a new course. 'How could it be otherwise?'

'If we agree on that, Zuhayr al-Fahl, then how can you resist my argument regarding the war against the occupiers of Gharnata? Our Sultan was built of straw, whereas Ximenes de Cisneros is a man of iron! The old style of war ended on the night the Christians destroyed al-Hama. If we want to win, we must learn from them. I know that al-Zindiq thinks it is too late, but he may be wrong. Al-Andalus could have been saved a long time ago if only our wretched rulers had understood the teachings of Abu'l Ala al-Ma'ari. That could have made them self-reliant, but no, they preferred to send messages to the North Africans pleading for help.'

'The North Africans did save us from the Christians more than once, did they not?'

'True. The only way *they* could save us was to destroy the foundations of what we had built. They saved us as the lion saves the deer from the clutches of the tiger. The Islam of which they spoke was neither better nor worse than Christianity.

'Our preachers are stumbling, Christians have gone astray,
Jews are bewildered. Magians far on error's way.
Humanity is composed of but two schools.
Enlightened knaves or religious fools.'

'Al-Ma'ari?' asked Zuhayr.

Everyone nodded.

'You sound like al-Zindiq,' commented Zuhayr. 'You must pardon my ignorance, but I have not read his work.'

Abu Zaid's outrage was genuine. 'Did not al-Zindiq educate you?'

'He did, but he never once lent me an actual book of al-Ma'ari. Simply recited his poetry, which I agree is a stronger stimulant than your date wine! Are you, by any chance, descended from him?'

'Before he died,' Fatima explained, 'he left instructions that a verse should be inscribed on his grave:

This wrong was by my father done
To me, but ne'er by me to one.

'He was so unhappy about the state of the world that he thought procreation was unwise. The species was incapable of curing itself. So you see we decided to act as though we were his children, and live by his teachings alone.'

Zuhayr was confused. Till this moment he had been sure that the path he had chosen was the only honourable course for a Muslim warrior, but these strange bandits and the philosopher who commanded them had succeeded in implanting a seed of doubt in his mind. He was only half-listening to Abu Zaid al-Ma'ari and his followers as they recounted the greatness of the freethinking poet and philosopher whom they had adopted as their collective father.

Zuhayr was floundering, his mind in turmoil. He felt on the edge of an abyss and in danger of losing his balance. He was overcome by an overwhelming urge to return to al-Hudayl. Perhaps the date wine had gone to his head. Perhaps a few more cups of coffee followed by a couple of hours in the hammam in Gharnata and everything would have become clarified once again. We shall never know, for in the midst of the intellectual haze which had overpowered him, Zuhayr heard them mock the al-koran, and this was something which he knew he could never accept. The blood rose to his head. Perhaps he had misheard the words. He asked Abu Zaid to repeat what he said a few minutes ago.

'What is Religion?
A maid kept hidden so that no eye may view her;
The price of her wedding gifts and dowries baffles the wooer.
Of all the goodly doctrine that from the pulpit I have heard
My heart has never accepted so much as a single word.'

'No! No!', Zuhayr shouted in frustration. 'Not his poetry. I've heard this one already. You mentioned the al-koran, did you not?'

Fatima looked him straight in the eye.

'Yes,' she replied. 'I did. Sometimes, but not always, Abu'l Ala al-Ma'ari could not stop himself from doubting whether it really was the word of God. But he truly loved the style in which the al-koran was composed. One day he sat down and produced his own version, which he called *al-Fusul wa-'l-Ghayat.*'

'Blasphemy!' roared Zuhayr.

'The *faqihs* certainly called it heresy,' explained Abu Zaid calmly and with the tiny glimmer of a smile, 'and it was a parody of the sacred book, but even our great teacher's friends declared that it was inferior in every way to the al-koran.'

'To which charge,' continued Fatima, 'our master responded by saying that unlike the al-koran, his work had not yet been polished by the tongues of reciters over four centuries.'

This gem from the master's treasury was greeted with applause and laughter. Abu Zaid was disturbed by the sombre expression on Zuhayr's face and decided to reduce the temperature.

'When he was charged with heresy he merely looked his accuser in the eye and said:

I lift my voice to utter lies absurd,
But when I speak the truth, my hushed tones are barely heard.

'Tell me, Abu Zaid,' Zuhayr asked. 'Do you believe in our faith?'

'All religions are a dark labyrinth. Men are religious through force of habit. They never pause to ask whether what they believe is true. Divine revelation is deeply ingrained in our mind. After all it was the ancients who invented fables and called them a religion. Musa, Isa and our own Prophet Mohammed were great leaders of their people in times of trouble. More than that I do not believe.'

It was this exchange that decided Zuhayr on his course of action. These people were impious rogues. How could they possibly hope to remove the Christians from Gharnata if they themselves were unbelievers? Once again he was irritated by Abu Zaid's voice, which indicated that his thoughts had been read.

'You are wondering how people like us can ever defeat the Christians, but ask yourself once again how it has come to pass that the most ardent defenders of the faith have failed in this very task.'

'I won't argue any more,' replied Zuhayr. 'My mind is decided. I will take my leave now and join my friends who await me in Gharnata.'

He rose and picked up his sword. Fatima and the others followed him out into the cold air. It was getting late and Zuhayr was determined to reach his destination before sunset.

'Peace be upon you, Zuhayr bin Umar,' said Abu Zaid as he embraced the young man in farewell. 'And remember, if you change your mind and wish to join us, ride to the al-Pujarras till you come to a tiny village called al-Basit. Mention my name to the first person you meet and within a day I shall be with you. May God protect you!'

Zuhayr mounted his horse, raised his cupped right hand to his forehead in a salute, and within a few minutes found himself back on the road to Gharnata. He was glad to be alone again, away from the illicit company of heretics and thieves. He had enjoyed the experience, but he felt as unclean as he always did after he had been with Umayma. He expanded his lungs and breathed in the fresh mountain air to cleanse his insides.

He saw the city as he reached the top of a hill. In the old days when he was riding to court with his father's entourage, they would stop here and drink in the view. His father would usually recount a tale from the days of old Sultan Abul Hassan. Then they would race down the slope in childish abandon. Once the gates were reached, dignity would be restored. For a moment Zuhayr was tempted to charge down the hillside, but better sense prevailed. Christian soldiers were posted at every entrance to the city. He had to behave in as calm a fashion as his brain would permit. As he reached the city gates he wondered what Ibn Daud would have made of his strange encounter with the bandits. Ibn Daud was such a know-all, but had he ever heard of al-Ma'ari?

The Christian sentries stared hard at the young man coming towards them. From the quality of his robes and the silk turban which graced his head, they saw that he was a nobleman, a Moorish knight probably here to visit a lover. From the fact that he openly carried a sword they deduced that he was no criminal intent on murder. Zuhayr saw them inspecting him and slowed his horse down even further, but the soldiers did not even bother to stop him. He acknowledged their presence with a slight nod of the chin, an action subconsciously inherited from his father. The soldiers smiled and waved him on.

As he rode into the town, Zuhayr felt serene once again. The confusion unleashed by that unexpected meeting with the heretics a few hours ago already seemed like a strange dream. In the old days or even a month ago, Zuhayr would have headed straight to the house of his uncle, Ibn Hisham, but today it was something that could not even be considered. Not because Ibn Hisham had become Pedro al-Gharnata, a converso, but because Zuhayr did not wish to endanger his uncle's family.

His dozen or so followers had reached Gharnata the previous day, and those who did not have friends or relations in the city were settled in rooms at the Funduq. To stay in a rest-house in a city full of friends and relations, and a city which he knew so well, seemed unreal. And yet it concentrated his mind on what he hoped to achieve. He did not wish to feel at home in Gharnata on this particular visit. He wanted during every minute of the day and night he spent here to be reminded of the tasks that lay ahead. In his fantasy, Zuhayr saw his future as the standard-bearer of a counter-attack which true Believers would launch against the new state under construction. Against the she-devil Isabella and the lecherous Ferdinand. Against the evil Ximenes. Against them all.

Later that evening Zuhayr's comrades came to welcome him to the city. He had been given one of the more comfortable rooms. A six-branched brass lantern decorated with an unusually intricate pattern hung from the ceiling. A soft light emanated from the oil burners. In the centre of the room stood an earthenware brazier, densely packed with burning coal. In one corner there was a handsome bed, covered with a silken green and mauve quilt. The eight young men were all sitting on a giant prayer mat which covered the floor in the corner opposite to the bed.

Zuhayr knew them well. They had grown up together. There were the two brothers from the family of the gold merchant, Ibn Mansur; the son of the herbalist, Mohammed bin Basit; Ibn Amin, the youngest son of the Jewish physician assigned to the Captain-General; and three of the young toughs from al-Hudayl who had arrived in Gharnata on the previous day. The reconquest itself had not changed the pattern of these young men's lives. Till the arrival of the man with a bishop's hat and a black heart, they had continued to lead a carefree existence. Ximenes de Cisneros had compelled them to think seriously for the first time in their lives. For this, at least, they should have been grateful to him. But the prelate had threatened their entire way of life. For this they hated him.

Nature had not intended any of these men to become conspirators. When they first arrived in Zuhayr's room all of them were feeling tense and self-conscious. Their faces were glum. Zuhayr saw the state they were in and made them feel at home by inaugurating a round of restorative gossip. Once they had dissected the private lives of their contemporaries, they became more cheerful, almost like their old selves.

Ibn Amin was the only one who had refrained from the animated discussion taking place around him. He was not even listening. He was thinking of the horrors that lay ahead, and he spoke with anger in his voice.

'By the time they've finished with us, they will not have left us any eyes to weep or tongues to scream. On his own the

Captain-General would leave us be. It is the priest who is the problem.'

This was followed by a chorus of complaints. Inquisitors from Kashtalla had been seen in the city. There had been inquiries as to whether the conversions which were taking place were genuine or not. Spies had been posted outside the homes of conversos to see whether they went to work on Fridays, how often they bathed, whether new-born boys were being circumcised and so on. There had been several incidents of soldiers insulting and even molesting Muslim women.

'Ever since this cursed priest entered our town,' said Ibn Basit, the herbalist's son, 'they have been making an inventory of all the property and wealth in the hands of the Moors and the Jews. There is no doubt they will take everything away unless we convert.'

'My father says that even if we do convert they will find other means to steal our property.' The speaker was Salman bin Mohammed, the elder of the gold merchant's two sons. 'Look at what they've done to the Jews.'

'Those bloodsuckers in Rome who set themselves up as Popes would sell the Virgin Mary herself to line their pockets,' muttered Ibn Amin. 'The Spanish Church is only following the example of its Holy Father.'

'But at our expense!' said Ibn Basit.

Ever since the fall of Gharnata, Zuhayr had been a silent witness at many such discussions in Gharnata and al-Hudayl. Usually his father or uncle or some village elder directed the discussion with a carefully timed intervention. Zuhayr was tired. The wind was beginning to penetrate the shutters and the brazier would soon run out of coal. The servants of the Funduq had gone to bed. He wanted to sleep, but he knew that the conversation could meander on in the quivering lamplight till the early hours unless he brought matters to a head and insisted on certain decisions being made tonight.

'You see, my friends, we are not difficult people to understand. It is true that those amongst us who live on landed estates in the country have, over the centuries, become cocooned in a world which is very different to life in the cities. Here your life revolves round the market. Our memories and hopes are all connected with the land and those who work on it. Often there are things which please us country people which none of you would care about. We have cultivated this land for centuries. We produced the food that fed Qurtuba, Ishbiliya and Gharnata. This enriched the soil in the towns. A culture grew which the Christians can burn, but will never match. We opened the doors and the light which shone from our cities illuminated this whole continent. Now they want to take it all away from us. We are not even considered worthy to be permitted a few small enclaves where we can live in peace. It is this fact which has brought us together. Town and country will die the same death. Your traders and all your professions, our weavers and peasants – all are faced with extinction.'

The others looked at him in astonishment. They felt that al-Fahl had matured beyond recognition. He noticed the new-found respect reflected in their eyes. If he had spoken like this even two years ago, one of them would have roared with laughter and suggested a quick visit to the male brothel where such loftiness of thought could be transcended by a more active choreography. Not today. They could sense that Zuhayr was not play-acting. They were only too well aware of the changes that had brought about this transformation in all of them. They had, however, no way of knowing that it was his curious encounter with the al-Ma'ari clan, even more than the tragedy of al-Andalus, which had sharpened his mind and alerted his senses. Zuhayr felt it was time to unveil the plan.

'We have had many discussions in our village. There are now twenty volunteers from al-Hudayl present in this town. The number may be small, but we are all dedicated. The first thing that needs to be done is to build a force of three or four hundred knights who will challenge the Christians to armed combat, every single day in the Bab al-Ramla. The sight of this conflict will excite the passions of the populace and we will have an uprising before they can send reinforcements to the city. We will fight the war from which our Sultan flinched.'

Ibn Basit was blunt in his rejection of the plan.

'Zuhayr bin Umar, you have surprised me twice this evening. First by your intelligence and second by your stupidity. I agree with you that the Christians want to destroy us completely, but you want to make it easier for them. You want us all to dress up and play their game. Chivalry is a thing of the past – that is, if it ever really existed and was not a chronicler's invention. Even if we defeated them – and I am not at all sure that our ardour could compete with their butcher's skills – it would still make no difference. None whatsoever. Our only hope is to prepare our men and take them out of the city to the al-Pujarras. From there we must send ambassadors to establish links with believers in Balansiya and other cities and prepare a rebellion which will erupt simultaneously throughout the peninsula. This is the signal for which the Sultan in Istanbul has been waiting. Our brothers will come to our aid.'

Zuhayr looked around for support, but none was forthcoming. Then Ibn Amin spoke.

'Both Ibn Basit and my old friend Zuhayr are living in a world of dreams. Basit's vision is perhaps more realistic, but equally remote from our realities. I have a very simple proposal. Let us cut off the head of the snake. Others will come in his place, but they will be more careful. What I am suggesting is not very complicated and is easy to accomplish. I propose that we ambush Ximenes de Cisneros, kill him and display his head on the city walls. I know he is guarded by soldiers, but they are not many and we would have surprise on our side.'

'It is an unworthy thought,' said Zuhayr in a very sombre tone.

'But I like the idea,' said Ibn Basit. 'It has one great merit. We can actually carry it out ourselves. I suggest we prepare our plan carefully over the next few days and meet again to agree on the timing and method.'

Ibn Amin's suggestion had enlivened the evening. Everyone present spoke with passion. Zuhayr reflected on the future and warned of a repetition of al-Hama in the old quarter of Gharnata. They could say farewell to any thought of victory, farewell to any notion of finding some support amongst the Dominicans. If Cisneros was killed he would become a martyr. Rome would beatify him. Isabella would avenge her confessor's death in an orgy of blood which would make al-Hama pale in comparison. Despite the intellectual strength of his arguments, Zuhayr found himself totally isolated. Even his followers from al-Hudayl were impressed by the stark simplicity of the plan to assassinate Cisneros. It was on the basis of this rickety enthusiasm that Zuhayr accepted defeat. He would not be party to a killing which went against every principle of chivalry, but nor would he try to obstruct their plans.

'You are too touchy and proud,' Ibn Basit said to him. 'The old days will never return. You are used to your shirts being washed in rose-water and dried with a sprinkling of lavender. I am telling you that everything will be washed in blood unless we decapitate these beasts which Allah has sent to test our will.'

After they had gone, Zuhayr washed himself and went to bed, but sleep would not come. Once again he was racked by doubts. Perhaps he should ride out of the city and link his fate to that of the al-Ma'aris. Perhaps he should just go home and warn his father of the catastrophe that threatened them all. Or, and this thought shocked him greatly, should he flee to Qurtuba and ask Great-Uncle Miguel to baptize him?

Chapter 10

'THE ONLY TRUE nobility I can accept is that conferred by talent. The worst thing in the world is ignorance. The preachers you seem to respect so much say that ignorance is a woman's passport to paradise. I would rather the Creator banished me to hell.'

Hind was in the midst of a flaming argument with her lover-to-be, whose affectionate mocking tone had suddenly begun to irritate her. Ibn Daud was taking a special delight in tormenting her. He had begun by posing as an orthodox scholar from the al-Azhar university and had defended the prevalent theology, especially in its pronouncements on the duties and obligations of women believers.

Hind's impassioned rejection of paradise was what he had really wanted to hear. The passionate Hudayl blood had surged up to her face as she stared at him with angry eyes. She was magnificent in her rage. Ibn Daud felt her power, for the first time. He took her hand and covered it with kisses. This spontaneous display of emotion delighted and excited Hind, but they were not alone in the pomegranate glade.

Ibn Daud's daring produced a spate of coughing from behind the nearby bushes where three young maid-servants were in attendance. Hind knew them well.

'Go and take a walk, all of you. Do you think I am deceived by all this nonsense? I know very well what happens when you first catch sight of the palm-tree that grows between the legs of your lovers. You begin to behave like a flock of hungry woodpeckers. Now go and take a walk for a few minutes and do not return until you hear me call! Is that clear?'

'Yes Lady Hind,' replied Umayma, 'but Lady Zubayda . . .'

'Have you told Lady Zubayda that my brother mounts you like a dog?'

Hind's bold retort settled the matter. A staccato outburst of laughter from Umayma's companions was the only response to this query. Fearing further indiscretions in front of the stranger, the maids moved away from the site. Hitherto their role had been to act as guardians of Hind's chastity and protect her honour. They now reverted to playing a part more suited to their temperaments and became, once again, the accomplices of their young mistress, keeping watch and making sure that the couple was not surprised.

Unknown to them, Yazid was close by. Soon after Ibn Daud's arrival at the house, Yazid had felt abandoned by his sister. He had also sensed the reason and, as a result, had begun to snub the newcomer with a ruthlessness only a child could deploy. He developed an irrational, but deep hatred for the stranger from al-Qahira.

At first Yazid had been fascinated by Ibn Daud's stories of the old world. He had been eager to learn, desperate to know more about life in al-Qahira and Dimashk; intrigued and curious as to the difference in pronunciation and meaning of certain Arabic words as spoken and understood in al-Andalus and in the land of the Prophet's birth.

The boy's thirst for information had, in turn, stimulated Ibn Daud. It forced him to think hard in order to explain facts which he had hitherto taken for granted. Yazid, however, began to notice that Hind would change colour, avert her eyes whenever Ibn Daud was present and put on an act of ultra-modesty. Once Yazid had realized that it was the Qahirene who was responsible, he began to avoid Ibn Daud's classes, or when compelled to attend them, made no attempt to conceal his displeasure and acted as if he were permanently bored.

He stopped questioning Ibn Daud. When the tutor asked him a question, Yazid either remained silent or restricted himself to monosyllabic replies. He even stopped playing chess with him. This was an enormous sacrifice, since Ibn Daud was new to the game and had not been able to defeat his pupil even once, till the point was reached when the latter had unilaterally broken off all personal relations.

When Hind asked him to explain his behaviour, Yazid sighed impatiently and stated in the coldest possible voice that he was not aware of any abnormality in his attitude to the hired teacher. This annoyed his sister and increased the tension that had built up between them. Hind, usually ultra-sensitive where Yazid was involved, was blinded by her love for Ibn Daud. And so it was her brother who suffered greatly. Zubayda, noticing the unhappiness on the face of her youngest child, understood the reason only too well. She resolved to settle the matter of Hind's marriage as soon as possible and decided to postpone any discussion on the subject with Yazid till that time.

Unaware that they were being observed, Hind and Ibn Daud had now reached a stage where certain crucial decisions had to be made. His hands had wandered underneath her tunic and felt her breasts, but retreated immediately.

'Two full moons upon a slender bough,' he muttered in a voice which she imagined was choked with passion.

Hind was not to be outdone. Her hands found a path from above his waist to the unexplored regions below which were covered by baggy silk trousers. She felt him underneath the silk. She began to stroke his thighs. 'Soft like dunes of sand, but where is the palm-tree?' she whispered as her fingers gently brushed the dates and felt the rising of the sap.

If any further advances were made, they would undoubtedly pre-empt the rites of the first night. But, Hind thought, if we stop now, the frustration, not to mention the long wait till our passion is finally consummated, will make life unbearable. Hind did not wish to stop. She had discarded every sense of propriety. With all her being, she wanted to make love to this man. She had taken so much vicarious pleasure from the unending descriptions supplied by maid-servants and giggling cousins in Gharnata and Ishbiliya, but now she wanted to know the real thing.

It was Ibn Daud who, realizing this, organized a hasty retreat. He withdrew his hands from her body and gently removed hers from inside his trousers.

'Why?' she asked in a hoarse whisper.

'I am your father's guest, Hind!' His voice sounded resigned and emotionless. 'Tomorrow I will ask to see him alone and request his permission to make you my wife. Any other course would be dishonourable.'

Hind felt the passion draining away.

'I felt I was on the edge of something. Something which is more than just pleasure. Something indefinably pure. Now I feel on the threshold of despair. I think I have misjudged you.'

A torrent of reassurances followed. Repeated declarations of his undying love. The high regard in which he held her intelligence. He had never met another woman like her, and all the while he was talking he was also kissing every toe on her feet and muttering a special endearment to each and every one.

She did not speak. It was a silence more expressive than anything she could have said, for the truth was that having lost her temporarily, he had won her back. And yet her instinct that she had misread him was not as remote from the truth as his gestures suggested.

Ibn Daud had never been with a woman before. His decision to disrupt the lovemaking was only partly explicable by his status in the household. He was surprised at how much Hind had succeeded in inflaming him, but the real reason he had pulled back was a fear of the unknown.

Till now there had been only one great passion in the life of Ibn Daud, and that was a fellow student in al-Qahira. Mansur was the son of a family of prosperous and long-established jewellers in the port-town of Iskanderiya. He had travelled so extensively and to so many cities, including a boat journey to Cochin in southern India, that his stories had Ibn Daud in a state of perpetual enchantment. Add to that the love they both felt for good poetry and the flute, and that each had striking features and a questioning mind, and the friendship which grew up between them seems inevitable. For three years the two men lived in close proximity. They shared a room in the *riwaq* overlooking the mosque of al-Azhar.

It soon became a triune relationship which concurrently fed their intellects, their religious emotions – they were disciples of the same Sufi shaykh – and, finally their sexual appetites. They had written poetry for each other in rhymed prose. This was composed in a language in which no pleasure was veiled from the other reader's sight. During the summer months, when they were separated from each other by the necessity of spending time with their families, they both kept diaries in which they recorded every detail of their daily lives as well as the effects of sexual abstinence.

Mansur had died in a shipwreck while accompanying his father on a trading mission to Istanbul. The inconsolable survivor could not bear the thought of living in al-Qahira any longer. It was this, more than any desire to study the works of Ibn Khaldun, that had brought him to Gharnata. He was drawn intellectually to al-Zindiq, but after several conversations felt that, while the crafty old fox was full of genius and learning, there was a lack of scruple in the stratagems he employed to outwit an opponent. At the end of one discussion of the poetry of Ibn Hazm, Ibn Daud had remembered a similar talk with Mansur. The memory had overpowered him. He had given way to unfeigned emotion. Naturally, he had not told al-Zindiq everything, but the old man was no fool. He had guessed. It was this that was worrying Ibn Daud. Al-Zindiq was a friend of this family. What if he confided his suspicions to Hind's parents?

As if guessing his thoughts, Hind fondled his hand and enquired innocently: 'What was the name of the woman you loved in al-Qahira? I want to know everything about you.'

Ibn Daud was startled. Before he could reply there was a scream and shouts of laughter as the maid-servants pounced on a mortified Yazid and dragged him into the glade.

'Look who we found, Lady Hind!' said Umayma, grinning shamelessly.

'Let me go!' shouted Yazid, the tears pouring down his face.

Hind could not bear the sight of her brother upset in this fashion. She ran to Yazid and hugged him, but he kept his hands firmly at his side. Hind dried his tears with her hands and kissed his cheeks.

'Why were you spying on me?'

Yazid wanted to embrace and kiss her, tell her of his fears and worries. He had heard how Great-Aunt Zahra had run away and never come back again. He did not want his Hind to do the same. If they had been alone he would have blurted all this out, but the smile on Ibn Daud's face stopped him. He turned his back and ran to the house, leaving behind him a bemused and bewildered sister.

Slowly it was beginning to dawn on Hind that Yazid's strange behaviour could only be explained in relation to her own state of mind. She had been so bewitched by those eyes, greener than the sea, that everything else had become secondary, even the voice of a lute. It was her carelessness that had upset her brother. She felt guilty. The intoxication of the embrace was all but forgotten.

The sight of a distraught Yazid reminded her of her own irritation with Ibn Daud.

'The truth is,' she told herself, 'that his honourable behaviour was nothing more or less than a refusal to recognize the beauty of our passion.'

This annoyed her so much that she, who had almost burnt him with her flame, now resolved to teach Ibn Daud a few elementary lessons. He would soon discover that she could be colder than ice. She still wanted him, but on her terms. For the moment her main concern was to repair the breach with Yazid.

The subject of Hind's thoughts was lying with his head buried in his mother's lap. He had burst in on Zubayda with the words: 'That man was playing with Hind's breasts. I saw them.' Yazid had thought his mother would be horrified. She would rush to the scene of the crime and instruct the male servants of the house to whip Ibn Daud. The upstart from al-Qahira would be sent home in disgrace, and on his way to the village to find transport to Gharnata he might even be attacked by wild dogs. Instead Zubayda smiled.

'Your sister is a grown woman now, Ibn Umar. Soon she will be married and will have children and you will be their uncle.'

'Married to him?' Yazid was incredulous.

Zubayda nodded and stroked her son's light brown hair.

'But, but, he owns nothing. He is . . .'

'A learned man, my Yazid, and what he owns is in his head. My father always used to say that the weight of a man's brains is more important than the weight of his purse.'

'Mother,' said Yazid with a frown. His eyes were like unsheathed swords and his voice reminded her so much of her husband at his most official that she could barely keep a straight face. 'Have you forgotten that we cannot harvest grapes from prickly pears?'

'True my brother,' said Hind, who had entered the room unseen just in time to hear Yazid's last remark, 'but you know as well as I that a rose is always accompanied by the thorn.'

Yazid hid his head behind his mother's back, but Hind, laughing and very much her old self again, dragged him away and imprinted dozens of kisses on his head, neck, shoulders and cheeks.

'I will always love you, Yazid and more than any man I happen to marry. It is my future husband who should worry. Not you.'

'But for the last month . . .' began Yazid.

'I know, I know and I am truly very sorry. I did not realize that we had not spent time together, but all that is in the past. Let's be friends again.'

Yazid's arms went round her neck and she lifted him off the ground. His eyes were shining as she put him down.

'Go and ask the Dwarf what he's cooking for supper tonight,' instructed Hind. 'I must talk to our mother on my own.'

As Yazid scampered out of the room, mother and daughter smiled at each other.

'How she takes after me,' thought Zubayda. 'I, too, was unhappy with love till I obtained permission to marry her father. In my case the delay was brought about by Umar's mother, unsure of the blood that flowed through my veins. Hind must not go through all that just because the boy is an orphan.'

Hind appeared to have divined her mother's thoughts. 'I could never wait as long as you did, while they discussed the impurities in your blood. It is something else that worries me. Be truthful now. What do you make of him?'

'A very handsome boy, with a brain. He is more than a match for you, my child. What more could you want? Why the doubt?'

Hind had always enjoyed a special relationship with her mother. The friendship that developed between them was due, in no small measure, to the relaxed atmosphere which prevailed in the house. Hind did not have to imagine what life could have been like had her father married again or kept the odd concubine in one of his houses in the village. She had visited her cousins in Qurtuba and Ishbiliya often enough to remember households in the grip of a permanently stifling atmosphere. Her cousins' accounts of indiscriminate and casual lechery reminded her of descriptions of brothels; the accounts of infighting amongst the women filled her vision with images of a snake-pit. The contrast with life at al-Hudayl could not have been sharper.

As she grew older, Hind found herself drawn closer to her mother. Zubayda, whose own upbringing, thanks to a freethinking father, had been unorthodox, was determined that the younger of her two daughters should not be subjected to the straitjacket of superstition or made to conform to any strictly defined role in the household. Kulthum, from her infancy, had been a willing prisoner of tradition. Hind – and even her father had noticed this when she was only two years old – was an iconoclast. Despite Ama's numerous forebodings and oft-repeated warnings, Zubayda encouraged this side of her daughter.

Because of all this there was no doubt in Hind's mind as to how she should respond to her mother's question. She did not hesitate at all, but began to describe everything which had taken place that afternoon, making sure that not a single detail was excluded. When she had finished, her mother, who had been listening very intently, simply laughed. Yet the merriment masked a real concern. If Umar had been present he would at once have noticed the nervous edge to the laughter.

Zubayda did not wish to alarm her daughter. Uncharacteristically, she embarked on an emollient course.

'You're worried because he would not let the juice of his palm-tree water your garden. Am I correct?'

Hind nodded gravely.

'Foolish girl! Ibn Daud behaved correctly. He is our guest, after all and seducing a daughter of the house while maid-servants kept watch would not be a very dignified way of responding to your father's kindness and hospitality.'

'I know that! I know that!' muttered Hind. 'But there was something more which I can't describe to you. Even when his hands were fondling me I felt the absence of passion in them. There was no urgency till I touched him. Even then he became frightened. Not of father, but of me. He has not known a woman before. That much is obvious. What I can't understand is why. I mean when you and Abu defied his parents and went to . . .'

'Your father was not Ibn Daud! He was a knight of the Banu Hudayl. And when we went to Qurtuba we had already been married for several hours. Go and lie in the bath and let me try and solve this puzzle.'

The sun was setting as Hind walked out into the courtyard. She stood still, hypnotized by the colours around her. The snow-covered peaks overlooking al-Hudayl were bathed in hues of light purple and orange; the small houses of the village looked as though they had been freshly painted. So engrossed was Hind by the beauty around her that her senses became oblivious to all else. A few moments ago she had felt cold and melancholy. Suddenly she was pleased to be alone.

'Only yesterday,' she thought, 'if I had found myself like this in the sunset I would have pined for him, wanted him to be here by my side so that we could share the gifts of nature, yet today I am happy to be alone.'

She was so deeply absorbed in her own thoughts that, as she began to walk slowly to the hammam she did not hear the sounds of merriment emanating from the kitchen.

Yazid sat on a low stool as the Dwarf played the tambourine and sang a *zajal*. The servants had been drinking a potent brew which they had distilled from the leftovers in the casks near the al-Hudayl vineyards. The Dwarf was mildly drunk. His three assistants, and the two men whose sole task it was to transfer the food from the pots to the dishes and place it on the table, had imbibed too much of the devil's piss. They were dancing in a circle while in the centre the Dwarf stood on a table and sang his song. Sitting on the steps outside the kitchen, a look of fierce disapproval on her face, was Ama. She had attempted to distract Yazid and drag him back to the house, but he was enjoying himself enormously and had refused to obey.

The Dwarf stopped playing. He was tired. But his admirers wanted the performance to continue.

'One last time,' they shouted, 'the song of Ibn Quzman. Sing it for our young master.'

'Yes please, Dwarf,' Yazid found himself joining in the chants. 'Just one more song.'

The Dwarf became very serious.

'I will sing the ballad composed by Ibn Quzman over three hundred years ago, but I must insist that it is heard with the respect due a great master. There will never be a troubadour like him again. Any interruptions and I will pour this wine on your beards and set them alight. Is that clear, you boastful babblers?'

The kitchen, which only a few seconds ago had resembled the scene of a drunken riot, became silent. Only the bubbling of a giant pan containing the evening meal could be heard. The Dwarf nodded to his assistant. The twelve-year-old kitchen boy produced a lute and began to test the strings. Then he nodded to his master and the tiny chef began to sing the *zajal* of Ibn Quzman in a voice so deep that it was overpowering.

> '*Come fill it high with a golden sea,*
> *And hand the precious cup to me!*
> *Let the old wine circle from guest to guest,*
> *The bubbles gleaming like pearls on its breast,*
> *It were as if night is of darkness dispossessed.*
> *Wa Allah! Watch it foam and smile in a hundred jars!*
> *'Tis drawn from the cluster of the stars.*
>
> *Pass it, to the melting music's sound,*
> *Here on this flowery carpet round,*
> *Where gentle dews refresh the ground*
> *And bathe my limbs deliciously*
> *In their cool and balmy fragrancy.*
>
> *Alone with me in the garden green*
> *A singing girl enchants the scene:*
> *Her smile diffuses a radiant sheen,*
> *I cast off shame, for no spy can see,*
> *And 'Wa Allah,' I cry, 'let us merry be!'*

Everyone cheered, and Yazid the loudest of all.

'Dwarf,' he cried in an excited voice, 'you should leave the kitchen and become a troubadour. Your voice is beautiful.'

The Dwarf hugged the boy and kissed his head.

'It's too late for all that, Yazid bin Umar. Too late for singing. Too late for everything. I think you had better return with the information the Lady Zubayda asked you to bring back from the kitchen.'

Yazid had forgotten all about his mother's request.

'What was it, Dwarf?'

'You have already forgotten the contents of my sunset stew?'

Yazid frowned and scratched his head but he could not remember a single ingredient. Bewitched by the wine song, he had forgotten the reason for his visit to the kitchen. The Dwarf began to remind him, but this time he made sure that the young boy's memory would retain the information and so he declaimed the recipe in a rhythm and intonation which was very familiar to Yazid. The Dwarf's sonorous voice was mimicking a recitation of the al-koran.

'Listen carefully all ye eaters of my food. Tonight I have prepared my favourite stew which can only be consumed after the sun has set. In it you will find twenty-five large potatoes, quartered and diced. Twenty turnips, cleaned and sliced. Ten dasheens skinned till they gleam and ten breasts of lamb which add to the sheen. Four spring chickens, drained of all their blood, a potful of yoghurt, herbs and spices, giving it the colour of mud. Add to this mixture a cup of molasses and, wa Allah, it is done. But young master Yazid, one thing you must remember! The meat and vegetables must be fried separately, then brought together in a pan full of water in which the vegetables have been boiled. Let it all bubble slowly while we sing and make merry. When we come to the end of our fun, wa Allah, the stew is done. The rice is ready. The radishes and carrots, chillies and tomatoes, onions and cucumbers all washed and impatiently waiting their turn to join the stew on your silver plates. Can you remember all this, Yazid bin Umar?'

'Yes!' shouted Yazid as he ran out of the kitchen trying desperately to memorize the words and their music.

The Dwarf watched the boy run through the garden to the house followed by Ama, and a sad smile appeared on his face.

'What will be the future of this great-grandson of Ibn Farid?' he asked no one in particular.

Yazid ran straight into his mother's room and repeated the Dwarf's words.

His father smiled. 'If only you could learn the al-koran with the same facility, my child, you would make our villagers very happy. Go and clean yourself before we eat this sunset stew.'

As the boy scampered out of the room Zubayda's eyes lit up.

'He is happy again.'

Umar bin Abdallah and his wife had been discussing the fate of their younger daughter. Zubayda had provided her husband with a modified version of the events in the pomegranate glade. Not wishing to upset him, she had excluded all references to palm-trees, dates and other relevant fruits. Umar had been impressed by the account of Ibn Daud's forbearance and sense of honour. This fact alone had decided him to give the young man permission to wed Hind. It was at this stage in the discussion that Zubayda had confided her fears.

'Has it not occurred to you that Ibn Daud might only be interested in other men?'

'Why? Simply because he rejected our daughter's kind invitation to deprive her of her virginity?'

Not wishing to give away too much, Zubayda decided to proceed no further. 'No,' she said, 'it was an instinct on my part. When you talk to him after we have eaten tonight it would help to set my mind at rest if you asked him.'

'What?' roared Umar. 'Instead of talking to him about his feelings for our Hind, I should become an Inquisitor, questioning him as if he were a filthy monk who had abused his position in the confessional. Perhaps I should torture him as well? No! No! No! It is not worthy of you.'

'Umar,' retorted Zubayda, her eyes flashing with anger, 'I will not let my daughter marry a man who will make her unhappy.'

'What if your father had asked me that question before permitting our marriage?'

'But there was no need, was there my husband? I did not have any doubts about you on that score.' Zubayda was playing the coquette, which was so out of character that it made him laugh.

'If you insist, woman, I will try to find a way of asking the young man without causing offence.'

'No reason for him to be offended. What we are talking about is not uncommon.'

The young man under discussion was in his room getting dressed for the evening meal. A strange feeling, hard to put into words, had overcome him and he was plunged in sadness. He knew that he had disappointed Hind. He was reliving the events of the afternoon and the sense of fear was being replaced by an excitement new to him.

'Can nothing drive her out of my head?' he asked himself as he put on his tunic. 'I do not wish to think of her and yet I cannot think of anything else. How can these images of her crawl into my mind against my will? I am a fool! I should have told her that the only lover I have known was a man. Why did I not do that? Because I want her so much. I do not want her to reject me. I want her as my wife. She is the first person I have loved since Mansur died. Other men have approached me, but

I rejected their advances. It is Hind who has aroused me again, Hind who makes me tremble, but what did she read on my face?'

On his way to eat, Ibn Daud was surprised by Yazid.

'Peace be upon you, Ibn Daud.'

'And upon you, Yazid bin Umar.'

'Should I tell you what the Dwarf has cooked for our meal?'

When Ibn Daud nodded, Yazid recited the list of ingredients in such a perfect copy of the Dwarf that his new tutor, not having heard the original, was genuinely impressed. They went into the dining-room together.

Ibn Daud was delighted by this renewal of friendship with his pupil. He felt it was a good omen. Everyone was extra kind to him during the meal. The Dwarf's sunset stew had been a great success and Hind insisted on serving him a second helping.

Miguel had returned to Qurtuba. Zahra was dead. Zuhayr was in Gharnata. Kulthum was visiting her cousins and future in-laws in Ishbiliya. The family presence in the dining-chamber was unusually depleted. This made the circle of which Ibn Daud was a part more intimate than usual. Zubayda had noticed him gazing into Hind's eyes with a smile, and this reassured her. Perhaps it had been a false alarm. Perhaps Umar's instincts had been closer to reality than hers. She began to feel guilty and wanted to tell her husband not to ask the boy any embarrassing questions, but it was too late. Umar had already begun to speak.

'Ibn Daud,' said the master of the house, 'would you care to take a short walk with me after you have finished your coffee?'

'It would be an honour, sir.'

'Can I join you too?' asked Yazid in a matter-of-fact voice, trying to sound as adult as he possibly could. Since Zuhayr was away, he felt he should be present at such an occasion.

'No,' smiled Hind. 'I want a game of chess. I think I am going to take your king in under ten moves.'

Yazid was torn, but his sister prevailed.

'On reflection,' he said to his father, 'I will remain indoors. I think it is getting cold outside.'

'A sensible decision,' said Umar as he rose from the floor and walked towards the door leading to the terrace.

Ibn Daud bowed to Zubayda, and looked at Hind as if he

was pleading with her not to judge him too harshly. He followed Umar out of the room.

'Go to my room and lay the chess pieces on the cloth,' Hind instructed her brother. 'I will join you in a moment.'

'I think we were wrong about Ibn Daud,' said Zubayda the minute her son had left the room. 'Did you observe him while we were eating? He had eyes only for you. He may be confused, but he is very attached to you.'

'What you say may be true, but the uncontrollable passion which I felt for him is gone. I still like him. I may even love him in time, but without the intensity I felt before. The afternoon has left me with a dull headache.'

'Not even our greatest physicians have been able to solve the riddles of the heart, Hind. Give yourself a chance. You are too much like me. Too impatient. Everything at once. I was like that with your father, and his parents mistook my simple desire for greed.'

'Surely, Mother,' said Hind in a very soft voice, 'we do not know how much time there is left for any of us. When you were young the Sultan was in the al-Hamra palace and the world seemed safe. Today our lives are governed by uncertainties. Everyone in the village feels insecure. Even the false magic of dreams can offer consolation no longer. Our dreams have turned sour. Do you remember when Yazid was crying and clinging to Zuhayr, pleading with him not to go to Gharnata?'

'Could any mother forget that scene?'

'The sight of Yazid in such distress angered me and I whispered some rudeness in Zuhayr's ear. Something stupid. Told him he had been selfish from birth. His face paled. He put Yazid down and took me to one side. Then he whispered fiercely in my ear: "There is nothing to be gained by becoming entangled in life and its daily routines. The only freedom left is to choose how we are to die, and you want to take even that away from me." '

Zubayda hugged Hind and held her close. They did not speak any more. In the silence they could hear the wind outside. Their bodies transmitted signals to each other.

'Hind! Hind!' Yazid's voice brought them back to the world in which they continued to live. 'I've been waiting. Hurry up! I've planned my moves.'

The two women smiled. Some things would never change.

Outside in the dark blue night, Umar and Ibn Daud were walking round the walls of the house. They, too, had been discussing the state of their world, though in more philosophical terms. Now that they were beyond the hearing of the night-watchmen who patrolled the perimeter of the house, Umar decided that no more time should be wasted.

'I have heard that you went for a walk with Hind after lunch today. She is a very precious treasure. Her mother and I both love her very much. We do not wish to see her hurt or upset.'

'I was very pleased when you asked me to come and walk with you. I love Hind. I wish to ask your permission to marry her.'

'Remember one thing, Ibn Daud,' said Umar in his most avuncular style. 'Only a blind man dares to shit on the roof and thinks that he cannot be seen!'

Ibn Daud began to tremble. He was not sure how much Umar knew. Perhaps Yazid had told his mother. Perhaps the maid-servants had talked. Perhaps . . .

'What I mean, my dear friend, is that there is no excuse for somebody to fall into the same hole twice.'

Now he understood.

'There is nothing I wish to hide from Hind and yourself or from the Lady Zubayda.' Ibn Daud spoke with a tremor in his voice. 'There was an incident some years ago. A fellow student. We loved each other. He died over a year ago. I have not been with any other man or woman. My love for Hind is stronger than it was for my friend. I would sooner die than harm her in any way. If, in your wisdom and with your experience, you and the Lady Zubayda feel that I am the wrong person for her, pray tell me so and I will pack my bag and leave your noble house tomorrow. Your judgement will be final.'

The wind had died, leaving behind a clear sky. Ibn Daud's honesty had dispelled the gloom of the night and Umar's heart had lightened. Zubayda's suspicions, even though he would not admit it to her, had discomforted him. There were far too many family stories of women made unhappy by men who lived only for each other, women who lived on withered dreams. Their sole function, as far as their husbands were concerned, was procreation. Umar's own grand-uncle, Ibn Farid's younger brother, had flaunted his male lover in this very house, but he, at least, had never bothered to get married.

'I am greatly impressed by your honesty. What you tell your future wife is between the pair of you.'

'Then I have your permission?' began Ibn Daud, but he was immediately interrupted.

'You have more than my permission. You have my blessing. Hind will carry a handsome dowry.'

'I assure you that the dowry is of no interest to me.'

'Have you any wealth of your own?'

'None whatsoever. Money has never played an important part in my life.'

Umar chuckled as they began to walk back to the house. The only thing to recommend poverty, he felt, was the way it ennobled some people with a dignity which wealth simply could not match.

'Never mind, Ibn Daud. You shall have the dowry nonetheless. My grandchildren will thank me for my foresight. Tell me, have you decided on where you want to live? Will you go back to al-Qahira?'

'No. That is the one place where I do not wish to live. I will naturally discuss all this with Lady Hind, but the Maghrebian town which pleases me the most is Fes. It is not unlike Gharnata, but without the presence of Archbishop Cisneros. Moreover Ibn Khaldun, if my grandmother is to be believed, commended it highly and wished to make it his permanent home.'

Whereas a few weeks ago the sight of Hind making eyes at Ibn Daud had only served to kindle Umar's irritation with the Qahirene, he now began to feel a kind of admiration for this young man. He no longer found him irksome and too clever for his own good, and had begun to share his confidence that he could survive materially simply on the basis of his intellect. As they reached the inner courtyard Umar felt that he was one of the few men with whom Hind could be happy. He embraced Ibn Daud.

'Peace be upon you and sleep well.'

'Peace be upon you,' responded the scholar from al-Qahira, his voice choked with emotions he was trying so hard to conceal.

When Umar entered his wife's bed-chamber he found Hind massaging her mother's legs and feet. Zubayda sat up the minute her husband entered the room.

'Well?'

'Who won at chess, Hind?' was Umar's only response, designed deliberately to provoke his wife.

'Umar!' demanded Zubayda. 'What happened?'

Umar, looking as resigned and calm as he could, stared at her with a smile. 'It was as I thought,' he replied. 'The boy truly loves our daughter. Of that I have not the slightest doubt. I gave him my permission. It is now up to Hind.'

'My fears?' pressed Zubayda. 'Were they totally false?'

Umar shrugged his shoulders. 'They were irelevant.'

Zubayda smiled in satisfaction. 'It is your choice and yours alone, my daughter. We are happy.'

Hind's face had acquired a flush as she heard this conversation. Her heart had begun to beat faster. 'I will think carefully about it tonight,' she said in a matter-of-fact tone, 'and tomorrow you shall all have my answer.'

She then kissed her parents in turn and, putting on her most dignified look, walked slowly out of the chamber.

Once she was in the safety of her own room, she began to laugh, first silently and then aloud. The laughter reflected her triumph, her joy, and there was also an element of hysteria. 'I wish you were not dead, Great-Aunt Zahra.' Hind was looking at a mirror and inspecting her own face, whose natural softness was enhanced by the light of the lamp. 'I need to talk to you. I think I will marry him, but first I must convince myself that his love is genuine, and there is only one way to find out. You told me so yourself.'

Having convinced herself of the righteousness of what she was about to do, Hind extinguished the lamp in her room and tiptoed out into the courtyard. It was pitch-black. The clouds had returned and covered the stars. She waited till her eyes had adjusted to the dark and walked nervously to the guest chambers.

Outside Ibn Daud's room she paused till she had stopped trembling. She looked around carefully. Everything was still. His light was still burning. She knocked gently on the door. Inside the room Ibn Daud was puzzled. He wrapped a sheet around him, got out of bed and unlatched the door.

'Hind!' His surprise was so great that he could barely hear his own voice. 'Please come in.'

Hind marched into the room, trying hard not to laugh at the

sight of this very proper young man trying to keep the sheet around him in place. She sat down on the bed.

'My father says that he has given you permission to marry me.'

'Only if you agree. Is that all your father said?'

'Yes. What else did you say to him?'

'Something I should have said to you many days ago. I was a fool, Hind. I think I must have been frightened of losing you.'

'What are you talking about?'

Ibn Daud recounted the whole story of his love for the dead Mansur, including the details most likely to cause pain to her. He described how they had shared a room at the al-Azhar university, how they had found each other's company the most stimulating and how, one night, their intellectual affinity had brought them together physically. He talked of their discovery of each other and then the death of Mansur.

'You were the person who brought me back to life.'

'I am glad of that. You have probably realized that I am one of those who prefer a heart pierced with anguish to a placid happiness, which is usually based on self-deception or deceit. The food of most marriages is a cold emptiness. Most of my cousins are married to brutes with the sensitivity of a log. Marriage for its own sake is something I could never accept. Can I ask you something?'

'Whatever you wish.' Ibn Daud's voice sounded eager and relieved.

'We could become great friends, write poetry together, join the hunt, discuss astronomy, but are you sure that when the sun sets you will desire a woman's body in your arms?'

'I have been yearning for you since the afternoon. I was confused and unsure, but the flow of your hands across my limbs was an experience I would happily repeat when the sun rises, never mind at night.'

As he stroked her face she felt moved again and embraced him, feeling his naked body underneath the sheet of pure cotton. When she felt his palm-tree stir she pulled the sheet off him and held him tight. Then she stepped back and shed her gown.

'The noise of your heartbeats will wake up the whole household,' she teased as she put out the lamp and fell with him on the bed.

'Are you sure, Hind? Are you sure?' he asked, incapable of further self-control.

She nodded. Gently he planted his tree in her garden. She felt the pain, which was transformed within seconds into pain-pleasure, and then she relaxed and joined him as their bodies began to heave in unison, reaching a climax together. All her cousins and the maid-servants had told Hind that the first time was the least pleasurable. She lay back and enjoyed the after-glow.

'Now are you sure,' he asked her, sitting up in bed and giving her a quizzical look.

'Yes, my lover, now I am sure. Are you?'

'What do you mean, you devil?'

'I mean was it as nice as it used to be with Mansur?'

'It is very different with you, my princess, and so it shall remain. A pomegranate can give as much pleasure as an oyster even though the taste of each is so completely different from the other. To compare them is to spoil both.'

'I am warning you, Ibn Daud. Even before we are married. If you desert me for a pretty young boy selling figs, my revenge will be public and brutal.'

'What will you do?'

In response she clasped his palm-tree.

'I will remove these dates and have them pickled.'

This made both of them laugh. The flame mounted again. They made love many times that night. He fell asleep before she did. For a long time she watched his sleeping body and relived what she had just experienced. She stroked his hair, hoping that it might awaken him, but he did not stir. Her palate wanted to taste him again, but sleep, tired of waiting any longer, over-powered her desire.

Just before sunrise, Zubayda entered the room, knowing what she would find. She put her hand on her daughter's mouth to prevent any startled screams which might embarrass her lover, then shook her vigorously till she opened her eyes. On seeing Zubayda she sat bolt-upright in the bed. Zubayda signalled that they should leave the room quietly.

'I love him. I will marry him,' whispered Hind drowsily as they crossed back into the inner courtyard.

'I am truly glad to hear the news,' replied her mother, 'but I think you should marry him later this afternoon!'

Chapter 11

XIMENES IS SITTING at his desk thinking.
My skin is perhaps too dark, my eyes are not blue but dark brown, my nose is hooked and long, and yet I am sure, yes sure, that my blood is without taint. My forefathers were here when the Romans came and my family is much older than the Visigoth ancestors of the noble Count, our brave Captain-General. Why do they whisper I have Jewish blood in me? Is it a cruel joke? Or are some disaffected Dominicans spreading this poison to discredit me inside the Church so that they can once again stray into the land of deceit and confuse the distinctions between ourselves and the followers of Moses and the false prophet Mahomet? Whatever their reasoning, it is not true. Do you hear me? It is not true. My blood is pure! Pure as we shall make this kingdom one day. I shall neither weep nor complain at these endless insults, but carry on God's work. The wolves call me a beast, but they dare not attack me for they know the price they will have to pay for my blood. The worship of Mary and the pain felt by Him who was crucified awakens mysterious emotions inside me. In my dreams I often see myself as a Crusader below the ramparts of Jerusalem or catching sight of Constantinople. My memory is rooted in the time of Christianity, but why am I always alone, even in my dreams? No family. No friends. No pity for the inferior races. There is no Jewish blood in me. Not even one tiny drop. No. On this I have no doubts.

A spy had informed Ximenes a few hours ago that at the conclusion of a banquet the previous night, after a great deal of wine had been imbibed and the assembled party of Muslim and Christian noblemen, together with Jewish merchants, were being entertained by dancing-girls, a courtier had remarked that it was a great pity that the Archbishop of Toledo could not be present to enjoy such pleasant company, upon which the Captain-General, Don Inigo, had been heard to remark that the reason for the prelate's absence might well be that in the candle-light it was impossible to tell him apart from a Jew. He had not stopped there, but insisted loudly, amidst general laughter that this could be one reason why His Grace shunned the company of Jews even more than of Moors. For whereas Moorish features were indistinguishable from those of Christians, the Jews had preserved their own special traits with much greater care, as a close inspection of Ximenes clearly revealed.

At this point a Moorish nobleman, stroking his luxuriant red beard and with a twinkle in his shiny blue eyes, had asked Don Inigo whether it was true that the reason the Archbishop was determined to destroy the followers of the one God had much more to do with proving his own racial purity than with defending the Trinity. Don Inigo had assumed a mock-serious expression and shouted that the suggestion was preposterous, then winked at his guests.

Ximenes dismissed the spy with an angry wave of the hand, to imply that he was not interested in these trivial pieces of malicious gossip. In reality he was livid with rage. That he was cursed and reviled by deceitful Moorish tongues was a well-known fact. Not a single day passed without reports of how he was being abused, by whom and in which streets of the city. The list was long, but he would deal with every single offender when the time was ripe. With such thoughts stirring in his head and increasing the flow of bile in his system, it is hardly surprising that the Archbishop's disposition that particular morning was not generous.

It was at this exact moment that there was a knock on the door.

'Enter!' he said in that deceptively weak voice.

Barrionuevo, a royal bailiff, entered the room and kissed the ring. 'With your permission. Your Grace, the two renegades have fled to the old quarter and taken refuge in the house of their mother.'

'I do not seem to be familiar with this case. Remind me.'

Barrionuevo cleared his throat. He was not used to declamations or explanations. He was given his orders and he carried them out. He was at a loss for words. He did not know the details of these two men. 'All I know is their names, Your Grace.

Abengarcia and Abenfernando. I am told they converted to our faith . . .'

'I recall them now,' came the icy response. 'They pretended to convert, but inside they remained followers of Mahomet's sect. They were seen committing an act of sacrilege in our church. They urinated on a crucifix, man! Bring them back to me. I want them questioned today. You may go.'

'Should I take an escort, Your Grace? There might be resistance without it.'

'Yes, but make sure that there are no more than six armed men with you. Otherwise there will be trouble.'

Ximenes rose from his desk and walked to the arched window from where he could see the streets below him. For the first time that day he smiled, confident in the knowledge that some of the more hot-headed Moors would be provoked by the bailiff and the soldiers to take up arms. That would be the end for them. Instead of taking his usual walk to inspect the construction of the new cathedral, he decided to stay at the al-Hamra and await the return of Barrionuevo. The unpleasantness occasioned by the report from last night's banquet had receded. In its place there was a feeling of burning excitement. Ximenes fell on his knees before the giant crucifix which disfigured the intricate geometric patterns on the three-colour tiles that comprised the wall.

'Holy Mary, Mother of God, I pray that our enemies will not fail me today.'

When he rose to his feet he discovered that the fire burning in his head had spread to just below his waist. That portion of his anatomy which had been placed out of bounds for all those who took the holy orders, was in a state of rebellion. Ximenes poured some water into a goblet and gulped it down without pause. His thirst was quenched.

From the heart of the old city, Zuhayr and his comrades were walking towards the site of the new cathedral in an exaggeratedly casual fashion. They were in groups of two, tense and nervous, behaving as though they had no connection with each other, but united in the belief that they were drawing close to a dual triumph. The hated enemy, the torturer of their fellow-believers, would soon be dead and they, his killers, would be assured of martyrdom and an easy passage to paradise.

They had met for an early breakfast to perfect their plans. Each one of the eight men had risen solemnly in turn and had bidden a formal farewell to the others: 'Till we meet again in heaven.'

Early that morning Zuhayr had begun to write a letter to Umar, detailing his adventures on the road to Gharnata, describing the painful dilemma which had confronted him and explaining his final decision to participate in the action which was favoured by everyone except himself:

We will set a trap for Cisneros, but even if we succeed in dispatching him, I know full well that we will all, each and every one of us, fall into it ourselves. Everything is very different from what I imagined. The situation for the Gharnatinos has become much worse since your last visit. There is both outrage and demoralization. They are determined to convert us and Cisneros has authorized the use of torture to aid this process. Of course many people submit to the pain, but it drives them mad. After converting they become desperate, walk into churches and excrete on the altar, urinate in the holy font, smear the crucifixes with impure substances and rush out laughing in the fashion of people who have lost their mind. Cisneros reacts with fury and so the whole cycle is repeated. The feeling here is that while Cisneros lives nothing will change except for the worse. I do not believe that his death will improve matters, but it will, without any doubt, ease the mental agony suffered by so many of our people.

I may not survive this day and I kiss all of you in turn, especially Yazid, who must never be allowed to repeat his brother's mistakes . . .

Zuhayr and Ibn Basit were about to cross the road when they saw Barrionuevo the bailiff and six soldiers heading in their direction. Fortunately nobody panicked, but as Barrionuevo halted in front of Zuhayr, the other three groups abandoned the march to their destination and turning leftwards, disappeared back into a warren of narrow side-streets as had been previously agreed.

'Why are you carrying a sword?' asked Barrionuevo.

'Forgive me sir,' replied Zuhayr. 'I do not belong to Gharnata.

I am here for a few days from al-Hudayl to stay with my friend. Is it forbidden to carry swords in the street now?'

'Yes,' replied the bailiff. 'Your friend here should have known better. Be on your way, but first return to your friend's home and get rid of the sword.'

Ibn Basit and Zuhayr were greatly relieved. They had no alternative but to turn around and walk back to the Funduq. The others were waiting, and there were exclamations of delight when Zuhayr and Ibn Basit entered the room.

'I thought we had lost you forever,' said Ibn Amin, embracing the pair of them.

Zuhayr saw the relief on their faces and knew at once that it was not just the sight of Ibn Basit and himself which had relaxed the tension. There was something else. That much was obvious from the satisfied expression on Ibn Amin's face. Zuhayr looked at his friend and raised his eyebrows expectantly. Ibn Amin spoke.

'We must cancel our plan. A friend in the palace has sent us a message. Ximenes has trebled his guard and has cancelled his plans to visit the city today. I felt there was something strange in the air. Did you notice that the streets were virtually deserted?'

Zuhayr could not conceal his delight.

'Allah, be praised!' he exulted. 'Fate has intervened to prevent our sacrifice. But you are right, Ibn Amin. The atmosphere is tense. Why is this so? Has it anything to do with the royal bailiff's errand?'

While they continued to speculate and began to discuss whether they should venture back to the streets and investigate the situation, an old servant of the Funduq ran into their room.

'Pray masters, please hurry to the Street of the Water-Carriers. The word is that you should take your weapons.'

Zuhayr picked up his sword again. The others uncovered their daggers as they rushed out of the Funduq al-Yadida. They did not have to search very hard to find the place. What sounded like a low humming noise was getting louder and louder. It seemed as if the whole population of the quarter was on the streets.

Through the fringed horseshoe arches of homes and work-shops, more and more people were beginning to pour out on to the streets. The beating of copperware, the loud wails and an orchestra of tambourines had brought them all together. Water-carriers and carpet-sellers mingled with fruit merchants and the *faqihs*. It was a motley crowd and it was angry, that much was obvious to the conspirators of the Funduq, but why? What had happened to incite a mass which, till yesterday, had seemed so passive?

A stray acquaintance of Ibn Amin, a fellow Jew, coming from the scene of battle, excitedly told them everything that had happened till the moment he had to leave in order to tend his sick father.

'The royal bailiff and his soldiers went to the house of the widow in the Street of the Water-Carriers. Her two sons had taken refuge there last night. The bailiff said that the Archbishop wished to see them today. The widow, angered by the arrival of soldiers, would not let them into the house. When they threatened to break down the door she poured a pan of boiling water from the balcony.

'One of the soldiers was badly burnt. His screams were horrible.'

The memory choked the storyteller's voice and he began to tremble.

'Calm down, friend,' said Zuhayr, stroking his head. 'There is no cause for you to worry. Tell me what happened afterwards.'

'It got worse, much worse,' began Ibn Amin's friend. 'The bailiff was half-scared and half-enraged by this defiance. He ordered his men to break into the house and arrest the widow's sons. The commotion began to attract other people and soon there were over two hundred young men, who barricaded the street at both ends. Slowly they began to move towards the bailiff and his men. One of the soldiers got so scared that he wet himself and pleaded for mercy. They let him go. The others raised their swords, which was fatal. The people hemmed them in so tight that the soldiers were crushed against the wall. Then the son of al-Wahab, the oil merchant, lifted a sword off the ground. It had been dropped by one of the soldiers. He walked straight to the bailiff and dragged him into the centre of the street. "Mother," he shouted to the widow who was watching everything from the window. "Yes, my son," she replied with a joyous look on her face. "Tell me," said Ibn Wahab. "How should this wretch be punished?" The old lady put a finger to her throat.

The crowd fell silent. The bailiff, Barrionuevo by name, fell to the ground, pleading for mercy. He was like a trapped animal. His head touched Ibn Wahab's feet. At that precise moment the raised sword descended. It only took one blow. Barrionuevo's severed head fell on the street. A stream of blood is still flowing in the Street of the Water-Carriers.'

'And the soldiers?' asked Zuhayr. 'What have they done to the soldiers?'

'Their fate is still under discussion in the square. The soldiers are being guarded by hundreds of armed men at the Bab al-Ramla.'

'Come,' said Zuhayr somewhat self-importantly to his companions. 'We must take part in this debate. The life of every believer in Gharnata may depend on the outcome.'

The crowds were so thick that every street in the maze had become virtually impassable. Either you moved with the crowd or you did not move at all. And still the people were coming out. Here were the tanners from the *rabbad al-Dabbagan*, their legs still bare, their skin still covered with dyes of different colours. The tambourine makers had left their workshops in the *rabbad al-Difaf* and joined the throng. They were adding to the noise by extracting every sound possible from the instrument. The potters from the *rabbad al-Fajjarin* had come armed with sacks full of defective pots, and marching by their side, also heavily armed, were the brick-makers from the *rabbad al-Tawwabin*.

Suddenly Zuhayr saw a sight which moved and excited him. Scores of women, young and old, veiled and unveiled, were carrying aloft the silken green and silver standards of the Moorish knights, which they and their ancestors had sewn and embroidered for over five hundred years in the *rabbad al-Bunud*. They were handing out hundreds of tiny silver crescents to the children. Young boys and girls were competing with each other to grab a crescent. Zuhayr thought of Yazid. How he would have relished all this and how proudly he would have worn his crescent. Zuhayr had thought he would never see Yazid again, but since his own plan of challenging individual Christian knights to armed combat had collapsed and the plot to assassinate Cisneros had been postponed out of necessity. Zuhayr began to think of the future once again and the image of his brother, studying everything with his intelligent eyes, never left him.

Every street, every alley, resembled a river in flood, flowing in the direction of a buoyant sea of humanity near the Bab al-Ramla Gate. The chants would rise and recede like waves. Everyone was waiting for the storm.

Zuhayr was determined to speak in favour of sparing the soldiers. He suddenly noticed that they were in the *rabbad al-Kuhl*, the street which housed the producers of antimony. It was here that silver containers were loaded with the liquid, which had enhanced the beauty of countless eyes since the city was first built. This meant that they were not far from the palace of his Uncle Hisham. And underneath that large mansion there was a passage which led directly to the Bab al-Ramla. It had been built when the house was constructed, precisely in order to enable the nobleman or trader living in it to escape easily when he was under siege by rivals whose cause had triumphed and whose faction had emerged victorious in the never-ending palace conflicts which always cast a permanent shadow on the city.

Zuhayr signalled to his friends to follow him in silence. He knocked on the deceptively modest front door of Hisham's house. An old family retainer looked through a tiny latticed window on the first floor and recognized Zuhayr. He rushed down the stairs, opened the door and let them all in, but appeared extremely agitated.

'The master made me swear not to admit any person today except members of the family. There are spies everywhere. A terrible crime has been committed and Satan's monk will want his vengeance in blood.'

'Old friend,' said Zuhayr with a benevolent wink. 'We are not here to stay, but to disappear. You need not even tell your master that you let us in. I know the way to the underground passage. Trust in Allah.'

The old man understood. He led them to the concealed entrance in the courtyard and lifted a tile to reveal a tiny hook. Zuhayr smiled. How many times had he and Ibn Hisham's children left the house after dark for clandestine assignments with lovers via this very route. He tugged gently at the hook and lifted a square cover, cleverly disguised as a set of sixteen tiles. He helped his friends down the hole and then joined them, but not before he had embraced the servant, who had been with his uncle ever since Zuhayr could remember.

'May Allah protect you all today,' said the old man as he replaced the cover and returned the courtyard to normal.

Within a few minutes, they were at the old market. Zuhayr had feared that the exit to the tunnel might be impossible to lift because of the crowds, but fate favoured them. The cover was raised without any hindrance. As seven men emerged from underneath the floor on to the roofed entrance to the market, a group of bewildered citizens watched in amazement. The men were followed by a disembodied weapon: Zuhayr had handed his sword through the hole to Ibn Basit, who had preceded him. Now he lifted himself up, replacing the stone immediately so that in the general confusion its exact location would be forgotten.

It was a scene that none of them would forget. They saw the backs of tens of thousands of men, women and children who had assembled near the Bab al-Ramla in a spirit of vengeance. This is where they had stood in 1492 and watched in disbelief as the crescent was hurled down from the battlements of the al-Hamra, accompanied by the deafening noise of bells interspersed with Christian hymns. This is where they had stood in silence last year while Cisneros, the man they called 'Satan's priest', had burnt their books. And it was in this square only a month later that drunken Christian soldiers had tipped the turbans off the heads of two venerable Imams.

The Moors of Gharnata were not a hard or stubborn people, but they had been ceded to the Christians without being permitted to resist, and this had made them very bitter. Their anger, repressed for over eight years, had come out into the open. They were in a mood to attempt even the most desperate measures. They would have stormed the al-Hamra, torn Ximenes limb from limb, burnt down churches and castrated any monk they could lay their hands on. This made them dangerous. Not to the enemy, but to themselves. Deprived by their last ruler of the chance to resist the Christian armies, they felt that it was time they reasserted themselves.

It is sometimes argued, usually by those who fear the multitude, that any gathering which exceeds a dozen people becomes a willing prey to any demagogue capable of firing its passions, and thus it is capable only of irrationality. Such a view is designed to ignore the underlying causes which have brought together so many people and with so many diverse interests. All rivalries, political and commercial, had been set aside; all blood-feuds had been cancelled; a truce had been declared between the warring theological factions within the house of al-Andalusian Islam; the congregation was united against the Christian occupiers. What had begun as a gesture of solidarity with a widow's right to protect her children had turned into a semi-insurrection.

Ibn Wahab, the proud and thoughtless executioner of the royal bailiff, stood on a hastily constructed wooden platform, his head in the clouds. He was dreaming of the al-Hamra and the posture in which he would sit when he received ambassadors from Isabella, pleading for peace. Unhappily his first attempt at oratory had been a miserable failure. He had been constantly interrupted.

'Why are you mumbling?'

'What are you saying?'

'Talk louder!'

'Who do you think you are addressing? Your beardless chin?'

Angered by this lack of respect, Ibn Wahab had raised his voice in the fashion of the preachers. He had spoken for almost thirty minutes in a language so flowery and ornate, so crowded with metaphors and so full of references to famous victories stretching from Dimashk to the Maghreb that even those most sympathetic to him amongst the audience were heard remarking that the speaker was like an empty vessel, noisy, but devoid of content.

The only concrete measure he had proposed was the immediate execution of the soldiers and the display of their heads on poles. The response had been muted, which caused a *qadi* to enquire if there was anybody else who wished to speak.

'Yes!' roared Zuhayr. He lifted the sword above his head and, with erect shoulders and an uplifted face, he moved towards the platform. His comrades followed him and the crowd, partially bemused by the oddity of the procession, made way. Many recognized him as a scion of the Banu Hudayl. The *qadi* asked Ibn Wahab to step down and Zuhayr was lifted on to the platform by a host of willing hands. He had never spoken before at a public gathering, let alone one of this size, and he was shaking like an autumn leaf.

'In the name of Allah, the Merciful, the Beneficent.' Zuhayr began in the most traditional fashion possible. He did not dwell for long on the glories of their religion, nor did he mention the past. He spoke simply of the tragedy that had befallen them and the even greater tragedy that lay ahead. He found himself using phrases which sounded oddly familiar. They were. He had picked them up from al-Zindiq and Abu Zaid. He concluded with an unpopular appeal.

'Even as I speak to you, the soldier who witnessed the execution is at the al-Hamra, describing every detail. But put yourself in his place. He is racked by fear. To make himself sound brave, he exaggerates everything. Soon the Captain-General will bring his soldiers down the hill to demand the release of these men whom we have made our prisoners. Unlike my brother Ibn Wahab I do not believe that we should kill them. I would suggest that we let them go. If we do not, the Christians will kill ten of us for each soldier. I ask you: is their death worth the destruction of a single believer? To release them now would be a sign of our strength, not weakness. Once we have let them go we should elect from amongst ourselves a delegation which will speak on our behalf. I have many other things to say, but I will hold my tongue till you pronounce your judgement on the fate of these soldiers. I do not wish to speak any more in their presence.'

To his amazement, Zuhayr's remarks were greeted with applause and much nodding of heads. When the *qadi* asked the assembly whether the soldiers should be freed or killed the response was overwhelmingly in favour of their release. Zuhayr and his friends did not wait for instructions. They rushed to where the men were being held prisoner. Zuhayr unsheathed his sword and cut the rope which bound them. Then he marched them to the edge of the crowd and pointed with his sword in the direction of the al-Hamra and sent them on their way. The incredulous soldiers nodded in silent gratitude and ran away as fast as their legs could take them.

In the palace, just as Zuhayr had told them, the soldier who had been permitted to leave earlier, assuming that his comrades would by now have been decapitated, had embellished his own role in the episode. The Archbishop heard every word in silence, then rose without uttering a word, indicated to the soldier that he should follow him and walked to the rooms occupied by the Count of Tendilla. He was received without delay and the soldier found himself reciting his tale of woe once again.

'Your Excellency will no doubt agree,' began Ximenes, 'that unless we respond with firmness to this rebellion, all the victories achieved by our King and Queen in this city will be under threat.'

'My dear Archbishop,' responded the Count in a deceptively friendly tone, 'I wish there were more like you in the holy orders of our Church, so loyal to the throne and so devoted to increasing the property and thereby the weight and standing of the Church.

'However, I wish to make something plain. I do not agree with your assessment. This wretched man is lying to justify falling on his knees before the killers of Barrionuevo. Not for one minute will I accept that our military position is threatened by this mob. I would have thought that, if anything, it was Your Grace's offensive on behalf of the Holy Spirit which was under threat.'

Ximenes was enraged by the remark, especially since it was uttered in the presence of a soldier who would repeat it to his friends: within hours the news would be all over the city. He curbed his anger till he had, with an imperious gesture of the right hand, dismissed the soldier from their presence.

'Your Excellency does not seem to appreciate that until these people are subdued and made to respect the Church, they will never be loyal to the crown!'

'For a loyal subject of the Queen, Your Grace appears to be ignorant of the agreements we signed with the Sultan at the time of his surrender. This is not the first occasion when I have had to remind you of the solemn pledges that were given to the Moors. They were to be permitted the right to worship their God and believe in their Prophet without any hindrance. They could speak their own language, marry each other and bury their dead as they had done for centuries. It is you, my dear Archbishop, who have provoked this uprising. You have reduced them to a miserable condition, and you only feign surprise when they resist. They are not animals, man! They are flesh of our flesh and blood of our blood.

'I sometimes ask myself how the same Mother Church could have produced two such different children as the Dominicans and the Franciscans. Cain and Abel? Tell me something, Friar

Cisneros. When you were being trained in that monastery near Toledo, what did they give you to drink?'

Cisneros understood that the anger of the Captain-General was caused by his knowledge that a military response was indispensable to restore order. He had triumphed. He decided to humour the Count.

'I am amazed that a great military leader like Your Excellency should have time to study the different religious orders born out of our Mother Church. Not Cain and Abel, Excellency. Never that. Treat them, if it pleases you, as the two loving sons of a widowed mother. The first son is tough and disciplined, defends his mother against the unwelcome attentions of all unwanted suitors. The other, equally loving, is, however, lax and easygoing; he leaves the door of his house wide open and does not care who enters or departs. The mother needs them both and loves them equally, but ask yourself this, Excellency, who protects her the best?'

Don Inigo was vexed by the Archbishop's spuriously friendly, patronizing tone. His touchy sense of pride was offended. A religious upstart attempting to become familiar with a Mendoza? How dare Cisneros behave in this fashion? He gave the prelate a contemptuous look.

'Your Grace of course has a great deal of experience with widowed mothers and their two sons. Was it not in pursuit of one such widow and her two unfortunate boys that you sent the royal bailiff to his death today?'

The Archbishop realizing that anything he said today would be rebuffed, rose and took his leave. The Count's fists unclenched. He clapped loudly. When two attendants appeared he barked out a series of orders.

'Prepare my armour and my horse. Tell Don Alonso I will need three hundred soldiers to accompany me to the Bibarrambla. I wish to leave before the next hour is struck.'

In the city the mood had changed a great deal. The release of the soldiers had given the people a feeling of immense self-confidence. They felt morally superior to their enemies. Nothing appeared frightening any more. Vendors of food and drink had made their appearance. The bakers had shut their shops and pastry stalls had been hastily assembled in the Bab al-Ramla.

Food and sweetmeats were being freely distributed. Children were improvising simple songs and dancing. The tension had evaporated. Zuhayr knew it was only a temporary respite. Fear had momentarily retired below the surface. It had been replaced by a festival-like atmosphere, but it was only an hour ago that he had heard the beating of hearts.

Zuhayr was the hero of the day. Older citizens had been regaling him with stories of the exploits of his great-grandfather, most of which he had heard before, while others he knew could not possibly be true. He was nodding amiably at the white beards and smiling, but no longer listening. His thoughts were in the al-Hamra, and there they would have remained had not a familiar voice disturbed his reverie.

'You are thinking, are you not, that some great misfortune is about to befall us here?'

'Al-Zindiq!' Zuhayr shouted as he embraced his old friend. 'You look so different. How can you have changed so much in the space of two weeks? Zahra's death?'

'Time feasts and drinks on an ageing man, Zuhayr al-Fahl. One day, when you have passed the age of seventy, you too will realize this fact.'

'If I live that long,' muttered Zuhayr in a more introspective mood. He was delighted to see al-Zindiq, and not simply because he could poach a few more ideas from him. He was pleased that al-Zindiq had seen him at the height of his powers, receiving the accolades of the Gharnatinos. But the old sceptic's inner make-up remained unchanged.

'My young friend,' he told Zuhayr in a voice full of affection, 'our lives are lived underneath an arch which extends from our birth to the grave. It is old age and death which explain the allure of youth. And its disdain for the future.'

'Yes,' said Zuhayr as he began to grasp where all this was heading, 'but the breach between old age and youth is not as final as you are suggesting.'

'How so?'

'Remember a man who had just approached his sixtieth year, a rare enough event in our peninsula. He was walking on the outskirts of al-Hudayl and saw three boys, all of them fifty years or more younger than him, perched on a branch near the top of a tree. One of the boys shouted some insult or other comparing his shaven head to the posterior of some animal. Experience dictated that the old man ignore the remark and walk away, but instead, to the great amazement of the boys, he clambered straight up the tree and took them by surprise. The boy who had insulted him became his lifelong friend.'

Al-Zindiq chuckled.

'I climbed the tree precisely to teach you that nothing should ever be taken for granted.'

'Exactly so. I learnt the lesson well.'

'In that case, my friend, make sure that you do not lead these people into a trap. The girl who survived the massacre at al-Hama still cannot bear the sight of rain. She imagines that it is red.'

'Zuhayr bin Umar, Ibn Basit, Ibn Wahab. A meeting of The Forty is taking place inside the silk market now!'

Zuhayr thanked al-Zindiq for his advice and hurriedly took his leave. He walked to the spacious room of a silk trader which had been made available to them. The old man could not help but notice the alteration in his young friend's gait. His natural tendency would have been to run to the meeting place, but he had walked away in carefully measured steps while his demeanour had assumed an air of self-importance. Al-Zindiq smiled and shook his head. It was as if he had seen the ghost of Ibn Farid.

The assembly of citizens had elected a committee of forty men, and given them the authority to negotiate on behalf of the whole town. Zuhayr and his seven friends had all been elected, but so had Ibn Wahab. Most of the others members of The Forty were demobilized Moorish knights. Just as Zuhayr entered the meeting a messenger from the al-Hamra kitchens was speaking in excited tones of the preparations for a counter-offensive under way at the palace.

'The armour of the Captain-General himself is being got ready. He will be accompanied by three hundred soldiers. Their swords were being sharpened even as I left.'

'We should ambush them,' suggested Ibn Wahab. 'Pour oil on them and set it alight.'

'Better a sane enemy than an insane friend,' muttered the *qadi* dismissing the suggestion with a frown.

'Let us prepare as we have planned,' said Zuhayr as the meeting ended and The Forty returned to the square.

The *qadi* mounted the platform and announced that the soldiers were on their way. The smiles disappeared. The vendors began to pack their wares, ready to depart. The crowd became anxious and nervous conversations erupted in every corner. The *qadi* asked people to remain calm. Women and children and the elderly were sent home.

Everyone else had been assigned special positions in case the Christian army tried to conquer the heart of the city. The men departed to their previously agreed posts. Precautions had already been taken and the defence plan was now put into operation. Within thirty minutes an effective barricade was in place. The kiln-workers, stonemasons and carpenters had organized this crowd into an orgy of collective labour. The barrier had been constructed with great skill, sealing off all the points of entry into the old quarter – what the *qadi* always referred to as 'the city of believers'.

How amazing, thought Zuhayr, that they have done this all by themselves. The *qadi* did not need to invoke our past or call upon the Almighty for them to achieve what they have done. He looked around to see if he could sight al-Zindiq, but the old man had been sheltered for the night. And where, Zuhayr wondered, is Abu Zaid and his crazy family of reborn al-Ma'aris? Why are they not here? They should see the strength of our people. If a new army is to be built to defend our way of life, then these good people are its soldiers. Without them we will fail.

'The soldiers!' someone shouted, and the Bab al-Ramla fell silent. In the distance the sound of soldiers' feet as they trampled on the paved streets grow louder and louder.

'The Captain-General is at their head, dressed in all his finery!' shouted another look-out.

Zuhayr gave a signal, which was repeated by five volunteers standing in different parts of the square. The team of three hundred young men, their satchels full of brickbats, stiffened and stretched their arms. The front line of stone-throwers was in place. The noise of the marching feet had become very loud.

The Count of Tendilla, Captain-General of the Christian armies in Gharnata, pulled his horse to a standstill as he found himself facing an impassable obstacle. The wooden doors lifted from their hinges, piles of half-bricks, steel bars and rubble of every sort had raised a fortification the like of which the Count had not encountered before in the course of numerous battles. He knew that it would need several hundred more soldiers to dismantle the edifice, and he also knew that the Moors would not stand idly watching as the structure came down. Of course he would win in the end, there could be no doubt on that score, but it would be messy and bloody. He raised his voice and shouted over the barricade: 'In the name of our King and Queen I ask you to remove this obstacle and let my escort accompany me into the city.'

The stone-throwers moved into action. An eerie music began as a storm of brickbats showered on the uplifted shields of the Christian soldiers. The Count understood the message. The Moorish elders had decided to break off all relations with the palace.

'I do not accept the breach between us,' shouted the Captain-General. 'I will return with reinforcements unless you receive me within the hour.'

He rode away angrily without waiting for his men. The sight of the soldiers running after their leader caused much merriment in the ranks of the Gharnatinos.

The Forty were less amused. They knew that sooner or later they would have to negotiate with Mendoza. Ibn Wahab wanted a fight at all costs and he won some support, but the majority decided to send a messenger to the al-Hamra, signifying their willingness to talk.

It was dark when the Count returned. The barricade had been removed by the defenders. Men with torches led the Captain-General to the silk market. He was received by The Forty in the room where they had held their meetings. He looked closely at their faces, trying to memorize their features. As he was introduced to them in turn, one of his escorts carefully inscribed each name in a register.

'Are you the son of Umar bin Abdallah?'

Zuhayr nodded.

'I know your father well. Does he know you are here?'

'No,' lied Zuhayr, not wanting any harm to come to his family.

Don Inigo moved on till he sighted Ibn Amin.

'You?' His voice rose. 'A Jew, the son of my physician, involved with this rubbish? What is it to do with you?'

'I live in the city, Excellency. The Archbishop treats us all the same. Jews, Muslims, Christian heretics. For him there is no difference.'

'I did not know there were any heretics present in Gharnata.'

'There were some, but they left when the Archbishop arrived. It seems they knew him by reputation.'

'I am not here to negotiate with you,' began the Captain-General after he had checked that the names of every member of The Forty had been taken. 'All of you are aware that I could crush this city in the palm of my hand. You have killed a royal bailiff. The man who executed a servant of the King cannot remain unpunished. There is nothing unusual about this procedure. It is the law. Your own Sultans and Emirs dispensed justice as we do now. By tomorrow morning I want this man delivered to my soldiers. From henceforth you must accept the laws laid down by our King and Queen. All of them. Those of you who embrace my faith can keep your houses and your lands, wear your clothes, speak your language, but those who continue to make converts to the sect of Mahomet will be punished.

'I can further promise you that we will not let the Inquisition near this town for another five years, but in return your taxes to the Crown are doubled as from tomorrow. In addition you must pay for the upkeep of my soldiers billeted here. There is one more thing. I have made a list of two hundred leading families in your city. They must give me one son each as a hostage. You seem shocked. This is something we have learnt from the practice of your rulers. I will expect to see all of you in the palace tomorrow with an answer to my proposals.'

Having uttered these words, more deadly than any soldier's blade, Don Inigo, the Count of Tendilla, took his leave and departed. For a few minutes nobody could speak. The promised oppression had already begun to weigh heavy.

'Perhaps,' said Ibn Wahab, in a voice weak with self-pity and fear. 'I should give myself up. Then peace will return to our people.'

'What he said could not have been more clear. If we retain our faith the only peace they will permit us will be the peace of the cemetery,' said Zuhayr. 'It is too late now for grand gestures and needless sacrifices.'

'The choice we are being offered is simple,' chimed in Ibn Basit. 'To convert or to die.'

Then the *qadi*, who of all those present, with the exception of Ibn Wahab, had felt the blow most deeply, began to speak in an emotionless voice.

'First they make sure they are in the saddle and then they begin to whip the horse. Allah has punished us most severely. He has been watching our antics on this peninsula for a long time. He knows what we have done in his name. How Believer killed Believer. How we destroyed each other's kingdoms. How our rulers lived lives which were so remote from those they ruled that their own people could not be mobilized to defend them. They had to appeal for soldiers from Ifriqya, with disastrous results. You saw how the people here responded to our call for help. Were you not proud of their discipline and loyalty? It could have been the same in Qurtuba and Ishbiliya, in al-Mariya and Balansiya, in Sarakusta and the al-Gharb, but it was not to be so. You are all young men. Your lives are still ahead of you. You must do what you think is necessary. As for me, I feel it in my bones that my departure will not be long delayed. It will free me from this world. I will die as I was born. A Believer. Tomorrow morning I will go and inform Mendoza of my decision. I will also tell him that I will no longer serve as an intermediary between our people and the al-Hamra. They must do their filthy work themselves. You must decide for yourselves. I will leave you now. What the ear does not hear the tongue cannot repeat. Peace be upon you my sons.'

Zuhayr's head was bent in anguish. Why did the earth not open and swallow him painlessly? Even better if he could clamber on to his horse and ride back to al-Hudayl. But as he saw the despondent faces which surrounded him he knew that, whether he liked it or not, his future was now tied to theirs. They had all become victims of a collective fate. He could not leave them now. Their hearts were chained to each other. It was vital that no more time was lost.

Ibn Basit was thinking on the same plane, and it was he who took the floor to bring the meeting to a conclusion. 'My friends, it is time to go and make your farewells. Those of you who feel close to our leading families, go and warn them that the Captain-General is demanding hostages. If their older sons wish to go with us we will protect them as best we can. What time should we meet?'

'Tomorrow at day-break.' Zuhayr spoke with the voice of authority. 'We shall ride away from here and join our friends in the al-Pujarras. They are already raising an army to join in the fight against the Christians. I shall meet you in the courtyard of the Funduq at the first call to prayer. Peace be upon you.'

Zuhayr walked away with a confident stride, but he had never felt so alone in his entire life. 'What a sad and gloomy fate I have assigned to myself,' he murmured as he approached the entrance to the Funduq. He would have given anything to find al-Zindiq, share a flask of wine, and confide his fears and doubts regarding the future, but the old man had already left the city. Al-Zindiq was on his way to al-Hudayl, where the very next morning he would present a detailed report on what had taken place in Gharnata to Zuhayr's anxious family.

'Zuhayr bin Umar, may Allah protect you.'

Zuhayr was startled. He could not see anyone. Then a figure moved out of the dark and stood directly in front of him. It was the old servant from his uncle's house.

'Peace be upon you, old friend. What brings you in this direction?'

'The master would like you to share his meal tonight. I was told to bring you back with me.'

'I will happily return with you,' replied Zuhayr. 'It would be a pleasure to see my uncle again.'

Ibn Hisham was pacing up and down the outer courtyard, impatiently awaiting the arrival of his nephew. The events of the day had made him sad and nervous, but deep inside himself he was proud of the role played by Umar's son. When Zuhayr entered his uncle held him close and kissed him on both cheeks.

'I am angry with you, Zuhayr. You passed through this house on your way to some other destination. Since when has my brother's son stayed at a lodging house in this city? This is your home! Answer, boy, before I have you whipped.'

Despite himself, Zuhayr was moved. He smiled. It was an odd feeling. He felt guilty, as if he was ten years old again and had been surprised in the middle of an escapade by an adult.

'I did not wish to embarrass you, Uncle. Why should you suffer for my actions? It was best that I stayed at the Funduq.'

'What nonsense you talk. Does the fact of my conversion mean that I no longer have any blood relations? You need a bath. I will order some fresh clothes for you.'

'And how is my aunt? My cousins?' enquired Zuhayr as they walked towards the hammam.

'They are in Ishbiliya staying in the same house as Kulthum. They will return in a few weeks. Your aunt is getting old and the mountain wind gives her rheumatism. It is much warmer in Ishbiliya.'

After being scrubbed with soap and washed by two young servants, Zuhayr relaxed in the warm bath. He could have been at home. Despite what Hisham had said, there was no doubt but that he was endangering his uncle's future. True, they had not been seen entering the house, but the servants would talk. They would boast to their friends that Zuhayr had dined with his converso uncle. By tomorrow it would reach the market in the shape of highly embellished gossip. Any one of the Archbishop's spies was bound to pick it up.

After their meal, which had been as simple and austere as usual, the conversation turned inevitably to a discussion of the plight in which their faith now found itself.

'Our own fault, my son. Our own fault,' declared Ibn Hisham without the shadow of a doubt. 'We always look for answers in the actions of our enemies, but the fault is within ourselves. Success came too soon. Our Prophet died too soon, before he could consolidate the new order. His successors killed each other like the warring tribesmen that they were. Instead of assimilating the stable characteristics of civilizations which we conquered, we decided instead on imparting to them our own mercurial style. And so it was in al-Andalus. Fine but thoughtless gestures, inconsequential sacrifice of Muslim lives, empty chivalry . . .'

'Pardon the interruption, Uncle, but every word you have spoken could equally be applied to the Christians. Your explanation is insufficient.'

And so the talk went on that night. Hisham could not satisfy his nephew and Zuhayr could not convince his uncle that it was time to take up arms again. It was obvious to Zuhayr that his uncle's conversion was only a surface phenomenon. He spoke and behaved like a Muslim nobleman. Pork did not defile his table. The kitchen and the house were staffed by believers, and if the old servant was telling the truth then Hisham himself turned eastwards every day in secret prayers.

'Do not waste your youth in mindless endeavours, Zuhayr. History has passed us by. Why can you not accept it?'

'I will not lie back and passively accept the outrages they wish to impose on us. They are barbarians and barbarians have to be resisted. Better to die than become slaves of their Church.'

'I have learnt something new in these last few months,' Ibn Hisham confided. 'In this new world which we inhabit there is also a new way of dying. In the old days we killed each other. The enemy killed us and it was over. But I have learnt that total indifference can be just as cruel a death as succumbing to a knight in armour.'

'But you who always had so many friends. . .'

'They have all gone their separate ways. If we went by appearances alone it would seem that individuals can effortlessly survive cataclysms of the sort that we are experiencing, but life is always more complex. Everything changes inside ourselves. I converted for selfish reasons, but it has made me even more estranged. I work amongst them, but, however hard I try, I can never be of them.'

'And I thought that in our entire family, only I understood what loneliness really meant.'

'One must not complain. I have the most patient friends in the world. I talk most often these days to them. The stones in the courtyard.'

The two men rose and Zuhayr embraced his uncle in farewell.

'I'm glad I came to see you, Uncle. I will never forget this meeting.'

'I fear it may have been our last supper.'

Zuhayr lay in his bed and reviewed the events of the day. How brutally the Count had deflated their hopes. The Archbishop had won. Cunning, tenacious Cisneros. The city now belonged to him and he would destroy it from within. Kill the spirit of the Gharnatinos. Make them feel ugly and mediocre. That would be the end of Gharnata. Far better to raze it to the ground, leaving only that which existed at the beginning: a lovely plain, furrowed by streams and clothed in trees. It was the beauty which had attracted his ancestors. And it was here that they had built this city.

His thoughts wandered to the evening spent with his uncle. Zuhayr had been surprised by Hisham's bitterness and abjection, but it had also comforted him a great deal. If his uncle Hisham, a man of great wealth and intelligence, could find no satisfaction in becoming a Christian, then he, Zuhayr, was justified in the course he had chosen. What use was the opulence and splendour if inside yourself you were permanently poverty-stricken and miserable?

That night Zuhayr was disturbed by a dream. He woke up in a sweat, trembling. He had seen the house in al-Hudayl swathed by a tent of white muslin. Yazid, the only one he could recognize, was laughing, but not as Zuhayr remembered him. It was the laugh of an old man. He was surrounded by giant chess pieces which had come to life and were talking in a strange language. Slowly, they moved towards Yazid and began to throttle him. The eerie laughter turned into a rattle.

Zuhayr lay there shivering. Sleep would not return. He stayed in the bed, wide awake, huddled in his quilt, desperately awaiting the first noises which come with the dawn.

'There is only one Allah and it is Allah and Mohammed is his Prophet!'

The same words. The same rhythm. Eight different voices. Eight echoes competing with each other. Eight mosques for the faithful today. And tomorrow? Zuhayr was already dressed. In the giant courtyard below he could already hear the sound of hoofs. His steed was saddled and a stable-boy, not much older than Yazid, was feeding it a lump of raw brown sugar. More hoofs entered the yard. He heard the voices of Ibn Basit and Ibn Amin.

They rode out of the Funduq, through the tiny streets, in the livid light of dawn, just as Gharnata was beginning to come to life. Doors were opening as groups of men made haste to their mosques. As they passed some open doors, Zuhayr could see people busy at their ablutions, trying to wash away the cumulative stench of sleep.

The city was no longer deserted, as it had been when Zuhayr had walked to the Funduq from his uncle's establishment late last night but it was immersed in despair. Ibn Basit could not recall a time when so many people had hurried to attend morning prayers.

Before the Reconquest it was the Friday afternoon prayers which had attracted the largest crowd – a social and political as well as a religious occasion. More often than not, the Imam would discuss political and military matters, leaving religion for those weeks when nothing else was happening. The mood was usually relaxed, in sharp contrast to the subdued silences of the people today.

'Zuhayr al-Fahl,' said Ibn Amin in an excited voice. 'Ibn Basit and I have two gifts to deliver at the al-Hamra. Would you care to ride there with us? The others are waiting outside the city. The Forty have become the Three Hundred!'

'What gifts?' asked Zuhayr, who had noticed the exquisite wooden boxes sealed with silken ribbons. 'The stench of perfume is overpowering.'

'One box is for Ximenes,' repled Ibn Basit, trying very hard to keep a serious face, 'and the other is for the Count. It is a farewell present which these grandees will never forget.'

Zuhayr regarded the gesture as unnecessary. It was taking chivalry to an absurd degree, but he agreed to accompany them. Within a few minutes they were at the gates of the palace.

'Stop where you are!' Two young soldiers drew their swords and rushed towards them. 'What is your business?'

'My name is Ibn Amin. Yesterday the Captain-General visited us in the city and invited us to have breakfast with him this morning. He made some requests and wanted our reply by this morning. We have brought a gift for him and for His Grace the Archbishop of Toledo. Unfortunately we cannot stay. Will you please convey our apologies and make sure that these gifts, a small token of our esteem, are delivered to the two gentlemen, the minute they have arisen.'

The soldiers relaxed and accepted the gifts in good humour. The young men turned their horses and galloped away to join their fellow fighters, where they had gathered just outside the city. Soldiers at the gate watched with grim faces as they passed through.

Three hundred armed men on horseback, most of them not yet twenty, cannot be expected to remain silent on the edge of change. There were screams, whisperings and excited laughter. The mountain air was chilly and both men and horses were swathed in steam. Anxious mothers, huddled in their shawls, were saying their farewells beneath the walls. Zuhayr frowned at the din, but his mood changed as he neared his troops. They were a magnificent sight, a sign that the Moors of Gharnata had not abandoned hope. As the three friends rode up to the assembled company, they were greeted by excited cries and a warm welcome. All were aware of the dangers that faced them, but despite that knowledge, spirits were high.

'Did you deliver the presents?' asked Ibn Wahab as they were leaving the city behind.

Ibn Amin nodded and laughed.

'In the name of Allah,' asked Zuhayr, 'what is the joke?'

'You really want to know?' teased Ibn Basit. 'Ibn Amin, you tell him.'

The son of the Count's personal physician laughed so much at this suggestion that Zuhayr thought he would choke.

'The stench of perfume! Your nose detected our crime,' began Ibn Amin after he had calmed down. 'In both those boxes, disguised by the attar of roses, is a rare delicacy for the consumption of the Archbishop and the Count. It has edible silver paper transferred on to its surface. What we have left them, Zuhayr al-Fahl, is a piece of our excrement. One, freshly delivered this morning from the bowels of this Jew you see before you, and the other, a somewhat staler offering, from the insides of a devout Moor, known to you as Ibn Basit. This fact, without mentioning our actual names, of course is made clear in a note addressed to both of them, in which we also express the hope that they will enjoy their breakfast.'

It was too childish for words. Zuhayr tried his best not to laugh, but found it increasingly difficult to contain himself. He began to guffaw uncontrollably. It did not take long for word of the prank to spread to the entire group. Within a few minutes the gallant three hundred were engulfed by a wave of laughter.

'And to think as I did,' said Zuhayr, as he tried to calm himself down, 'that you were being far too sentimental and chivalrous.' This made his friends laugh again.

They rode on for a few hours. The sun had risen. There was no wind at all. Capes and blankets were discarded and handed to the hundred or so servants who were attending their masters. It was after they had been riding for over two hours that they observed a small group of horsemen riding towards them.

'Allahu Akbar! God is Great!' shouted Zuhayr, and the chant was repeated by the young men of Gharnata.

There was no reply from the horsemen. Zuhayr ordered his troop to halt, fearing an ambush. It was when the horsemen drew close that Zuhayr recognized them. His spirits rose considerably.

'Abu Zaid al-Ma'ari!' he shouted with pleasure. 'Peace be upon you! You see I followed your advice after all and brought some other friends along.'

'I am happy to see you, Zuhayr bin Umar. I knew you were headed this way. You had better follow us and get away from this particular track. It is too well known, and by this time there will already be soldiers on your tail, trying to determine where you will camp for the night.'

Zuhayr told him about the gifts they had left behind for the Count and the Archbishop. To his surprise Abu Zaid did not laugh.

'You have done something very stupid, my friends. The kitchen in the al-Hamra is probably enjoying your joke, but they are the least powerful people in the palace. You have united the Count and the Confessor. A gift to the priest would have been sufficient. It might even have amused the Count and delayed the offensive. Did you really think that you were the first to have thought of such an insult? Others like you, all over al-Andalus, have executed similar pieces of folly. It is getting late. Let us get out of this district as soon as possible.'

Zuhayr smiled to himself. He was a courageous young man, but not completely bereft of intelligence. He knew that his capacities did not extend to leading an irregular mountain army. Abu Zaid's presence had relieved his burden considerably.

As they rode the day was in full progress and the sun, unfiltered by even a single cloud, was warming the earth, whose scented dust they inhaled as they climbed the mountain. Ahead of them there lay an irredeemable landscape.

Later that afternoon, al-Zindiq delivered Zuhayr's letter to Umar and described the events of the last two days. He was heard in silence. Even Yazid did not ask questions. When the old man had finished, Ama was weeping loudly.

'It is the end,' she wailed. 'Everything is over.'

'But Ama,' replied Yazid, 'Zuhayr is alive and well. They have begun a *jihad*. That should make you happy, not sad. Why do you cry like this?'

'Please do not ask me, Ibn Umar. Do not torment an old woman.'

Zubayda signalled to Yazid that he should follow her and Umar out of the room. When Ama saw that she was left alone with al-Zindiq she wiped her tears and began to question him about the details of Zuhayr's appearance that morning.

'Was he wearing a rich blue turban with a crescent made of gold?'

Al-Zindiq nodded.

'That is how I saw him in my dream last night.'

Al-Zindiq's tone was very soft. 'Dreams tell us more about ourselves, Amira.'

'You do not understand me, you old fool,' Ama retorted angrily. 'In my dream Zuhayr's head wore that turban, but the head was lying on the ground, covered in blood. There was no body.'

Al-Zindiq thought she was about to cry again, but instead her face turned grey and her breathing grew loud and irregular. He gave her some water and helped her back to her room, a tiny chamber where she had spent most of her nights for over half a century. She lay down and al-Zindiq covered her with a blanket. He thought of their past, of words left half-spoken, self-deceptions, the pain he had caused her by falling in love with Zahra. He felt that he had been the ruin of Ama's life.

Instinctively, the old woman read his thoughts.

'I don't regret for a single moment the life that I have lived here.'

He smiled sadly. 'Somewhere else you could have been your own mistress, beholden to no one but yourself.'

She stared up at him with a plea in her eyes.

'I have wasted my life, Amira,' he said. 'This house has cursed me forever. I wish I had never set foot in its courtyard. That is the truth.'

Suddenly she saw him at eighteen, with thick black hair and his eyes full of laughter. The memory was enough.

'Go now,' she told him, 'and let me die in peace.'

For al-Zindiq the very thought of dying quietly, passing on without a last scream of outrage, was unthinkable and he told her so.

'It is the only way I know,' she replied as she clutched her beads. 'Trust in Allah.'

Ama did not die that day or the next. She lingered for a week, making her farewells at her own pace. She kissed Umar's hand and dried Yazid's tears, told Zubayda of her fears for the family and pleaded with her to take the children away. She remained calm except when she asked Umar to remember her to Zuhayr.

'Who will make him his heavenly mixtures when I am gone?' she wept.

Ama died in her sleep three days after Zuhayr's flight from Gharnata. She was buried near Zahra in the family graveyard. Yazid grieved for her in secret. He felt that as he was approaching manhood he should be brave, and not display his emotions in public.

Chapter 12

EVERY MORNING AFTER breakfast, Yazid would take his books and retire to the tower.

'Stay here and read with me,' Zubayda would plead, but he would give her a sad little smile.

'I like reading on my own. It is so peaceful in the tower.'

She never insisted, and so what had started as an assertion of the independence associated with approaching manhood had become a regular routine. It had begun two months ago when they had first heard the news of the events in Gharnata and the flight of three hundred young men with Zuhayr at their head.

Yazid had felt so proud of his brother. His friends in the village had been full of envy and he could not fully understand the sadness which had descended on the house. Even Ama, who had died so peacefully in her sleep, had expressed her misgivings.

'Nothing good will come out of this adventure, Ibn Umar,' she had said to Yazid, who could not have known then that these were virtually the old woman's last words.

It was her caution which had made Yazid rethink the whole affair. It was Ama who, in the past, had defended every daring deed, however foolhardy, carried out by any male member of the family. She had filled his head with seamless stories of chivalry and courage which naturally featured his great-grandfather, Ibn Farid, in a prominent role. If Ama was worried about Zuhayr, then the prospect must be really grim.

From his tower, Yazid saw a horseman riding towards the house. Every day when he went up there he would hope and hope and pray that he would see such a sight and that it would be his brother. The rider was at the gates of the house. His heart sank. It wasn't Zuhayr. It was never Zuhayr.

Yazid had never known the house so empty. It was not just Zuhayr's absence or Ama's death. These were heavy losses, but Zuhayr would return one day and, as for Ama, he would see her, as she had promised him so often, in Paradise. They would meet in the seventh heaven, by the banks of the stream which flowed with the tastiest milk imaginable. He missed Ama more than he would admit, but at least her place had been taken by al-Zindiq, who knew much more about the movement of the stars and the moon. Once when he had told al-Zindiq about his projected reunion with Ama, the old man had chuckled and said something really strange.

'So, Amira thought she would go straight to the seventh heaven, did she? I am not so sure, Yazid bin Umar. She was not without sins you know. I think she might have problems getting past the first heaven and, who knows, they might even decide to send her in the other direction.'

No, it was Hind's marriage and departure which, while not a surprise, had nonetheless come as a devastating blow. He was closer to Hind than to anyone else in his whole family. But she had gone. True, she had begged her parents to let Yazid go across the water with her for a short time, swearing to bring him back herself after a few months, but Zubayda would not be parted from her son.

'He is all we now have left in this house. I will not let my most precious jewel be stolen from me. Not even by you, Hind!'

And so Hind had left without her brother. It was this, much more than the leaving of her ancestral home, that had made her weep like a child on the day of departure, and again a day later when she and Ibn Daud had boarded the vessel in Malaka for the port of Tanja.

Someone was running up the steps to the tower. Yazid abandoned his thoughts and began his descent to the house. Halfway down he encountered his mother's maid-servant, Umayma, her face flushed with excitement.

'Yazid bin Umar! There is a messenger here from your brother. He is with the Lady Zubayda and your father, but he will not speak until you are present.'

Yazid brushed past her and flew down the stairwell. When he reached the ground he ran through the outer courtyard like a whirlwind as Umayma, cursing under her breath, discovered that she could not keep up with him. She was no longer the slim gazelle who could outpace even al-Fahl. She had become round-wombed over the last few months.

Yazid appeared breathless in the reception room.

'This is Yazid,' said Umar, his face wreathed in smiles.

'Your brother sends you hundreds of kisses,' said Ibn Basit.

'Where is he? Is he well? When will I see him?'

'You will see him before long. He will come one evening, when it is already dark, and leave the next morning before it is light. There is a reward for his head.'

Umar's face became transformed with anger.

'What? Why?'

'Have you not heard?'

'Heard what, boy?'

'The events of last week. Surely you have heard? It is the talk of Gharnata. Zuhayr thought that his uncle Hisham would have sent a messenger.'

Umar was getting more and more impatient. He was twirling the edge of his beard and Zubayda, who knew this was a signal that an explosion was on the way, tried to pre-empt his wrath.

'We do not know any of this, Ibn Basit. So please enlighten us quickly. As you can see we are starved for news of Zuhayr.'

'It all happened some nine days ago. Abu Zaid al-Ma'ari was leading us to a hideout in the mountains when we sighted the Christians. They had seen us too and a clash was unavoidable. There were just over three hundred of us, but from the dust raised by their horses we knew they were double our size if not more.

'An unarmed messenger rode over to us from them. "Our leader," he began, "the noble Don Alonso de Aguilar, sends you his compliments. If you surrender you will be treated well, but if you resist then he will return to Gharnata bringing only your horses." We were trapped. For once even Abu Zaid had no clever scheme to see us through. It was then that Zuhayr ibn Umar rode out in front of us. He spoke in a voice that could be heard for miles. "Tell your master that we are not a people without a history," he roared. "We are Moorish knights defending what once belonged to us. Tell him that I, Zuhayr ibn Umar, great-grandson of the knight Ibn Farid, will fight Don Alonso in a duel to the death. Whosoever wins today will determine the fate of the others." '

'Who is Don Alonso?' interrupted Yazid, his face tense with fear.

'The most experienced and accomplished of the knights in the service of Don Inigo,' replied Ibn Basit. 'Feared by his enemies and by his friends. A man with a terrible temper and a scar across his forehead, imprinted by a Moorish defender at al-Hama. They say that he alone killed a hundred men in that ill-fated city. May Allah curse him!'

'Please go on,' begged Zubayda, trying to keep her voice calm.

'To our great surprise, Don Alonso accepted the challenge. The Christian soldiers began to gather on one side of the meadow. Two hundred of us went and occupied the other side.'

'Where were the others?' asked Yazid, unable to suppress his emotions.

'You see, Abu Zaid had decided that whether we won or lost an element of surprise was necessary. He took a hundred men and placed them at different points of the mountain, overlooking the meadow. The plan was that immediately the combat was over we would charge down on the Christians before they had time to prepare for battle.'

'But that is against the rules,' Umar protested.

'True, but we were not playing a game of chess. Now, if I may continue. Zuhayr carried an old, beautifully embroidered standard which had been given him by an old lady in Gharnata who swore that Ibn Farid had carried it in many battles. On his green turban there was a shining silver crescent. He planted the standard in front of his men. At a distance we saw a golden cross put into the earth by Don Alonso. At the agreed signal, Don Alonso charged, his lance glinting in the sun and pointing straight at Zuhayr's heart. Both of them had disdained the use of shields.

'Zuhayr unsheathed his sword and rode like a madman. His face was distorted with an anger I had never seen before. As he neared Don Alonso the entire company heard his voice. "There is only one God and Mohammed is his Prophet." They were close to each other now. Zuhayr avoided the lance by almost slipping off his steed. What a display of horsemanship that was. Then we saw Ibn Farid's sword flash like lightning. For a minute it seemed as if both had survived. It was only when Don Alonso's horse came closer that we saw that its rider had lost his head. They don't make swords like that in Tulaytula any more!

'An almighty cheer went up on our side. The Christians were

demoralized and preparing to retreat when Abu Zaid charged down towards them. They suffered heavy losses before they managed to escape. We took fifty prisoners, but, on Zuhayr's insistence, they were given Don Alonso's body and his head to take back with them to Gharnata. "Tell the Count," Zuhayr told them, "that this war was not of our doing. He has lost a brave knight because the Captain-General is nothing more than a mercenary in the service of a cruel and cowardly priest!" '

Yazid had been entranced by the tale. He was so filled with pride on behalf of his brother that he did not notice the concern on the faces of both his parents. It was al-Zindiq, equally worried by the consequences of Zuhayr's victory, who questioned Ibn Basit further.

'Did Abu Zaid say anything about the reaction of the al-Hamra?'

'Why yes,' said Ibn Basit, looking at the old man in surprise. 'He said a great deal two days later.'

'What was it?' asked Zubayda.

'The Count was so enraged that he has offered a thousand pieces of gold for the head of Zuhayr bin Umar. He is also preparing a force to crush us forever, but Abu Zaid is not worried. He has a plan. He says that where he is taking us not even the Almighty would be able to find Zuhayr.'

'There speaks the voice of Satan,' said Umar.

'Go and bathe, Ibn Basit,' said Zubayda, looking at the dust on the young man's face and the state of his clothes. 'I think Zuhayr's clothes will fit you. Then join us for the midday meal. Your room is prepared and you can stay as long as you wish.'

'Thank you, Lady, I will gladly bathe and eat at your table. Alas, I cannot permit myself the luxury of a rest. I have messages to deliver in Guejar, and by sunset I must be in Lanjaron, where my father awaits me. Why do you all look so uneasy? Zuhayr is alive and well. For myself I am convinced that we can recapture Gharnata within six months.'

'What?' shouted Umar.

Al-Zindiq did not permit the discussion to continue any further. 'The tongue of the wise, my dear Ibn Basit,' he muttered, 'is in his heart. The heart of the fool is in his mouth. The attendants are awaiting your pleasure in the hammam, young man.'

Yazid escorted their guest to the hammam. 'Enjoy your bath, Ibn Basit,' he said as he pointed Zuhayr's friend towards the baths and hurried to the kitchen where the Dwarf, Umayma and all the other house servants were gathered. For their benefit he repeated, word by word, the story of Zuhayr's duel and the decapitation of Don Alonso.

'Allah be thanked,' said Umayma. 'Our young master is alive.'

Looks were exchanged, but nothing was said in Yazid's presence. The excitement on the face of the story-teller had captivated even the most cynical members of the kitchen staff. The Dwarf alone appeared unmoved. It was only after Yazid's departure that the cook gave expression to his feelings.

'The Banu Hudayl are courting death and the end will not be long delayed. Ximenes will not let them live in peace.'

'But surely our village will be safe?' interjected Umayma. 'We have not harmed anyone here.'

The Dwarf shrugged his shoulders.

'That I do not know,' he said, 'but if I were you, Umayma, I would go and serve the Lady Kulthum in Ishbiliya. It is best that your child is not born in al-Hudayl.'

The young woman's face changed colour.

'The whole village knows you are carrying Zuhayr's foal.'

A crude cacophony of laughter greeted the remark. It was all too much for Umayma. She ran out of the kitchen in tears. Yet she could not help thinking that the Dwarf might be right after all. She would ask Lady Zubayda tonight for permission to wait on Kulthum in Ishbiliya.

Yazid was lost in his own world. He was in the pomegranate glade, pretending to be a Moorish knight. His sword was a stick, whose end he had sharpened with his knife – the knife Zuhayr had given him on his tenth birthday and which he proudly wore in his belt whenever there were visitors. He was galloping up and down in a frenzied fashion, waving his make-believe sword and decapitating every pomegranate within reach. Soon he had tired of the fantasy and sitting down on the grass, he split open one of the vanquished fruits and began to drink its juice, spitting out the chewed seeds after every mouthful.

'You know something, Hind? I think Zuhayr will die. Abu and Ummi think the same. I could tell from the way they looked when Ibn Basit was telling them about the duel. I wish Ummi had let me go with you. I've never been on a boat. Never crossed the sea. Never seen Fes. They say it's just like Gharnata.'

Yazid stopped suddenly. He thought he had heard footsteps and the rustling of the gorse which surrounded the glade. Ever since he had been surprised by Umayma and the other servants that day he had become much more cautious and always on the look-out for intruders. He wished he had never seen Ibn Daud and Hind kissing each other. If he had not told his mother, she would not have spoken to Hind and, who knows, perhaps the wedding might have been delayed. Hind might still have been here. What a strange wedding it had been. No feasts. No celebrations. No display of fireworks. Just the *qadi* from the village and the family. He giggled at the memory of how he had almost dropped the al-koran on Ibn Daud's head, bringing a smile even to the face of the *qadi*. The Dwarf had excelled himself that day. The sweetmeats, in particular, tasted as if they had been cooked in paradise.

Three days later Hind had gone. It had been a time of sadness, but Hind had spent more time with him than with Ibn Daud. They had gone for long walks. Hind had shown him her favourite haunts in the mountain and by the river and she had, as always, talked to him seriously.

'I wish you could come with me for a while. I really do,' she had told him the day before she left. 'I'm not leaving you, just this house. I could not bear the thought of living here with Ibn Daud. We must live where he feels comfortable and in control of the surroundings. This is Abu's house, and after him it will belong to Zuhayr and you and your children. You do understand me, don't you Yazid? I love you more than before and I will always think of you. Perhaps next year when we come to visit we can take you away for a month or two.'

Yazid had not been able to say very much in response. He had simply clutched her hand tight as they walked back to the house. Yazid did not wish to think about it any more, and was quite relieved at the interruption.

'Ah! It is the young master himself. And pray what are you doing here on your own?'

The familiar, hateful voice belonged to his father's chief steward Ubaydallah, who, like his father before him, kept a record of every single transaction enacted on the estate. He had a much better idea of the exact amount of land which Umar owned, or how much rent had accrued in which village, or the exact amount of money from the sale of dried fruits last year, or how much wheat and rice was stored in underground granaries and their specific locations.

Yazid did not like Ubaydallah. The man's blatant insincerity and his exaggerated show of unfelt affection had never deceived the boy.

'I was taking a walk,' replied Yazid in a cold voice as he rose and assumed the most adult posture he could manage. 'And now I am returning to the house for my midday meal. And you, Ubaydallah? What brings you to the house at this time?'

'I think the answer to that question had better be given directly to the master. May I walk back with you?'

'You may,' replied Yazid as he put both his hands behind his back and strode back towards the house. He had heard Ama say a hundred thousand times that Ubaydallah was a rogue and a thief, that he had stolen land, food and money from the estate for decades and that his son had opened three shops on the proceeds – two in Qurtuba and one in Gharnata. He had decided not to speak to the man for the rest of the journey, but he changed his mind.

'Tell me something, Ubaydallah.' Yazid spoke in the unique and infinitely superior tone of a landowner. 'How are your son's shops doing? I am told that one can buy any and every luxury in them.'

The question took the old steward by surprise. The insolent young pup, he thought to himself. He must have picked something up from the cartloads of kitchen gossip. Umar bin Abdallah would never stoop to discuss such matters at his table. Aloud he was unctuous to the point of absurdity.

'How nice of you to think of my boy, young master. He is doing well, thanks be to Allah and, of course, to your family. It was your father who paid for his education and insisted that he find work in the city. It is a debt which can never be repaid. I am told that you are a ferocious reader of books, young master. Everyone in the village talks about it. I told them: "You just wait. Yazid bin Umar will soon begin to write books of learning." '

Without looking at the man, Yazid smiled in acknowledgement of the remark. The flattery made no impact on him at all.

This was not just because Yazid did not trust Ubaydallah. In this respect the boy was very much like his father and mother. Words of praise slipped off him like water off leaves in the fountain. It was a sense of inherited pride. A feeling that the Banu Hudayl was so naturally advantaged that they did not need anybody else's favours. For Yazid, like his father and grandfather before him, an offering of wheat-cakes sweetened with the syrup of dates from a poor peasant meant much more than the silk shawls showered on the ladies of the house by Ubaydallah and his son. It was what the gift meant to the giver that determined their attitude.

Ubaydallah was babbling on, but the boy had stopped listening. He did not believe any of this nonsense, but the very fact that he had forced Ubaydallah to speak to him as he would have addressed Zuhayr was, he felt, something of a triumph. As they walked through the main gate, known in the village after its builder as Bab al-Farid, Ubaydallah lowered his head in a half-bow. Yazid acknowledged the gesture with an imperceptible nod of his head as they went their separate ways. The elderly man hurried to the kitchen. The boy maintained his posture and did not relax till he had entered the house.

'Where have you been?' whispered Umayma outside the dining-room. 'Everyone else has finished.'

Yazid ignored her and rushed into the room. The first thing he noticed was Ibn Basit's absence. This depressed him. His face fell. A distant look appeared on his face as he fingered the medallion Hind had left him as a token of her love. Inside it, black like the night, was a lock of her hair.

'Has he gone, Abu?'

His father nodded as he picked at a dark red grape from the silver tray bedecked with fruit. Zubayda served Yazid some cucumbers cooked in their own water with a dash of clarified butter, black pepper and red chilli seeds. He ate it quickly and then consumed a salad consisting of radishes, onions and tomatoes, soaked in yoghurt and the juice of fresh limes.

'Did Ibn Basit say anything else? Did he give you any idea when Zuhayr would visit us?'

Zubayda shook her head.

'He did not know the exact day, but he thought it would be

soon. Now will you please have some fruit, Yazid. It will bring the colour back to your cheeks.'

As four servants entered to clear the table, the most senior amongst them knelt on the floor and muttered a few words close to his master's ear. A look of disdain appeared on Umar's face. 'What does he want at this time? Show him to my study and stay there with him till I arrive.'

'Ubaydallah?' asked Zubayda.

Umar nodded as his face clouded. Yazid grinned and described his encounter with the steward.

'Is it true, Abu, that he now owns almost as much land as you?'

The question made Umar laugh.

'I don't think so, but I'm the wrong person to ask. I'd better go and see what the rogue wants. It isn't like him to disturb me just as we are about to rest.'

After Umar had left them, Zubayda and Yazid walked up and down the inner courtyard holding hands and enjoying the winter sun. She saw the look in Yazid's eyes when they passed the pomegranate tree, under which Ama had spent many a winter day.

'Do you miss her a lot, my child?'

In reply he tightened his grip on her hand. She bent down and kissed his cheeks and then his eyes.

'Everyone must die one day, Yazid. One day you will see her again.'

'Please, Ummi. Please not that. Hind never believed in all that stuff about life in heaven. Nor does al-Zindiq and nor do I.'

Zubayda suppressed a smile. She did not either, but Umar had forbidden her the right to transmit any of her blasphemous thoughts to the children. Well, she thought, Umar has Zuhayr and Kulthum to believe with him, and I have Hind and my Yazid.

'Ummi,' he was pleading, 'why don't we all go and live in Fes? I don't mean in the same house as Hind and Ibn Daud, but in our own house.'

'I would not exchange this house, the streams and rivers which water your lands, the village and those who live in it, for any city in the world. Not Qurtuba, not Gharnata and not even Fes, even though I miss Hind as much as you. She was my friend,

too, Yazid. But no. Not for anything would I change all this . . .
Peace be upon you, al-Zindiq!'

'And you, my lady. And you, Yazid bin Umar.'

Yazid began to walk away.

'Where are you . . . ?' began Zubayda.

'To the tower. I will rest there and read my books.'

Al-Zindiq looked with affection at the boy's disappearing
back. 'This child has an intellect which puts many old people to
shame, but something has changed, my lady, has it not? What
is it? Yazid bin Umar looks as if he is in permanent mourning.
Is it Amira?'

Zubayda agreed with him. 'I have a feeling that this child
knows everything. As you so rightly said, he knows more than
many who are older and wiser. As to his ailment, I think I know
the cause. No, it is not his Ama's death, though that upset him
more than he revealed. It is Hind. Ever since she left the shine
has gone from the pupils of his eyes. My heart weeps when I see
them so sad and dim.'

'Children are far more resilient than we are, my lady.'

'Not this one,' continued Zubayda. 'He is having great diffi-
culty in managing his pain. He thinks it is unmanly to show
emotions. Hind was his only confidante. Fears, joys, secrets. He
told her everything.'

Umar's return deprived her of the old man's advice.

'Peace be upon you al-Zindiq.' As the old man smiled, Umar
spoke to his wife in a light-hearted vein. 'You will never guess
why Ubaydallah came to see me.'

'It wasn't money?'

'Would I be right in thinking,' suggested al-Zindiq, 'that our
venerable chief steward is being troubled by his conscience on
matters of the spirit?'

'Well spoken, old man. Well spoken. Yes, that is exactly his
problem. He has decided to convert, and wanted my permission
and my blessings. "Ubaydallah," I warned him. "Do you realize
that you will have to confess all your misdemeanours to a monk
before they admit you to their Church? All of them, Ubaydallah!
And if they find out that you've been lying, they'll burn you at
the stake for being a false Christian." I could see that this worried
him. He made a quick mental calculation as to how many of his
petty crimes the Church could uncover and decided that he was

safe. Next week he visits Gharnata, and he and that imbecilic son of his will go through that pagan ritual and become Christians. Blood of their blood. Flesh of their flesh. Seeking salvation by praying to the image of a bleeding man on two pieces of wood. Tell me something, al-Zindiq. Why is their faith so deeply marked by human sacrifice?'

A full-scale discussion on the philosophy of the Christian religion was about to begin, but before the old man could reply a scream rent the air. Yazid, out of breath and his face red from the exertion, had come running into the courtyard.

'Soldiers! Hundreds of them. Like a ring round the village and our house. Come and look.'

Umar and Zubayda followed the boy back to the tower. Al-Zindiq, too old now to climb the stairs, sat down with a sigh on the bench underneath the pomegranate tree.

'Our future was our past,' he muttered in his beard.

Yazid had not been deceived. They were surrounded. Trapped like a hunted deer. As Umar strained his eyes, he could make out the Christian standards as well as the soldiers who carried them. A man on horseback was riding excitedly from one group of soldiers to another, obviously giving out instructions. He seemed very young, but he must be the captain.

'I must go to the village immediately,' said Umar. 'We will ride out to meet these men and ask them what they want of us.'

'I'll come with you,' said Yazid.

'You must stay at home, my son. There is no one else to guard your mother.'

As Umar came down from the tower he found all the male servants of the house gathered in the outer courtyard, armed with swords and lances. There were only sixty of them, and they were of varying ages which stretched from fifteen to sixty-five, but as they stood there waiting for him he felt a surge of emotion sweep through his body. They were his servants and he was their master, but at times of crisis their loyalty to him transcended everything else.

His horse had been saddled and four of the younger men rode out to the village with him. As they rode through the main gate, an eagle flew over the house in search of prey. The servants exchanged looks. It was a bad omen.

At a distance they could hear a chorus of dogs barking. They, too, felt that something was wrong. For a start nobody was at work. The men and women who toiled in the fields every day from dawn till sunset had run away on seeing the soldiers. The tiny streets of the village were filled with people, but the shops were shut. The last time Umar had witnessed such a scene was the day his father had died after being thrown by a horse. That day, too, all activity had ceased. They had followed the body in silence as it was carried to the house.

Greetings were being exchanged, but the faces were drawn and tense. It was the fear which is born out of uncertainty. Juan the carpenter was running towards them.

'It is a cursed day, Master,' he said in a voice breaking with anger. 'A cursed day. The Prince of Darkness has sent his devils to harass and destroy us.'

Umar jumped off his horse and embraced Juan.

'Why do you speak in this fashion, my friend?'

'I have just returned from their camp. They knew I was a Christian and sent for me. They asked me all sorts of questions. Did I know Zuhayr al-Fahl? Did I know how many men from the village were fighting by his side in the al-Pujarras? Did I know that they had killed the noble Don Alonso when his back was turned to them? To the last question I replied that the version I had heard was a different one. Upon which their young captain, whose eyes burn with an evil flame, came and slapped my face. "Are you a Christian?" I replied that my family had never converted and that we had lived in al-Hudayl from the day it was built, but that nobody had ever suggested to us that we should embrace the faith of the Prophet Mohammed. We had lived in peace. Then he said to me: "Would you rather stay with them or come and live with us? We even have a chapel set up in that tent, and there is a priest to hear your confession." I said that I would happily confess to the monk, but that I wished to stay in the house where I had been born and my father and grandfather before me. At this he laughed. It was a strange laugh and straight away it was imitated by the two young men at his side. "Do not bother with your confession. Get you back to your infidels." '

'If they wish to question anyone about Zuhayr they must deal with me,' said Umar. 'I will go and see them.'

'No!' barked another voice. 'That you must not do under any circumstances. I was on my way to the house to talk to you.'

It was Ibn Hasd, the cobbler, who as Miguel's natural brother was Umar's uncle, but this was the first time he had ever spoken in the capacity of a family member. Umar raised his eyebrows as if to question the reasoning behind such a peremptory instruction.

'Peace be upon you, Umar bin Abdallah. But the blacksmith Ibn Haritha has just returned. They dragged him off this morning to attend to the horseshoes which needed repair. He did not hear anything specific, but the eyes of the young captain frightened him. He says that even the Christian soldiers fear him as though he were Satan himself.'

'And,' continued Juan, 'that wretch Ubaydallah has taken fifteen villagers with him to their camp. One can only imagine the stories he will tell to save his own neck. You must return to the house, Master, and seal the gate, till this is over.'

'I will stay in the village,' replied Umar in a tone that brooked no dissent. 'We shall wait for Ubaydallah to return and tell us what they demand. Then, if necessary, I shall go and talk to this captain myself.'

Chapter 13

THE RED-HEADED beardless captain had not dismounted. Why is he still on his horse? This question was nagging Ubaydallah. His work over the last fifty years, as a manager of estates and human beings, had equipped him with an all too rare experience and knowledge which books alone can never provide. He had become an acute observer of human psychology. He had noticed that the captain had been cursed by his maker. His height, not an unimportant matter for a soldier, was not at all in keeping with his fierce disposition. He was stout and short. He could not be more than sixteen years of age. The facts, Ubaydallah was sure, could not be compensated for even by the officer's military skills.

Once he had surmised this, Ubaydallah fell on his knees before the commander of the Christians. This act of self-abasement nauseated the villagers who had accompanied him. 'Pig's pizzle,' one of them muttered under his breath. Ubaydallah was unworried by their reaction. He had made the captain feel tall. Nothing else mattered on that day. Years of service to the lords of the Banu Hudayl had prepared the steward well for the task he now sought to accomplish.

'What is it you want?' the captain asked him in a nasal voice.

'My lord, we have come to inform you that the whole village is prepared to convert this very afternoon. All it requires is for Your Excellency to send us a priest and to honour the village by your presence.'

At first the request was greeted by silence. The captain gave no sign of life. He looked down through heavy-lidded, dark blue eyes at the creature kneeling before him. The captain had just turned sixteen, but he was already a veteran of the Reconquest. He had been commended for his courage during three battles in the al-Pujarras. His fearless savagery had brought him to the notice of his superiors.

'Why?' he snapped at Ubaydallah.

'I do not understand, Excellency.'

'Why have you decided to join the Holy Roman Church?'

'It is the only true path to salvation,' replied Ubaydallah, who was never renowned for discriminating between truth and falsehood.

'You mean it is the only way to save your skins.'

'No, no, Excellency,' the old steward began to whine. 'We Andalusians take a long time to decide anything. It is the result of being governed for hundreds of years by rulers who determined everything. On everything that mattered, they made our decisions for us. Now we are slowly beginning to make up our own minds, but it is not easy to discard an old habit. We are deciding for ourselves, but we take our time and we split hairs . . .'

'How many of you are there in the village?'

'At the last count we were just over two thousand.'

'Very well. I shall think of the most appropriate response to your proposal. You may return to your village and await our decision.'

Just as Ubaydallah was about to rise, the captain hurled another question at him and the steward went back on his knees.

'Is it true that an old standard depicting a blue key on a silver ground above some gibberish in your language still hangs in the palace of Abenfarid?'

'It does, Excellency. It was a gift from the King of Ishbiliya to one of the great ancestors of Ibn Farid. The inscription in Arabic reads: "There is no other Conqueror but God." '

'The key symbolized the opening of the West, did it not?'

'Of that I am not sure, Your Excellency.'

'Are you not? Well, I am,' said the captain in his most aloof and arrogant tone, indicating that he did not wish this conversation to meander any longer. 'The Archbishop wishes to inspect it with his own eyes. You may inform the family of Abenfarid that I will call on them to collect the banner. You may go now.'

After Ubaydallah and the others had left, the captain, still on his horse, rode over to the two officers who had been listening from a distance and instructed them to round up all the soldiers. He wished to address them before they went into the village.

226

When the men had gathered, the captain began to address them. His tone was friendly but authoritative.

'Our objective is simple. You will erase this village and everything that it contains. Those are my instructions. There are no more than six or perhaps seven hundred able-bodied men in the village. They are unlikely to put up even a token resistance. It is not a pleasant task, but soldiers are not trained to be kind and gentle. His Grace's orders were very clear. Tomorrow morning he wishes to instruct the cartographers to obliterate al-Hudayl from the new maps which they are preparing. Is that clear?'

'No!' cried a voice from the middle of the throng.

'Come forward, man.'

A tall, grey-bearded soldier in his early fifties, whose father had fought behind the banner of Ibn Farid, strode to the front and stood facing the captain.

'What is it that you want?'

'I am the grandson of a monk and the son of a soldier. Since when has it become a Christian practice in these lands to kill children and their mothers? I tell you here and now that this arm and this sword will not kill any child or woman. Do with me as you will!'

'It is obvious, soldier, that you were not with us in the al-Pujarras.'

'I was at Alhama Captain, and I saw too much. I will not go through that again.'

'Then you would have seen their women pour pots of boiling oil on our men. You will carry out your orders or suffer the consequences.'

The soldier became obstinate.

'You have said yourself, Captain, that you do not expect any resistance. Why ask us to kill innocent people? Why?'

'Old fool!' replied the captain, his eyes flashing with anger. 'You are not long for this world. Why be generous with our lives?'

'I do not comprehend you, Captain.'

'If you kill their men, the women and children will become filled with a blind hate of everything Christian. To save their lives they will convert, but it will be a poison. Do you hear me? A poison, permanently embedded in our skins. A poison which will become increasingly difficult to remove. Now do you understand?'

The old soldier shook his head in disbelief, but it was clear that he would not obey. The captain curbed his natural instincts. He did not wish to demoralize his soldiers just before they went into battle. He decided not to punish the mutineer.

'You are spared your duties. You will return to Gharnata and await our return.'

The old soldier could not believe his luck. He walked to where the horses were grazing and untied his mount.

'I will return,' he said to himself as he rode away from the encampment, 'but not to Gharnata. I will go where neither you nor your cursed monks can ever find me.'

The gates which breached the wall surrounding the house were the only point of entry to the ancestral home of the Banu Hudayl. They had been firmly sealed. Constructed of solid wood, four inches thick and reinforced with strips of iron, their function had been largely ceremonial. They were not built to withstand a siege. They had never been shut before, since neither the village nor the house was considered to be of any military significance. Ibn Farid and his ancestors had gathered knights and soldiers under their command from this and surrounding villages. They had assembled outside the gates and marched off to wars in other parts of the kingdom.

When Ubaydallah had conveyed the young captain's message, Umar had smiled grimly and understood. This was not the time for the flamboyant gestures which had caused the death of so many members of his own family. He had ordered that the banner of the silver key on a sea of blue be removed from the wall in the armoury and hung over the gates.

'If that is all they want,' he told his steward, 'let us make it easy for them.'

Several hundred villagers had sought refuge behind the walls of the house. They were being fed in the gardens, while the outer courtyard was filled with children playing games, blissfully unaware of the evil that was stalking them. Yazid had never known the house so full or so noisy. He had been tempted to join in the fun, but decided instead to retreat to the tower.

Like everyone else, Ubaydallah had been offered the sanctuary of the house, but he preferred to return to the village. Something deep inside told him he would be safer in his own house, independent of the family he had served for so long. In this he was tragically mistaken. Even as he was walking back to the village, a cavalryman, egged on by his friends, unsheathed his weapon and sword-arm raised, charged towards the unsuspecting Ubaydallah. The steward had no time to react. Within seconds, his head, neatly severed from his body, lay rolling in the dust.

Yazid was tugging at his father's robe. Umar had just given orders for the armoury to be unlocked and arms handed out to all able-bodied men and women. Zubayda had insisted that they would fight. Memories of al-Hama were burned into her consciousness.

'Why should we wait helplessly for them, first to despoil our bodies and then thrust their swords in our hearts?'

'Abu! Abu!' Yazid's voice was insistent.

Umar picked him up and kissed him. This spontaneous display of affection pleased the boy, but also annoyed him, since he was trying so hard to be a man.

'What is it, my child?'

'Come to the tower. Now!'

Zubayda sensed the tragedy. She refused to let Yazid return to the tower with his father.

'I need your help, Yazid. How do I use this sword?'

The distraction worked. Umar ascended the stairs alone. The higher he climbed, the more quiet it became. And then he saw the carnage. The houses had been set on fire. He could see the litter of bodies, near where the mosque had stood. The soldiers had not completed their task. They were riding up the nearby hills in pursuit of those who had attempted escape. As he strained his ears, Umar thought he heard the sounds of wailing women, punctuated by the howling of dogs, but soon there was complete silence. The fires were blazing. Death was everywhere. He looked at a map of the village on the table through a piece of magnifying glass. It was too much, and he let the glass drop to the floor and shatter. Now Umar bin Abdallah dried his eyes.

'The broken glass has no saviours,' he told the two servants who had been keeping watch. They stood in place like statues, observing the grief that had overcome their master. Words of comfort were on their tongues, never to be spoken.

Umar slowly descended the stairs. From the tower he had surveyed everything. There was no longer any room for doubt. He cursed himself for not having permitted Yazid to go with his sister. As he reached the giant forecourt he was greeted by an eerie silence. The children had stopped playing. No more food was being eaten. All was still, except for the occasional noise of the blacksmith sharpening swords. They had all caught sight of the fired village and now sat on the ground, watching the flames melt into the setting sun on the horizon. Their homes, their past, their friends, their future, everything had been destroyed. The vigil was interrupted by a woeful cry from the tower.

'The Christians are at the gates!'

Everyone was galvanized into action. The older women and children were sent into the outhouses. Umar took the Dwarf to one side.

'I want you to take Yazid and hide with him in the granary. Whatever else happens, do not let him come out unless you are sure that they have gone. May Allah protect you.'

Yazid refused to be parted from his parents. He argued with his father. He pleaded with his mother.

'Look,' he said, waving a blade which the blacksmith had prepared for him. 'I can use this sword as well as you.'

It was Zubayda's entreaties which finally moved him to accompany the Dwarf. He had insisted on taking his chess pieces with him. When these had been retrieved, the cook took him by the hand and led him towards the formal garden. Beyond it, just below the wall, there was a cluster of trees and plants of every variety. Close by, carefully camouflaged by a circle of jasmine bushes, was a small wooden bench. As the Dwarf lifted it, the stone on which it was placed rose as well.

'Down you go, young master.'

Yazid hesitated for a second and looked back at the house, but the Dwarf nudged him and he began to climb down the tiny stair. The cook followed, carefully replacing the cover from below. In these dark vaults there was enough wheat and rice to feed the whole village for a year. These were the emergency stocks of al-Hudayl, to be used if the crops failed or in the case of unforeseen calamities. The Dwarf lit a candle. Tears were pouring down Yazid's face.

Above the ground, everything was now ready to receive the

Christian soldiers who were now using battering rams to break down the gates. When the doors finally gave way, the first soldiers rode into the forecourt, but this was simply an advance party and their captain was not at their head. The rapid destruction of the village, and the fresh corpses which their horses had trampled over in order to reach the house, had engendered in them a false sense of security.

Suddenly they noticed Moorish knights, also on horseback, poised for action on both their left and right flanks. The intruders tried to race through the forecourt into the outer courtyard, but they were not fast enough. Umar and his improvised cavalry unit bore down with blood-curdling cries. The Christians, unprepared for resistance, were slow to react. Each one was unhorsed and killed. A loud cheer and cries of 'Allah is Great' greeted this unexpected triumph.

The bodies of the dead soldiers were loaded on to their horses and the animals were whipped out of the forecourt. There was a long wait before the next encounter, and the reason soon became obvious. The army from Gharnata was widening the breach in the wall so that they could charge three abreast through the gate.

Umar knew that it would not be so easy the next time. 'It is our downfall,' he told himself. 'All I can see now is death.'

Barely had this thought crossed his mind when he heard the tones of a voice not yet fully broken: 'No mercy on the infidels.' It was the captain himself, at the head of his soldiers. This time they did not wait for the Moorish attack, but charged straight at the defenders. Fierce hand-to-hand fighting was the result, with the courtyard resounding to the noise of clashing steel and the thud of blows, intermingled with screams and alternating cries of 'Allah is Great' and 'For the Holy Virgin, for the Holy Virgin!' The Moorish archers stationed on the roof could not use their crossbows for fear of hurting their own side. The Moors were outnumbered and their resistance was soon bathed in blood.

Umar's horse was hamstrung and the fall concussed him. Soldiers dragged him to the captain. As the two men looked at each other, the captain's eyes gleamed with hatred. Umar dispassionately studied his young conqueror.

'You see before you the wrath of our Lord,' said the captain.

'Yes,' replied Umar. 'Our village emptied of its people. Women and children put to the sword. Our mosques given to the flames and our fields desolated. Men like you remind me of the fish in the sea who devour each other. These lands will never be prosperous again. The blood I see in your eyes will one day destroy your own side. There is only one Allah and he is Allah and Mohammed is his prophet.'

The captain did not reply. He looked at the soldiers on either side of his prisoner and nodded. They did not need further urging. Umar bin Abdallah was forced to his knees. Then the archers struck. Two arrows found their targets as Umar's would-be-executioners were felled. The captain screamed: 'Burn this place down.' Then he ordered two other soldiers forward, but by this time Umar had caught up a sword from one of the fallen men and was fighting once again.

It took six men to recapture the chief of the Banu Hudayl. This time he was beheaded at once, and his head skewered on the point of a pike. After being paraded round the forecourt it was taken into the outer courtyard. Screams and wails burst forth, followed by cries of anger and the clash of blades.

An archer who had witnessed Umar's death ran from the scene and informed Zubayda. Tears poured down her face. She took a sword and joined the defenders in the courtyard outside.

'Come,' she shouted at the other women, 'we must not let them take us alive!'

The women, to the great astonishment of the Christians, displayed a boundless courage. These were not the weak and pampered creatures of the harem about whom they had been told so many fanciful stories. Once again it was the element of surprise which aided the women of al-Hudayl. They were responsible for decreasing the size of the captain's army by at least a hundred men. Ultimately they succumbed, but with swords and daggers in their hands.

After two hours of fierce fighting, the killing was done. All of the defenders lay dead. Weavers and rhetoricians, true believers and false prophets, men and women, they had fought together and died in view of each other. Juan the carpenter, Ibn Hasd and the old sceptic al-Zindiq had refused Umar's offer to hide in the granary. They too, for the first time in their lives, had wielded swords and perished in the massacre.

The captain was angry at having lost so many men. He gave the order for the house to be looted and burnt. For another hour the men, drunk on blood, celebrated their victory in an orgy of plunder. The children, who had been hidden in the baths, were decapitated or drowned, depending on the mood of the soldiers involved. Then they set the old house alight and returned to their camp.

Lingering with his two aides, the captain now dismounted and sat down in the garden, watching the house burn. He took off his boots and dangled his feet in the stream which bisected the garden.

'How they loved the water!'

Beneath the ground, Yazid would wait no longer. It had been silent for a very long time. The Dwarf insisted that the boy must stay, but he was adamant.

'You stay here, Dwarf,' he whispered to the old man. 'I will go and see what has happened and then come back. Please don't come with me. Only one of us should go. I'll scream if you disobey me.'

Still the Dwarf would not budge and Yazid, feigning exhaustion, pretended to settle down again. As the grip on his arm relaxed just a little, he broke loose. Before the Dwarf could stop him he had climbed up the ladder and forced up the cover enough to slip through. When he stood up, it was to see a litter of corpses and his house on fire. The sight unhinged him. He lost all his fear and began to run towards the courtyard, screaming the names of his parents.

The captain was startled by the noise. As the boy ran through the garden, the two aides seized him. Yazid kicked and flailed.

'Let me go! I must see my father and mother.'

'Go with him,' the captain told his men. 'Let him see for himself the power of our Church.'

When he saw his father's head impaled on a pike, the boy fell on his knees and wept. They could go no further because the flames were overpowering, as was the stench of burning bodies. If they had not held him back, Yazid would have rushed through the flames to find his mother and perished in the fire. Instead they dragged him back to the captain, who was now ready to mount his horse.

'Well boy?' he asked in a jovial tone. 'Now do you see what we do to infidels?'

Yazid stared at him, paralysed by inexpressible grief.

'Have you lost your tongue, boy?'

'I wish I had a dagger,' said Yazid in a strangely distant voice. 'For I would run it through your heart. I wish now that many centuries ago, we had treated you as you have treated us.'

The captain was impressed despite himself. He smiled at Yazid and looked thoughtfully at his colleagues. They were relieved at his reaction. They did not have the stomach to kill the boy.

'You see?' he said to them. 'Did I not say earlier today that the hatred of the survivors is the poison that could destroy us?'

Yazid was not listening. His father's head was talking to him.

'Remember, my son, that we have always prided ourselves on how we treat the vanquished. Your great-grandfather used to invite knights he had defeated to stay in our house and feast with him. Never forget that if we become like them, nothing can save us.'

'I will remember, Abu,' said Yazid.

'What did you say, boy?' asked the captain.

'Would you like to stay at our house and be my guest tonight?'

The captain gave his aides the signal they knew only too well. Normally they carried out his orders at once, but it was clear that the boy had lost his mind. It was like cold-blooded murder. They hesitated. The captain, enraged, drew his sword and plunged it into the boy's heart. Yazid fell to the ground with crossed arms. He expired on the spot. There was a half-smile on his face as the blood, full of bubbles, gurgled out of his mouth.

The captain mounted his horse. Without a glance at his two lieutenants, he rode out of the gate.

Night came on. The sky which had seemed like a burning abyss a few hours ago was now dark blue. First two and then a pleiade of stars began to fill the sky. The fires had gone out and everything was dark, the way it must have been a thousand years before when the land grew wild and there were neither dwellings nor creatures to live in them.

The Dwarf, his eyes rigid with horror, was sitting on the ground with Yazid's body in his arms, swaying gently to and fro. His tears were falling on the face of the dead child and mingling with his blood.

'How did it come to pass that of all of them I alone am still alive?'

He repeated this phrase over and over again. He did not know how or when he fell asleep or when the cursed dawn announced a new day.

Since the moment Ibn Basit had told him that he had seen a force of several hundred Christian soldiers outside al-Hudayl, Zuhayr had almost killed his mare by riding without stop till he reached the approaches to the village. Deep lines marked his face, descending from the side of his eyes to the edge of his lips. His eyes, usually black and shining, seemed colourless and dull in their deep hollows. Two months of fighting had aged him a great deal. It was a clear night as Zuhayr galloped through the gorse, his thoughts not on his men, but on his family and his home.

'Peace be upon you, Zuhayr bin Umar!' cried a voice.

Zuhayr reined in his horse. It was a messenger-spy from Abu Zaid.

'I am in a hurry, brother.'

'I wanted to warn you before you reached al-Hudayl. There is nothing left, Zuhayr bin Umar. The Christians are in their cups and telling anyone in Gharnata who will listen to them. They are senseless tonight.'

'Peace be upon you, my friend,' said Zuhayr looking blankly into the distance. 'I will go and see for myself.'

Within fifteen minutes he had reached al-Zindiq's cave, half-hoping, half-praying that the old man would be there to calm his fears. It was deserted. Al-Zindiq's manuscripts and paper were lying there, neatly tied into bundles, as if the old man were preparing to leave forever. Zuhayr rested for a few minutes and gave the horse some water. Then he rode on. He pulled in the horse as he rounded a spur of hillside and looked upward in the familiar direction. The pale light of dawn shone upon charred remains. He rode in a trance towards the house. The worst was true. When he saw the ruins from a distance, his first thought was of revenge. 'I will seek them out and kill them one by one.

I swear on my brother's head before Allah that I will avenge this crime.'

As he rode into the courtyard he saw his father's head mounted on a pike stuck firmly in the ground. Zuhayr jumped off the horse and removed the pike. Gently he looked his father in the face. He took the head to the stream and washed the blood off the hair and face. Then he took it to the graveyard and began to dig the earth with his bare hands. In his frenzy he did not notice a spade lying a few feet away. After he had buried his father, he walked back into the courtyard and saw, for the first time, the Dwarf swaying gently with Yazid in his arms. For a second Zuhayr's heart leaped into his mouth. Was Yazid alive, after all? Then he saw his brother's still face, bloody at the edges.

'Dwarf! Dwarf! Are you alive? Wake up, man!'

Startled, the Dwarf opened his eyes. His arms were as stiff as Yazid's body cradled within them. On seeing Zuhayr, the Dwarf began to wail. Zuhayr embraced the cook and gently took Yazid's body from him. He kissed his dead brother's cheeks.

'I have buried my father's head. Let us bathe Yazid and put him to rest.'

Gently, they undressed the body and bathed it in the stream. Then they lifted Yazid and took him to the family graveyard. It was when he was under the ground and after they had refilled the grave with freshly dug earth that Zuhayr, who had displayed superhuman calm, broke down and screamed. The unblocked anguish released the tears. It was as if rain had fallen on Yazid's grave.

The two men embraced each other and sat down on the grassy knoll, near the new graves.

'I want to know everything, Dwarf. Every single detail. Anything that you can recall I must know.'

'If only I were dead and Yazid alive. Why should I be still alive?'

'I am happy that anyone survives. Tell me what happened.'

The Dwarf began his account and did not pause till he reached the stage where he had let go of Yazid. Then he began to wail and pull out his hair. Zuhayr stroked his face.

'I know, I know, but it is over.'

'That is not the worst of it. He had left the cover slightly open and I heard them grab him and begin their questions. How proud you would have been if you had heard him reply to their captain, that prince of evil who was intent on murdering us all from the very beginning.'

After the Dwarf had finished his story, Zuhayr sat with his head between his hands for a long time.

'Everything is finished here. They have eclipsed our moon forever. Let us go away. It is no longer safe.'

The Dwarf shook his head.

'I was born in this village. My son fell here, defending your palace. I, too, wish to die here, and I feel that it will not be long. You are still young, but I have no desire to live any longer. Leave me alone and let me die in peace.'

'Dwarf, I was born here as well. Too many have died here already. Why add to their number? Besides I have a task which only you can accomplish. I need you.'

'While I am here, I am at your service.'

'I will take you to the coast and put you on a boat destined for Tanja. From there, make your way to Fes and seek out Ibn Daud and my sister. I will write a letter to her and you can tell her whatever she wishes to know.'

At this the Dwarf began to weep once again.

'Have pity on me, Zuhayr bin Umar. How can I face the Lady Hind? With which mouth should I say that I let her Yazid die? It is cruel to send me to her. Let me go to the Lady Kulthum in Ishbiliya. You should go to Fes and live there. They will not let you live on this peninsula.'

'I know my sister Hind very well. More so than even she understands. It is only you she will want to hear, Dwarf. She will feel the need for someone from the house to remain at her side. Otherwise she will go insane. Will you not do this as a last favour for the Banu Hudayl?'

The Dwarf knew he was defeated.

'My father said that there were a few bags of gold always kept in the vaults. We had better take them with us. I will use them to fight our wars, and you take one for the journey and to set yourself up in Fes.'

Once the five leather bags containing gold coins had been uncovered, Zuhayr saddled his horse and rounded up another for the Dwarf. He adjusted the stirrups to accommodate the man's short legs. As they rode away from the house and left the village behind them, Zuhayr broke his silence.

'Let us not stop and look at it again, Dwarf. Let us remember it as it used to be. Remember?'

The cook did not reply. He did not speak till they reached the coastal town of al-Gezira. They found a boat which was departing early the next morning and booked a passage on it for the Dwarf. After a brief search they found a comfortable funduq, which provided them with a room and two beds. As they went to bed, the Dwarf spoke for the first time since they had left the forecourt of the house in al-Hudayl.

'I will never forget the fire or the groans and screams. Nor can I forget the look on the face of Yazid after the savages had killed him. That is why I cannot remember the more distant past.'

'I know, but that is the only past I want to remember.'

Zuhayr began to write his letter to Hind. He gave her an account of his duel with Don Alonso and its tragic consequences. He described the destruction of the village and the house and he appealed to her never to return:

How lucky you were to find a man as worthy of you and as farsighted as Ibn Daud. I think he knew a long time ago that we would lose our battle against time. The old man who brings this to you is full of remorse for the crime of being alive. Look after him well.

I have been thinking of you a great deal over the last few days and I wish we had spoken more to each other when we lived in the same house. I will confess to you that one part of me wanted to come to Fes with the old man. To see you and Ibn Daud. To watch you bear children, and to be their uncle. To begin a new life away from the tortures and deaths which have taken over this peninsula. And yet there is another part of me which says that I cannot desert my comrades in the midst of these horrors. They rely on me. Mother and you always thought that I was weak-willed, readily convinced of anything and incapable of firmness. You were probably right, but I think I have changed a great deal. Because the others depend on me I have to wear a mask, and this mask has become so much a part of me that it is difficult to tell which is my real face.

I will return to the al-Pujarras, where we control dozens of villages and where we live as we used to before the Reconquest. Abu Zaid al-Ma'ari, an old man you would like very much, is convinced that they will not let us live here for much longer. He says that it is not the conversion of our souls which they desire, but our wealth, and that the only way they can take over our lands is by obliterating us forever. If he is correct then we are doomed to extinction whatever we do. In the meanwhile we will carry on fighting. I am sending you all the papers of our old al-Zindiq. Look after them well and let me know what Ibn Daud thinks of their contents.

If you want to reach me, and I insist you let me know when your first child is born, the best way is to send a message to our uncle in Gharnata. And one more thing, Hind. I know that from now till I die, I will weep for my dead brother and our parents every day. No mask I wear can change that in me.

Your brother,
Zuhayr.

The Dwarf had not been able to sleep for more than a couple of hours. When dawn finally came he rose and left the room for his ablutions. When he returned, Zuhayr was sitting up in bed, looking at the morning light coming through the window.

'Peace be upon you, old friend.'

The Dwarf looked at him in horror. Overnight, Zuhayr's hair had turned white. Nothing was said. Zuhayr had noticed the box containing Yazid's chess pieces amongst the Dwarf's belongings.

'He left them with me when he went up to see if he could find the Lady Zubayda.' The Dwarf began to weep. 'I thought the Lady Hind might like them for her children.'

Zuhayr smiled, biting back the tears.

An hour later, the Dwarf had embarked on a merchant vessel. Zuhayr was on the shore, waving farewell.

'Allah protect you, Zuhayr al-Fahl!' the Dwarf shouted in his old voice.

'He never does,' Zuhayr told himself.

Epilogue

TWENTY YEARS LATER, the victor of al-Hudayl, now at the height of his powers and universally regarded as one of the most experienced military leaders of the Catholic kingdom of Spain, disembarked from his battleship on a shore thousands of miles away from his native land. He strapped on the old helmet which he had never changed, though he had been presented with two made from pure silver. In addition, he now wore a beard, whose redness was the cause of many a ribald jest. His two aides, now captains in their own right, had accompanied him on this mission.

The expedition travelled for many weeks through marshes and thick forests. When he reached his destination, the captain was greeted by ambassadors of the local ruler, attired in robes of the most unexpected colours. Gifts were exchanged. Then he was escorted to the palace of the king.

The city was built on water. Not even in his dreams had the captain imagined it could be anything like this. Boats ferried people from one part of the city to another.

'Do you know what they call this remarkable place?' he asked, to test his aide, as the boat carrying them docked at the palace.

'Tenochtitlan is the name of the city and Moctezuma is the king.'

'Much wealth went into its construction,' said the captain.

'They are a very rich nation, Captain Cortes,' came the reply.

The captain smiled.

GLOSSARY

Abu	Father
Ama	Nurse
al-Andalus	Moorish Spain
al-Hama	Alhama
al-Hamra	the Alhambra
al-Jazira	Algeciras
al-Mariya	Almeria
al-Qahira	Cario
bab	gate
Balansiya	Valencia
Dimashk	Damascus
faqih	religious scholars or experts
funduq	hostels for travelling merchants
Gharnata	Granada
hadith	sayings of the Prophet Mohammed
hammam	public baths
Iblis	devil: leader of the fallen angels
Ishbiliya	Seville
Iskanderiya	Alexandria
jihad	holy war
Kashtalla	Castile
khutba	Friday sermon
madresseh	religious schools
Malaka	Malaga
maristan	hospital/asylum for the sick and the insane
qadi	magistrate
Qurtuba	Cordoba
riwaq	students' quarters
Rumi	Roman
Sarakusta	Zaragoza
Tanja	Tangier
Tulaytula	Toledo
Ummi	Mother
zajal	popular strophic poems composed impromptu in the colloquial Arabic of al-Andalus and handed down orally since the tenth century